Books by John Leggett

WILDER STONE

THE GLOUCESTER BRANCH

WHO TOOK THE GOLD AWAY

WHO
TOOK
THE GOLD
AWAY

John Leggett

WHO
TOOK
THE GOLD
AWAY

Random House

NEW YORK

First Printing

Copyright © 1969 by John Leggett

All rights reserved under International and Pan-American
Copyright Conventions.
Published in the United States by Random House, Inc.,
New York, and simultaneously in Canada by
Random House of Canada Limited, Toronto.
Library of Congress Catalog Card Number: 69-16464
Manufactured in the United States of America
by H. Wolff, New York, N.Y.

for Tim, John, Tony

PART ONE

New Haven

1938

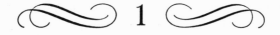

1

Considering what Yale was like in 1938, it is remarkable that Pierce Jay and I should have known each other at all.

In that year, when we were both freshmen, Yale was a goldfish bowl in which we fluked about, earnestly unfurling our aspirations. The telling marks on a man were his prep school, his dress and what he did with his leisure. Grace, detachment, not seeming to care and, above all, being with acceptable companions—these were prized.

Imagine. It was a fall in which the nation was convalescing from its grave illness of the early thirties. A few of our fellow citizens were in the north of Spain with the Lincoln Battalion of the International Brigade; some of them dying for the Republic on the banks of the Ebro. Chiang Kai-shek was quarreling with the Reds and destroying the cities of North China as he retreated from the Japanese army. In Munich, Chamberlain and Daladier were bartering Czechoslovakia to Hitler for his promise of peace, while his countrymen burned thirteen of the twenty synagogues in Berlin and passed a law that Jewish physicians must henceforth be known not as doctors but as Jew-treaters. There was even a hurricane to devastate the Atlantic Seaboard and welcome us to New Haven by splitting the trunks of the city's most venerable elms.

But as the undergraduates of Yale's 238th year stepped over the fallen limbs, their concern was less for these insane and distant sounds of strife than for being left out of the world at hand. That was unthinkable punishment—for just in being here we were heirs to a Christmas package of American promise. For a young Yale man, life streamed with possibility. We were the elected, the chosen, the princes.

It may be the passing of the years has betrayed me, but I don't recall a middle ground. One aspired to be "white-shoe" or else one didn't know any better. That most unenlightened of oafs was described in some lyrics for a Dramat show of the time:

> *There's a meatball who lives in Calhoun.*
> *His hometown is Hamden, Connecticut.*
> *He's not only a terrible goon,*
> *He's lacking in breeding and etiquette.*

Even I felt that some rather splendid destiny awaited me and I must not jeopardize it by indiscretion. I was in illustrious company. What an assembly of American resources Yale seemed to be. Just a list of her undergraduates and their hometowns started a glow of pride. There was a Ford from Grosse Point, a Pillsbury from Wayzata, a Rockefeller from Greenwich, a Biddle from Philadelphia, an Armour from Lake Forest, a Dillingham from Honolulu. Names. Names and places. Getting to know the thundering names and then the inside names was not the least of our education.

As a high school graduate, a bursary student and the son of a not-so-successful Providence doctor, I provoked little envy in my 844 classmates. To someone like Pierce Jay, whose celebrated father had recently died in the spectacular Andes crash of one of his own airplanes, I was an untouchable. We might sit side by side in Geology 10, spin the combinations on adjoining mailboxes at Yale Station, pass daily on campus paths, share shower and lavatory facilities—and never speak.

I roomed with Morton Wolfe, a big fellow with warm eyes in a sad clown face. He had gone to Peddie, a school somewhere in New Jersey, and he was out for wrestling because he had the strength and weight for it. He told me with solemn mischievousness that there was something stubborn about wrestling that appealed to him. It didn't call for the cleverness of boxing and fencing. "It's a nice little irony," he said, "and I like that." But his real love was cards—poker or, even better, bridge. I might find a penny-a-point game under way in our room, any time, even on the glorious fall afternoons. Silent, anxious fellows came to play—for the money, and because they had found little else to do.

The room we shared on the ground floor of Bingham was an inexpensive one because it gave on Chapel Street, where the streetcars groaned and squealed as they rounded the corner into College Street. We grew sensitive about noise, and in the middle of the fall semester began to take a sterner view of a more irritating disturbance—the beer-can bowler. Someone in the entry had discovered that an empty beer can (they were a novelty that year) properly launched from the top landing would roll down the nearly spiral stairs, one stone step at a time—*kaplonk, kaplonk, kaplonk*—taking some three minutes for the descent to arrive outside our door. It occurred at odd times, but generally in the late evening while we were studying or in the early hours of the morning when we would be awakened by the clatter.

The good humor with which we first received the sound of the tumbling can soon gave way to protests and an investigation. It was discovered that the Chapel Liquor Shop delivered beer by the case to Pierce Jay, and although he denied it, he was thought to be the bowler. Jay roomed with Aldrich in what had been a faculty suite on the third floor.

Their room was one of the rallying places of the churchschool faction. Jay and Aldrich had both gone to St. Paul's, though only Aldrich had graduated. Throughout the fall I had been aware of the comings and goings of their friends. They had cowled, underwater voices, some nasal, some deeply gargled, and Harris tweed jackets they had brought along from prep-school wardrobes, so unlike the ungainly garments recently acquired by many of us from the college shops of hometown department stores. They were knowledgeable, laughing at incomprehensible jokes and funny nicknames as they jostled one another on the stairs to Jay's room. They drank ostentatiously. And I was often roused at one and two in the morning by the racket overhead—those haughty bloods ending an evening of boozy vaingloriousness in a full-throated rendering of "Wake, Freshmen, Wake!" In their laughter, even their retching, which invariably wound up their revels, there was unmistakable scorn for the rest of us. They could look right through you—as though you didn't exist. They really knew how to do that.

Another reason we were permissive with Jay was that we held him in awe because he was an athlete. He was on the freshman football squad and had played in three early games, though not so adroitly as to be singled out in the *News* coverage. Still, it was further distinction. He was a member of that radiant, loose-limbed, confident fraternity of the Ray Tompkins field house. If you played football for Yale, you were true, traditional, blue Eli. There was a spot for you on the old fence. You were in there with Hinkey and Heffelfinger and Booth and Kelley and Frank—and you never could do wrong. You owned the place.

But one night as I paused over my *Richard II* to note the tinny tumbling commence overhead, I felt that Jay intended to go on launching his empties down the stairwell forever. Wolfe stirred and grumbled in his Morris chair, but in the hallway there were no outcries. The entry was ignoring the nuisance.

What irked me was not the noise itself, which was a small fraction of what those screeching trolleys could produce, but that this incessant prank which at first had seemed funny to me—ordinary college waggishness, as exuberant and friendly as it was silly—now appeared to be malicious.

It was his rubbish that he rained down upon us nightly. That was indignity enough. But more important, he was invading our privacy with, presumably, no desire for any other communication with us. This is what really burned me—that without knowing us, or even wishing to know us, he would continue his everlasting harassment. What *colossal* contempt.

Closing the book, I said to Wolfe, "You know what I'm going to do? I'm going up there and shove a beer can down his throat. He has no right."

"Save your strength." Wolfe didn't even look up. "He's a snotty bastard. I said hello to him the other day, to make sure, and he just nodded—you know, as if I was the porter. Besides, he's big. He'd cream you."

"Well, what do you propose to do, for God's sake? Sit here and let him annoy us forever?"

"I wouldn't give him the satisfaction," Wolfe said.

Then I began to think about what kind of guy would get pleasure out of this. Jay did not look sick or deranged. Nor could I believe that arrogance alone would sustain such a persistent program. No—I thought it must be more elaborate, some kind of experiment perhaps. In some way he was rolling his cans down in hopes of response.

I went into the vestibule and met the can just as it arrived on the bottom step. Seizing it, I climbed the stairs to the third floor and knocked on Jay's door.

It swung ajar on a sitting room whose walls were hung with framed pictures of schoolboy teams and an oar from a Halcyon boat, a winning time painted on its blade. There was a huge red leather sofa and at its far end a record player filled the place with trumpeting.

Jay appeared in the doorway of one of the bedrooms. He seemed huge to me, six-foot-one, with long legs and arms— and with a fierce, predatory look about him. His nose was slender, with a pronounced arch that added to the hawklike illusion. Beneath it was a curving voluptuary's mouth which put me in mind of eating. I supposed it would have put a woman in mind of kissing.

His shoulders, clad in a blue Y.A.A. sweatshirt, seemed to fill the doorway but there was nothing heavy about him. He was taut and muscular, as though he was vain of his body and gave thought to its training. He was shod in worn patent-leather evening pumps and from one hand dangled a copy of *Yachting*. Deep brown eyes darkened, indignant at intrusion.

"May I come in?" I asked.

"All right," he said without cordiality.

As I entered I saw that Aldrich was in his bedroom, seated at a desk. He surveyed me briefly and turned back to his writing.

"I'm Moseley," I said. "I live below you, on the ground floor."

"Oh?"

"I'd like to talk to you about bouncing the beer cans down the stairs." I held out the sample in my hand.

"Yes." His voice was penetrating, polished yet without accent, and he squeezed off phrases like bullet bursts. "It is a nuisance, isn't it?"

"I know the guys came up and asked you about it and that you denied it. But we're convinced it's you. You're the one that gets this stuff delivered."

"How do you know it isn't Aldrich? He's a pretty sneaky-looking character."

Aldrich looked around with a ghost of a smirk, then turned away.

"May I look in your room?"

He shook his head.

"Well, I tell you, Jay. It was funny the first few times, but now, after a month of it, everybody's getting sore—and that seems to be exactly what you want. Do I have it straight?"

"It's the persistence of the noise that bothers you?"

"Not the noise itself, though that is a pain in the ass if you're studying or sleeping, but there's something really infuriating about its being a one-way joke. I mean, you don't know any of us down there and clearly you don't want to. What you want to do is roll your beer cans at strangers. You see what I mean?"

He nodded at the big red leather sofa. "Have a seat, Moseley." I sat down on it while Jay slumped into the big armchair beside the record player. "You want a beer?"

"No thanks."

The record finished and he watched the tone arm cross the record and begin again. "It's the Count," he said. " 'One O'Clock Jump.' You like that?"

"Yes. It's okay. You were going to tell me whether you understood about the beer cans."

"I'd like to help you, Moseley, but it's impossible." His smile prickled with cunning. "You see, our biddy here disapproves of my drinking the stuff and I've got to get rid of the evidence."

"I see. Still, there ought to be some way to work it out. She must be the same one that does our room. Maybe we could have a talk with her or— I don't suppose you'd want to *carry* the cans down?"

"No. I wouldn't want to give up the noise." He looked into Aldrich's room to see how he was enjoying the exchange. Aldrich was oblivious.

"You haven't explained to me about your purpose. Why do you want to antagonize us?"

He made an indifferent face. "I don't see why you should take it that way. Why not think of it as an alarm, reminding all the grinds down there of the hour—that it's getting late for all their tests and reports. Tell them that."

"I think you'd better tell them." I watched Aldrich rise from his desk and thought he was coming to join us, but instead he closed the door on us firmly.

"That's not very hospitable," Jay called to him. "Don't you know we have a guest?" There was no answer, and Jay said, "Rude fellow. He gets cranky when he's answering his invitations."

"I'm curious about another thing," I said. "Aren't you in

training? I always thought the football team didn't drink at all during the season."

He was amused by that awkward flattery. "Freshmen football isn't that demanding." He leaned into the chair, clasping his hands behind his head. "What are you out for, Moseley?"

"Body building." He looked puzzled, and I explained, "The physical-fitness classes."

"Shit." He gave the word its full gutter-loving expressiveness and dropped the facetiousness which had hung like a curtain between us.

"I don't have the physique or the time for the freshman squad, if that's what you mean."

"What are you so busy with—grinding?"

"I have a job. I'm a bursary student."

His eyebrows raised. "What do you have to do?"

"I work at the Student Agencies."

"Where's that?"

"Chapel Street."

"I haven't noticed. What is it?" He looked pained. "The laundry and dry cleaning?"

"Oh it's not that bad. I don't scrub or press. It's a regular office. We solicit business and collect bills . . . but yes, it's laundry and dry cleaning that occupies me."

He nodded without interest. "Tell me, Moseley, how did you happen to come to Yale?"

"A scholarship. I got a Providence area scholarship."

"Do you like Yale?"

"All except for the noise. Do you?"

"Do *I?*" It surprised him, and he reflected for a moment. I thought I would get a facetious answer, but instead he replied, "It's something I've never questioned. My father went here—and so did my grandfather. Did yours?"

"No."

"At school—and I went to several—I hung around with the Yale people. I simply accept it, like"—he wiggled his fingers in rough count of his blessings—"many things."

"The football? Surely you get pleasure from that."

His glance was guarded, questioning if I was being sarcastic or genuinely curious. "Well, no. I'm not an idiot about it. I *like* it well enough. I like sports. I'm a good athlete and I like to prove to myself I can do anything. I can, you know. But hell, no, I don't love college football for itself the way some of these jerks do. No." He shook his head as some new and rather troublesome thought seemed to cross his mind. "As a matter of fact, this freshman team is a big disappointment."

"Oh? I thought we were doing very well. We've won a couple of games."

"Schoolboy games. Wait till we hit Dartmouth."

"What's the trouble—we don't have the players?"

"No. That's not it. There's good material out there. It's just not being used properly."

"How come? What are we doing wrong?"

Jay stirred uneasily in his chair, thrusting his hands deep into his pockets. "I don't like to knock Root, you know. We're all new to him—that's the thing about a freshman team. But the season's going to be over before he gets it shaken down. He doesn't know what he's got, still doesn't have the right guys in the right spots. You'd think he'd have done a little homework on us, wouldn't you? You'd think he'd have a clue about what his players have done in school . . ."

"He doesn't?"

"I'll tell you what he knows. He knows Andover and Exeter. If you've played for one of the big schools, you're in. You start every Saturday. If you went . . . if you're from a high school, oh Jesus, are you ever set. Any high school. If you're from East Quincy High, your old man must run a drill press at the ironworks, so it stands to reason you *must* be tough and you play the whole goddam game. Look, I don't want to be disloyal, but I don't get along very well with Root. It isn't that he discriminates against the small schools—he just doesn't know about them. They don't count with him. He asked me where I went to school, and when I told him Brooks, he didn't . . . That was the last place. It's very com-

plicated, my schooling. That was all he wanted to know. He
didn't want to know that at S.P.S., I was playing first Isthmian
in my fourth-form year, and that after I got kicked out and
went to Brooks, in my fifth-form year I scored in both the
Middlesex and the Nobles games. He doesn't even *know* that.
He does know that I've played in the backfield. He knows
that because I've told him about twenty times, but he's got
me at end. I oughtn't to be in the line. I can pass and I can
run with the ball. Christ!"

"Doesn't he see his mistakes after he's watched a game or
two?"

Jay regarded me sullenly. "No."

"I see. Well, I can't think of much to do. How about some
other sport? There must be about a dozen. Soccer? Lacrosse?
Is it too late to go out for one of them?"

He laughed. It was the donkey-bray I was going to know
well. Jay kept it cocked for the preposterousness he saw about
him so profusely. "Oh Jesus, you're kidding aren't you?"

"No. Why not? If you don't like the football coach—it's a
perfectly reasonable suggestion."

"I'll tell you something, Moseley. One of the reasons—I
suppose it's the most important reason most of the people are
out for the freshman squad—is because the good guys do it. It
so happens that the good guys in any class go out for freshman
football."

"*All* of them?"

He shrugged uncertainly but replied with a dogged "Yes,
all of them."

"How do you know that?"

"Well, I mean it's common knowledge. I've heard it from
everybody—from a dozen old Elis, from upperclassmen, from
my father's friends, even from my father. It's the first important sorting-out. Didn't anybody ever tell you that, Moseley?"

"Never before. I must be very naïve. I just naturally supposed you went out for football because you liked it."

"The football captain is always the last man tapped for

Bones. You know that, don't you? You know about *that* surely?"

"Yes. I know about that." We sat, eying one another, our subject presumably exhausted, hearing Count Basie once more. "What I'd like to know is what you mean by the good guys. What are the qualifications?"

"Oh come on, Moseley. Are you kidding me? You can't be that innocent. If you really don't know—if you want me to define it as though it were an exam question . . ."

"I want to know about the sorting-out," I said. "Who passes and who flunks and why? I'd like to know how those boys from East Quincy High make out."

Jay seemed relieved, finding me not altogether simple-minded. "Some of them," he said earnestly, "the cream of them, will do fine. A couple of them will go straight to the top. Yale's democratic, for Christ's sake. If you don't like that, you go to Harvard. This is the land of Horatio Alger. You know. It's why you're here."

"It is?" I laughed. "Perhaps you're right. I don't know. But if you're telling me I've already missed the main chance by not going out for football, you're wrong. I'd be in traction by now."

"Well, it isn't the *only* way. There's the *News*. A few guys, the best of them—the editor in chief, the managing editor, the business manager, the good columnists. They all make it, and after graduation they all go straight down to Harry Luce and get on with it."

"There must be other activities too. The Political Union?"

"The what?"

"The Dramatic Association, then?"

"Flits. The airdrome. Everybody knows that."

"Well, there are other ways, I'm sure. Maybe I'll even get somewhere pressing pants."

"Maybe," he said with overwhelming doubt and lingering condescension. But then he must have reflected on my lack of choice, for he added with unexpected charitableness, "I don't

try to make any sense out of it, but it's how it is. In every class
there are the guys who run it—maybe ten or twenty of them.
By the end of freshman year everybody has a pretty good idea
of who they are, and by sophomore year there's no doubt at
all. They're the ones having the best time. They're in Fence
and Deke and they're deciding who's going to follow them in.
They're the ones who get tapped in Branford Court, and in
senior year they're the ones that decide who's coming into
Bones and Keys, and the year after that they're passing judgment on you again and it goes on all your life. They're deciding who's getting the good jobs and running for office, getting
into the clubs and getting the big chances downtown. My father had a staff of Yale guys around him and he was always
counting on the Yale guys in Washington. They all help one
another.

"Your father was . . ."

"Bones."

We sat quietly in a field of gravity and I had the impression
we had passed beyond decorum, that these delicate, yet vital
matters were seldom discussed *in situ,* never so frankly, even
with Aldrich. Conceivably, his need to impress me had led
him to unseemly revelation and he now suffered remorse.
Nevertheless, he continued, "They say no Bones man ever
fails in life—that if one of them gets into financial difficulty,
the other fourteen guys in his delegation bail him out."

"That's a cruel sort of kindness."

"Yes. It is, isn't it?"

"You know it for a fact?"

"I've heard it many times."

"Your father?"

"My father never talked about it. He couldn't. He
wouldn't be allowed."

"I see."

He watched the record finish and this time turned the machine off, terminating my interview and allowing the sounds
of our community to be heard. The heavy-tongued bell in

Harkness tower solemnly counted out midnight and there was a scuffling and some laughter in the courtyard below.

"Well," I said, getting to my feet, "there must be some advantages to coming here uninformed—traveling light and unencumbered. What I don't know won't hurt me, will it? Maybe I'll get through without knowing what I'm missing."

He shook his head slightly. "You're in—unless you really don't give a shit." It was a question.

"I do."

"Then you're playing. Ignorance of the rules is no excuse. The four years we're going to spend in this place is our test flight. You work the fucking thing out right here so everybody can see what kind of stuff you've got. I suspect that very few of us are going to learn enough from the experience to change the pattern—to change what happens afterwards. If you make it here, you make it later—if not . . . Oh, unless you're a real kook—an Einstein or something."

"And I'm not that." I rose to go. In the doorway I paused and said, "Thanks a lot."

Jay watched my departure with a preoccupied stare. It was not unfriendly, but there was no farewell, no indication that our talk had separated me, in his view, from the greasy grinds who lived in the well below.

I closed the door firmly on his patronizing and started down the stairs. But on the way, following the route of the beer cans, I discovered my indignation had been undermined. I hesitated outside the door to my own room, wondering if this didn't reveal some shoddiness in my own character.

Curiously, it was Jay's self-absorption, his indifference to my feelings, that fascinated me most. He had touched some formless yearnings, and the effect was not unlike that of falling in hopeless love. I had never encountered a fellow of such arrogance, and yet, combined as it was with his youth and looks, that manner, that careless manifestation of money and its willfulness, I was intrigued by it. I tried to persuade myself that I was moved by curiosity about him, but in a rare flash of candor I admitted that my bedazzlement was simple envy—the sense that nothing had, and nothing ever would be, denied him and a belief that some of the plenty in which he flourished would rub off on those about him.

I supposed that this in turn was rooted in my father's numbness to opportunity, my own sensitiveness to it, and the belief (absorbed from him) that Yale was its touchstone.

In any case, it was the end of the beer cans. They did not roll again.

*　　　　*　　　　*

During the next weeks I looked in vain for Jay's name in the weekly line-ups. He was not even among the substitutes who streamed into the final quarters of the Princeton and Harvard games so they could claim letters, and I was aware that his football career had fizzled.

Throughout the football season, each Saturday afternoon, the Connecticut Company would recall from pasture its eighty open streetcars to shuttle the crowds to the game. Beginning at one o'clock they would appear on Chapel Street, and although their normal capacity was ninety, nearly twice that number would find a toehold for the journey to the Bowl. A stranger might have guessed the scene was one of refugees fleeing before the Turkish onslaught.

It was the return to the university, though, that was the real trial for the harassed trolley crews. To gather fares in their pistol-grip receptacles, the conductors had to spider around the flanks of camelhaired and fur-bearing youths, each bent on proving himself no less exuberant than undergraduates of prior football seasons.

On one such golden autumn day I saw Pierce Jay run along the track behind one of the cars, unfasten the guide halyard and deftly dislodge the trolley pole from its overhead wire. With the car stalled in the back streets of New Haven and blocking a cortege of football specials, I watched Jay shinny up onto the roof, some cheering students boosting him while others tugged at the hem of his black bearskin coat.

From his perch he called encouragement to the exasperated motorman and conductor as they seated the trolley, then waited until the motorman had resumed his station up front before disconnecting the trolley again. Meantime he encouraged the mutinous passengers to rock back and forth, calling out like the coxswain of a crew, "Lean to port! Now to starboard!" in an attempt to derail the car.

The police came quickly—and with a ladder. They were, I realized, prepared for Jay, and my estimate of them was never higher—though he did escape them by leaping from the roof of the car to the street and making off into the gallery of spectators, pulling a lovely blond girl after him. I can still recall her face, laughing and flushed with the excitement of being with him.

*　　　　　*　　　　　*

With the coming of winter, New Haven turned sooty and gray. The streets seemed to narrow and become like those of any industrial city in the East. The bleakness of the food in Commons and of the New England sky drove us undergraduates to the meager urban pleasures that New Haven yielded. There was solace at the Poli and Roger Sherman, where the Marx Brothers gave shape to our comic fantasies, Betty Hutton and Claudette Colbert and Jean Arthur, to our romantic ones; and at the Strand, where we went to be cheated (that was the fun of it) by *Marihuana, the Weed with Roots in Hell.*

It was not costly diversion. Admission to the movies was only thirty-five cents, and a beer at the Hofbrau House, the fumy barnlike tavern on Crown Street, was a dime, and a steak sandwich, grilled by a chef in a white mushroom hat over a bed of flaming charcoal, was a quarter. A reasonable man's debauch could be had for a dollar.

Late one frosty Friday night I was at the Hofbrau bar with Wolfe and a pair of his bridge players, splurging on a schooner of the velvety dark, when I saw Pierce Jay come in. I had not seen him here before. His Chesterfield collar was turned up and there was a sparkling of snow on his thick, curling brown hair. He was with some bloods. I had learned to recognize them by the prevalence of cluster-striped school ties and red-soled white buck shoes.

They took a booth in the rear of the taproom, but presently I was surprised to find Jay at my elbow. He called me by name. "Hello, Moseley," he said. "How are things over at the laundry?"

"Simply ripping." It was our Chapel Street wheeze, enfeebled by months of wear, but Jay laughed—so appreciatively that I realized he had been drinking the whole evening. His eyes, their whites tinged with pink, kept slipping away as though I eluded him. Ordering a Cuba libre, the mixture of rum and Coca-Cola that was a national beverage of the late thirties, he looked over his shoulder at his friends but was in no hurry to rejoin them.

"You come in here often?" he asked.

"Once or twice a week."

"On your way to Savin Rock?"

"What?"

He grasped a handful of my jacket. I remember the suit with a mixture of feelings. It was a lustrous silver-gray gabardine which I had chosen for its progressive style and the sunny splendor of its fabric. *Snappy* was the word I had in mind for it, and until that moment I had worn it with pride, assuming that its very uniqueness made it acceptable, even enviable.

"I understand they like these bi-swings down at the Rock," he explained with a great wink. "The high-school girls down there really go for them. You ought to do all right."

The humiliation was instant, for I was not sure of my taste, but my anger trailed uncertainly. He was grinning. It was a joke. But I couldn't be certain of his intent—whether he was making fun of me or guiding me in the ways of his sophisticated world.

But through the numb of whiskey he sensed my warming

indignation and his long arm embraced me, firmly, across the shoulders. It was a disconcerting gesture. I am wary of any demonstrativeness and I stood stiff and awkward under the weight of his arm until he removed it.

"Seriously," he asked, "where are you going?"

"Nowhere. I'm going to have another beer. Then I'm going back to my room and go to bed."

"You want to come with us? We're going to the Knick to look over the pigs."

"No."

"Come on, Moseley. Don't be a poop all your life. There'll be laughs all around."

"Thanks all the same."

"Are you drinking alone?"

"No." I nodded to the others up the bar. They nursed their beers in narrow heavy-bottomed glasses, pretending not to notice Jay, who squinted at them through roseate eyes, his head weaving slightly.

In the smoky light their faces were pale, colorless. They looked unfinished, rough-cut, some bark still on them. I saw an ungainly slope of forehead, a stubborn heaviness of jaw, an abrasive crinkling of forelock. The one handsome face appeared to be made of soap or custard, some insubstantial material.

Why, I wondered, does the character in a face here seem to go with money? Why is an ugly rich boy interesting-looking; how does he turn his twisted nose and undershot jaw to advantage? Surely it's not the wrapping—not those snug Brooks shoulders and heathery Shetlands; more likely, that knowledgeableness, the sureness of step and voice that my friends in their hesitant self-consciousness lack. Or is it, for God's sake, some illusion Pierce Jay has put in my susceptible eye?

"All right," he was saying, "but you're missing the fun."

"I'm sure of it."

"Two more," he said to the bartender.

"I'll buy a round, then," I said.

"You'll come out on the short end," Jay said.

"That's okay." I watched him in the mirror; his eyes blinked as though weighted. "I've been wanting to ask about the football. What happened to you?"

The bland grin, that rhythmic bobbing of his head as though to some inner tune which put me in mind of an elephant looking over the Saturday crowd at the zoo, the occasional thirsty licking of his lips, all ceased abruptly. His dark eyes went black. "What do you mean?"

"You didn't play again. You'd about persuaded me to come out for the squad. What happened—did you meet all the good guys?"

"No." He frowned at the drinks as they were set before us. "No, I quit." He lifted his glass, took a swallow and savored it. The tongue licked his lips again. "Root had it in for me, you know. Everybody could see that. It was plain as hell. I was as good as anybody out there, but he didn't start me for Dartmouth. I don't put up with that shit, you know." He looked at me for some encouragement, and I nodded.

"I'm not one of these nuts about college football," he continued. "It beats me how anyone but a fool can care that much about the game today. It's all a big fraud now, you know." He shook his head and his laugh was low and derisive. "Old Seymour makes a speech about it once a week, you notice—how Yale doesn't exist for football. But by God, there's that Bowl they built out there and it's got fifty thousand seats to fill every Saturday. Think of it—at three bucks a seat, that's real jack. That's big business." He winked and rubbed his fingers together. "That's the change since the old man's day. We've gone commercial. Well, fuck 'em. Let them buy a load of ringers with unpronounceable names out of the Scranton high schools. But it's the end of Yale's greatness and they won't fill the Bowl that way. Who'll come to see a bunch of hunkies play. You can put Yale jerseys on eleven Polacks, but it doesn't make a Yale team."

I nodded thoughtfully. There seemed no point in argument. "I can see how you'd feel about that. Sounds like you're well out of it."

He looked at his reflection in the mirror for a moment and then said carefully, "You know, Moseley, Yale's built on six generations of American men. They're what made it a great place. They left New Haven to go out and run the country. It's their money, you know, not public funds, that built it— men like Harkness and Sterling and Whitney and hundreds of others, my old man among them. He left Yale a cool half-million. No, goddam it. Yale isn't meant to be a big city university like NYU or Columbia. That wasn't what he had in mind. Yale is supposed to keep the American tradition pure —like a spring. You understand what I mean?"

"I think so, but what about you? I mean—getting ahead here? What about the Yale ladder? Have you quit that too?"

He looked at me with a sly smile. "You bastard," he said. "I know what you're doing. Don't think I've forgotten all that shit I told you a couple of months ago. By God, it sickens me, Moseley—hearing myself played back like that. Forget it. I'm ashamed."

"But it isn't shit. It's all true. I believe you. You haven't really changed your mind about the system?"

He gave a colossal shrug. "No, I haven't. It's there for all the clucks who want to play it. It's just not for me, that's all. Now that's what I've learned at Yale so far. That's something in three months, you know. By God, you *do* get an education here after all. Anybody who says you don't is a liar. Once you know that, Moseley, how you really get an education around here, there's no need to go to class. Of course, you've got to get the cut list fixed before it gets to the Dean's Office. I'm working on that now. When I get it perfected I'll let you in on it because you're a good fellow, by Christ." He kneaded my shoulder with affectionate brutality. "You know what? I haven't been to class in a week and I think I've got it fixed so the cuts don't show."

"No sports? No classes?" I asked. "You must have plenty of

time on your hands. Just the Knick? You never told me about that. Is there a letter for it? Do they let you into Bones if you score high in pigs?"

He clapped me on the back in a travesty of appreciative fellowship. "You're all right, Moseley, goddam it."

"Seriously—are you really cutting all your classes? You're not doing anything? Nothing at all?"

"By God, you're a serious, conscientious fellow. You ought to go far here." He looked at me intently and burst out laughing. "You sure you don't want to go to the Knick?"

2

"I make a loose interpretation of the freshman rules," Jay was saying as we swept out of New Haven onto Route One. "I don't drive it up to Phelps gateway and give the bulls a good look. I keep it at a garage downtown and just use it for emergencies like this. Discretion"—he winked at me as he fed the big Packard gas—"that's the ticket."

It was a grand car, a convertible the color of sand, with massive hardware and brown leather upholstery that was soft to the touch and faintly perfumed, like a woman's glove. Swooping in to the trolley stop where I had been clutching a valise and doubting I could catch the 3:50 train, it had seemed no ordinary machine for getting places, but a destination. It was a supership that cowed pedestrians and stirred envy wherever it plied the traffic, thus assuring its passengers of their supremacy. The motor sang in a deep bass voice as it reached up the twin lanes of concrete into the Connecticut hills.

"No, I didn't drop it," he said of the course we took together. Recently I had missed the back of his head with its dark curls twining to the collar, an arrestingly shaggy sight in an era when close shearing was the fashion. "But I don't go to the lectures much any more. Christ, what a bore Carmody is. I can't stand bores. You put up with one because you don't want to hurt his feelings and the next thing you know you're immune to boredom. You accept it everywhere and then you become a bore yourself—boring other people. I detest bores. I'd rather be dead than a bore. Doesn't he bore you, Moseley?"

"Well, yes. Only I didn't expect Geology 10 to be exciting. I took it to satisfy the science requirement. It's supposed to be the easiest way."

"That's why they put the dullest men in the department on the survey courses—because the freshmen are just satisfying the requirement. But that's no excuse for a stupid man like Carmody putting a hundred people to sleep in the middle of the day. If any one of us had the slightest interest in geology, Carmody would strangle it with obtuseness. 'A fault, gentlemen' "—Jay gargled in a convincing mimicry—" 'is a break in the earth's crust.' I expect sometime he'll announce the earth is round like a tennis ball. Jesus. Well, I'm not putting up with it."

"But you didn't drop the course?" I took my first apprehensive glance at the speedometer and watched it climb past sixty. Jay seemed in no way daunted by thoughts of ambush.

"Why? The zoology and the chem are just as bad. They're hurdles you're supposed to jump to get to the good men. The system is terrible, but there it is. And thank God for the tutoring schools or the whole crummy freshman year would collapse. You take advantage of the higher education up at Elm City and Rosenbaum's?"

"No. Not yet."

"No kidding, never been to Rosie's? Jesus, Moseley, you're missing Yale. On the night before the Geology 10 exam, Rosie gives you everything in two hours. I mean everything that oaf Carmody has said in three months."

"That's okay if you can afford it," I said. "Except you know what they say about cramming, that you only retain it for the exam. It doesn't stick."

"Good. I wouldn't want to clutter my mind with all those eskers and fossils. What good does that do you? Rosie gives you the questions they're going to ask on the exam and then he gives you the answers. They must have been giving the same exams for years. I mean if they're that stupid it stands to *reason* they couldn't be teaching you anything worthwhile. You know what I think—they should get Rosie to teach every freshman course in the university. He could do the whole year in a couple of weeks and we could all go home by the first of November. You know what I got in my midterm? I got seventy-six—every point of it Rosie's. What did you get?"

"Seventy," I said. "Have they been more generous with you on cuts? They only gave me seven for the whole year and they take doubles for a last class on Friday."

"Same here," Jay said, skirting a truck on the upgrade. We narrowly avoided an oncoming car, and its horn could be heard blowing resentment as we sped past. "No special privilege."

"But no one's been in your seat."

"There's always a way . . ." He turned to me, smiling.

My own eyes went to the road ahead. There was an inevitability, like the realization of some dimly recollected nightmare, to our passage through Orange. Sensing my anxiety, Jay was provoking it. The needle of the speedometer touched the 70 mark and he seemed as much intoxicated by my quailing as the speed itself. The posted limits flashed by so fast I could not read them. I clutched the door handle and looked ahead for the constable.

Though I had no experience of it, I dreaded arrest. The sight of a policeman, even traffic lights, sobered me. Once touched, however lightly, by the finger of the law, a man was not only subjected to a heartless legal process and its petty tyrants, he was also infected with the virus of criminality. Who knew where it might end? That was *my* heritage.

So when the police car, a sinister black Ford, jumped from its lair at the roadside, I felt doomed. Even though it was Jay, not I, who was the lawbreaker, I could not avoid the feeling of complicity. The whining siren behind us was a dirge to which I junked my weekend plans in favor of a court appearance.

Jay was equally aware of pursuit. He studied the road behind him in the mirror but without slowing at all. We swerved to pass a farm truck just emerging from a side road and then leaped onward.

"Pierce, you can't, for Christ's sake. You can't get away from him."

"The hell I can't. That heap of his can't do better than eighty."

"He's got the license. He was close enough for that." My feet forced mightily at the floorboards and it occurred to me that Pierce was really insane. Losing all my own nerve, I cried out, "For God's sake, stop, Pierce. Let me out!"

He reacted slowly—first with a glance at me to see that I really was frightened, and he took an instant's satisfaction from that, then another in the mirror to assure himself that he could, that we were drifting away from the now petulant wailing behind us—and having scored twice, he said coolly, "Okay," and let the big car slow down.

Once stopped on the gravel shoulder, Jay reached for my rigid leg and grasped it just above the knee. "Oh, Moseley!" He laughed. "You're a tonic, you are. You're good for me." Then, joyously, he leaped from the car to trot back for his interview with the Orange constable.

I could see him through his windshield, a narrow, foxy man, and I sensed the menace in him, in his obdurate refusal to look up at Jay. He seemed rooted there behind his wheel. Frowning at Jay's credentials, he seethed as though he had chased us on foot.

Alongside, Jay was admiring a pair of dusty draft horses as they cropped away at some yellow stubble. While I trembled, Jay looked as unconcerned as if he were ordering breakfast at the Smoke Shop.

Then, bewilderingly, the man smiled. There was a round of nodding and a shaking of hands as though they had found kinship, and in the next moment Pierce Jay was strolling back to join me. Without a word he started the Packard's engine and resumed the road westward. I looked behind to see the police car make a brisk U-turn and head in the direction from which it had come.

"Now what was that all about? What happened?"

"Nothing. He thought we were driving too rapidly. They've got a lot of chickens around here and he didn't want us to frighten them. I told him we'd be careful. That's all."

"Come on, Pierce. I want to know. Don't you have to go back? What did you say to him? Did you give him some money?"

Jay had the car up to sixty, but he looked over at me, still bubbling with self-pleasure, and again kneaded my leg. "Oh, Mose. Oh, Morosely boy—that would be telling."

*   *   *

Just as we were getting onto the parkway in Westchester, Jay produced a pint bottle of whiskey from the dash compartment and handed it to me to break the seal. I took a swallow and hoped that would be the end of it, for I've never liked whiskey straight and particularly from the mouth of the bottle. Jay took a gulp and smacked his lips theatrically in a way that suggested he didn't enjoy it greatly either. Then he asked what was taking me to New York.

"Some dance at Barnard."

"Barnard?" It was as though he had never heard of it.

"A girl from home asked me."

"Ahh. *The* girl? Childhood sweetheart?"

"No. Matter of fact, I don't even know her very well. She's tall and plays tennis. She just wrote and asked me. It's Yale, I guess. They like to have Yale guys take them."

"I can understand how you got asked—but why go? Does she screw?"

I laughed. "I suppose she's capable. I have my doubts about it this weekend."

"Well, there you *are*. Why would you want to go to Barnard? Sounds gloomy."

"It was the best offer I had."

"Jees, I think I can better that. There's a dinner I might be able to get you into and a big dance at the St. Regis."

"I don't see how I can."

"And afterwards, after dumping the jailbait, I could take you over to meet Julie at the Orph. Ever been to the Orph? No kidding—Well, you ought to meet Julie. It was Julie, you know, I had up to the S.P.S. dance. Did you know that? Oh, was that ever something. She doesn't look like a whore, you know. She was a little older than all the prim little cunts from Farmington and Walkers but she'd picked up the look. She goes down to Princeton all the time and she keeps her eyes open. She wears her hair in the pageboy, and she arrived in this tweed skirt and sweater and the virginal string of pearls, and if it weren't for the way she walks and a little too much make-up—she wears that deep purple kind—she'd have got home free. But at the tea, you know, the Rector's wife looked her over—sniff, sniff—and then she wanted to know, 'Oh, Jay, is your girl from New York? Gravawicz? Now that's an interesting name. Is her family . . . Czechoslovakia, I see. The diplomatic? And school . . . Oh, I see, studying art. I see.' She was chilly and suspicious now, watching all the time because Julie was overcompensating on the accent. And oh, Morosely, when she turned up at the dance in a white satin dress with one of these low-cut fronts, honest to God, right to the edge of her nips, and when the Rector's wife saw Julie coming down the receiving line with her big well-handled bubies practically falling out—Oh, Morosely, you've never seen anything so funny in your life. The Rector's wife groaned and scooped up a sweater from the chair behind her and wrapped it around Julie like she was going to explode any minute and hustled her out of the gym, all in eight seconds flat. When Julie got back to the dance she was in a black tent that belonged to the Rector's wife and covered her from her Adam's apple down. In the morning, when I got called into the

Rector's office for my walking papers, some guys made a big
ice sculpture of her, Queen of Concord, you know, and Julie
was still laughing when she got back to Times Square."

"You were kicked out for that? Bringing a girl they didn't
like to the dance?"

Jay shrugged. "There were other matters. We didn't get
along, S.P.S. and me. We didn't go for one another's attitudes.
Now *you* might get along fine there . . ."

"Julie thought it was *funny*—your getting kicked out on
her account?"

"Oh, Morosely. You get so tense, boy." He nodded
thoughtfully. "You've got to loosen up if you're going to get a
liberal education. You haven't been to the Orph. You haven't
been to the Knick to meet Cathy, the girl who took on seventeen guys the night of the Columbia game. I mean it. This is
an important part of your education—more important than
old Carmody's lectures in the igneous and sedimentary.
You're neglecting it shamefully. You ought to do something
about it." He laughed and thrust the bottle toward me.

"No thanks."

Tilting it, he took a mouthful, swished it bravely between
his cheeks before swallowing and wiped his mouth with the
back of his hand. "The Barnard prom—Jesus. You ought
to meet a girl I was out with last week—the nymphomaniac
debutante. She's only seventeen but *built*. She's a little Venus
and she absolutely loves it—takes it right out of your pants.
She felt me up under a table at the Stork Club."

"I don't believe it!" It burst from me angrily. "I don't believe half the stuff you're telling me." He gave me a blank
glance and returned his attention to the road. "I really don't.
You're just pulling my leg, aren't you?"

"You want to come and see?"

"I can't stand this girl up, and anyway I've only got about
fourteen bucks."

"It's on me. I'm taking your education in hand."

The temptation was formidable. I *did* half believe him and
there was plenty of prurience in me, plenty of inquisitiveness

about the high and low life I suspected I was missing. I was equally curious about him. I yearned to know if I was calling his bluff. But, as he anticipated, I didn't. My qualms prevailed.

"Another time, maybe," I said.

"There may not be another time. Never count on tomorrow."

"I always do and so far it hasn't failed me."

"It will." He was looking out at the sooty, apathetic houses of Yonkers. "That's what all the poor saps out there are doing. They're boring people and they live boring, starving lives. You know why? Because they're saving themselves for tomorrow—misering out their spirit in drops and pinches, putting pennies in the piggy bank against a rainy day. For what, Mose? For more of the same."

"You sound as though you don't have long to live," I said. "Is something wrong with you?"

"I'm going to live forever."

"Then why do you want to do everything tonight? It'll be tomorrow and you'll have done everything—drunk all the whiskey and laid all the girls. There'll be nothing left to do."

"There's always more."

"I'm not so sure. Not if you're sated. Not if you've burned yourself out."

"Don't preach at me, Morosely. I don't go for sermons."

"Then what about survival at Yale? What about getting ahead? Remember? You make your bed in freshman year. From the first moment they're passing judgment on everything you do."

"Did I say that? Really? Well, as you must know, it's a lot of shit and it's unkind of you to keep bringing it up. I don't think I believed it at the time. I must have been trying it out on you to see how impressionable you were. And, brother . . ."

"But it isn't shit. Basically it's true. We are being watched and we do have to conform."

"To what?" he asked. "To what everybody else is doing? Well, fuck that."

"It's no longer important to impress the upperclassmen? Friends? Your crowd from school?"

"Listen, Moseley. Let me tell you something. Right after I quit the squad, I'd hear them going out, yelling at one another in the afternoon, and I'd walk over to the Taft bar and have a couple of drinks. Very dark in there and nobody much around. I'd be thinking of what they were doing out at practice. I'd look at my watch and figure it would be passing drill now, or blocking, or it was about time for the scrimmage. The days were still warm and long then, and at the end of the third one I was ready to go out to the field, wringing my cap, and ask Reggie to take me back. I would have, I guess, if I hadn't run into George Vandevanter. It was about five o'clock, just after the bus came in with the freshmen, and I found George on the fence outside Yale Station getting a shine and I walked over and perched there beside him. You know Vandevanter?"

"No."

"Well, I do. From way back. From school and a lousy summer camp we went to in Switzerland when we were kids. I was asking George what they'd done today—when he jumped up, suddenly, like he had to go to the can, and he tried to pay the shine boy, only the shine boy wouldn't let go of George's shoe. He hadn't finished, see. He'd brushed it but he hadn't polished it with his cloth. A regular perfectionist, he was. It was very funny—George finally prying himself loose from this crazy colored kid and tearing off. Then I noticed the varsity bus had come in and guys were piling out and crossing Elm Street toward us—Humphrey and Anderson and all of them—and as they went by into Yale Station, they looked like they'd smelled something bad." Jay's laughter rang out in a contemptuous bark. "I had a little dose of leprosy, see—and nobody'd even told me."

"You imagined it."

"No," he said. "No mistake. Believe me, until then it hadn't even occurred to me. But now all of a sudden my best friends—the guys I'd known all my life, who were always hanging around the room wanting to walk over to Commons, as though they didn't know the way yet—were no place around. Vanished. Pouf! Very magical."

"Then why didn't you go back to practice?"

"Because the stupidity of my comrades of the gridiron had become exquisitely clear. It was total—like their brains were permanently frozen. They had minds so narrow, nothing bushy, only the skinniest, worn, threadbare ideas, could get in there. I could see them as old guys, going down to their Yale clubs to watch the films and coming back to games until they're seventy, grim as death when the old team loses and getting on the wire first thing Monday, trying to fire the coach. Jesus. You've got to watch these guys, I'm telling you, Ben. They'll smother you if they can."

His spirit was persuasive but I was bewildered by the logic. Disgust—first with the new Yale, then false friends—was leading him to an impossible confrontation.

I knew that Jay had made a spectacular run against Exeter but was undependable, and Root had been seeking to discipline his performance by keeping him on the bench. In this first, comforting awareness of a legacy's burdens, I understood that Jay might find that impossible to endure. But what I could not grasp was why he must go to such lengths of alienation. The drink, the wanton girls, the fast-and-loose with the Dean's office was a courting of disaster that appalled me.

I took Jay, who seemed sprung from another planet, at face value—and yet rolling into New York in that great Packard, his cloak of pride had parted just long enough for me to recognize the paradox. In that instant I had a glimpse of vulnerableness. My reaction was embarrassment, as though I had accidentally happened on Jay in some shameful act, and tacitly agreed with him that I had seen nothing.

"Even so," I said, "I think you do care very much about Yale."

After a moment's reflection, in which he gave great concentration to the traffic ahead, he said, "What matters, Moseley, is to be your own man, you understand? *I'm* going to be my own man. I'm going to do nothing because it's been done by all the poor saps." He began to bray, tunelessly, the line from "The Whiffenpoof Song"—*Lord have mercy on such as we—ba-a, ba-a, ba-a.* "Only when I believe in it—you understand?"

"All right. But that's no excuse for not going to class."

"It gives me pleasure. That's the excuse."

"How do you expect to get *away* with it? You can't beat the cut system. Some hawkshaw at the Dean's office is going to figure it out sooner or later. The odds are against you."

"I'll lay you a little three-to-one on it. Take me?"

"What if you get caught?"

"So be it. I'll have had my fun. I'm always ready to pay for fun."

We passed under the great arm of the George Washington Bridge reaching for the Palisades, and the towers of Riverside Drive came into view, wearing in the dusk the faintly colored glow that preceded their kindling.

"And the girls? What's the belief about them?"

"Ah—that you have to *ask.*"

"Don't put me off, goddam it. I mean your nymphomaniac debutante and Julie the Orph girl. If you really are the big swordsman you say and you're not just crapping me . . ."

Jay rolled his eyes.

"Well, isn't there a high price on that too?"

"Now there you go preaching again. What have you been up to—reading George Frederick Gundelfinger? Come on, level with me. You've been worrying about John Barleycorn and Nat Nicotine and Sally Syphilis all lurking about trying to get at the white altar of your body—isn't that it?" He turned to appraise a girl driving a station wagon in the inner lane. He waved at her and she turned away.

"Well, what about it? You were the one who took such pride in his body. Remember? It was important that it be in perfect working order—important you could do anything with it."

"Now, *that* I'll own up to. The body is nothing in itself. It's just a machine for giving and getting pleasure and for carrying the mind around, and like any machine it should be tested from time to time, not kept in the garage to deteriorate." In illustration he released a burst of the Packard's energy and passed four cars in startling fashion. "You've got to see what it will do, what its capacity is, what you can deprive it of, you know, of sleep and food and warmth, of how much it can eat and drink and copulate. That's what your ding-dong is for, you know. It's for spreading the joy around. If you don't know about that, what's the use of having it."

Jay turned off at Seventy-ninth Street and started across town. "Got a place to stay?"

"A room at the Biltmore."

"You want to save the five bucks? There's a bed at my joint."

"Wouldn't that be some trouble?"

"There's only Ma and she'll see right away what a good influence you are." He laughed.

"Yes, if you're sure." Some barrier seemed to have broken between us and I felt relaxed with Jay for the first time. "I hope it's all right that I'm acting on some of your castoff advice. I'm going to heel the *News* in the next competition."

"No," he said incredulously. "Can you do that—and the Student Agency job?"

"I've got it all fixed. They're going to give me some time off."

"That's great. Really." We had stopped for a light at Central Park West and Jay leaned forward on the wheel to gaze at me with a slowly evolving smile, and then he said, "By God, Moseley, you *are*, aren't you? You're going to make it."

"I don't know that I will," I said. "It's stiff as hell. Do you know how tough the competition is? It's six weeks of running your ass off."

He shook his head. "I didn't mean the *News* competition.

Of course you'll make that." The traffic light changed and we
sped forward into the cut. "Why do you really want to make
the *News?*"

"You talked me into it. Yes—really, you did. You told me a
freshman has to make some kind of mark in an extracurricular field. That's how you prove yourself. Why do you make
that funny face. It's true, Pierce. You know it is."

"If I were you, I wouldn't take my word for a thing."

"Henry Luce then. Henry Luce says heeling the *News* is
the best training for business of any kind—for whatever work
you go into. It seems too valuable an experience to pass up,
that's all."

We rushed on across the park, toward the great cliffs of
Fifth Avenue soaring above the bare trees and the fretful
streams of traffic, and I saw in the lights of an oncoming taxi
that his face had turned thoughtful.

"Why don't you heel too?" I asked, and there was a moment before he laughed.

 3

I recall little of that Saturday evening in New York, possibly because it was just as forgettable as Pierce had warned, but more likely because what happened the next day so dwarfs it in my recollection. On Sunday, before we drove back to New Haven, I met Angela Rice.

With another girl she came to the Jays' apartment in the Savoy Plaza. They wore identical short silver-fox jackets, a uniform with New York girls that year, but Angela was small and blond, with the fairest skin I had ever seen. From my corner I watched her move about the room, attracted by her appearance, a combination of youth (she was barely seventeen) and worldliness I had not encountered in Providence. She seemed to be at that moment in life when a girl teeters between child and woman, one toe in each world, delighting in, reluctant to part with, the naïve joys of flirting, yet drawn toward the mysteries of womanliness and first acquaintance with passion and grief.

There was an innocence about her mouth. Its upper lip was rather narrow and came to a point, like the prow of a tiny boat, while the lower was full and round. She laughed easily and too frequently, and yet it was true laughter, rippling with a love of pleasure. There was a rubbery, infant plumpness to her body, especially her calves, still tanned from a tropical vacation. But there was also a cosmopolitanism about her—in her style of course, in that expensively simple black dress and plain pumps, the gold bracelet and the flawless symmetry of her shiny hair, but more essentially in her eyes. They were elliptical, with rather heavy, S-curved lids which gave them a sexy look of indolence. She gave the impression of being unshockable, that for all her youth she was beyond illusion.

There was luncheon for eight in the small yellow dining room of Melissa Jay's apartment. From its windows I had a dizzying view of the garden with miniature ponds and bridges that the park made some thirty floors below.

Melissa Jay, pale and queenly in widowish lavender, exchanged apprehensive glances with me from the head of the table. She was chatting energetically about acquaintances common, it seemed, to all but me. "Minnie" had given a dinner at which the soufflé never rose. "Frederica" and "Jim" had been divorced and remarried. "George" had suffered an attack of indigestion on the floor of the Stock Exchange and been helped to a taxi by "Amos"—which struck everyone as funny.

Pierce, at the opposite end of the oval table, sensed my awkwardness, and despite the gray hangover which was so clearly tormenting him, gave me an expressive roll of his eyes. He had flanked himself with Angela and a tall, dark-skinned girl whose insouciance had further intimidated me. Their interest in Pierce and natural competitiveness had overwhelmed their manners and neither paid me much attention. But before the bisque cups were cleared, Pierce reached for the reins of the table conversation. He did this naturally, in any situation, for he loved to show off, but I believe his purpose here was to see I was included.

"Hey, Ma. I want you to know how much we appreciate this good home cooking," he said. "The food in Commons is wholesome, you know, particularly that corned beef hash and the battleship-gray string beans, but it can't touch your grub for flavor. Would you agree, Ben?"

I grinned foolishly.

"It must be the saltpeter they put in everything up there that gives the food that flat taste. You don't put saltpeter in the soup any more, do you, Ma?"

Far from being distressed at this absurdity, Melissa Jay was delighted. She laughed, unreasonably, I thought, and appeared to take as much pleasure from her son's attention as did the two girls.

"Oh, darling," she said, "I wish you weren't just teasing. I wish you did come home more often. It seems I *never* see you any more. Even these few hours are such a treat for me." Melissa turned to plead with her table of guests. "I always hope when Pierce comes home for a weekend that *this* time I'm going to catch up on all the things he's doing at Yale, and of course I'm lucky to catch a glimpse of his coattails." Her hands flew up in despair. "After waiting all week to see my son, he's scarcely dropped his valise before he's off again. He takes a shower bath and in the next instant he's out the door to a party and I don't set eyes on him again until it's time for him to go back to New Haven, and I haven't discovered one single thing about what he's learning or all the fine new friends he's making"—there was no acknowledging glance for me—"or what he's doing in athletics. I used to go to all the football games with his father, you know. Pierce was the most loyal old Blue."

"Oh, Ma, cut it out. You hate going to the games. I remember that time at St. Paul's when it rained. Even wrapped up in fur robes and your feet in that electric warmer you were miserable."

"Of course I was, dear. But it wasn't the rain. It was the spectacle of all you boys hurtling at one another. I can still hear the sounds you made—thud and crack and grunt. I was certain every time they untangled one of those huge stacks of bodies, they were going to find yours, crushed, on the bottom.

No, I certainly didn't enjoy it. I used to go with your father because he loved it so. But I never enjoyed watching *you* play at school. I was too afraid you were going to be the next one hurt. I think watching one's children play rough sports is absolutely terrifying. Do you remember the boxing at Buckley? Oh, Angela, it was frightful—all we mothers watching our children turning bloody in the nose and crying as if their tiny hearts had broken. Oh, I remember the faces of the mothers of the boys who were winning; how they, too, grew brutal. I can still recall that." She laughed and clapped her hands in delight. "Oh, dreadful!"

"Well, you can relax now, Ma," Pierce said. "Now that I'm twenty, I'm getting too brittle for the rough stuff. No more boxing. No more strife on the playing fields for me. No kidding. You can put away your anxiety."

"Oh, darling, I'm afraid we mothers never do that. I'm just as anxious now as I was when you were little." She looked hopefully at the bald man on her right, and he smiled. "I'm so frightfully anxious about the driving and the drinking. I'm not so concerned about the million other ways there are to get into trouble." She sipped from her wineglass and looked mischievously over its rim at the two girls. "Of course, I wouldn't like it at all if he should bring home a wife I didn't approve of, some lady from the circus perhaps, but"—and now she beamed at Pierce—"I'd try desperately not to let you know."

The girls, who had been exchanging sly, encoded glances, were sobered by this and gave her their full attention. "But oh yes," Melissa Jay continued, "I am frightened of highways. Not of you, dear. I know you're a good driver and a careful one, but you can never be sure of the others—and you are precious to me."

"You're a worrier, Ma. I'm Mr. Safety on the road. Really careful, aren't I, Ben?"

"Yes," I said. "Very careful."

Pierce grinned at my perjury and then addressed a thoroughly bewildered audience about me. Like a press agent, he announced my plans for the *News* competition and explained its significance in Yale's social and power structures, and summed up by advising Angela and Bettina, the other girl, to rescue me from the enwebbing of a junior Eastern States tennis champion who had been quick to recognize how much I had on the ball.

This facetiousness evoked a mild but tangible acknowledgment of my existence from Angela, which pleased me. In Melissa Jay, it stimulated a new curiosity, which did not. "Providence?" she asked. "But I have some dear friends there —Edgar and Cynthia Hopkins. I wonder if . . ."

"No. I don't know them."

"I'm sure your parents would. I think Edgar is head of your big insurance company."

"Providence Mutual."

"Yes—that's it."

"Now, Ma, that's a perverse thing you're up to. It's comforting, isn't it, to think everything interesting is part of your experience. But the truth is there's been a lot going on, even in Providence, and particularly in doctoring—Ben's father is a doctor . . . No you don't!" Pierce nipped off a new question of his mother's. "You parents—always trying to relate your own past to the children's future. It's a desire to limit them—you know that?"

Melissa Jay smiled helplessly. "But it's nothing of the sort. I was simply interested in Ben's . . ."

"Well, no more inquisition. Ben's a man of tomorrow and he has no past. The past limits, suggests he will follow familiar patterns, that history repeats itself. Well, that's not true of Ben."

I murmured a protest in behalf of Melissa Jay, who, though still enjoying his attention, was looking slightly dazed under the siege of her son's headlong argument. It was typical of Pierce, assailable, vulnerable, yet carrying just enough acuteness and crashing impetus to scatter reasonable opposition until he had escaped. Besides, it was occurring to me that his motive was less to harass his mother than to divert her from thoughtlessly embarrassing me.

I think Melissa Jay recognized this in the same instant, for she hurriedly accepted me. Those capricious, yet unmanning eyes rested on me just long enough for a new judgment and promptly I felt a touch of the warmth she held for her son. From that moment she included me as Pierce's friend and a possible ally of her own.

Presently, linking her arm through Pierce's, she led us from the table into her living room, where we were to have coffee and brandy. The others grouped themselves around the fireplace, where to my surprise there burned a real fire of split oak. I was just about to take a chair somewhat apart when Melissa Jay beckoned me to the place beside her on the sofa. Nevertheless, as I watched her fill cups from a tall silver coffeepot and listened to the ebb and flow of conversation around me, I found I was tongue-tied. I caught sight of my socks, bright argyles contrasting sharply with the creamy shades of the rug, and had second thoughts about their appeal, but it was my continued inability to find words that troubled me.

Soon I retreated behind my smile, observing the others as though through a sheet of plate glass, reasoning that my muteness was due to having no substance here, that I owed my existence in this mauve room with its delicate French furniture to accident, to Pierce's whim.

As the shadows lengthened, a curious, drowsy constraint enveloped me. I felt overfed and numb, bound like Gulliver with a multitude of fine threads and mildly drugged with melancholia. I was watching Angela Rice, watching how her silken knees crossed, the toe of one black pump swinging to and fro, negligently, but to a dance step surely, to some tune in her pretty head, and was ever more poignantly aware that I was invisible to her.

Pierce gave her a cigarette, and as he held a light for her, his hand trembled. She laughed at that and steadied it affectionately, and at that moment it occurred to me that Angela might be the wanton girl of the Stork Club. The possibility was agonizing and yet beguiling.

Pierce, at his drollest, was telling another story at his

mother's expense—how she had been persuaded by her hair-dresser to invest in a Connecticut chinchilla ranch. Angela listened attentively, cheek cradled in a smooth, possibly bone-less hand whose carmined fingertips disappeared into her golden forelock. From time to time she pursed her lips, as though sipping, to blow little feathers of smoke. When she laughed, tossing back her hair, the heavy-lidded eyes crinkling in delight, I coveted her desperately and yet I knew that feeling to be the kind which was more likely to make a clown of me than an acceptable suitor.

It was Bettina who suggested a movie, a particular film playing at the theater nearby, and Pierce, who thought it sounded too frivolous for Sunday and his own penitent frame of mind, deferred to me.

"It's nearly four," I pointed out. "We'd never get back to New Haven."

"Oh, must you go so soon?" Melissa Jay protested. "Couldn't you stay and have an early dinner and a good night's sleep? Pierce darling, you do look tired. I think it would be *so* good for you." Quickly she turned to me. "Wouldn't you like that, Ben?"

"I'd like that. Of course I would." Both girls were looking at me. I had not anticipated my time at the fulcrum, but now I took it gratefully. "But I have an eight-o'clock in the morning. We'd have to leave before six. I don't think we could do that. Besides, I've left some reading to do for it."

Pierce laughed. "You see, Ma? You see about Ben?"

*   *   *

Through the window of Pierce's bedroom I was watching the western sky, a wide banner of lemon-colored silk, turn a deeper citrus hue, the tangerine of its border. The massive towers of the midtown hotels and offices which half an hour ago had seemed the gray battlements of an impregnable fortress now shone in the soft light like the minarets of an enchanted city where old corsairs lay dreaming of their youth—and the plunder of the world might be had for the taking.

On one of the twin beds, my suitcase stood packed and ready. Pierce, still in shirt sleeves, lay sprawled across the other, his foot and hand dangling to the rug as he eyed the ceiling from under fluttering lids.

"I had no idea what it would be like, living in a tower," I said. "It's fairyland. Though I suppose it gets real around the first of the month."

"I suppose it does." Pierce shaded his eyes to squint at me against the sunlight. "And I guess it is. I guess that's why Ma likes this joint, poor old bat. She's always one for getting as far from where they keep the garbage as she can."

"You can hardly blame her for that."

Pierce raised his hand from the floor and examined the smoldering stump of a cigar it held and took a puff on it. "Well, yes I can. That's why I have at her all the time. It worries me, her dodging unpleasantness. She sees people the way she wants them to be and that's what makes her the pushover she is. Some flit decorator just sold her a boatload of furniture—carted off the old stuff, which was perfectly good, and put in all this crap. He even, for Christ's sake, was going to make off with the old man's barber chair."

"Barber chair?"

"Yes, you want to see it? Come on—" And Pierce was off the bed, all nervous energy, leading the way along a corridor, past the bedroom where Melissa Jay had disappeared for a nap, toward the back of the apartment. Just short of the pantry he paused before a narrow door and opened it on a darkened room.

He entered, beckoned me after him, closed the door behind us and turned on the light. It was a small bedroom, probably a maid's, and although carpeted, curtained and sparsely furnished, it was clearly untenanted, a room for storage, the makeshift attic of the Jays' winter home. Dress and hat boxes were stacked on the vanity table, and in the closet, which stood open, I saw the kind of luggage—the cases for golf clubs, top hats, guns, fishing rods and photographic equipment— that clutters the checkrooms of men's clubs.

In the very center of the room stood a piece of furniture unlike any I had ever seen. It was a narrow, spidery chair tilted in semi-recline. Its frame was of slender, dark lengths of fine-grained mahogany. Beneath its seat some brass rods, a great cogwheel and a long crank with an ivory handle suggested further ingenuities. The seat, back, head, arms and footrests were of worn cowhide, the color of roasted coffee.

"You want to try it?"

I stepped into it gingerly, for it looked so fragile I feared it might give way, but once I was seated I found myself gently and firmly supported, and as Pierce manipulated the crank beneath me, raising my legs and lowering my head and shoulders, I had the agreeable feeling of being tenderly cradled in some giant hand.

"He bought it in Honduras," Pierce said. "Right out of the barbershop in Tegucigalpa. He stepped out of this thing and told the barber he'd never had a more comfortable shave and he wanted the chair, so the price of it should be added to his bill and he'd take it along. And by God, he walked out with it and brought it back on the plane and he had it set up in his room in a house we used to have on Seventy-ninth Street. His regular barber, Emil from the Racquet Club, came up and gave the old man a shave in it and me a haircut. And after that it just sat there, but we used to get in it now and then and talk about how superior it was to the big chromium thrones they have every place and how we would form a company someday and make a bunch of them. He could fall asleep in it right away—and he used to have a lot of trouble sleeping."

"It's great," I said, trying to rise.

"Wait," he said and cranked me upright.

The moment I was clear of the chair, Pierce stepped into it, and leaning over its side, deftly cranked himself into a steep recline. "By God, that's all right, isn't it? It beats that Louis Quinze stuff out in the living room. It not only feels better, it's better-looking. You know what, Mose? I'm going to take it back to New Haven. Wouldn't it be a good thing to have in the room? What do you think?"

I had been watching the tilted supine Pierce from the window sill. He had closed his eyes momentarily, and the effect was so strongly that of an anesthetized patient, or possibly a corpse, upon a table that when he raised the cigar stub to his lips, there was something richly comic in the gesture and I laughed.

"What?" he asked.

"I don't know," I said. "Are you going to be there long enough to bother?"

"Where?"

"In New Haven."

"Sure. What makes you say that?"

"I have the impression you're trying to get kicked out."

"Do you?" He answered sharply, warning me I had touched the quick. He left the question unanswered, plainly posting an area of no trespass. Eager to comply, I spoke of the chair again. "No, I wouldn't take it back to college," I said. "It's too important. It means too much to you to have it around as a kind of curiosity, you know what I mean? I can imagine guys climbing over it, making fun of it, maybe damaging it. It's a wonderful contraption and it's irreplaceable."

"You're right, Mose. We'll leave it."

"Anyway, it's part of the magic here in your cloud house. If you took it away, the whole spell up here might break."

"You've never been in a joint like this?"

"I've been in hotels and offices, but never anything quite like this, never quite this view of my fellow man and his works. The city, even the ugliness of it, looks like a game for kids from up here, doesn't it? Something you could hold in your hand. Simple height, maybe—military advantage. Looking at the world from up here makes it all seem so easy, doesn't it?"

"What all?"

"Oh—having your way, I guess. Getting what you want."

"A girl?"

"Well, not entirely. Not . . . yes. I suppose, yes. A girl."

"Too bad you didn't go for the ginch today," he said drowsily. "Shame. They were imported for your personal gratification, Morosely. If you'll give me some idea of your tastes, I'll try and do better next time."

"They were fine."

"They were?" Pierce raised his head from its rest to look at me. "Then why didn't you want to stay? We could have gone out dancing someplace. The Stork maybe. Come to think of it, the Stork is pretty good fun of a Sunday night." He brought the stub of cigar to his mouth again and puffed languidly. "Found time for a bit of intimacy and still got you back to New Haven for your eight-o'clock."

"Well, now you mention it, there *was* one trouble with the girls. They both liked you."

"Oh, Morosely, don't be an ass." He raised himself awkwardly on an arm now to see me better. "Could you have gone for one of them?"

"Sure."

"Which?"

"Angela." I smiled, discovering relief, a rich pleasure just in speaking her name. "Angela Rice."

"Well, for Christ's sake, why didn't you say so? They've *gone.*"

"Look, was Angela the girl . . . I had the feeling she was the one you were talking about, the one who was so eager . . ."

Pierce laughed. "No, she's not the nymph. Not Angela." His discovery of my vulnerableness gave him exquisite pleasure. He peered at me through eyes asquint, chortling like Old Scratch himself. "But supposing she's gone off into a nunnery. She seemed to have every intention, Morosely. Here you've gone and blown your chance again."

"I've blown nothing, Pierce. Angela wasn't for me and you know it. She couldn't take her eyes off you long enough to know if I was in the room."

"Oh, Morosely, you idiot. You just met her. What did you expect her to do, strip to the bolocky bare-ass and leap in your lap? She *was* attracted to you."

"You're lying." He had dropped back into repose, still smiling, puffing contentedly on the moist cigar stub, and I watched him with suspicion. "You're lying and you're taunting me."

"But I'm not. She asked about you."

"When?"

"Just as they left. That's what we were talking about in the hall—*you.*"

"What did she want to know—where I'd been to school?"

"No, stupid, nothing specific. She was just curious about you. I think she asked if we lived near each other. She wanted me to talk about you. Jesus, Morosely, I don't think you understand much about women. Remind me to fill you in."

I was thoroughly bewildered. I wanted to believe that there was truth in what he was telling me, that my timidity alone was the barrier I saw around Angela, that she had been aware of me and only lacked the opportunity to let me know. Perhaps I had crossed the threshold into this giddy world where improbable pleasures were effortlessly attained. And yet a sober, inner voice told me not to be deceived, that here, just as on the road, there was a law for Pierce Jay and another one for me.

"Do you think, if I asked her up to New Haven for something, for Derby Day maybe, that she'd come?"

"Yes, Morosely. I think she would. Yes sirree. I'll bet you and Angela could do big things for one another." He smiled with a flickering lasciviousness, like some cynical old-world matchmaker. Then his eyes closed and in a moment he was fast asleep.

*　　　　*　　　　*

The bursar was as mindful as any man of campus prestige, and knew its benefits to his boys and to their homely enterprises. So I was encouraged, as much for the laundry's sake as my own, to enter the *News* competition.

During the week which followed my trip to New York, I put my obligations to the Associated Student Agencies into the hands of one of the secretaries, much as a businessman might on the eve of a vacation, and promising to drop in frequently and keep an eye on my real livelihood, I went on down York Street to the organization meeting for the spring competition.

It was held in the vaulted copy room of the Britton-Hadden Memorial Building at the east end of Fraternity Row. There, some thirty prospective heelers filled the hard benches and the shelf, one continuous typewriter table projecting from the three stone walls. One by one, the owlish, seasoned staff members, the juniors who would manage and edit the paper until the middle of the following year, spoke to us, outlining the hardships we would endure, warning off the academically weak and the irresolute. Only a few of us could hope to survive. For the thirty freshmen present, there was room for less than ten on the *Oldest College Daily*'s board.

The chairman talked about policy, the *OCD*'s relation and responsibility to the university. The managing editor described the nature of the competition and the point system of survival. The two chiefs were followed by the department heads, who told how each separate arm of the organization— production, business and advertising, sports, university and general news, features, photography and entertainment— went about its work.

It was all grim enough, purposely so, and when it was over, half a dozen of the would-be competitors rose, gathered up their belongings and made quietly for the door.

"All right, if the rest of you are crazy enough to stay, I'll take your names. It was the managing editor, his sleeves rolled up, tie askew and clipboard in hand. "Speak up when I point to you."

"Moseley," I said as his finger sought me out. "Benjamin Moseley . . . *e*-y."

A moment later a voice announced: "Jay. Pierce Jay . . . a-y." I turned, and to my amazement, found Pierce grinning just behind me. He wore, collar turned up, an elaborate trench coat bristling with superfluous flaps, straps and grommets. It was faded and worn, as though a veteran of a dozen hazardous assignments. Pierce winked. "May the best man win, Morosely."

 4

I can recall the anxiety of the eight-week novitiate. The dungeon we knew as the heelers' room, an achievement of Yale's collegiate Gothic years, was fashioned from great chunks of granite. There was stone underfoot, overhead in three menacing barrel vaults and facing us from buttressed walls. These last were pierced by such narrow vine-laced slits that at noon on a bright day I typed my copy by the light from a gooseneck lamp and began to develop that wariness for unseen obstacles peculiar to the blind.

High in the east wall, some fifteen feet above our bent heads, there was a single opening, the top of our well. When its battened door flew open, a shaft of light fell from it upon our blinking, upturned faces. Like laboratory mice, never knowing if the signal foretold the cheese or the electric shock, we tensed for further developments.

The trumpet voice was that of Logan, the assignment editor and our scourge. "Moseley? You down there? What the hell do you *mean* there's no Budget Drive story. We've got a hole for it and there's nothing else to put in. Get your tail up here!"

Or later, toward the dinner hour, the door would bang open and disdainful fingers would release some sheets of yellow copy paper, the fruit of a day's foraging and best efforts at composition. Heavily slashed with grease pencil, the pages floated down accompanied by editorial advice. "You've got it all bassackwards, Blodgett. We don't find out what Reverend Lovett's sermon was about until the third paragraph, and nobody's going to read that far in this crud. Try it again." And the door shut with a bang as Blodgett groped in the murk gathering the scraps with which he must rebuild his hopes and self-esteem.

Outside the heelers' room, a rocky tunnel led to the editorial floor above, and we wore away at its granite treads bearing our offerings up to Logan's sacrificial block. Waiting there for some crumb of encouragement, we could view the leisurely, fraternal order of the arrived journalist. Briggs, the sports editor, had crossed his feet on his desk to confer with an assistant coach just back from Cambridge and a scouting of the Harvard baseball team. The movie reviewer tapped out another taunt at Hollywood and paused to gloat.

In the middle of the floor and, in our view, at the center of the university web, sat Bailey, the managing editor, assurance enough that despite our ineptness there would be an edition tomorrow. The dummy of it, already ruled and scrawled with his expectations, lay before him. Puffing serenely on his straight-stem pipe, he further pruned the stories that had got past Logan. He received a basket of prints, still gummy from the vats of the basement darkroom, and after a moment's deliberation with the photographer, selected a picture for the front page.

Sometimes the great paneled door beyond would open a few inches, just wide enough to release a narrow view of the chairman's office, with its big desk, two phones, flag, trophies —all bathed in a cascade of ecclesiastical light from the Gothic windows opening on York Street—and rarely, to release the chairman himself.

This was Butterfield, narrow as a giraffe, with a grave, equine face, who to our unabating amazement wore suits, not only a matching jacket and trousers, but a vest as well.

Butterfield clearly regarded the heelers' room as infectious and did not make an appearance there throughout the competition. But this was no surprise, for I had been warned by two survivors of the previous one that he would not address us by name and that if he were acquainted with our individual aptitudes and progress he would keep it, like everything else, to himself.

The errands which brought Butterfield out invariably had to do with the editorial page, most likely one of the serious columns—*Views on the News* or *Cabbages and Kings*—which he did not write but whose authors made up his cabinet. They sauntered boldly into the chairman's office to make their deliveries, possibly interrupting the composition of to-morrow's editorial, and Butterfield would personally see each column, marked with his majestic C. B., each carefully selected letter to the editor and, finally, the editorial itself, safely into Bailey's desk basket.

He might tarry a moment, sucking on his own curved-stem, to peer over Bailey's shoulder, to frown, to point a finger, but the racket outside seemed to impinge on his global and metaphysical reflections and he would soon retreat into his sanctuary, where, we believed, he communicated daily with President Seymour, Henry Luce and God.

The noise level in the *News* building varied with the hour. In the forenoon it centered in the business office where Miss Brown presided over the stenographers. Toward midday the order of the building was broken by the swinging of the oak entrance door and the first shufflings on the stone steps as the heelers straggled in, pale and punchy from their three-hour sleep, for the shape-up at Logan's desk.

At this early phase of the cycle, the phone bells summoned us at discrete intervals, bringing word of stirrings in the university's outposts. In the subbasement of Osborne Zoological Laboratory on far-off Prospect Street, the Science Club was to smash an atom, and on the cloud-embraced seventh floor of Payne-Whitney Gymnasium, fencers were to clash.

But as the afternoon wore on and the typewriters sputtered their first strangled words—*A gallant Mitre sextet went down to final period defeat*—the bells, the cries of the community we served, became insistent. In the hours ahead there would be endless trysts in the name of sport, health, song, worship, drink, fellowship, art, improvement of the mind or helping the needy. Bells encroached, one upon the other, then three at once, impolite now, urgent and demanding, as though a fire had broken out or, at last, the war in Europe, which the nabobs had been predicting since Christmas.

And voices, which had begun the *News* day tired and cross, were finding their strength. "Heel-*er!*" Logan would cry, cracking open his cupboard door. "On two—take a U-notice!" or "Heel-*er! Trip to the Toasty!*"

The peak, unless there was some big story coming in late, occurred about six, just before the board members loped off to the Zete and Deke bars for their predinner drink. By this time the paper was made up. There was rewriting to be done and a couple of stories were still developing, but save for emergencies, all was within the scope of the night editor, who would return from his fraternity grill at eight to oversee the final rewrites and the headline composition. Then, toward midnight, he would decamp with a pair of heelers for the printers.

Beyond the university's landscaped realm, where reason, fair play and sanitation ruled, lay the real New Haven, with its rail yards, auto-body shops and all-night diners. In its black heart stood a loft building which sheltered the Quinipiac Printing Company. Twice a week I would take my turn there and would slip like a prowler through its darkened front office, past hooded machines and shuttered desks whose tenants, indeed the rest of the world, as nature intended, were sleeping the night away. Under a cone of blue light at the back of the shop, an aproned, ink-stained alchemist received my armload of final copy dourly, never looking up from his linotype machine as it jingled out slugs minted from its reservoir of molten metal, slugs of university news, at last bright as sterling and for the moment too hot to handle.

As the hands of the big-pendulumed clock crept across the graveyard hours, I read yard-long galleys of proof against the original copy, and at the compositor's instructions, cut or padded stories to make them fit the space available yet, hopefully, retain their sense. Then, as I watched the edition, still crawling with my blunders, locked into its forms and the rollers of the big press spread a first coat of ink across its bed, I was free to go.

Cycling through the dark streets, where I shied at a gust-blown ball of paper or a scuttling cat, I noted the first gray streaks in the sky and shuddered at the thought of my eight-o'clock English class. By the end of the second week I had begun to lose weight and to assume a greenish pallor—but it was obvious that Pierce Jay was thriving.

In its sixty-one years the *OCD* had never seen a heeler like him. In his costume trench coat, battered hat, flashing a counterfeit press card, he seemed at first to be satirizing the intense professionalism that prevailed in the stony corridors of the Britton-Hadden Memorial Building; yet he exuded such ebullience, such zest for his chores, that doubts about his sincerity were swept aside.

Pierce arrived at the printer's as though for a party, unloading from the back of his Packard touring car a bagful of beer and pretzels to hearten us and to loosen the tongues of those grumpy union men. And they fell, not so much for the beer as for Pierce's pervasive good humor. The linotypist, who like Tenniel's carpenter capped his bald head with a paper box, was soon swapping obscenities with Pierce, vying with him in coarseness and laughing as he was outdone.

Pierce seemed to be exposing the fraternity of prurience between us college types and these meaty old men—and they loved it. Here was an okay Yale kid—nothing snotty or stand-offish about this one. And he *was* friendly. He really enjoyed them, I was sure of it. Occasionally, after I left, he would remain for some hands of pinochle and take on their chore of delivering the bales of printed papers to Yale Station, never getting to bed at all. But as I pedaled home through the night I would recall his wink for me and I sensed the printers were wrong, that just behind the Pierce who was all equality and fraternity, stood another, busily pulling their legs. I wondered they didn't detect it.

I had a special distaste for the bullying of local merchants the business department required of us. I dreaded the wheedling and shakedown, the forecasts of blight which befell the shopkeeper's trade who failed to take his quota of space, the collections from those lean, hungry cash registers along Church and Chapel streets and the unending disappointment with my performance which guttered in the eyes of Canby, the business manager.

But to Pierce, it was no effort at all. He danced through this part of the ordeal. He neither pleaded nor blamed his own competitive needs, but like some drummer possessed, whirled through the tailor shops and haberdasheries in a parody of supersalesmanship. Hypnotized, jollied and tempted with thoughts of Pierce's own custom, the inflexible merchants joyously doubled their commitments.

As a writer, Pierce was not gifted. He lacked that discipline, one that came more easily to me, of selecting from what he had seen and heard and putting it in order. Logan's reaction to confused, garbled copy was outrage, and he did not spare Pierce.

"Christ, what a mess!" he would bray. "We don't want to know about the quarter when nothing happened. Where were you when Branford scored, Jay? In some cathouse?"

Yet Logan's irascibleness was no match for Pierce's good-humored perseverance. Pierce pasted the who-what-why-when-and-where formula for lead writing onto his typewriter, and with difficulty but with unsinkable self-confidence, rewrote his stories a dozen times.

Shaking his head, Logan would throw him a life line. "I know this freshman commons story's boring, but you don't have to make it unreadable, for crying out loud. Now this mile of spaghetti business. That's kind of interesting. Couldn't you string the whole business on that?" And thanks to Logan's rough resuscitations, Pierce's first stories limped, groggy and mutilated, into Bailey's basket.

Pierce did excel in another, and I must confess a more significant, area of reporting. He had good journalistic imagination. As Bailey had told us at the outset, the highest premium was on origination. Unassigned stories counted double on our point scores. At the end of the first week Pierce proposed a series of interviews with minor campus figures—maids and waitresses (beds were made for us and we were waited on at table in those days), barbers, tailors, shine boys and bartenders.

His style was without whimsy. It was formal and deferential, suitable for interviewing a prime minister, so that at first reading, the stories seemed simple-minded. Yet he frequently caught the significant direct quote, one that gave the university reader a fresh and often devastating glimpse of the subject, or himself. It was only in retrospect that one sensed there *was* a point of view—an artful, mocking one.

And for some reason, the rest of us did not resent it when Pierce's role in the competition began to change from that of the bungler and clown to that of an erratic but dazzling performer. Perhaps it was because *he* did not change. Just as he was undismayed by his failures and Logan's harassment, he was unaltered by his first taste of success. He went right on entertaining us, though now it was more by what he said than by what he did.

He made preposterously lewd proposals about what Butterfield was really doing behind his closed door. Each evening he read aloud to us from his favorite articles, those prepared by the Health Department for the regular hygiene page. "How's this?" he would cry as he rushed in with the latest. "Cow called mother of human race." Or "Acne affects many young adults, beginning shortly after the age of puberty and terminating spontaneously when full sexual development has been attained."

When Pierce discovered that the *News* annually made a profit of twenty thousand dollars, which was carved up by the board without a penny to the heelers who had done all the donkey work and who, if they should fail of election, would never participate in *News* prosperity, he took time from the deadline rush to mount his bench for a seditious outburst.

"Heelers, hear me," he concluded his speech. "We toil in a serfdom—so flagrant an exploitation of us by the capitalists upstairs that it is a mercy poor Marx did not live to see it. By comparison, a coal mine is a worker's paradise. Arise. Now is the time for action. Demand your rights!"

From his crow's nest, Logan was scowling down on Pierce's performance, and Bailey, who had paused on his thirsty way to Zeta Psi to watch from the doorway, applauded. Pierce bowed and finished with the exhortation: "You have nothing to lose but the competition."

Logan soon became permissive of Pierce's copy. His stories would disappear at first draft, and if they were altered, it was by editorial hands. Then Bailey began to dote on Pierce. He would pause in the cavern's doorway to ask for him with a twinkle in his eye, as though there were delightful mischief in just mention of his name. In the fourth week of the competition we discovered that Pierce had talked him into a three-part series on the A.A. But the crusading tone of his first article on Yale Club scholarships, for which he had composed the head *Ringers in the Woodpile,* was too much for the sports editor, who gave the better part of an hour to explain to a disappointed Jay that his was a vulnerable stand and that if the story were to run, it would surely jeopardize alumni relations.

Pierce wasted no time sulking about it, and within another day he had bamboozled Bailey into a cheeky, unlikely expedition to Washington. Pierce had no special entrée—only the forged press card he had bought from a man at the New

Haven *Register*, but he was convinced he could get an interview with President Roosevelt. None of us believed he had a chance and thus we wished him well.

To our astonishment he did get admitted to the general press reception at the White House, where he dutifully recorded the President's answers to queries—news which would be on the stands by nightfall. When, at the conclusion of the conference, he approached the presidential desk and asked Mr. Roosevelt the question with which he had armed himself —"How can the college student of today protect himself from all the dangerous 'isms'?"—he was set upon by Stephen Early, the press secretary, and encircled by humorless men in blue suits. Just before he was hustled away, the amused President did give him an exclusive, if brief, story. "I would like to give the Yale *News* an interview," he told Pierce, "but I fear reprisal from the *Crimson.*"

Although Pierce felt he had failed in his mission, the account, that of an anonymous *News* reporter's experience at the hands of the Chief Executive, made Monday's front page, chalking up fourteen points for him. And as if that weren't enough reward, just outside the *News* building we encountered the chairman, who looked up from the cobbles to throw Pierce a salute. "Nice job at the White House, Jay," he said. The miracle. Stupefied, we watched Butterfield vanish down Fraternity Row.

When, in midcompetition, the news grew thin (Mermen Seek Eastern Crowns, Volleyball Tourney Announced), we eyed each other's scores warily and turned to grim research. Stories began to appear which compared Yale to other colleges, the ratio of students to instructors, say, culled from the pages of the *World Almanac;* or the number of books in Sterling Library (third most—Widener, irritating old wound, had twice as many).

When these chestnuts met resistance at Logan's desk, we sought the final, desperate resort of invention. Our time had come to produce the works which in truth were the children of our journalistic necessity but to the world outside would seem the seasonal manifestations of collegiate moon-madness.

In that year we had already experienced the goldfish-eating at Harvard. Lothrop Withington, Jr., a freshman there, had eaten a live goldfish. By reporting it, the *Crimson* had set off a chain of imitation. Campuses across the land vied for the consumption record until a sophomore at Oregon State choked on his forty-sixth (he had found that dipping them in ketchup made them go down easier, but even so, there proved to be a physiological limit). On the tail of the goldfish craze came that of eating Victrola records, which, understandably, did not become so widespread.

At Yale we had the Michigan co-ed affair, the concept of an ambitious heeler in the fall competition. He had invented a caravan of girls willing to follow the Michigan team from Ann Arbor to New Haven, not only to cheer it to a victory, but if only the formalities of introduction could be arranged, to undertake amorous adventures with Yale men.

It was the first time Yale had played one of the Big Ten colleges and few of us were familiar with the customs of the Midwest, but we were not entirely indifferent. We had seen provocative drum majorettes strut across the screen at the Poli and nursed a suspicion that girls in the big Western universities were generally handsome, healthy, sexually promiscuous (from watching the farm animals and being around boys all the time), and like most women, socially ambitious. It stood to reason they would prefer a polished, worldly Yale man to one of those clumsy cornhuskers in their sleeveless sweaters and porkpie hats.

Thus did the *News* readership follow avidly the reassurances that the girls from Ann Arbor were coming—the preparations, a map of the bus route and an estimate of the size of the party and its time of arrival.

The pairing was to be done by the *News* itself, according to height and hair color ("State second preference in case of shortage in your size"). One story reported on how severely the *News* planned to deal with an applicant who attempted to return, exchange or in any way evade delivery of his co-ed on sight.

Sixty-three applications were received, most of them expressing doubts that the girls would come, and yet on the morning of the Michigan game a crowd of several hundred undergraduates milled around in the Vanderbilt gateway awaiting the arrival of the buses. For the *News* photographer they held up the numbered cards that had been distributed ("Look for the girl with a corresponding number") and a banner reading *Welcome Michigan Eves—This Way to Paradise.*

There were cries of "Here They Come!" and laughter for each local bus that turned the corner and each bewildered woman on a Chapel Street errand. The exuberance continued into the lunch hour—long after it was clear there was no caravan of eager maidens on the way and never had been, and that everyone had been taken in. The eager applicants lingered to laugh at one another's gullibility, and their own. As they straggled off they were less disappointed than amused by their folly.

But of course that wasn't the point. Over at the *News* a heeler had pushed his score high enough to assure his election to the board.

*   *   *

At the beginning of our fourth week I agreed with Pierce to probe, over lunch, the possibilities of invention, but arriving at his room, I found only Aldrich—as usual, busy with his correspondence.

"More invitations?" I asked.

"No," he said civilly, "the ghastly old b-and-b. I'd prefer to do the Classical Civ, wouldn't you?"

I settled down with the *News* to reread my story on recent gallery acquisitions. "B-and-b?"

His glance, sly and curious, put me on guard. "Bread-and-butter letter—for last weekend."

"Oh? You always do that?"

He looked as though I had just trampled the flag. "Yes. Of course."

I turned a page and scanned it before asking, "Just for spending the night?"

"Yes. Why?"

"Oh, I don't know. As a rule I don't, that's all." I waited in vain for more information. "If it were for a week, or even a few days, I might—but not just for one night."

But Aldrich was wholly absorbed, sealing and addressing his letter, and I was alone with an uncomfortable awareness of a blunder. When another few minutes had passed without Pierce, I left for Commons, but on the way, turned into the library and requested, as though it were contraband, a copy of *Emily Post.*

In a dark corner of the reading room, I studied the rituals observed by guest and hostess and learned my note was already three weeks overdue. I dwelt, momentarily, on the extent of my mother's innocence and wondered how many similar omissions lay in my schooling. There was an inclination to blame her for that insistence on packing me off with rubbers and warm underwear while omitting this essential. But the thought had barely formed when I was shamed for so splenetic a notion. My mother would never admit to a need for that kind of equipment. She herself would not have slept in the house of someone she knew so slightly as to require niceties for their own sake. If she knew the term "bread-and-butter letter" she would surely scoff at it, for in her homely, comfortable world of durable friends and relations, the response would emerge, nameless, from the promptings of a full heart.

On the back of an envelope I tried a letter to Mrs. Jay, but its awkward formality made me destroy it, and I went off to the *News,* lunchless and irresolute.

"Where did you go?" Pierce asked, catching me on the stairs. "Why couldn't you wait a minute? I chased you over to Commons and couldn't find you. Well, never mind—let's have dinner. It's Monday, after all, Whiff night. I'll meet you at Mory's around seven."

*   *   *

It was the first time I had been within that enveloping, mellow womb of Mother Yale and observed her mementos—the ancient oars and trophies, the fading likenesses of her departed hero sons, all bathed in yellow satin light. As we were seated at an initial-furrowed table in the back room, I said to Pierce, "You know, what with the competition and all, I completely forgot to write your mother a bread-and-butter note."

"Oh Jesus, you don't need to write her."

"That's all very well for you—but she probably thinks I don't know any better."

Pierce was watching the Whiffs as they mustered at their big table. "All right, go ahead, write her a letter. She'll think you're hot stuff, if that's what you want." He shrugged as though this challenged comprehension, and gave a word to the waiter.

With the arrival of a tower of buttered toast, oysters and schooners of ale, he spoke of the competition. "I think Blodgett and Wyeth are shoo-ins—and you look fair, particularly if they take five of us, but we could use a scoop, Mose, something that would really wow the boys. What about societies? Now there's something people feel strongly about. Maybe we could do a big story on them."

"Like what?"

"An exposé. You know—what goes on inside Bones."

"What does?"

"Jesus, I don't know. We'd make it up. Needlework . . . whatever you like. A black mass?"

"Yes. That's a dandy suggestion for a heeler who wants to avoid all the anxieties of Tap Day himself."

"If we didn't get too close to the truth, they'd probably love it." Pierce pulled at the prow of his chin and nodded. "But we'd never get it by the juniors. They've only got six

weeks to go. They'd all faint, wouldn't they? Pity, though. It's
an opportunity for some real crusading journalism, the kind
of thing that would have interested Steffens. Well . . ."

With a sigh he produced the green drawstring bag in which
he carried his several notebooks and, on occasion, spirits, por-
nography and sporting goods. From it he now brought forth a
roll of *News* back issues and spread them on the table.

"A really good hoax has to do with something that's on
everybody's mind," he announced, "something the reader desires, like a co-ed. Or possibly . . . something he fears. The
idea already exists, see—it's just not expressed. I've been looking over these things because the *News* doesn't miss much. If
it does, you can't print it anyway. It's probably right here,
staring at us—in the color stories, maybe, or on the editorial
pages." He leafed through several.

"There's a lot of drool," he went on, "about what an intellectual desert Yale is—but what's really bothering Butterfield
and the columnists is that they've talked themselves into
keeping free of foreign entanglements and all that Oxford
Pledge crap, and they don't really believe it. You know, Mose,
a generation ago the guys were busting to get out of here and
get in on the excitement. Some of 'em were flying those coffins
against the German air force before the U.S. declared war. My
old man quit in the middle of his junior year to go with the
Yale unit. You know about that? It was a private air force
they started. They trained down at Trubee Davidson's on
Long Island, and when Josephus Daniels wouldn't let 'em in
the Navy, they bought their own planes and Rodman Wanamaker gave 'em an air station in Palm Beach, and by God,
Mose, before they were through, the Navy had to join *them.*"

"It's a different age, Pierce. More sophisticated. We can see
in the light of history how the Americans got sucked into
fighting somebody else's war for 'em. And it didn't do a damn
bit of good. Europe's back in the same trouble. War never
settles anything."

Pierce was now putting away a broiled steak with fastidious

pleasure, watching me obliquely, smiling as though he knew better. "Listen . . . if there's a fight going on, and you have any guts at all, you want to be in on it—right?"

"No. Call me anything you want, but that's the kind of excitement I can pass up."

"You wait, Mose. Wait till they press the button and you'll find out what makes you mad." Pierce finished his ale and whistled at the waiter, who had his back to us. With his thumb he ordered replenishment for both of us, though my schooner was half full. "I wouldn't want to think our generation had gone yellow, for Christ's sake."

"No," I said, "I don't think that at all. There's a full quota of red blood in here tonight—but I hope to God we've grown a little more sophisticated than the last generation. Jesus, if we haven't learned anything from history . . ."

He wasn't listening. He sat quietly, licking his upper lip, and then said, "That would be something worth knowing, though, wouldn't it, Mose? What kind of thing would make these guys mad. You think we could do that?"

"Propaganda? Is that what you mean? I would hope not."

He nodded. "Probably right. That old junk about helping our British friends wouldn't work. And the atrocity—chopping off the hands of the little Belgian babies while their mothers look on and get raped at the same time—while that's got a certain durable pull, it's suspect, I'll have to admit. We're too smart for that."

The fresh schooners arrived and he took his up to sip from it meditatively. Then, with new preoccupation, he riffled through the pages again until he came upon a story about Henry Gries, the German janitor of Timothy Dwight. From his basement room, which he had decorated with Nazi posters, Gries had directed the New Haven Bund. It was his attempt to start a Bund camp in Southington that had provoked Assistant Professor Ernest Bronson to attack the New Haven movement. The story reported that after receiving some mysterious parcels, Henry Gries had departed for the Fatherland, leaving T.D.'s heating system unmanned.

"How about that?" Pierce began to nod. "*I* think we have an obligation to find out. Yes sirree." As I raised my glass, he clapped me smartly on the back and argued on with accelerating enthusiasm. "I'll bet it's good for a whole series. We could alternate writing 'em and split a thousand points between us. That's our story, Morosely. We're going to bring Henry Gries back to New Haven."

"Don't be ridiculous," I said, blotting my collar with a napkin. "It isn't even funny."

But Pierce did not seem to hear me. From that moment his plan for a Henry Gries story possessed him, and toward the end of the week he brought me up to his room, where he closed the door on his inquisitive roommate to show me the handbills he had had printed.

MONSTER RALLY!

Welcome Home, Henry Gries

New Haven Bund Celebrates Triumphal Return
of Its Leader and Grand Opening
National German-American Fund Drive

The Old Campus
6:30 P.M. Thursday March 3

ALL WELCOME!

"It's going to be a bust, Pierce. There isn't going to be a show. You can't produce Gries."

"Oh, but I *can*," he said.

*　　　　*　　　　*

I remember shivering at my sentry duty, keeping a nervous watch over the bleak moonscape of the Old Campus where balloons of ghostly light floated over empty paths and patches of dirty snow. It was five in the morning, and as I yearned for the warmth and oblivion of my bed I could hear Pierce in the entry above, whistling lightheartedly as he sowed his handbills.

I was rooted to the steps of Farnum by his spell, by his fresh exuberance and his inexhaustible vitality. He was even finding time for geology lectures. Scorning the Rosenbaum review session before our last hour test, he had gotten a seventy on it. But he was quick to assure me his scholastic attitudes were unchanged. Tossing the blue book into the wastebasket, he said, "If I'd gone to Rosie, I'd have got a ninety."

The new Pierce, Pierce under full journalistic sail, I found irresistible. I missed him when I was not with him and sought his company like shelter from the rain. In just a few months I had passed from a resentful wariness of him to fascination and admiration. I felt he liked me too, that by my very contrast I supplied some solid ground which he found a useful, even necessary, foil to his aerial performances.

I was more drawn to Pierce than to any of a dozen classmates who offered a simpler relationship. Still, for all its intensity, I suspected Pierce's favor was fickle and might be withdrawn as quickly as it was given. I felt under continuous examination for worthiness. Part of his enthusiasm for this jape was clearly a qualifying of my blood. Was it sludged with bourgeois qualm and caution—or could it leap? And he had me there. I didn't know either—nor did I want to disappoint him.

Pierce came swinging jauntily through the door to join me and sweep aside my latest misgivings. We resumed a corkscrew course which led us through J. E., Saybrook and the Law School in a flurry of handbills, and as dawn broke over New Haven we climaxed our journey with a ceremony in Hewitt Quadrangle. Beneath the window of the president's office in Woodbridge Hall, I stood at a smart attention and saluted while Pierce cut the downhaul on Ledyard flagstaff and raised a small Nazi flag.

*   *   *

Pierce had decided that the less people in on the deception, the greater its persuasiveness, and when Logan accused him of originating the handbills, he denied it. This produced suspicion on the editorial floor, and then a nearly fatal apathy toward the story, but toward the deadline, Bailey relented and permitted a box on page one.

It reported a resurgence of Bund activities—the discovery of a Nazi flag by a janitor on his way to work, and then, by students, the handbills, scattered like autumn's elm leaves, telling of the Thursday rally. No one from the Bund was available for comment, but Inspector Gill of the campus police stated that though he knew of no plans for a rally, he would see that an adequate force was on hand to maintain order.

The second story was to be mine, and on Tuesday I set out for some interviews. My first call was on Assistant Professor Ernest Bronson, the historian whose militancy against Fritz Kuhn and Father Coughlin had brought him notice on our editorial page and provoked a testy full-column letter-to-the-editor in reply.

My first impression was of imperviousness to York Street notions of dress. Ernest Bronson's shapeless once-blue suit was turning purple. There was ungainliness in the pug nose and receding woolly hair. Even here in his own disheveled nest of books and papers, he seemed to be in some mild but persistent discomfort—constipation perhaps.

He seemed reluctant to make my acquaintance. His distant eyes worked around behind me, not meeting mine. "You're not one of my students." It was question and accusation.

"No, sir. I'm from the *News.*"

"The *News?* Is it more about my letter?" His voice was faintly evangelical in tone yet it brought to mind the struggle for survival in vast, steamy urban high schools. "I think we have had about enough of that. Altogether tautological at this point. Well—sit down if you wish."

I did and produced a handbill. "It's this, sir. We wondered if you had seen one of these."

Mr. Bronson's eyes lingered on my necktie, as if he found it distasteful, and then he drew from under the card file on his desk a duplicate of the handbill I held. "This, you mean? What about it?"

"We know of your strong feeling about Bund activity here and wondered if you had some comment."

Now he looked at me, sharply, his glance like an ice pick. Then he laughed, with a great rumbling in his chest and a shaking of his upper body which ceased as suddenly and surprisingly as it had begun. "You want me to make some comment, is that it, Mr. . . . ."

"Moseley."

He waved the handbill at me. "Did you write this, Mr. Moseley?"

"Write it? I don't understand."

"Then let me explicate. This is an obvious prank and in very questionable taste. It offends me that you and your associates think me so obtuse as not to recognize it as such and that you imagine I would cooperate in making a fool of myself. Is this your idea, Mr. Moseley, this colloquy? Because if it is I would guess that your career in journalism is not promising."

"Would you tell me why you doubt this, Mr. Bronson?"

"Because the ignorant and misguided people of the Bund are workingmen from the city of New Haven," he explained with a strained patience. "It is inconceivable they would hold a meeting on the campus."

"May I quote that?"

"No. I will not give you anything. No statement at all, do you understand?" He was on his feet, bounding toward the door to be sure I found the way.

I then wandered over to Davenport, where a junior, president of the *Deutscher Verein,* was annoyed at my suggestion that his organization might participate. They were planning a *Wanderung* and *Singfest* with Mt. Holyoke over the coming weekend—and that was *all.*

*   *   *

Pierce's door was locked but I could hear band music within. I rapped several times before he opened it a suspicious crack.

"Ah, good," he said, pulling me in and relocking the door. The music was coming, not from the Magnavox but a steamer trunk from which spilled coils of insulated wire and an assortment of electrical devices.

"What's that awful noise?" I asked.

"It's the 'Horst Wessel.' Exciting, isn't it? Doesn't that set the old feet atapping? Make you want to get out to a pogrom or something?"

Books were scattered on the floor, and he crossed the room on them, like stepping stones, pausing on a copy of *Mein Kampf* to say, "You came in answer to my summons—you know that? Not ten seconds ago I thought to myself, I wish Ben was here. I've got some terrific new ideas for the rally and I want to try them out on him—and by golly, you rapped on the door. What do you make of that?"

"I came because the story is falling apart on me. It had nothing to do with your summons."

"That's what you think."

He heard my history of disappointments, nodding in time to the music, and promptly dismissed them. "But of course you have a story, Mose. All we need is some attention. Look— why not skip Bronson? Let's save Bronson and hang it on your friend in Davenport. *Deutscher Verein* to boycott rally. How does that sound? Indignant leader of German cultural affairs says he and his followers will stay away from the giant Bund rally planned for Thursday night."

"He's going to be pretty sore," I said. "I wonder what else he belongs to."

"Nothing you'd want to join would let anybody in from the *Deutscher Verein*. Now, the reason I sent for you"—he rummaged in a clothes box—"is to find out if this is any kind of a fit." He drew forth a blue tunic with a high collar and festoons of gold braid, along with a garrison cap.

"What's that?"

"Well, actually it's half a band costume, but in the dark, with a swastika here on an armband and maybe on the cap, I

hope it will make a convincing Hitler suit. Perhaps also"—
reaching out, he lay a finger across my upper lip—"a little
black toothbrush right here."

"*Oh* no." I edged for the door.

"Wait. You don't understand yet." He began to search
among the books on the floor. "He's dead—did you know
that? He was poisoned just before Munich." Selecting one, he
held it so I could read the title: *The Strange Death of Adolf
Hitler.* "That's why Chamberlain got confused. He knew, see,
the man he was talking to wasn't Hitler. Did you know that,
Mose—that there are four guys impersonating him now—
that they take shifts? Hell, one of them had time to write this
book. So why wouldn't one of them have time to come to our
rally?"

"Maybe he would," I said, getting the door open at last.
"But he isn't going to be me."

*   *   *

Sometime Thursday morning a small platform with three
chairs and a lectern was set up on the turf facing Wright Hall.
A picture of Hitler was tacked to the edge of the lectern, and
while it had attracted mild curiosity earlier in the day, now,
as dusk and the hour of the rally approached, it flapped unnoticed in a chill, wet wind.

There was no sign of an audience. A few lights had come on
in Durfee and I could see freshmen at their windows, absorbed in day-end ceremonies—one toweling his hair, another
putting away his laundry, a third, curled in a window seat,
reading a newspaper. The basement doors of Wright Hall
swung in the traffic of the broke and lovelorn—wistfully into
Yale Station, and out again, disappointed—yet not a man tar-
ried by our display. No sooner did a cluster form than it
moved off, bent on some private purpose.

As planned, Pierce brought the Packard, with its exceptional cargo, to the High Street gate. Beside him was a gray-
haired graduate student from the Drama School who had
agreed to impersonate Bundmeister Gries and to deliver the

preposterous speech Pierce had prepared. In the back was the trunk of sound equipment, a mounted Nazi flag and a clothing dummy, mustached and dressed in the uniform, now complete with armband swastika, that I had declined.

Canaday, the graduate student, mounted guard at the car while we lugged the trunk across the campus. At the platform, we uncoiled a length of insulated wire and led it to an outlet in the nearest entry, connected the loudspeaker and attached a microphone to the lectern. Still, no one paused.

By custom our classmates herded at any excuse—the flimsier the better. They knew no greater joy than the heady one of their unison, no more gratifying freedom than to surrender their ill-fitting identities to the many-legged beast and to commit outrages in its name. But tonight there was such an obstinate indifference to our preparations, I gave some weight to Pierce's view of the class numbness to politics.

When Pierce, who had been occupied with adjustments to the sound system, produced a puffing in the speaker, he said, "Okay, Mose, let's go." And as I ran off to the car, his voice boomed forth, "One-two-three, testing."

Returning, Canaday with the flag and I with the dummy over a shoulder, we heard the band music blare into Wright courtyard. At this end of the campus some windows were flung open and figures straggled toward the noise. Pierce himself had attracted half a dozen spectators. At their center he was talking to a stout Irishman, instantly recognizable (he bulged uncomfortably in his camouflage of reversible coat and snuff hat) as a campus cop.

"Free right of assembly guaranteed us by the Constitution of the United States," Pierce was explaining over the trumpeting "Horst Wessel." "I think I have a copy of it here somewhere in case you're unfamiliar with it."

This conflict was amusing the gathering and made good cover for Canaday and me, allowing us to get both flag and dummy displayed on the platform without attention. But when I joined Pierce, I found his sovereign manner, that which had sent many a bureaucrat and minor functionary slinking like a coward before battle, had not yet worked its magic.

"You can assemble all you want," the unmoved campus cop was telling him, "but you'll have to turn that noise off. That's a damned nuisance, that noise."

As I counted our circle of grinning onlookers, wondering if we could hold them now, I was startled to find the man beside me was Ernest Bronson. The effect was like a wading encounter with something active underfoot.

"Yes," he said. "I am not surprised to find you here, Mr. Moseley. I expected you would disregard my advice."

"I'm not disregarding anything, sir. I'm just here to see what happens. I'm covering it."

"You don't really expect me to believe that, do you?" he asked, and drew a hostile glance from Pierce.

"Can't you shut that thing off?" It was the campus cop, still amiable but determined. Pierce bent over the trunk and presently the music stopped. Our attention turned to the platform, which was now seen to be flying the Nazi flag and supporting two seated figures.

"You in charge of this business?" the campus cop wanted to know, and while Pierce considered his answer, Mr. Bronson stepped into the center of our circle.

"I think you will find no one has permission for it," he told the campus cop. "Permission has to be granted by the university authorities for a political meeting. We all know that."

"That's right," Pierce said. "The permit's coming. The people in charge of the rally are bringing it." He peered toward Phelps gateway. "They should be here any minute."

Mr. Bronson smiled. "I don't believe that for a moment." Then, turning to the campus cop, he said, "If there's any doubt in your mind about whether this disturbance should be allowed to proceed, I suggest you get hold of Inspector Gill."

A second campus cop, who had just joined us, said, "Chief's coming."

Mr. Bronson received this news with a gratified bobbing of his head. He stepped closer to the platform and examined the seated figures, exchanged glances with Canaday, knocked experimentally on the dummy's knee, and then laughed contemptuously. Turning, he addressed us all. "Is there a single one of you who reads the papers? No one *aware* of what is going on in Germany? No one? Well, I tell you—to make a community joke of it reveals precisely how insensitive you are."

"We'll just go get a bite to eat until the permit comes," Pierce announced and busied himself with closing up the trunk. Leaning close to my ear, he panted, "You bring Schicklgruber. Hoopla!" Then he hopped on one foot, laughing as though this were the most exhilarating of possible developments. While the spectators watched, he seized the trunk, and listing precariously, ran toward the car. Canaday and I followed closely—he bearing the flag across his chest and I the dummy, slung once more across my shoulder.

"Death to the bulls!" Pierce said as we drove off. "May they all contract exquisitely painful doses of clap and give it to their wives. Goddam, but they have a lot of nerve interfering with our freedom of assembly—eh? As an all-American boy, doesn't that gall you, Ben?" He reached around and patted the dummy's knee. "Just like home, isn't it, Shickey?" He scowled at his watch and the increasing darkness. "Nobody ever gets a permit. Well, okay, if the bulls don't want a nice peaceful Nazi rally, we'll give them something they have to call out the National Guard for. You don't need a permit for a riot, do you? Just let me have a minute to think."

"Now you know I wasn't bargaining on any trouble . . ." said Canaday.

"No, no, Mr. Canaday. No need for concern. We're just changing the plan slightly, that's all. There'll be no trouble."

Pierce was driving slowly but purposefully up College Street, peering at the pedestrians. "I don't quite get it, Mose. We've activated the wrong bunch. Why the campus cops? Why should they care all of a sudden? I've never seen the slobs off their asses before."

And it *was* puzzling. Neither of us had anticipated more

than a token appearance from the campus police. Their function was to prevent serious bloodshed, damage to university property and the infiltration of bogus magazine solicitors. Thus far and no further did university authority encroach on undergraduate life.

Official, corporate, pedagogic Yale—that so well portrayed by awesome, waxy President Seymour in his fur-collared tycoon coat as, walking stick aswing, he strode up the steps of Woodbridge Hall—rarely encountered callow, heedless, boisterous, delinquent undergraduate Yale. They occupied the university grounds and buildings in uneasy truce, meeting as required in classrooms and, when it could not be avoided, in college dining halls, yet successfully resisting every effort—including Mr. Edward Harkness' fifteen million dollars—toward communication.

Pierce and I arrived at the answer—Ernest Bronson—simultaneously. "Of course," I said. "He was more than just an officious busybody. He must have turned out the cops."

Swinging into York Street, Pierce nodded. "Well, by golly, there's a discovery. *Bronson* cares. Maybe we'd better find out what course he gives and sign up."

"I don't know. He gives the impression of having a long memory."

"Pity." Pierce looked at me while the car proceeded past Deke and the University Theatre. "But *why* does he care? Why does he go to the trouble? He must have something better to do than traipse around the Old Campus on a chilly night."

"Maybe it's me that put the bur up his ass," I suggested. "Me, or the *News,* or just undergraduates in general."

"Bronson—Bronson. Could that be Jewish?"

"I don't think so. He doesn't *look* Jewish. He's a homely duck, but I wouldn't say . . ."

"Must be, though. That would explain . . ." Pierce was silent, pondering.

"We'd better call this thing off."

"Call it *off!*" Pierce cried in indignation. "Now why would

you say a thing like that? It's all the more reason. Oh, I'm *for*
Bronson, sure. I'm all for spirit. That makes him a worth-
while adversary, but let's not lose sight of our objective,
Mose. Bronson's standing in the way. He's trying to thwart us.
Besides, the poor fellow has no sense of humor. *That's* inex-
cusable."

Pierce paused in front of the *News* building and honked his
horn at Alonzo Ferguson, who, camera in hand, had just
crossed through our headlights. "Here we are, Alonzo. Get
aboard. Better climb in front. We're obliged to make a little
change in the plan," he explained, making a U-turn in York
Street and heading back toward Elm. "Different auspices. It
seems the sentiment is running against totalitarianism tonight, and we're nothing if not flexible, you understand. It's
going to be an anti-Bund rally. Maybe Professor Bronson will
say a few words."

On Wall Street we pulled up in front of the Bureau of Ap-
pointments, where we could see the façade of Freshman Commons. The twin glass doors of its lobby were already swinging
with hungry freshmen drifting in from Hewitt Quadrangle,
the scene of our Monday morning flag-raising. Pierce handed
me a carton, and then, shouldering the dummy, he led us
across the courtyard, instructing Canaday as he went.

The carton contained auto safety flares, and these I placed
at intervals around the base of the flagstaff while Pierce
mounted the stone bench which circled it and arranged the
dummy, whose arm could be raised in salute but, it turned
out, who could not be made to stand without support. Thus
Canaday embraced its waist and began to declaim. Satisfied
with this opening of the performance, Pierce hurried after
me, lighting the flares.

"Louder, Mr. Canaday," he called. "We can't hear you."

Increasing his efforts, Canaday could be heard, chanting in
the fashion of a barker, "Step right up, gentlemen, and kick
Herr Hitler in the pants. Ten cents is all. One dime. The
tenth part of a dollar."

"What an utter lack of noise," Pierce said. "I would give

my left testicle for a horn right now. We've got to sing, Mose."

"What?"

"It doesn't matter. Anything—just so it's loud. Alonzo? Come over here. We're going to sing now. We're going to sing 'Over There.' Ah-one, ah-two . . . *Ohh-verr tha-a-ayre* . . ."

Our three voices tottered forth on the night, uncertainly, like a trio of skaters on membrane ice, more alert to first warnings of danger than to performance, but Pierce's booming bass heartened us and soon the curious did begin to gather. They multiplied, a second row begetting a third of grinners and neck-craners.

A church-school voice identified Pierce. "It's Jay! Look at Jay, there! Hey, Jay, what is it, a game rally? Football season's over, didn't you hear?"

The dancing red light of the flares licked at the tiers of faces, revealing our crowd—picked one member, then another from the shadowy pack, held him with a fiery finger long enough for us to read indifference and contempt or the hyena-look of mockery and derision.

The night had become total, stealing away Woolsey's dome and enveloping the quadrangle. Pale, vaporous light, falling through the spiderweb windows of Commons, silhouetted its soaring Corinthian columns, the massive chain of the balustrade and the war memorial itself, a marble sepulcher the size of a stagecoach. Red, sulfurous flare light danced here too, revealing the names of the luckless whose footsteps led from where we stood to some muddy ditch in France. The inscription read: Men of Yale . . . True to Her Traditions Gave Their Lives That Democracy Might Not . . . Somme, Chateau Thierry, Ypres, St.-Mihiel . . .

And from the towering portico our voices were returning in unfamiliar echo—from somewhere as far as the Argonne Forest itself—and my voice caught in my throat. I stood in the center of the spectacle—terrified.

It seemed as though I had stolen time's perspective and snatched a chilling, supernatural glimpse of all of us. In the making of his flimsy farce, Pierce had wrought some magic. Here in this eerie amphitheater of the dead he had evoked a terrible truth about us. While we rejoiced in the certainty that we chose our destinies as surely as our neckties, history's wheel had just been tripped and it seemed to shake the ground as it commenced its turn. While we jeered at one another here and scoffed at sucker heroes, it was singling us out again—the cynical and the credulous, the willing and the unwilling—just as before, thrusting us forth to places and fates we had no plan or wish for.

The spell was broken by a meaty voice vaulting the crowd. "Okay, boys, the show's over now. Let's everybody get along. That's right."

"Hang him!" Pierce cried out, falling back to the bench and pointing to the dummy in horror. "They're trying to protect him, don't you see? Hang the Führer! Don't let the bulls save him! String him up, boys!"

There was silence all around. Even the campus cop was immobilized by Pierce's zeal. Deliberately, Pierce uncleated the halyard and held it forth. "Here! Swing him!"

Making a guttural noise, a bark, one boy lunged forward and a dozen followed.

"Alonzo, for Christ's sake!" Pierce cried, backing away from the scrimmage. "Where are you?"

Ferguson's reply came in a reassuring flash, and a moment later Pierce was walking away, reassuring Canaday and turning to see Ferguson bring another instant's blue glare to the tug of war over the dummy. It had been torn down from its scaffold before it had fairly swung and its remains were now being disputed by a dozen souvenir hunters as the campus cop tried to separate them.

"Okay," Pierce said, "we've got a story. We can go."

*   *   *

"But you *can't,* Pierce. You really can't." Across the composing room, Thornton, the night editor, was supervising the lockup of page one and smack in the center of it was a cut of

Ferguson's photograph, six students scuffling over the effigy while two others sought to raise it. Beneath was Pierce's story —a galley of which had just appalled me:

With the assistance of an alert, disciplined corps of campus police, it read, *Yale's anti-Nazi movement repulsed every effort of the Bund to hold a meeting on the Old Campus last night and countered with a demonstration in Hewitt Quadrangle, hanging the German Chancellor, Adolf Hitler, in effigy.*

In an exclusive interview with the News, *the leader of anti-Nazi activity here, Assistant Professor Ernest Bronson, described the Bund plan to welcome home ex-T.D. janitor Henry Gries as in "very questionable taste." Although he dismissed Bund activity here as ineffective and confined to "workingmen from the city of New Haven," he was observed operating with police patrols in defense of the Old Campus last night. Later, at the Hewitt Quadrangle demonstration, he was not available for comment.*

"He's going to be furious, Pierce. He'll kill us."

"Fine. That'll make another good story."

Thornton, who had become curious about my turning up on an off-duty night, watched us from under his green eyeshade. "Come on outside," I said.

Pierce called to Thornton that he would be right back, and we passed through the darkened front office to stand in the entranceway.

"We don't know what Mr. Bronson was doing there, Pierce. For all we know he was just out for a walk."

"A pretty funny coincidence."

"But you can't pin the whole thing—campus cops, hanging the effigy and all—on Bronson."

"I haven't. If you'll read the story carefully . . ."

"But oh brother, have you ever implied it. And *I'm* the one who's going to catch it. You don't seem to realize that Bronson is serious."

"Oh, but I do. I admire him for getting sore and doing something about it—but he doesn't have a monopoly on righteousness. How does he know our Bund meeting wouldn't have been an interesting development? What right has *he* got to say who can assemble on the Yale campus and who can't. And goddam it, he lacks style. The way a man does a thing is just as important as what he does, Mose. If a man does a right thing the wrong way, it's the same as if he hadn't done it. The one cancels the other, you know what I mean?" He found my bicycle leaning against the corner post and straddled it. "He tried to louse up our story. That's a score to be settled. What's more, he thinks of us as The Foe—and I'd hate to disappoint him." He pedaled off on my bicycle, and laughing gloriously, he made sweeping circles in the deserted street.

"Sometimes, you know, I think you're cracked."

He bumped up on the sidewalk and stopped beside me, balancing for a moment on his toes, then got off the bicycle and held it, a servile groom, while I mounted.

"Have faith!" He added a slap on the back, and I headed off for Bingham Hall with very little.

*   *   *

I thought we were going to get away with it. Throughout the morning I noticed people, strangers, reading the story and overheard talk and laughter about it in the jostling coatrooms and corridors of my academic rounds. When we assembled for assignments, Pierce and I began accepting the congratulations of envious competitors.

The first alarm came as a phone call from Logan, summoning me from a travel agency where I was collecting material for a spring-vacation story. At the *News* building, the hush of crisis was in the air. Logan passed me on to Bailey with an it's-not-for-me-to-tell-you solemnness, and presently I was thrust into the chairman's office. There, alongside Butterfield's desk, still wearing his funereal purple suit, sat Ernest Bronson.

He welcomed me with a puckering smile. "Mr. Moseley, I would like you to confirm what I have been telling your chairman, namely, that you broke an agreement with me. I made it explicit that I would not give an interview. There could be no doubt. Yet you went straight ahead and quoted me."

"I didn't realize everything you said was off the record," I contended. "I thought—just about the handbills."

Studying his interlaced fingers as though reading something there, he said, "That's not true, I'm afraid. I know journalistic practice. What you have done is dishonest." He glanced up to observe the arrival of a grave Bailey escorting Pierce, who, though in custody, smiled dauntlessly.

"I want to make clear," Ernest Bronson continued, "that you are guilty of irresponsible journalism, and it reflects, not just on your newspaper, but on me."

"I'm sorry, sir." Pierce spoke up, giving the *sir* an ironic inflection as though Bronson were not entitled to it. "I don't think I heard all that you said, but if you're talking about the rally story this morning, I'll have to disagree with you. There is nothing irresponsible about it. I know because I wrote it."

A wire of hostility snapped taut between them. I could feel it humming in the close air.

"A confidence was broken by Mr. Moseley." Disconcerted, he glanced at me, then back to Pierce. "Well, I don't want to argue . . ." His voice lost some of its smoothness and climbed in pitch and stridence. "Just which one of you is the more to blame doesn't matter to me. As far as I am concerned, you are all equally guilty."

"Of what, sir?"

"I gave no interview. Surely I have a right not to give an interview."

"On the contrary. You're the spokesman for the anti-Nazi people. You've had plenty to say in the past, and your views are public property."

Momentarily dazed, Mr. Bronson took a copy of the morning's *News* from Butterfield's desk and waved it at Pierce. "But this isn't true." I saw little pearls of moisture sprouting on his forehead. "Your story is all lies, from the first to the last word."

"What lies, sir?"

His woolly head quivered. "Innuendo. There is not one word of truth in all this."

"I'll have to disagree with you again, sir. There's a lot of truth in it—induced perhaps, but still an indication of student feeling toward totalitarianism."

"What are you *talk*ing about? What are you trying to say?" His self-control yielding at last to Pierce's obfuscations, Mr. Bronson trembled in hand and lip. "It was a hoax, pure and simple."

Bailey broke into their inflammatory dialogue, bearing the hose of arbitration. "As I'm sure you're aware, Professor Bronson, we have a tradition here of occasional foolishness . . ."

"That's precisely why I'm angry—at foolishness."

"Yes, Harry." It was Butterfield at last. "As Professor Bronson points out, we are a college newspaper, but no less bound by professional standards. No question about that. Now let's get this straight." He turned ponderously to Pierce. "You two invented the rally—handbills and all?"

"All of it."

"Who else knew the story wasn't genuine?"

"No one."

"I suspected it wasn't entirely true," Bailey said.

"Never mind, Harry. That was an error, Jay, not taking the editors into your confidence. I feel sure that if we had been aware of Professor Bronson's objections . . ."

"I hope you will keep that in mind, that I have been ridiculed," Mr. Bronson interrupted. "But what none of you seems able to grasp is that your sophomoric frivolousness is wholly inappropriate to matters of such gravity. You reveal a complete lack of discrimination, all of you. What's going on in Germany is no different to you from eating goldfish."

"I feel sure," Butterfield protested, "that if you were to read our editorial page . . ."

"I have."

In the stillness, Butterfield was seen to swallow this taunt, to assess the potential of Mr. Bronson's wrath, to look long-ingly at one of the telephones and, finally, to have another try at conciliation.

"Supposing we run a retraction in tomorrow's edition? Either a box, somewhere up front, indicating the story was untrue, or if you prefer, an apology on the editorial page. You can write it yourself if you like." Butterfield smiled. "Will that square matters?"

Ernest Bronson's keen protuberant eyes roved the room as he considered, then came to rest on Pierce. "Quite frankly, that's all I came for, but meantime, it's occurred to me that it is my duty to bring legal action."

Butterfield gave moderate voice to our dismay at this appall-ing thought. "Professor, I do hope you'll reconsider. Practi-cally, it wouldn't be worthwhile. The *News* itself has no money, and individually, at least in this year of our lives, none of us is of much consequence." He produced a thin smile. "We're all potential, I'm afraid."

Mr. Bronson's gaze again moved around the room to fasten on Pierce. "I could close you up."

"I wish you'd try that, Professor," Pierce said.

Ignoring Pierce, Butterfield hurriedly said, "But I think you would find that well beneath your dignity, Professor."

"What you mean is that I may not take you seriously—right? That as college boys you're privileged. It is yours to make havoc of the grown-up world and at the same time be invulnerable to it. You refuse to be adults, and frankly, it makes me sick. You may have a surprise this time."

Whereupon Mr. Bronson arose and left us.

*   *   *

For the rest of the afternoon I expected to be called back to the *News,* but nothing happened until early evening when Pierce turned up in my room looking wilted, rather like a man who's had a hard day at the office. He groaned as he set-tled into the collapsed end of our sofa.

"What a pretentious worm Bronson is," he said. "How did

somebody like that get in here? That's what I want to know. Who goofed? He doesn't belong at Yale."

"What happened?"

"You're all right. I'm out."

"Of the competition?"

He nodded. "They suspended me from it. No more points. I'll be last man by this time tomorrow. I suppose I could heel again in the spring, but starting all over . . . the hell with it. It was my tail or a libel action—really."

"What lousy luck, Pierce. I'm sorry."

"Not only would Bronson be the joke of the year if he sued the *News*—he doesn't even have a *case*." Leaping up, Pierce pounded the paneled door with such violence, I thought he must break a bone. "Goddam, *why* didn't Butterballs let him?" He dropped into the window seat and looked glumly into Chapel Street. "He didn't want a feud with the university is why. Hell, I see that. I don't even blame Butterballs. But oh, how I hate to be pushed around by that *teacher*."

There was a sound at the door, and Wolfe came in with an armload of books from the library. He said "Hi" and nodded to us both, but despite Pierce's determined overtures, Wolfe was still wary of him and he went into his bedroom, leaving us alone. Through the door Pierce watched him arrange the books, in order of height, on his desk.

"Hey, Wolfie," Pierce called to him. "What do you think of a Jew who changes his name?"

Wolfe went on moving his books around, and for a moment I thought he might not answer, but then he said, "I don't admire it. But a Jewish name stands out. It can be unpleasant." Then he turned to face us, and coming to the door, looked at Pierce evenly. "If a man's name bothers him—if it makes it easier to get along, why shouldn't he change it?"

"If you don't understand why," Pierce said, "I couldn't explain it to you."

"Oh, do I ever understand," Wolfe said. "Do *you?* Do you have any notion? No. You wouldn't know. A fellow like you wouldn't want to know."

"Like me?" Pierce asked.

"I tell you, Jay. I was brought up in a family with a lot of pride, enough of it to kill a man when some trust is broken. They're the kind of people who bring their kid up very carefully, with a belief he's as good as anybody, but also with the thickness of skin to live with bigotry, the kind he's going to find in a place like this. They teach him to laugh at it when he can, or to sense it coming and duck it. There are all kinds of defenses Jewish kids learn while a fellow like you is learning to dance and play tennis."

"You really believe that, Wolfe?" Pierce asked. "You really believe that people around here have it in for you? I don't believe anybody even thinks of whether so-and-so is Jewish or not. I don't, goddam it. It never occurs to me. I've never thought about it one way or another."

"Oh, listen, Jay." Wolfe folded his arms and leaned in his doorway. "I've heard you on football and the guys with the peculiar names you can't pronounce. *Why should they want to come here?* That's what you said. I've heard you on Yale and who built it and how it's important to keep the tradition pure, like a spring, and not let it get to be just like a big city college. Don't you recognize that for what it is? How do you think that sounds to somebody whose father is working for an odd-lot trader who just happened to be luckier than him on Black Tuesday—not liking it, mind you, but going down every day so his son can go to Yale? Can you imagine that, Jay, or do you just keep on wondering why would I want to *come* here?"

Pierce kept shaking his head in denial, but he kept an eye, a puzzled eye, on Wolfe.

5

But the spectacle of his seven-week endeavor washing over the falls of the rally story did not overwhelm Pierce nor, so far as I could see, even disconcert him. With no loss of verve, he applied himself to the plots and intrigues of admission to a residential college.

Silliman, now nearing completion, would accommodate another two hundred applicants, but even so, there would be room within the architectural ingenuities and the massive, sybaritic splendor of the nine colleges for only two thirds of our class; the rest would wait in line. Moreover, there were subtle differences of caste between these great manors, and the choice of, and by, one was our introduction to the barbarities of the annual roundup and branding. In many ways it was as painful as the fraternity rushing we would undergo as sophomores, and junior year's agonizing preliminaries to Tap Day, for this was our first real evaluation. No longer could we sustain illusions of promise and desirability. An accurate measure of these qualities could now be read, as though painted on signs around our necks. Who would have us and who would not told our past, and making a small allowance for error and luck, our future as well.

The factions which had arrived, already politically sophisticated, from the big prep schools were dividing, absorbing odd lots of desirables from the smaller ones and even an occasional high-schooler who had grasped the knack of mobility. These new groups proliferated along specialized lines of geography, wealth, extracurricular activity and social expertise. The last was vital. The word most often used to praise a peer was *genial*. There was none higher.

Round the clock we bulled about colleges, arguing advantages of one over another, retelling the day's rumors of deals and entry packs, while assignments went unread and ashtrays overflowed. It was earnest talk, as though we were confronting a marriage in eternity.

"It's regal, Mose," Pierce, who had joined an entry pack for Timothy Dwight, was crowing. "It's a regular flat. It used to be a fellow's suite, with this fancy paneling and its own can. You'll have to come and visit us weekends."

His customary good fortune was especially irritating since Morton Wolfe and I awaited, with scant hopes, a favorable word from Branford. "How'd you arrange it?" I asked. "The old school friends? The gang from the field house?"

For answer I had his brazen, oh-if-you-only-knew grin, duplicate of one I recalled from the speeding episode on the Orange turnpike.

"Well," I said, "I must say it's remarkable how those wounds of yours heal up. I thought you had it in for the false friends from school."

He was riffling the pages of a history text, glancing at the pictures. "I tell you, Ben, I have an absolutely elephantine memory and I've forgiven no one. However, I understand them now—which is not the same thing at all. It makes it easier to live with them, though, and I've got to do that. But it's no compromise. You understand?" He raised his eyes long enough for an icy warning. "And this isn't going to be any gold-coast entry. It's going to be very democratic—mostly Andover and Exeter guys who with their usual political awareness have already got the whole joint wired. By the way, it's a three-bedroom layout. Curious—everybody in the class trying to get into the brick colleges and no singles around. Know anybody whose roommate's not coming back?"

I watched him turning pages, and to my own surprise asked, "Would you want me?"

He looked up. "You and Wolfie splitting?"

"No." I laughed and took it back. "No, Wolfie and I get along. He's a good egg, regardless of what you may—"

"I know," he said quickly.

"Well, you know how some guys' roommates get on their nerves—their sniffing or scraping their throats, or how they leave their junk around, or borrow their clothes or money and forget about returning it. But Wolfie and I don't bother each other. We can read, side by side, and while I know he's there, it's no strain. We know when to leave each other alone, and when to talk. And I *like* him—I've gotten used to him. I don't think I could say to Wolfie, I'm quitting you—you know what I mean?"

Pierce nodded. He seemed amused by this argument with myself.

"Besides," I went on, "I don't really go for Aldrich. I know you see something in him and I suppose his mother does—but *Jesus!* Did you hear him this afternoon . . . talking about Antibes? He's always doing that—Antibes or Old Westbury or someplace like that. It's the church-school boy's way of reminding the rest of us not to get too chummy, I suppose."

Pierce laughed. "Well, I know. They do make a piss-poor first impression. They're really determined to live up to the reputation."

"And you know what you're *talking* about," I said. "I used to think you were trying for the record."

"Me? No kidding. Well, you know better now. But it's hard for them, Ben. They've been in the incubator for five years, learning about their responsibilities, and they're still in awe of the big world outside. First time they've been on their own. All that freedom—my gosh, they can go to the movies and drink beer any time they *want*. It's scary and they don't really like it. At least the stupid ones don't, and believe me, three quarters of them are apes—too witless to try anything the Rector didn't explain to them. Poor bastards had to check in with him every time they took a leak. Oh, I know all about it. What really shakes them up is the idea they might make a disgrace. Just the thought of it, boy! And the surest way around that is to lay off any new people. New people might have some ideas that would lead to trouble, and the next thing you know, God or Dr. Drury or somebody will have them up to the office and there'll be a letter home to the folks. But they're wising up. Don't despair of them, Mose. As for Aldrich—when I was down with the leprosy last fall, he picked up a touch of it too. You know how it is with these communicable diseases. When the guys went to the movies or out drinking, they didn't come by for Aldrich either. But it didn't bother him, and there at the end of term, when I was trying to drain the Bacardi out of Connecticut, he hauled me off the floor one night and put me to bed. That really threw him, my spending a night on the floor. Then in the morning he gave me this sermon—the old brimstone—might have been the Rector himself. It was comic—me with this pile-driver of a hangover, so I couldn't fight back—but good, you know what I mean?" He frowned at me. "That's interesting you don't care for Aldrich—he likes you all right."

I nodded. "Sometimes . . . I think he *is* trying."

At that moment Aldrich came through the door. He greeted me with perceptible affableness and drifted into his own room, where I could see him getting out his brushes and oxblood creams, preparing to add a fresh and loving luster to his loafers.

Pierce had paused in his skimming, to read, and I realized he was stealing a moment from our conversation to prepare for his eight-o'clock. "You seem these days," I said, "like a man with new zest for the old Yale game."

"That so?"

"Yes." I gave Pierce one of his own sly winks. "I thought

you'd like to know. I also wondered what you attribute it to—
Reggie Root, spring, the *News* competition, or what?"

He shrugged. "Oh well, you have to play. You start off
playing with all your heart, as though it's the *only* way.
Everybody's doing that, so it *must* be right. Then something
happens, like say you get cut from the squad, and so you have
to question the whole system." He laughed. "There has to be
something wrong with the system because otherwise there'd
be something wrong with you, right? That's when it occurs to
you maybe the old Yale game is a joke on everybody. What
you win is this onion. For every score you get to peel a layer,
and underneath you find another, a little smaller one, and
there's supposed to be a pearl there at the center—bonded
friendship and *lux et veritas,* which is Latin for getting ahead.
But *maybe* there's nothing. Well, there's one way to find out
—go on peeling and keep your eyes open."

"With an onion?"

Pierce laughed and kneaded my knee. "Ah, Mose—you
flinty-nosed fellow. You're good for me, you are. I'm going to
hate to lose you to Branford."

"Look," I said. "If you really want me . . ."

Aldrich, in the doorway, examining the loafer in his hand,
said, "Sure we do, Ben."

A half-hour later I was saying to Wolfe, "I don't think
we're going to get into Branford. It's arranged through these
packs. Somebody knows a guy on the allocations committee.
And even if we do get in, I'm not sure Branford is the place
for us. The *News* guys are all getting into the brick colleges."

Morton Wolfe had the drift at once, and when he asked
what I had in mind, I confessed, "Well, yes, I am thinking
about it. They have this single, Jay and Aldrich do, and I was
wondering, just hypothetically, if you wouldn't be happier
with some of your guys. I mean, there's nobody in the class I'd
rather room with than you, Wolfie. Honestly. If we ever did
break up, it would only be for convenience, for getting more
out of college. I mean, it probably would be helpful—if I

make it—to live in one of the *News* board pockets. You know how they bull all night over some problem about the paper, and that would bore the hell out of you, particularly when you want to have some peace to study or some guys in for a bridge game. If we were to split up—and I'm not saying we should—but if we did, could you find somebody to go to Branford with?"

Morton Wolfe's first response was the mature one I expected. His wide, rather gentle eyes studied me while he thought about it, and then he said, "Well, sure, okay, Ben. If you don't want to come to Branford, that's all right with me. I'll make out."

But he did not take up his reading again. For a while he sat very still, chain-smoking, a single furrow in his steep forehead conveying the withdrawal of his warm regard. Just beneath his detachment I recognized the opening wound. Though I had no intention of it, he felt betrayed. He did not speak again. He left me for his bedroom, closing the door firmly, yet through it I could feel a contempt for my ambition and a warning I would be the errand boy and general suck-up in any entry of Pierce Jay's.

Despite the hour—it was after one—I went out into the still, dark Old Campus and walked around it, disliking myself. I seemed to be at the forks, one road climbing to a regular Olympus of opportunity, the more alluring for its vagueness, the other descending into Branford's dungeon. Yet I shied from the disloyalty to Mort, whom I genuinely liked. Above all, I had no wish to pare any thinner that unusually sensitive skin of his.

I pushed open the door to Pierce's room and found him in his pajamas, still at the history. "I can't do it, Pierce," I told him miserably. "I can't dump Mort. You know how badly I want to come along with you, but I can't face myself. I've never felt such a shit."

Clapping the book shut, he paced the room, hands clasped behind and flashing me an intermittent grin. "Is it that you don't want to be a shit—or *appear* to be one? Can you tell me that?"

"It's the same," I said. "The appearing—the reflection in somebody's eye is what's going to remind me all the time."

He smiled at that, and still enjoying my dilemma, moved from a curiosity about it to a taunting, as though I were a likable but tiresomely backward pupil. "What you want from me is some pious excuse for the disagreeable act, right? Well, let's see—that it would be better for your marks? How's that? Or—you might be honest and say to him: Why should I spend another three years living like a mole? Branford? It's a regular all-American of meatballs. Why should I bury myself in *any* of these Gothic dumps if I don't have to? In three years I'd turn green and slimy. I'm going to do all right around here. I'm going to make the *News* board. Might even be a wheel over there—who knows. I'm certainly going to walk off with the student agency thing. I can have whatever I like out of Yale, for Christ's sake, if I don't go straggle off with the unwashed. How's that sound to you?" He watched me, then stretched. "Well, if it's not clear to you now, you'd better go to bed. It's late and your courage is failing you. Maybe tomorrow."

The next day Pierce told me casually, as though it was the easiest thing in the world, that he had paid a call on the Master of Timothy Dwight and secured half an entry—there would be room enough for all.

I argued half that night with a sullen Wolfe, who saw small advantage in T.D.'s gracious Georgian courtyard when you "have to walk halfway to Hartford" to see it. It was a discouraging journey from Lindsey-Chittenden and the library stacks, he pointed out, and worse, our entry mates would include Jay and Aldrich.

Wolfe capitulated when he was permitted to bring along his bridge game, a pair of mournful A.S.U. members, Sudermann and Chwast, who were unable to get into any college at all.

Only one thing bothered me. I had been made to recognize myself at that unflattering angle, with my willingness to dump old Mort and my lack of courage for it showing. And this had pleased Pierce, as though until that moment he had not been sure of my own share of human weakness. Whereupon he had provided me, indeed all of us, with this miraculously facile solution. So effortless, it seemed to cost him nothing. Yet just because it was an act of such princely bounty, one that only he could perform, I felt bound to Pierce by yet another cord—and the least bit possessed. It was a just perceptible stone in my shoe.

*   *   *

In early April, Pierce goaded me into inviting Angela Rice to New Haven. I fully expected to be turned down, and when she replied, accepting, I could not believe it. If Angela Rice would come to New Haven at my bidding, capricious fairies had surprised the committee that governs human probability, bound its dour members to their chairs and made a havoc of its laws. *Nothing* was impossible.

What can ever surpass a first letter from a pretty girl? There is such an incredible promise in the round, even strokes. How remarkable that so fair a creature could be so accomplished as to create on this matchless blue notepaper these incomparably lovely marks, so evocative of all that is mysteriously, satisfyingly feminine.

Such a multitude of opportunities—dark sacks shared with common bills, threats, advertisements, invitations, the heedless hands of sorters and carriers, trains fanning to an infinity of destinations—to go astray. What a miracle that it should have made its hazardous way from her fingertips to my mailbox, gloomy with neglect, to illuminate it and spread an exquisite, exalted glow throughout the postal system.

I carried it like a talisman. I would steal it out in class to read a few lines and drift away from the lecture in a bubble of bliss.

I had so trimmed her with my fancies that I hurried by the

real Angela on the station platform and afterward wandered about the sooty hangar of the waiting room, feeling the fairies had been deposed or had turned their mischief against me. I felt more kin to the derelicts and the huge colored woman with her painful feet watching from the bench than to the girls trailing ribbons and the boys in beer jackets and straw hats who pranced to and fro and then, through the doors, to the fresh spring day outside.

A forgotten-looking girl stood by the information booth. She wore a short pale-blue coat, and although she looked at me expectantly, a slight smile breaking her lips, she was imperfect—noticeably plump, her eyes squinty—and a slump in posture gave away her uncertainty. I took a step forward, and she laughed, raised her hand and waved. To my astonishment it *was* Angela.

I had given much thought to the effect I would have on her. Mindful of the strong currents of tradition, I would borrow copiously from the reliable environment, be an indispensable part of the ivied scene here, the very incarnation of it. But more—I would be worldly-wise and amusing, old wisdom and new wit, astonishing and delighting her with this downy collegiate countenance.

But instead of an accomplished entertainer I was a mute beside her. It had not occurred to me that she would bring, and I would have to carry, the baggage of her welfare and right to happiness, nor had I any idea it would weigh me down so. There were no more cabs and we boarded the trolley. As we rattled past the warehouses and tire shops of downtown New Haven, I stole glances at her suspecting I had been deluded. She was not a beauty, after all. Without her frame of metropolitanism she was a vulnerable-looking girl, one who would scarcely turn a head on a New Haven street. It was even possible she would be regarded by my classmates as something of a dog.

She was talking, tossing off great, girlish beach balls of conversation that I tried in vain to catch. Not only did she make no sense, she had no intention of it. Her chattering was more release from her nervousness than an effort at communication, and of what use was my stored-up wit and wisdom against that?

The prospect was unendurable and I was enough coward to consider bolting her. The impulse overcame me in front of Connecticut Hall, where Angela hailed and ran to greet friends, an upperclassman and his girl from Spring Lake, where she summered. But the very warmth of their reunion overcame my irresponsible thought, and by the time Pierce arrived to join us I had a more charitable view.

Pierce had brought a reticent but stunning blond model and he had put the Packard's top down and decked it with patriotic bunting. By some sleight of hand, an elaborate courtesy toward Angela, a suggestion of delights to come, he changed our anxiety about ourselves into anticipation. I found my tongue. Angela's bursts of purposeless laughter abated. I remembered some of the things I had planned to tell her about Yale and myself, to which she listened attentively, and all at once the day became the exuberant welcome to spring we had planned.

Explaining we must celebrate Derby Day in the Olympian manner, Pierce provided a hamper of curious Greek sandwiches and a jug of *retsina,* and we picnicked under a hazy, adolescent sun on the boggy bank of the Housatonic. Golden mists rose from the warming earth, and steeped in them we welcomed the newcomers—more youths and maidens come to join in the vernal rites.

There were striped blazers and peg-top pants with wide suspenders, bowlers, skimmers, top hats and a German helmet with a tall spike. "Genial" nymphs skittered about like slippery puppies, young breasts making an erotic spectacle of a varsity sweater. They came on bicycles and tandems and in trucks filled with hay and mattresses, each with its beer keg and musicians, to watch the rowing of the Blackwell Cup regatta.

I have no recollection of the intercollegiate races but I do remember two ancient scows, one the *Record*'s, the other the

News's, and Pierce, in a burlesque of collegiate behavior, wading into the river after them up to his waist; and a lone fellow mired to his ankles, a beer can in one hand and a rose in the other, desolately calling, "If anybody sees my mother, tell her I'm lost." Best of all I remember Angela, urban, indoor creature that she was, coerced by Pierce into a softball game, a flap of her blouse pulled out of her skirt, a lock of blond hair dangling across her eye, a helpless but beguiling first baseman.

In the evening we roamed Fraternity Row, listening at the windows to the music and fetching noises of the dances. But we were recognized as freshmen and barred from every doorway, and when a light rain began to fall, Pierce herded us toward the car with a cry of "On to the Stork!"

Misgivings over another breakneck New York excursion with Pierce were swept aside by his offer to let me drive, and as we started down the Post Road, I realized what had sparked his generousness. He had decided to seduce his handsome model on the way.

Angela talked steadily—first about her father, a manufacturer of pumps, and his belief that between Hitler and *that man in the White House,* this summer would be a last chance to see Europe; then about the schoolgirl tour—ugh—he was urging on her. I felt she was truly asking my view of her pretty dilemma, but simultaneously doing her best to cover up the plaintive murmurings of crumpling resistance in back.

As nearly as I could tell, Pierce succeeded shortly after we entered Westchester, but I was unable to pay it, or Angela, full attention, for the rain had been increasing steadily, driving in at the edges of the side curtains and sluicing across the windshield.

On the parkway, just below the George Washington Bridge, our headlights dimmed and then, confirming this ominous symptom, the motor faltered and I felt the power drain out of it. Within a hundred yards we had chugged to a stop. It was clear the ignition system had failed, for we had no lights. The rain seemed to beat harder on the Packard's hood and I had a moment's illusion of being in a remote and peaceful place, some sleeping porch or tent of my childhood, during a storm. But Pierce's reaction to our peril was instant. "Hoopla!" he cried, and emerging from the steamy dark of the back seat he leaped out into the weather. In the mirror I could see him silhouetted by onrushing headlights as he opened the trunk and ran backward along the road, stooping to set a flare. He had difficulty lighting it in the continuing downpour and had to jump to safety from time to time as headlights approached.

When he did get a flame burning he came loping back to us, and opening a door, cried, "Out—everybody out! We're going to catch it here, for sure." As he spoke, I saw the car coming— fast, straight down our lane. I leaped from behind the wheel and up onto the center island in time to see the speeding car strike the flare and send it bouncing, then swerve, but too late by seconds, and come crashing into the rear of the Packard with a tremendous grinding and tearing of metal. Door handles and bumpers snatched at my coat as they sailed by, and the two cars, coupled, mounted the center island, and straddling it, ground an agonizing twenty feet before they came to rest.

Pierce tugged the back door open and was leaning in. "All right?" he was asking. "Are you all right? Does anything hurt? Can you walk?" And in the next instant he had them out, frightened but unharmed, and was leading them to the comparative safety of the roadside.

Instead of an evening of dancing in Angela's environment, we spent it in mine, or at least one in which I was more at home than she, waiting in bare rooms and walking the soiled, indifferent labyrinth of all-night garages and police stations. Pale at the thought that death, having almost caught us, was unwilling to let us go—we could still hear its wrenching impact and the grumey taste of it was in our mouths. A vulnerable Angela seemed lovelier than ever now. The beauty of almond eyes, fair child's skin, tiny waist and contrasting bounty of her bosom was fully restored. Moreover, I felt her drawn to me with all the power of this terrifying aftermath to our idyll at the riverside.

When at last I brought her to her apartment, watched her let herself into a hall hung with tapestries and brass escutcheons, I wondered if our adventures entitled me to a kiss. While I waited uncertainly for some indication, she said, "Don't go."

"I should have told Pierce not to wait, shouldn't I? It crossed my mind there in the cab and then I thought it would be obvious and you wouldn't like that."

"I don't mind obviousness"—Angela smiled—"sometimes."

"Next time, then, I'll be more obvious."

"You'll come back?"

"Yes."

She offered me her unbelievably soft hand and then, so easily I scarcely knew what had happened, her warm, yielding mouth. And thus our love affair began—the first serious one in both our lives.

*   *   *

At eighteen, when the circulatory system is pristine, alcohol has real possibilities. It is not just a solace then, balm for the day's wounds or chloroform for a man who cannot bear the strong light of his wakefulness. At eighteen you can climb tall trees with it—run right up them in a wink. On just a cup you can soar and glide among the stars. From up there you can see forever and the view is endless and green. When you do come down, it makes more of a mess, but it doesn't hurt so much.

The night of the heelers' banquet Bailey prepared a vat of fishhouse punch, sly amber stuff which he served us as we gathered in his Berkeley rooms. To my surprise, Pierce was there. He had come on an invitation that would not have given me much hope of election, but he leaped about, reciting obscene limericks and slopping punch over heelers and board members, as though he were a sure thing.

The banquet itself took place in the Captain's Room, the largest of the private dining rooms upstairs at Mory's, and here the vinous tide rose higher and gurgled across our long table. Huge horn-handled trophies sloshing with Green and Velvet Cups, the classic blends of still and bubbly wines with liqueur, passed from dripping mouth to dripping mouth.

Looking around the table at my comrades, ordinary fellows really, capable as anyone of stupidity, ungainliness and unkindness, they appeared uniformly handsome, the loyalest friends I should ever have—and clever too. Everything they said was funny. There was a rising surf of laughter; waves of it crashed, one upon the other, not leaving me time to catch my breath, and as I struggled to retain the excruciating things that were said, I thought I might drown in mirth.

Even when Butterfield arose to announce who among us had reached the masthead, order was attained with difficulty. The lingering cries were a protest, a reluctance to break the perfect circle of our fraternity. This oneness with each other was what we were here for. In a moment of clarity and alcoholic penetration, it seemed what life itself was all about. God, how we loved each other at that moment. What could ever be so true as our fellowship of the heelers' bench and the long night watch at the printer's? And here were our taskmasters, Bailey, Logan, even the joyless Butterfield, now out from their masks and our true companions too. With all my heart I willed it not to end for me.

Through the heavy anesthetic of my hope and dread I heard Butterfield say that after an argument of some heat and length over which of us was most dispensable to the future of the *News*, they had been able to settle it only by taking us all.

There was a moment's numbed silence and then a great lusty cheer went up, starting a demonstration of noise and stomping that must have made the diners below think we were coming down on top of them. Blodgett stood on a chair to make a speech, indifferent to a fusillade of rolls and balls of vanilla ice cream, while Balfour and Selby, locked in each other's arms, waltzed round and round the table and two

waiters tried to restrain Pierce from taking a stuffed moose-
head off the wall.

Floating south on York Street, I seemed to move effortlessly
on a cushion of air while from my throat spiraled silvery filaments of melody to blend with our chorus, astonish me with
their perfection and make me wonder if I oughtn't to be out
for the Glee Club too.

In front of the College Toasty, I found the gliding sensation due in part to the support I was getting from Bailey.

"Great guys—every last one of you." In front of Langrock's
show window, Bailey was trying to focus on me. "Why, we
had to take the whole gang. Never do that—but had to on
account of all such great guys."

"Jay was the surprise. I guess you had something to do with
that."

Bailey blinked his heavy lids as he concentrated on getting
it straight. "Jay was a squeaker. He didn't have the points—
nowheres near enough points. But he'd made himself the goat
for Bronson. He wanted *all* the blame, you know. None for
the *News*. None for you. He told Bronson that after the interview you tried to kill the story. Hell, we couldn't leave him
behind—not Jay. Not that wild man." He laughed. "He's got
heart." Bailey frowned as though he had received a threat
from his stomach. "Don't know if that's all to the good or not.
But I do know when he was in trouble he didn't want to share
it with anybody. Don't forget that, Moseley. Wanted it all
himself."

The others had veered past us, singing and shouting with
growing disunity, and we trailed after their bibulous sounds,
catching up in the Fence Club, temporarily and unexplain-
edly open to us.

Here the celebration resumed. With a fresh drink in hand I
was thumped and welcomed into one of the rival quartets.
Bailey sat tailor-fashion in the center of a round table, conducting with a splintered chair rung for a baton. Arms interlaced, hands grasping shoulders, shirts soaking with sweat and

drink, bodies steaming and faces purpled—we strained to drown each other out.

Abandonment, rare in my colleagues, flourished all around. One leaned in the doorway, urinating down the steps into the garden. Another, having splashed his trousers with vomit, removed them and leaned unsteadily against the fireplace in striped undershorts.

I must have looked debauched myself, for a wet and disheveled Pierce laughed at the spectacle I made, clapping me on both shoulders in approval.

In the same moment I witnessed Seymour Ripley's spectacular descent from the skies of his imagination. In the belief he could soar and that the floor of the bar, two flights of stone steps below, would receive him like a goose-down pillow, he stretched his arms and, with a cry of *Ooooleee,* leaped—and landed in a still heap at our feet.

When we turned him over, his eyes lolled under slightly open lids and blood flowed from his lips. Norman, the bartender, called an ambulance while the rest of us stood about in a sobering circle. But long before aid arrived, Ripley wakened, slowly, as though from drugged sleep, seemed temporarily puzzled by his surroundings and then, with some difficulty, got to his feet.

Brushing his way past well-meaning hands he went to the bar, where he ordered another drink. While downing a mixture of whiskey and his own blood, he assured us he was all right and threatened to go back up the stairs and try his flight again. Perhaps it was because of who we were and where—in sanctuary—that we accepted his diagnosis, and indeed, when the doctor came, Ripley was repaired with only some stitches in his lip. The bacchanal resumed.

*   *   *

At two in the morning I was sitting on the fence outside Branford, Pierce beside me, still drinking from a metal mug. I had retched in the gutter in front of Wolf's Head and now, despite a bad taste in the mouth and a world still unsteady, I felt purified and possessed of exceptional perceptions.

"You seemed to know," I said. "You seemed so sure you were going to make it. Did someone tell you?"

He shook his head. "Nobody told me. But this is Yale, Mose."

"Bronson is Yale."

"Oh no, Mose. No, he's not. He doesn't exist. You know, for a while I was going to launch a big Bronson vendetta, really let him know what a mistake it was butting in here, and send him back where he belongs, but then I realized he wasn't worth the trouble. He's an unimaginative, stupid man. I can even feel sorry for him—but a fellow like that couldn't screw me. That's all I knew." Pierce laughed and swigged from the mug. "My old man used to say, 'Never get in a pissing contest with a skunk'—but he never gave in to one. No, you can't do that, Mose. Not if you want to scale the walls." He looked down the wide path between us and Saybrook, then up at the pinnacled silhouette of Harkness tower, its black lace spread on a luminous, moon-drenched sky. "And I do, Mose. I'm going to be a good *News* man—as good as any that ever was. How about you, Mose? Want an office? You want to be M.E.?"

"M.E.? Jesus, Pierce. Let's wait till tomorrow and check our wings. Remember Ripley."

"I'd like to be chairman. I'd be a good one. What do you think of my chances?"

"I don't know. I suppose it depends on who else wants it and what you do next year."

He looked disappointed, as though he thought I might have assured him of it on the spot. "Yes, there's no telling, is there? Well, I don't want to be vice-chairman. I don't want any other office. I'd rather have a column. That would be okay—a political column. I think I could do that as well as anybody. I might take some political history next year. I might take that course of Sherman Kent's or maybe Rudine's or Driver's, guys like that. I might go to Europe this summer and see for myself. Yes, I'd almost as soon run a really good column."

"You heeling *Time?*"

There was such a long pause I thought I must have offended him. And then he said, "The old man was Bones. I'd like to go there. Not as a legacy, though. I'd want it to be all on my own."

6

In August of 1939 Germany jettisoned the anti-Communism
that had been a Nazi watchword and made its surprising pact
with Russia. I followed these developments indifferently in
the Providence *Journal* and consoled myself for a summer of
law-clerking by a wistful correspondence with Angela Rice.

I pinned the picture postcards—Leaning Tower, the David
copy, Bridge of Sighs, Eiffel—to my bedroom wall and doted
on the thin gray leaves of hotel-de-luxe stationery with their
breathless accounts of doing the cathedrals and galleries, gar-
lic-scented waiters, obliging concierges, and the ingenuity of
her companions in outwitting the vigilant Miss Baldweg.

The *Veendam* docked on the first of September, and the
papers that morning bore fat black headlines reporting that
the German army had crossed the border into Poland. The
swarming Holland-America Line pier seethed with the extra
excitement and gratitude of safe return. Even here on the
shore of the quiet Hudson you could feel the mounting pressure of vacationing Americans funneling toward Europe's
embarkation ports.

I discovered Angela awaiting her turn with customs, and

thought her blonder and thinner than she had been in June. In her grand-touring she had lost the urban, every-hair-in-place look and acquired an appealing abandonment—as though she really *had* seen the world. This time she struck me as ravishing.

At the sound of my voice she turned and sent a gray butterfly skirt swirling out from tanned legs and she laughed at the sight of me waving and blushed gloriously as she came toward me. We hesitated, then kissed across the picket fence that separated passengers from visitors, both of us aware of the other girls' regard. I realized with some pride that I was on exhibit, the now tangible excuse for her regular absorption with the mails and, perhaps, some passed-up flirtations.

The Rices' apartment on Sutton Place had been closed up for the summer and we found it pleasantly cool and dark on this warm, muggy day. It was a somber place, with its plum-hued French tapestries and huge, lustrous arms slung from walnut paneling, but in its very contrast, the background for Angela. Her blondness, the frivolous sound of her slender heels on bare floors, the jingle of her bracelets seemed ultimately, perishably exquisite against it. It was also a foretaste of the elaborate life I had imagined for her and about which I was the least bit apprehensive.

My thoughts reached backward to that schooling. By Aldrich, in the bread-and-butter letter, recalling how I had scrapped the textbook model and written Mrs. Jay a wholly original one, including, as excuse for the delay, an account of what Pierce and I had been doing in the competition. A week later I had received a surprisingly ardent reply. I had delighted her and was to revisit whenever I chose. It provided me with a stripe of confidence now. I felt I could rely on candor. I sensed its remarkable power, particularly in a young hand. It was a kind of passkey that had seen me safely through the formidable gate to Pierce's mother and earned me that cordial response. Guilelessness came naturally to me. I was beginning to feel sure of its effect and guessed it would serve me equally well wherever I wished to go. I wondered, though, what would be required of it next.

While Angela flung clothes from one suitcase to another and rattled about in long closets where I had an awesome glimpse of her wardrobe—shoes enough for a ballerina, a rainbow of frocks, filed like the leaves of a long memory—I stood among the ghostly dust covers and wondered about making love to her.

I felt she would not resist. She would hardly have brought me here if she had wanted to prevent it. I yearned to. I was light-headed at the prospect. Yet I had a reluctance toward the overtures, toward shattering the agreeable companionship of our reunion with the heavy-breathing, possibly clumsy, grapplings of love-making. Besides—the whole weekend lay ahead. There was no need to rush. So although I was alone with Angela for an hour, I did not touch her.

At the garage on Fifty-sixth Street we asked for her car and found it still in storage. They could not have it ready for us until later, possibly by midevening. We wandered west, along hot streets and into the Weylin Bar for a drink and listened for a while to the sly aphrodisiac of the piano. Flushed and exuberant, Angela told about one of the girls whose crush on a young American painter in Paris had caused her defection, how she had stolen off from an inspection of the Cluny Museum for a Pernod with him and did not get back to the hotel until the following day. She had spent the night in his ghastly little garret room, horrifying Baldweg, who had her in virtual chains for the balance of the trip, and creating a monumental envy among the other girls.

"And you?" I asked. "The way you tell these stories, you always seem to be the duenna. Didn't you have any fun at all? Weren't there any boys for you?"

We were strolling uptown now along nearly empty summer streets toward La Rue, where Angela had asked to go for dinner. She paused to look in at a dress shop and said, "Oh sure. There always *seemed* more of us than there were boys, but there were lots of them around, really. There were some Princeton boys on the boat going over, cute ones, but they drank a lot and we knew about them anyway. We were going all that way to see *Eur*ope."

"And did you find *them* attractive?"

She laughed in sudden recollection. "Oh, *some,* yes. There were three Italian boys in Rapallo that we swooned over. They had those huge big eyes and satiny skin and that lovely curly hair, and they were just boys, you know—only seventeen or eighteen—but they were so very proud-looking, we thought they must be at least dukes and so terribly knowledgeable, as though they were *born* blasé about everything, and at the same time they were laughing and having such a good time showing off for us." She gave a mock sigh for Rapallo. "And there were some French boys at the Deauville Casino. You should have seen them dancing, such absolutely wild joy. They were just beautiful, that's all."

"Really, Angie?" I was indignant. It struck me as not only unwholesome but unpatriotic. "You really think Frenchmen and Italians are beautiful?"

"Sure. Some. Oh, *yes.*"

"Not too slick? Don't you think they're slick and greasy-looking?"

Angela shook her head firmly as she sprinted ahead through the restaurant's doors, then turned to laugh at my expression. "What's the matter?"

"Did you actually *fall* for one of the French boys?"

"Oh no, Ben. I just looked. Isn't that all right—just looking?"

"You said they were dancing. Who with . . . themselves?"

"They had girls with them. We didn't even get to *talk* to them."

"Did you fall in love with—anyone?"

She turned her almond eyes upon me and they smiled and welled with pleasure. She formed a *no* with her lips and put her hand in mine. "Did you?"

I shook my head.

"Then dance with me."

We went out on the tiny waxed floor, where I sensed I had arrived at dead center of Angela's neighborhood, the little world of the East Fifties, with its tail-wagging headwaiters and the pomaded leaders of stringy, accordion-laced bands, their ears cocked for the debutante's wishes, invariably "From Now On" or "This Can't Be Love." Though I doubted my gifts for it, some circuit closed and the slippery syncopation coursed through me like current, possessing me and thrusting my cautious, untutored toes to a recklessness that turned out to be charmed. I was tasting the joys of Angela's French boys. I was all male, dominant and supremely deft. She answered, moving airily to my very thought, the incredible softness of her body against me. We were in the music, responding like one animal. It seemed we had made a fresh discovery about it, that it was really up there all the time, a regular flashing airstream of it, and together like this, we could hear it, share it with stomping Watusis, dervishes and gypsies around the world, all of us tuned in on the fertile rhythm of life itself.

The music stopped and we clung to each other in the middle of the floor, feeling like some creatures left on a sand bar as the sea receded. I made another discovery—that I was no longer in love with an abstraction but with the real girl in my arms.

When it was time to go Angela paid the bill with one of her remaining traveler's checks, assuring me her trip was not yet over and that her father would want to finance the evening as a necessary expense of returning her safely to the Rice doorstep.

Walking east in the cooling evening, I was regretting my cautiousness of the afternoon and hoping the car would not be ready, but it stood, a Ford phaeton with our luggage already loaded, in front of the garage, and Angela called her mother to say we were on our way.

When at an early hour of the morning we said goodnight in the upstairs hall of the Rices' quiet, rambling house in Spring Lake, I tried to kiss her. To my dismay she turned aside with

a smile, more of amusement at my thwarting than coquettish-
ness, and her door closed firmly. I went down the hall to my
own room and hours of wakefulness with my failure and disappointment, doubting my own senses and wondering if the
rebuff was an aspect of virtue I did not comprehend, or a punishment.

On Saturday night there was a dance at the Bath and Tennis Club, and while Angela enjoyed the attentions of old
beaux and flirted with one in particular, my misery grew
until it was unbearable and I cut in angrily.

"Hi," she said. "Having a good time?"

"You know damned well . . ." I shuffled grimly around
the floor.

"What's the matter? Do you want to meet some girls?"

"I want to talk to you. Will you come outside?"

She frowned at the unreasonable request. "We can talk
here."

"No we can't." I released her and walked off the floor.

Angela followed me through the lobby and paused as I did
in front of the clubhouse, then followed me silently into the
parking lot. In the shadows at the far side I put my foot on
someone's bumper and smoked half a cigarette before I spoke.

"What I don't understand is why you brought me down
here."

"I'm sorry. I didn't know you were unhappy, Ben."

"Watching those guys paw you? My God, Angela. I saw
what that fellow was doing to you. Windy—is that his name?"

"He's a little drunk."

"You were loving it—every squeeze. Is he the big romance?
Are you in love with him?"

"Oh, Ben, I've known Windy forever. He just does that. It
doesn't mean anything."

"It does to me, goddam it. It's disgusting."

"What do you want me to do, Ben, refuse to dance with
him?"

"Whatever you like," I said. "I'm going back to your house
now and in the morning I'll walk to the station."

I could hear music from the club and the sound of someone laughing, but Angela, though she had not moved from where she stood by the fender of the next car, did not speak. It heightened my anger that she could not find a reply, but when I looked into her face, I found to my astonishment that she was crying soundlessly. I was so moved at the sight of her streaming face that I drew her to me, and at the slippery-salty taste of her mouth, pushed her back across the fender and hood of the car and kissed her with a bruising violence that seemed to bring relief to us both.

From that moment Angela accepted my claim upon her. She did not flirt with anyone in my presence. When we were alone we kissed and touched one another with endless delight. Her mother, though mild as milk, had shared some of her more formidable father's initial and understandable suspicion of me. Now this was swept away and I was accepted as a provisional member of the household, with easy access to its comforts and privileges. I fell into the agreeable habit of expecting to see Angela every weekend, in New Haven during the football season, or as her habitual escort and weekend guest in New York.

*   *   *

Pierce had brought back from Berlin a huge oil painting and had hung it over the fireplace of the splendid new quarters in Timothy Dwight. On a severe iron bedstead a pair of life-size lovers were represented, naked but for a blanket that covered them to the hips. The man lay sleeping, face down, his powerful arm sprawled across the girl's stomach. She was a long-haired blonde, and her exalted, love-sated face had just turned to the window for a view of dawn as it broke over snow-crowned mountains of the New Germany. For all its carnality, the intent was clearly spiritual. The canvas was drenched in religious light. Just as it attracted, it repelled me. I found it continuously disturbing, although Pierce made great fun of it.

"It's for recruiting offices," he told us exuberantly, patting the magnificent, lovingly detailed breasts. "That's the New Germany for you. Every good storm trooper will be issued one of these automatic Brunhildes."

Armed with introductions from friends of his father, one from Colonel Lindbergh, he had been received with warm, traditional hospitality everywhere he went. Over the Piesporter, friendly Germans scoffed at Hitler's importance and tried to persuade him that Nazi rule was repugnant to most of them, and left to themselves, they would see it was temporary. The only incident that cheered him was a talk with a German flier he met in Vienna. He was on leave from a post in Moravia, where, he told Pierce, he never felt safe except in his barracks. One of his fellow officers had been caught in the street alone at night. The Czechs had bludgeoned him to death. Also, he confessed, the Czechs had an effective underground railway, smuggling their aviators into France.

But before Pierce sailed for home, the Germans launched their blitzkrieg into Poland and that nation of thirty-four million citizens fell to the German army in just three weeks.

In New Haven, the fall of Poland did not change, but rather reinforced, the thinking of most of us—that the United States was well out of it. In that fall of 1940 we were of one mind—that the war in Europe, no matter how real or hot it grew, was no concern of ours.

There were daily reminders in the columns of the *News* about what suckers—that was the word—our fathers had been, how they had "snapped at the bait of humanitarian propaganda only to find themselves impaled on the rusty old hook of European self-interest." No sir, the way to preserve Democracy was to make a bastion of it here, three thousand miles away. Totalitarianism could not be impressed on a healthy, contented, prosperous place like ours.

I remember going with Pierce to hear Ray Bridgman—a World War I ace who had flown with Pierce's father—tell an audience that when he quit in his sophomore year to join the French air force, he believed he had enlisted in an idealistic crusade but had found it a bath of hatred and propaganda.

The youth of today had better see there was no heroism in war. It was more heroic to go to prison than accept a draft call. The pacifists were right. They had to be.

Pierce fumed. He would not even speak to Bridgman afterward.

But Pierce's most intriguing souvenir of Europe was the film he had taken. Night after night we insisted he show it on the wall of his ground-floor suite in T.D. Friends from all over the campus came to squat on the floor and view the chronicle of his summer abroad.

It began in Hamburg, recording a Wehrmacht parade and youth rally, complete with girl gymnasts. In Berlin, he had photographed an air show with planes stunting over the heads of a crowd, young aviators looking skyward in front of ranks of Messerschmitt pursuit planes. There were young boys in a work battalion fixing a road down the Rhine valley. But the film's primary appeal, what made us whistle and laugh with vicarious concupiscence, was the profusion and variety of girls he had photographed in his obviously triumphal progress across Europe. There were proud, long-legged, elegant ones enjoying outdoor cafés and tennis courts and pigeon shoots, and coarse, sensual ones in the courtyard of a bordello who invariably seemed impatient for him to put his camera aside.

There was one girl in particular, a lovely dark Argentinean he had found in Como and taken along to Rimini in his little Bugatti. On a deserted stretch of beach he had persuaded her to take off her clothes for a swim in the Adriatic and had photographed her coming out of the waves, first trying to cover herself with her hands, then running into the camera, her imploring arms outstretched.

On the Grande Corniche, near Menton, he was nearly killed in a collision with a truckload of carnations. The girl with him was hospitalized for a week and the Bugatti totally destroyed, but his own recuperation took place at the Negresco, thanks, he told us with a significant wink, to a pretty Niçoise, who was miraculously accomplished at massage.

He had some footage of handsome girls beckoning from the

windows of a house in Paris, and these, he explained, were decoys. Inside, the girls were different. Alas, he had no record of an *exhibition* he saw in a little hotel near Pigalle. It was an erotic performance by a man and two girls, and we never tired of its details.

Pierce did three stories for the *News* on his trip—one on what he had seen in Germany, with some observations about the mystical German nature, the old myths of power built around Wotan and Thor, and how Hitler played on this, believing himself divinely ordained. The others were on the war at sea, about which he had picked up some first-hand knowledge.

His passage home had been booked on the *Aquitania* sailing from Southampton, but when on the third of September Britain declared war, he was warned in a telegram from Ambassador Kennedy that the Germans planned to sink it. He managed to get a single berth in a crowded stateroom aboard the U.S. freighter *Wocasta,* which sailed from Glasgow on September 8.

The morning of the second day out, he had come on deck to find a submarine lying in the haze a quarter-mile away. A shell had splashed in the sea some forty feet off the *Wocasta's* bow and she was reversing her engines obediently.

A boarding party arrived, and while two German officers remained on deck scanning the horizon, another pair examined the ship's papers, passengers and cargo—fifteen thousand cases of Scotch whiskey and twenty tons of tulip bulbs. The Germans made jovial apology, and the raider U-27, its crew on deck waving good-bye, passed them onward.

His third story was an interview with a passenger on the *American Farmer,* who was an eyewitness to the spectacular sinking of the British carrier *Courageous.*

It looked to me as though Pierce, who had signed up for Cecil Driver's Comparative Government and Sherman Kent's Nineteenth Century Liberalism and Nationalism, and at midterm got B's in both, was well on his way to his goal of Oracle at the *News.*

*   *   *

With early October came the social grading and labeling event of the year, the two weeks of junior fraternity rushing. It was a time of life when a young man could get an idea of the female anxieties, the terror of being left out and the pleasures that come wrapped in an invitation. Oh, to be chosen! When a man is young, surely the primary yearning is to be recognized—and if not admired, then loathed—as an individual. Anything is preferable to serving more time in that gray ooze from which, since first consciousness, he has been struggling to emerge.

During the first week we had learned how welcome we were. Now, at the beginning of the second, Morton Wolfe and I stood on the steps of Battel Chapel, awaiting the hour of eight when we could appear at the house of *our* first choice. Meanwhile we viewed the ancient rites of Calcium Night. Snaking columns of hooded, torch-bearing Lucifers were chanting their largos and making hellish arcs in the night.

Wolfe, torn between curiosity and scorn for these aspects of higher education, sneered away. "Where do you suppose they got the idea for those hoods," he was saying. "If I was a member of some minority group, a jig, say, this would scare hell out of me."

"Another vestige," I suggested, "of a time when sophomores were more impressionable." Looking closely I saw signs that the marching brothers were eager to be done with the ceremony. "They don't seem to have much heart for it."

"There's my bunch." He pointed out the straggling Sigma Gams in purple robes, flimsy as children's costumes. "They don't even know their song. Well, that's an encouraging sign. Maybe I'll drop by there after all."

"Will you?"

Hands in pockets, he shook his head at the spectacle. "Well, I tell you, Ben. Shutting people out and giving them labels to wear is a ghetto—assbackwards maybe, but still, in principle, a ghetto. It's a bad joke and I despise it with all my heart. And yet it's interesting, isn't it, that they want me." He laughed at himself and his dilemma.

A particular respect and fondness for Wolfe overcame me. Sometimes the sight of him, alone, walking across the campus, was a reproach, but tonight I felt especially close to him and I believed he had forgiven me my defection of the spring.

"You want to know what I think?"

He hesitated before his careless "Sure."

"You should go Sigma Gam."

"Because they'll take me?"

"No, for God's sake, Wolfie."

"All right, why? Why should I go?"

"Because you'll make friends there."

His mouth twisted with skepticism.

"There'll be forty guys in there you'll drink and eat with. You're bound to find some you'll like."

"I tell you, Ben. In all this"—he waved at the retreating columns with their now-guttering torches—"there's only one person I admire—the one who won't have anything to do with it, who doesn't need any of this crap to make him feel important."

"All right, Wolfie. I admire that too, but this is a real world and you join up in it because if you don't you get left out. The loners get left out of everything."

He gave me a not unfriendly but a disappointed look. "Ben," he said, "you've been had."

I was fond of Morton Wolfe. He was intelligent and totally honest. Yet I felt his vulnerableness, his fear of humiliation, made him unnecessarily wary, and his diffidence was becoming habitual. But just before eight I watched him stroll toward Sigma Gam.

*   *   *

Wolfe's scorn had its effect on me, though less as an argument against joining a house than as a fresh reminder of my own minimal self-confidence. The fear of being left out still haunted me then. I could not shake off a recollection of being laughed at for the fatness which had afflicted me when I was a child, of being whispered about for (I imagined) odors of breath and body and of being spurned by high school class-mates. I had a recurring dream of distant laughter, overheard from my darkened room, and of a sprint toward a departing boatload of excursionists who, over a widening gap of water, ignore my cry of "Wait!" I seem to be held in a dark thicket, glimpsing the light, hearing the joy of others, just out of reach.

*   *   *

Architecturally the houses of Fraternity Row were very simi-lar, small stone manor houses, replicas of the *News* building. The row wound like a cowpath from disheveled Park Street, where Sigma Gam stood, past the P.U. house, abandoned years earlier by some marginal brotherhood, past Chi Psi, then through the gate which joined Beta Theta Pi and Zeta Psi and made a social as well as physical threshold over which it debouched into the very center of the campus, the court-yard which embraced the Fence Club and, at the University Theatre's left flank, Delta Kappa Epsilon. According to my values, they were increasingly desirable in that order—Fence and Deke sharing the crown.

I had not received an eight-o'clock invitation to either. Al-though predominantly athletic, Deke was a *News* enclave and I felt a real injustice had been done me there. I don't know whom I had offended, who had weighed the ordinariness of my background, but I was wounded by the rejection. I re-sented the two or three upperclassmen I suspected had cast the blackball against me.

I was less resentful of Fence, for it was predominantly so-cial. Almost exclusively church-school and stud-book, its rolls glittered with names made formidable by their forebears. Perhaps it was my very lack of qualifications that made Fence so attractive. I was strongly impressed by the grace, the lack of anxiety, with which they had entertained us. In the bar, the athletes had talked to me about the *News*, with nary a men-

tion of *the team.* If there were grinds about, they were disguised. There was a *News* contingent in Fence and they com-
plimented me by *not* talking shop, but rather discussing
drinking and the leisurely pursuit of girls. It was amusing and
effortless conversation, in the Fence manner, focusing at last
on the proper selection of gut courses—Pots and Pans, Cow-
boys and Indians, and a course called The Twelve Great Living Religions for which the final examination was invariably
the single question: *Name* the twelve great living religions.

I liked the look of the place—all the immaculate button-
down shirts and soft white buckskin shoes, each with its bit of
grass-stain from Northeast Harbor or Palm Beach. I noticed a
Fence smell too. It was the prevalence of Harris tweed, and I
imagined that on a rainy night the clubhouse would be peaty
as a Hebridean croft.

But there was a less tangible attraction to Fence. It was a
force that moved me, and later, much later, when I had
gained some perspective on my generation, I sensed it had
touched us all. I think we were some bewitched by the aristocratic ghost of old Yale. Though he had been no more than a
wraith for half a century, we could feel his presence fleeting
ahead of us along the old corridors and assuring us we were
young American princes awaiting our sovereignty.

Under his spell there was little we could do wrong, provided we lived by the code—poise, style in clothes and behavior, good manners (a kingdom might be lost by a breach of
manners) and a particular indifference (at least outward) to
intellectual pursuits. Yes, it was more appearance, of seeming-
not-to-care than of not-caring, for we admired accomplishment. But great deeds must be performed without effort, for
that was the way, as we understood it, of aristocrats.

We were drawn to Leslie Howard's portrayal of *The Scar-
let Pimpernel,* for there was our *beau ideal;* there was a figure
to emulate—the fop who danced expertly and made the ladies
laugh while his vast underground thwarted the Revolution
itself. And for all our anti-intellectualism, we doted on *Henry
IV. To be Hal!* And by God, as the ale trickled down our

throats of a Saturday night and our dreams steamed up through the smoke in Mory's back room, we were. We were certain there was a kingdom out there somewhere, awaiting us.

All that was woven into the Fence tie. It was a field of black with clusters of four parallel gold stripes. It was worn proudly, like a flag, and I was convinced that in its four-bar amulet was the assurance that its wearer would never be left out, for it was princely raiment. This belief swept away my last suspicions of the bloods and made me wish for the camouflage that would make me one with them.

But real welcome, evidence of desire for my company, began a third of the way down the row, at Zeta Psi. Zete was a good place for me. With only a few swimmers and hockey players, it was athletically weak, but socially—with a wide representation from the Massachusetts and New Hampshire schools and a discriminating taste in girls—it was only a jump behind Fence. If any fraternity did, Zete maintained an academic reputation. Members of the P.U. who washed were Zetes, as were the majority of the nabobs at the *News*—and that was my entrée. Bailey had seen to my welcome and urged me to accept the bid. As I made my courtesy calls at Chi Psi and Beta, and then stood on the steps of Deke waiting for Pierce, I had very nearly decided on it.

Pierce's was a more complex decision. He was welcome every place, and as we walked toward T.D., I congratulated him on his freedom of choice. "I suppose you're going Fence," I said.

"The Dekes have been giving me a lot of pleasure lately." He paused in front of George and Harry's window to count attendance at the pinball machine. The same forlorn seven were at their endless marksmanship, and gratified by the sight, Pierce resumed the way. "I'm sorry you missed Deke tonight. I'd have given a month's allowance to have you watch those big furry locker-room types jollying me up. The same guys wouldn't have peed on me a year ago. I think you'd have enjoyed seeing Coleman and Hammond patting me on the back and rubbing my ears as though I were Handsome Dan himself."

"You like that?"

"Well, of course I like it." At the sound of our footsteps in the entryway a campus cop looked up from his newspaper, and at Pierce's obscene gesture, laughed and waved. "Why wouldn't I like it? I've known Hammond since third-form year, but what I remember best about him is that he was by the bench talking to Reggie Root when I got pulled from the Exeter game—and he laughed at me. You'd like it too if you'd been in the field house with those guys and taken their shit."

I followed him into his ground-floor rooms, grateful to find Aldrich still out. "You're going Deke?"

"I didn't say that, Mose. No, I think Fence. I think I like that best. It was Psi U then, but the old man was there."

I declined an Italian crook, a bent, evil-smelling twist of tobacco he swore he enjoyed, and watched him settle into his big armchair, light one and take some self-satisfied puffs. "Explain about the legacy thing, Pierce. I don't quite understand why you would want to do something because your father did. If your father was alive, of course it would please him, but . . ."

Pierce blew a series of tiny smoke rings. "He's not as dead as you'd think, Mose."

We sat quietly, listening to the night sounds, the chain of a heavy truck toiling by, someone playing "St. James Infirmary" in the courtyard. "Well, it's an important choice," I said. "These are the guys we'll be eating and drinking with for the next three years and I suppose they'll be our friends for the rest of our lives. We'll be working with them in some office, playing golf with them on Sundays, marrying their sisters, borrowing their political opinions. It's pretty goddam intimate when you come to think about it."

His eyebrow arched. "Who told you that?"

"You. Just a year ago."

He smiled, puffed on his crook. "That was an eon ago. This year I don't believe anything I believed last year. Clean

sweep. All new merchandise, Morosely. You want to know
what I think? I think—assuming you're not a creep or an an-
archist of some kind—you've got to join one of them. It's like
wearing a tie. You do because everybody else does, and if you
don't you have to take a stand on it—and that's not worth the
bother. If you can, you avoid the far end of the row, but in
choosing between Zete, Fence and Deke—oh, they do vary
in"—he made a spiral in the air—"character. But if you're
not a legacy, you go where people you like are going." In the
courtyard, someone whistled, the same notes repeated, like a
signal, then called "Hey, Bunny!" Jay rose and closed the
window on it. "Where you going, Ben? You want to go Zete?"

"Well, it'll make Bailey happy. He's about persuaded me.
'Ideal compromise between geniality and purpose. No meatballs. Zete dances are as much fun as Fence's and there's always a good crowd at the bar. At the same time you don't have
to be ashamed of getting caught in the library.' "

"You *don't?* First time I ever heard that. You ever hear
that before, Mose?"

I laughed. "Never."

"Sounds a pretty shameless crowd. What else did Bailey tell
you?"

"He mentioned the Dean's Cup. He said nobody gave
much of a shit, but they do win it every year."

"The what?"

"It goes to the house with the highest academic average."

Pierce frowned. "You really want to go Zete?"

"I'm not in such demand as you, Pierce."

"Someone blundered. There are fatheads everywhere.
Where would you go if you had your choice?"

"I don't know—not Deke, anyway."

"Fence?" He seemed amused.

"What's wrong with that—goddam it?"

"It strikes me funny, that's all."

"Why? Too grand for a bursary boy?"

"No, but I thought you didn't like the church-schoolers."

"All right. I've got over all that. I scarcely remember where people went to school any more. We've all overcome that jumpiness." I nodded at Aldrich's empty room. "I can even see the human side of him. He and Wolfe are speaking now, you notice? We're all growing up."

"Still—I'd hate to think you were going soft on Episcopalianism." Pierce shook his head. "Fence—fancy. You were impressed by the brothers?"

"Well, yes. They struck me as very"—I was about to say *genial*—"casual, the way they go about things, sports, *News*, Dramat, whatever it is. And yet on Tap Day they look as good as anybody. Yes, I was impressed. Oh, they do have a reputation for thinking they're pretty hot stuff, but to be honest about it, the whole fraternity idea is snobbish. Why pretend it's democratic like some kind of craft union? If you're going to be a snob, you might as well go at it with guys who've been brought up to do it right—know what I mean?" Jay was delighted. Grinning, he wagged his shaggy head at me. "And the girls are aware of it all right. I mean, what girls think isn't a vital reason for choosing a fraternity, but they do know all about Fence. They recognize that tie a block away."

"Angela? Angela would approve?"

"All right. Yes, Angela. She'd like it."

Pierce puffed on his crook. "If they knew you thought so highly of them over there, I think they'd be glad to reconsider."

"No thanks. I really don't want that." But for his questioning eye, I granted, "What could you do?"

"They probably figure you're all sewed up at Zete. I could do them a favor."

When I went upstairs Pierce came along to reclaim a history book, and we found Wolfe listening to Bessie Smith's "Empty Bed Blues." Hands caging his face, he didn't even look up. It was unusual—his having no sly taunt for us, and I thought he was absorbed in the music.

"So—is it all set?" I asked. "You a Mystic Night of the Sea?"

Wolfe blinked at us, and then as though at last he saw

something amusing about the two of us, smiled—an old man's weary smile. "No. Not quite. I'm giving serious thought to forgoing some of those good friends you told me about, Ben." The record ended and he held up the tone arm to examine the needle, then set it to play over. "You want to know what happened? The shots—Black, MacGregor and Arlen—took me off to an office upstairs. Very special treatment, very cordial, as though they were going to give me the brass ring or something. Arlen, the head of the house, did the talking. He's very smooth. I predict great things for Arlen. They're waiting for him in sales somewhere. He sat on the corner of the desk and folded his arms and said, 'Mort—we want you here very much. Every one of us does. It's important you understand that. But . . . there's one slight complication. We're a national fraternity, you know, with forty-seven chapters all over the country and there are certain regulations, binding, I'm afraid, on all of us.' 'No Jews?' I ask. 'What is this? You knew what kind of a Wolfe I am. I made that clear the night I was here for dinner.' 'Yes, we know—and we don't care. And it's our feeling that what the national committee doesn't know won't hurt it. You understand?' He reached around and pulled a card out of the desk drawer and held it out to me. My name on the top in fancy gothic type, and below, everything filled in except a blank for religious affiliation. 'What can we put in there, Mort?' This big grin, you know, as though we were in cahoots and he's doing me the biggest favor. 'How would you like to be a Unitarian?'" Wolfe shook his head. "That's when I knew it was time to blow the Sigma Gam house."

"But they do want you, Wolfie," I said. "They want you bad enough to break their own rules for you. And it's them, Arlen and the guys who run the place, that are pulling the fast one—not you."

Wolfe rebuked me with his sorrowful eyes.

"I understand," I said. "Only I hate to see you pass up seeing what goes on inside a fraternity house for a principle, an abstract idea that might not seem so important to you later."

"Abstract?" Wolfe shrugged. "My father isn't a religious man, but you've seen him, Ben. You know. When I was a little kid he warned me that people would try to persuade me I wasn't as good as they were, but that I mustn't ever believe them."

"If I were you, Wolfie," Pierce said, "I wouldn't urinate on Sigma Gam."

* * *

Effortlessly, as though I had only to wish it, I was pledged to the Fence Club, and for the first time at Yale, began to feel an individual, even something of an eminence. In February, when Pierce and I had been members for four months, came the second, the clean-up, rushing when we who were in assessed our classmates who were not. The Fence council chamber was a windowless room in the eaves of the clubhouse, with stalls like church pews running around four sides, so that we faced each other in a hollow square. The tall boxes in which we sat dignified us dramatically, lending a notion that we were playing at these assizes, and we giggled at each other, like schoolboys in church. Yet for me, as for most of us, it was a first experience at sitting in judgment of my peers and I found it subtly exhilarating. Likings and aversions, heretofore a private burden, now had formal weight, and for a young man it was a fragrant whiff of importance.

Our search was so relentlessly for good Joes, round pegs for Fence's round holes, that the possibility of my roommate's candidacy never occurred to me until Pierce proposed him.

The idea must have come to him suddenly, for otherwise he would have prepared me to support him. Nevertheless, Jay grew enthusiastic about Wolfe as he talked.

"You know him. I don't have to tell you he's one of the few really mature guys in our class. He goes his own way—never asks any favors of anybody—and he has a real wit. I mean he's an exceptional fellow, and at the same time, the kind who's likely to be overlooked."

Plaice, one of the Grotties, stood. "Well, I'm not against him, but we have to think about precedent, Pierce. We take Wolfe, you know, and where do we stop?"

"Because he's a Jew, you mean?"

"That's right," Plaice replied with a determined smile. He had a stock of New England stories which he told in Down East dialect, thus establishing himself as our wag.

"We stop wherever we want to stop." Pierce leaned out over the rail, liking this, drawing fresh enthusiasm from the concern on the faces of our delegation and enjoying the tilt with Plaice. "It isn't precedent either. There've been plenty of Jews in Fence—some known, some not. But that's not the point. I wouldn't want to think we could behave with any of the shabbiness of the Siggies. I didn't like that, did you? Wolfe's a guy with a lot of pride. You understand about that? He probably wouldn't come here even if we asked him. But we *can* ask him. We don't have other chapters or an alumni to tell us what to do—and I goddam well think we should." Pierce turned to me. "He's your roommate, Ben. Say something."

"Yes . . ." I got to my feet, struggling to find the right words to supplement Pierce's conviction, yet after listing Wolfe's accomplishments, only flimsy platitudes were coming to my lips. "Yes, I certainly agree he'd be an addition here. I can't really say enough for him. He often seems gruff, Wolfe does, but actually he'd give you the shirt off his back."

"What size does he wear?" Plaice asked, and it broke the tension. There was a roar of laughter during which I slumped to my seat, feeling I had blundered and failed both Pierce and Morton Wolfe.

But Pierce was banging his fist on the rail, demanding they be quiet and hear him out. "Listen, goddam it," he said. "I don't care what a guy is—Jew, Mohammedan, Buddhist or what—if he's got guts. Wolfe has them. You want to know anything more, Plaice—or shall we put it to a vote?"

He sat down in the awed silence his fervor had made, and

when the box, a little birdhouse with a divided porch for black and white balls, was passed around and opened, it was found that Morton Wolfe had not received a single black one.

We went happily, Pierce and I, to deliver Wolfe's invitation. But he seemed only momentarily pleased by it. I don't think he even considered it. He thanked us and declined. "Maybe I ought to be ashamed of myself for not coming right over with you and joining up and being one of the regular fellers," Wolfe said, "but I'm not. I'm going to keep on being suspicious of crowds. I feel safer that way."

7

Angela and I had been dancing our way steadfastly into that comfortable yet precarious relationship for which no name more ennobling than *going-steady* has been found. Those first indications of the deepening relation between us are among the sweetest, most gratifying experiences of my life. We wrote one another daily—newsy letters at first, cataloguing our activities. Then our formal endearments gave way to boldness, to unguarded confessions that we were in love. "I miss you, miss you, miss you" we wrote each other, and then felt sure enough of our privacy for some smoky, promissory eroticism.

It was a sign of the growing confidence we felt. The strands of trust wove round and round, and as we permitted each other further access to the privacy of our hearts and the most personal of our thoughts and concerns, we felt the less vulnerable.

Angela was silently attentive to my accounts of student behavior at Fence and the *News* and dutifully shared my elation at being elected sophomore manager of the Student Laundry, with its assurance of twelve hundred dollars a year for the balance of my undergraduate career. She absorbed it all like a sponge, and I never quite knew if it impressed, interested or simply bewildered her.

At the same time I was totally fascinated by her accounts of the qualifying skirmishes and jousting for the debutante lists, involving, as they did, charitable works, the loyalty and spite of her own school friends, the limited leverage of her mother on the lionesses of the Colony Club and, over the pink table-cloths at Giovanni's, the endless turning of conspiracies which nested, one within the other, like Japanese bowls and brought womanly light to teen-age eyes.

Yet Angela was surprisingly apathetic about such things. She cared about being included in the major cotillions and balls only insofar as she did not disappoint her friends and family and, lately, me.

One Saturday night in early December we paused on our way to a movie to watch young people in evening clothes pouring from taxis and limousines into the ballroom entrance of the Ritz Carlton. The marquee lights shone brilliantly on the babbling, waving throng of partygoers and I recognized some classmates and a girl who was a friend of Angela's.

"It's the Grosvenor," Angela said. "I didn't get asked to that."

"I'm sorry," I said as we moved along. "But it's probably not a very important one."

"Oh, but it *is*." She laughed in that tender, vulnerable way that suggested she did know something of disappointment. "It's a terribly important one. But I don't care, Ben. Honestly I don't. I'm having a much better time here with you than getting lost at a big fracas like that."

"That's very sweet," I said. "But you can go to the movies with me any old time."

"Oh, Ben, *you* want to go, don't you?"

"Of course I don't. I don't like those big brawls any better than you do." I had a last glance over my shoulder for the ballgoers and linked my arm with hers.

There was a new joy in every phase of our developing intimacy. I loved to go along with her to buy clothes, to pass judgment on a pair of shoes or a sweater, have the salesgirl defer to me as possessor of this blond creature with a taste for soft raiment, and I loved to stalk about in her bedroom, that fluffy sanctum of pillows and perfume bottles, gratified at the snapshots of us, the one of me alone, tucked into the frame of the vanity-table mirror. I would catch her sometimes in the lovely vulnerableness of her dressing to make playful love to her.

Even the spending of the Rices' money didn't bother me then. I would come to town with ten or twelve dollars for the weekend, and when there were no parties to go to, Angela supplemented this, diplomatically, with the price of a restaurant dinner or an evening of dancing at La Rue's.

Actually, this act of taking money from Angela seemed to me one kind of ultimate intimacy. I can remember the curious excitement of her soft fingertips touching mine beneath the table as she palmed me a ten-dollar bill. I was wholly aware of the gigolo aura it lent me but this was offset by a feeling that the secret act was a notable breach in the wall of her independence and made her more my possession than ever. In her paying for our food and drink, I felt not kept, but more a man for the exhilarating, worldly and the least bit depraved mastery over so young and desirable a creature.

I had told Mother and Father that I had a girl in New York and they were politely curious but did not press me about her, sensing, I guess, that she was well-to-do and that I might be embarrassed to bring her home. It was Angela who insisted.

While I knew there would be no unpleasantness (my family would be a bit dazzled but polite—and Angela accepted everyone without criticism), still I felt apprehensive about the joining of two worlds altogether separate. It was as though I were an actor who could behave perfectly well in two separate plays—one by Chekhov, say, and another by Philip Barry —but who was obliged to bring the characters of both together on a single stage and foresaw in it his undoing, that in the multiple confrontation he would be shown up as faithless, or worse—a cipher.

She came to Providence for just a night during Christmas week, bringing Mother a little blue china vase and me a silver cigarette case with my initials engraved on the lid, and hers covertly within. We had considered having a party, gathering some presentable young people, but we settled on a family dinner with no pretense at all.

Angela, proudly wearing the little circle pin I had given her, sat beside me on the kitchen table watching the homely preparations, and then insisted on helping. Father, with rare playfulness, tied her into an apron and handed her some plates that had been warming on the stove, indeed, were so warm on the side she grasped that they seared her soft white hands. Curiously, she held them firmly and mutely, suffering as her flesh bubbled, and we could never wholly understand why she had neither dropped them nor cried out.

Late in the evening, while Angela had gone off for another application of salve, leaving me alone with Mother and Father, they both said how pretty she was and how they liked her.

"And it's plain," Mother added with a sentimentality bordering on the tearful, "that she adores you, dear."

I remember nodding and thinking about what she had said, agreeing of course but bridling at the familiar pressure. I knew how fond of me Angela was and that she was never far from my own thoughts, but there was this gentle pushing all the time. Angela's mother had taken to asking my advice about her education, if I thought she oughtn't to apply herself to a more demanding course of study than the art and music appreciation she pursued so diffidently, and to admitting me to family secrets as though certain conclusions had already been determined.

Upstairs I heard Angela's footsteps on the floor of the guest room and recalled the dalliance we had stolen on one of the twin beds there earlier in the day. The purple chintz of its cover, the musty smell, the glazed texture, the kewpie-cuteness of the dust ruffle had evoked a gallery of aunts and uncles whose frames had gathered strength here, and their company

soon caused our moist, panting love-making to seem unnatural
and involuntary.

Now, overwhelmed with a wish to put an end to this uncomfortable line of inquiry, I heard myself reply, "Well, yes,
Mother. I guess she's that all right—but . . ."

"But what, dear?"

"She's too sexy."

The effect was immediate. Shock and embarrassment stilled
the house for a moment, and then Father recovered enough to
smile and say, "Well, that needn't be such a terrible thing in
someone you're fond of."

"I know," I said and felt miserably guilty at the sound of
Angela's light step on the stair.

The truth of it was that although we slept together—liter-
ally—tiptoeing to each other's room the moment the Rices'
house was still, although we joyously explored each other's
bodies and learned sophisticated ways of giving each other
pleasure, we had not yet had sexual intercourse. Though I
made a great show of consideration for her in this much-
magnified matter, the self-denial was, I think, one last slender
root clinging to the crumbling bank of my own independence. I was reluctant to see it part.

I *had* grown to love her totally. At times I felt like an
empty skin into which Angela had crept and filled to bursting
with the warmth and perfume and laughter of her feminine-
ness. There were no other girls in the world. When we were
apart I starved for the light of her eyes and the touch of her
hand.

And I knew with glorious certainty that she was equally,
passionately in love with me, that her resistance to the final
act of possession, full matrimonial right to her body, was as
thin and transparent as tissue paper. Oddly, it was Angela's
very permissiveness, and her family's, for they must have
heard the creeping about and the muffled closing of doors at
midnight and again at dawn, which inhibited me. The lack of
resistance, the run of the Rice house, which meant just that,
hoisted the whole load of responsibility for Angela's welfare

onto me. The trust was complete, and the result, inhibiting. I began to feel that however enviable and velvety my situation, it was a trap.

The thought weighed on me, made me newly serious with Angela, turned my concern to such gravities as the war in Europe. I might call her attention to the repeal of the arms embargo, permitting cash-and-carry exports to belligerents, or Russia's invasion of poor little Finland, and was rewarded with an irritating inertness. Talk of war glazed her pretty eyes. The more I sounded like a news commentator, the more childish and irresponsible an audience she became. She wanted to stay and dance until they closed or drive to Montauk and see the moon come up and sometimes she would drink too much.

In my uncertainty I would consider Pierce Jay and his contrasting ideas of the relation between the sexes. I knew precisely what his advice would be and laughed aloud at the thought. With envy I realized his irresponsibility gave him the kind of strength I lacked—made him potent as I felt impotent and put upon. And really, just as he claimed, he did spread joy around. His swagger and insolent eye were all the warning any girl needed, and I suspected he harmed no one. It made me question my Providence chivalry as too heavy a burden for these swift thoroughfares. I wondered if I might cut free of its encumbrance and knew of course that I could not—ever.

This was not all lost on Angela, whose habitual mild sunniness could disappear under clouds of prickly obstinacy, and in late January she stunned me by an elaborate begging-off from our weekend together. It was obligatory, a classmate's brother in town, but it left me forlorn in New Haven.

When I saw her next we had our first serious argument, but made up quickly and passionately, thus taking an elementary lesson in the exquisite pleasure of lovers' pain. It was a whole world we had yet to explore.

Angela was an adept pupil. As the winter progressed I was thwarted by a succession of her slight illnesses (even a three-day case of ptomaine poisoning had not stood between us in the fall), and then to my dismay, prior engagements. I was no longer to take our weekends for granted. I made formal application for all of February and imagined the worst was over, but one late afternoon while we sat in the Carlyle bar trying to decide what to do, she told me casually, yet with a sparkle of cunning in her almond eyes, that Pierce had asked her out.

It was as though I had been hit hard from behind while drowsing. I could not grasp it at first and yet I felt it was true, that she was not inventing it to taunt me, that Pierce had, in some unfathomable quirk of perfidy, wanted her.

"And you went?" Agony fluttered like a hummingbird in my throat. "I'm sure you did."

"Yes, I did." She laughed, ducked her head and sipped through a cellophane straw at her daiquiri.

"There was nothing to stop you, was there?"

"Oh, Ben, don't be like that. It wasn't anything. He was down about his father's estate and he had a few hours to kill. That was all."

"In the middle of the week? I didn't think you went out on school nights."

"It was just for dinner. Really, I'm sorry I told you."

"Did he kiss you?"

With an angry toss of her head she put her cigarettes back in her purse, stood up and left me. At the door she turned around and came back to the table.

"Do you have enough money?" she asked.

"Yes, goddam it." Rage made a wooden block of my tongue, so that I spoke thickly as well as absurdly. "I can buy this place if I want."

Angela moved off. Through the glass door to the lobby I watched her stop and chat with two girls, well-groomed and rich-looking as she, and then part with that bland laugh of hers as though nothing was the matter and sail through the revolving door onto Madison Avenue in a swirl of blond hair and fox jacket.

I was let into the Rice apartment by a maid, to find Angela

still out. I packed like a man drunk, leaving some ties over
the mirror and including a bath towel. In the foyer I rang for
the elevator and stood waiting and drowning, clinging to my
empty heroics, knowing them for the pitiful, empty, bluster-
ing things they were and yet the last salvation of my pride.
But worse, I was already ruing the privation, the barbaric destruction, I was imposing on myself as well as on Angela.

The elevator arrived with Angela, who stepped off, gave
my valise a scornful look, and puckering her forehead, said,
"You poor idiot. We talked about *you.*"

Swamped, but with the sail of rescue now in sight, I followed her back into the apartment, there to accuse her of
purposely arousing my jealousy. She denied it, and rather
than acknowledge the seediness of my suspicions, I shook her,
ripping the shoulder seam of her dress. And after a moment
in which we were equally stunned by what I had done, Angela collapsed in my arms and we forgave one another for
what then seemed a preposterous misunderstanding.

But I could not help returning to the thought. I asked for
details—how he had put it when he called, how and where
they went, what they drank and ate—and after hours of this
interrogation, even as she lost patience with me, Angela surprised me again by revealing that my instincts had not entirely played me false.

Her confession came at some dark hour of urban morning
when the room, apartment, building, the whole East Side
were as still as polar wastes. You would have thought no creature lived short of the miles-off, terrified wailing of a siren.
Beneath the covers we whispered, sharing what we knew of
truth. I had taken off the top of her pajamas, and as I stroked
the firm flesh of her back she told me in little bursts, punctuated by childlike gasps as though in fear of punishment, that
Pierce *had* tried to make love to her, had tried to kiss her in
the cab and again when he came upstairs with her.

Oh God no, she hadn't let him. Oh *please* no. How could I
even think such a thing. No, she hadn't slapped him. That

was supposed to be the worst, didn't I know? She held him off—and laughed. Laughter was the thing to turn away a man, to make a joke of it and not hurt the male thing so. She had laughed and run away. No—he wasn't angry. It was just habit with Pierce.

"Habit with you?" I asked. "Had there been anything before?"

"No, no, silly." She gave me a kiss, then, a little rosebud of reassurance. "He's that way with every girl. You see, it didn't *mean* anything. And you must never—never, never—speak to him about it. He's probably forgotten already. And I'm miserable. I'm such a fool for telling you, sweetie."

And I promised.

There is a clubhouse loyalty between males, perhaps a clause of the double standard, which takes itself as enduring and the loyalty with *any* woman as makeshift. It was in part this code which suppressed my resentment of Pierce. Whatever he had in mind—whether to test Angela's fidelity, to prove his invincibleness or simply to relieve the tedium—I felt, in his presence, bound to condone.

Moreover, I could not wholly believe it had taken place as the assault Angela had seen it. To be sure, he went about his seductions like a probationary Comanche after scalps, but he was both devoted to me and incapable of harming anyone he cared about.

In any case, accusing Pierce of poaching would have only added a ludicrousness, the cuckold's indignation, to the impotence I already saw in my reflection. So there was no rupture of our comradely parading of the winterbound campus. When he proposed that I come to Florida for spring vacation and bring Angela along, I scarcely hesitated. I wanted to see Willow Cay, the Jays' house in Del Ray, and the wonders of the Gold Coast—Worth Avenue, the Alibi, the Bath and Tennis, the Everglades Club, Colonel Bradley's—and to see if I passed among the young who made up the Palm Beach court.

"Oh, but I can't," Angela protested. "I mean, it sounds absolutely divine but our vacations don't coincide. Mine's two weeks later."

"I'll talk to your mother," I said. "I'll go over and interview that finishing school and explain. We'll get the work they're going to do while you're away and I'll tutor you. There are untold cultural advantages to travel. You'll see."

But getting Angela's release was not so easily accomplished. Persuasions and reassurances were required for the Rices, a long-delayed invitation from Melissa Jay and clever deceptions for Angela's dean—all planned and executed by me. Angela rode the wave of my eagerness with a puzzling indifference.

It was the same lack of curiosity over what lay beyond the hedges of her agreeable garden that she had shown toward Europe. As March and the time of departure approached, she neglected the simplest of her own preparations and even quarreled with plans I had made as though she would as soon not go at all.

When I found I could afford the Seaboard's Silver Meteor, which would carry us to West Palm Beach for twenty-three dollars in as many hours (the incident at the Carlyle when Angela had returned to make sure I had enough for the check lingered humiliatingly), she developed a contrary notion.

"But that's so dreary, sitting up all night. Squalling babies and drunken sailors. I hear it's perfectly ghastly. Why don't we go on the plane. Pierce is going on the plane."

"Because I am not Pierce and I don't want to spend the money. Besides, we can have a good time. We can bring some books and read and we can talk and even bring a jug and get smashed. A lark. It'll be good for you to see how real America lives. Part of your broadening experience."

"Oooh," she said as though she could already smell our fellow passengers and their cast-off orange peels.

*   *   *

The aisle still churned with pushy passengers, anxious for a better seat if they had one or any seat at all if they hadn't, when a classmate leaned across my lap. It was Anthony Cates, whose dissolute looks were amplified by a smear of lipstick on his mouth and another on the stuffed animal he carried.

"Where are you going, Moseley? Nassau?"

"We're going down to visit Jay."

"Oh my." He perched on the armrest beside me and beamed, moistly and lippily, at Angela. "When you get tired of dressing for dinner, come over to Nassau. That's where everybody's going to be, you know, with the rugby team. You get in on all the parties and stuff. Get Jay and come on over. You ought to do that, Moseley."

"Maybe." I reached overhead into the rack and got down the book—Alsop and Kintnor's *American White Paper*.

"Seen the bar on this thing? Pink flamingos—flocks of 'em all over the walls. Boy, it's going to be pretty frightening in there. I bet they take off after the third drink and fly around. It's full of tawdry Miami types but it's going to be pretty jolly. You want to come back and have a couple? I've got a place staked out. What do you say?"

I opened the book and smoothed some pages.

Angela edged forward and her lovely knees, smooth as peaches, emerged from her skirt and her charm bracelet tinkled as she touched a lock of hair into place. "It sounds like fun."

"Somebody might take our seats. We're lucky to have two together."

"If we put a coat across, nobody will take them, Ben."

"You go if you want."

"You don't mind?"

I ducked my head to cover my irritation and shook it slightly.

Over an hour later, as I was staring spitefully through the rain-streaked window at North Philadelphia, Angela returned. I did not acknowledge her "Hi! Why didn't you come?" but there was an admission of naughtiness in her laughter, like optimistic tail-wagging at signs of discipline.

Her voice was furry and as she crossed in front of me she slipped. I guessed she had had at least three.

"I kept thinking you were going to come." She sat down carefully in the window seat, smoothed her skirt, looked at me, then propped her chin in her hand and stared out at Pennsylvania disappearing under the evening. "Oh? We're not speaking? I'm going to be punished now, is that it?" After a while she added, "Oh, Ben, please. If you didn't want me to go, why didn't you say so?"

I turned a page. "You like Tony Cates?"

"At least he's fun. He makes me laugh."

"Why don't you go back to the bar car then?"

"Oh, you *are* mad, aren't you?"

"Yes."

"This is going to be a grand trip. I can see that."

We rode across Delaware without a word, swaying slightly against one another, slowly inflating our separate rancor like two balloons.

"You never think about the money," I said, breaking the silence at last. "It never even occurred to you that I have only seventy bucks to last me the whole vacation. I did not want to blow it in the bar car when the train was barely out of Penn Station. How many did you have?"

"I don't remember."

"You don't remember?"

"Two. He paid. He had plenty of money."

"But that doesn't make it any better, that he paid and has plenty of money. You're with me."

"Oh, please let's don't be so glum and horrid about it. Money doesn't matter that much, not on a vacation. Oh, I do know how you feel, that you oughtn't to be sharing mine—but it does give me pleasure and there's nothing wrong with it, really there isn't. There's always money for what you want to do, and if there isn't, that's all right, you get along without it."

"Not all of us can afford that point of view."

"Now that's really mean, damn it. I'm not a spoiled rich girl. I'd be happy without *any* money, I honestly would. I could live some dreary place if I had to, but while I don't, there's no reason to be guilty and miserable about it, is there? Please don't let's start the trip worrying about it. Daddy gave me some money for us to have fun with. It's ours. Yours." Angela opened her purse and took out two one-hundred-dollar bills folded together. "Will you keep it?"

She tucked them into my hand, and when I tried to give them back she pushed my hand away so abruptly the bills fluttered to the dirty floor of the coach. They stayed there at our feet like something alive and threatening, and we resumed our silence and listened to the wheels cluck against the rail joints, rhythmically counting off the miles. A woman in the seat across the aisle anxiously pointed out the bills to me, and though I only nodded, Angela reached down and picked them up.

"I'm going to throw it away unless you take it," she said, and when I didn't, she brushed by my knees and into the aisle. There was no slight doubt in my mind that she would do it. Angela rode an impulse with a glorious recklessness, and I watched her progress toward the head of the car, wondering if she would turn into the ladies' lavatory or offer me a last chance.

In the vestibule I caught her hand as it reached to push the two bills under the accordionlike curtain connecting the cars. "That would be foolish," I said. "I'll keep it for you."

This resolution calmed us. Back in our seats we drank moodily of the rum collins in our thermos. When the car-length queue for the diner discouraged us, we dined on sandwiches bought of a Baltimore candy butcher and were lulled by the rocking of the train and the droning of voices and the whisper of blowers into a traveler's euphoria. I observed our neighbors and wondered about their relationships and destinations. They were the middle-aged and middle class for the most part, bound for some sun deck in North Miami. But I also recognized first evidences of the war, a pair of young soldiers, a pretty woman alone with her baby, an older one knitting an endless khaki scarf—each one with a pathetic expression of being uprooted and in transit to someplace they didn't want to go. And then I thought about my own destination and relationship.

I smelled Angela's perfume, her mother's Bellodgia, and I turned to admire her. She had got out the copy of *A Handful of Dust* I had been urging her to read, and I watched her soft fingers at play in the coils of her hair, that perfect leg in a stocking so filmy it was invisible, no more than a dusting of silk.

"Liking the Waugh?"

"Yes," she said. "Oh yes." She looked at it as though surprised to find it in her lap.

"You're in the same place you were last week. Maybe you ought to try something else. Not everybody likes Waugh. It's a special taste."

"No, I *like* it. Only it's hard to read on the train. It jiggles and kind of hurts my eyes."

"Why don't you wear your glasses? You brought them, didn't you?"

She nodded, shrugged, looked in her purse. "I can read as well without them. They're really no help."

"Put them on. Go ahead, please." I watched her take a pair of slightly elliptical horn-rims out of their case, put them on shyly and smile. Protruding from the wings of blond hair, they lent a pleasing angularity, a curiosity and earnestness, to the soft flesh of her face. "Well, you know, I think you should wear them—for looks."

"For *looks?*"

"Really. You look sexy in them." I was pleased to see her blush and fold her arms contentedly. "Maybe I'm a spectacles fetishist, but right away I'm excited." The lady across from me was dozing and no one was in the aisle. I leaned over and kissed Angela and she laughed in delight. "Sometimes I wish you'd leave the glasses on and take everything else off. Wow."

"Oh, you're just being funny."

"I'm not. I really mean it. I think glasses—and I don't care what Dorothy Parker said—make a girl look more interesting. More intelligent."

A shadow of disappointment crossed Angela's eyes. She took the glasses off, looked at them doubtfully and slid them back in their case. Then she glanced at the book in my lap. "For a course?"

"No. Pleasure."

She tilted up the cover. "I didn't know you were all that interested in history. I thought you were getting a D in it."

"All right, information then. I *hope* to get some information about what's going on in the world, maybe learn something about the forces that may well destroy me, could even destroy our whole civilization in the next couple of years."

"Do you think you can *change* anything?"

"That's not the point. The point is that soon, it could be next week, you know, I'll probably be called on to go fight somewhere, maybe give my life for some ideal or other, just like they did the last time, and I'll have to decide whether to go to the parade or to jail. I mean, the way I feel right now I'd go to jail. Oh yes . . . any day. I can't see any reason . . . look, what do *you* think? Would you be ashamed of me? What do you think about being a conscientious objector?"

"I wouldn't care."

"Oh, come on. You would. Goddam it, you're not even thinking about it. I don't think you really believe the Germans are wiping out whole regiments of Poles, real people like you and me, and that right this minute people in London are stumbling down into the subway in the dark to get away from the bombs and not knowing if their house is going to be there when they come back up. Hitler's going to be in England by August, Angela. Jesus, you were there last summer. I don't understand."

"What can I do?" She made a helpless gesture.

"I don't know. Knit something. Can you knit?"

"Anybody can knit. It doesn't take any particular competence to knit—if that's what you're trying to say."

"Why don't you then—because the other girls don't?"

"If you're going to jail, why do I have to knit?"

"You don't have to knit. You don't have to do anything. I just wish you'd react in some way. Couldn't you say, 'You'd be a rotten, lousy coward not to defend your country. How could you ever take any pride in yourself? What would your children think of you?' Couldn't you say something like that? So I'd have some way of knowing how you feel?"

"But that's not the way . . ."

"Okay. Then back me up. Tell me it's a good idea to go to jail for the belief that war is wicked and its only purpose to protect somebody's investments."

"I don't believe that either—do you?"

"I don't know," I said, "but there's supposed to be a hill in Luxembourg where you can sit and look up the Moselle valley and see guns firing, French and German guns firing at each other, while in the foreground two trains pass. One is leaving with iron ore for Germany, and the other is arriving from Germany with coke for the French mills right below."

"I don't get it."

"Luxembourg is neutral—and the German businessmen are supplying French businessmen with the fuel to make guns to shoot Germans, just as the French businessmen are supplying German businessmen with the ore to make guns to shoot Frenchmen."

"Oh."

"You understand that, don't you?"

She nodded vacantly.

"What?" I insisted.

"That they oughtn't to *do* it," she said crossly. "The businessmen."

"Well, yes, of course. But I mean about not wanting to die for some big cartel." She had turned to look out the window again, although it was dark there now, and what was irritating

me was not that she didn't understand. I kept thinking it was
that and that all I had to do was explain it to her. But she did
understand. It was that she didn't, or couldn't, care about
anything so abstract as a war that had not yet hurt her.

She looked resentfully at the Alsop book still open in my
lap. "You're not making a lot of progress there yourself."

"It's not easy stuff."

She smiled and then laughed at me.

"I never made any claims about being a big brain or anything. I just wish to know more than I do. I don't want to be
like an animal prodded along without any knowledge of what
it's all about."

"Yes. That's exactly how I feel sometimes, like an animal
you're trying to prod somewhere. That's what you're really
doing with the book, goading me with it. You do that kind of
thing all the time, do you know that?"

"I don't at all."

"You don't? You didn't about this trip? You want to know
something? You never once asked me if I wanted to go."

"Didn't you?"

"Yes. But not this way—being pushed all the time."

"If I hadn't pushed, we wouldn't even be here. We'd be
back in the Carlyle talking about it like a couple of lotus-
eaters. Really, Angie, there were times when I felt I was carrying you and you were making yourself extra-heavy, the way a
child can when he wants to."

"If that's true—I'm not saying it is, but *if* it is—it's all your
fault. It makes me livid sometimes when I know you're trying
to make me over into someone else"—she choked on a bubble
of resentment—"as though I didn't please you . . . make me
over according to some crazy idea that you just thought of,
not even because you like it particularly, but just to see if you
can. It makes me want to . . ." She shook her head in frustration and turned to the solacing window.

"My God. I'm sorry, Angie."

The car was darkened now for the night, and to the rhythm
of wheel on rail, the sigh of the blower and someone snoring,

we rocked gently and silently for miles. Then she blew her nose, and a glimpse of her face, flushed and swollen-eyed, touched me.

"It seems the closer we get, the harder we are on one another, doesn't it?" I said.

"It needn't be, you know. It doesn't have to be that way."

"But, Angie, I'm afraid it does."

She shook her head defiantly. "Girls I know say all the terrible things people do to one another, all the strains, you know, just disappear when you get married."

"Oh, Angie, how could they? People are just the same whether they're married or not. They go on being themselves."

"There's at least one thing that's different."

"The sex, you mean?" Together we regarded the outskirts of Richmond. "But I don't think you can count on that. I mean, it's quite possible it would just get boring after a while."

"Oh no." She faced me now, filling with indignation. "It gets better and better."

"Angie love, how would you know about that?"

Her eyes widened. "But it does. I know. They've told me. Girls I know that are married."

"Do you know so many?"

"Lots. There were two didn't come back this fall. One of them's already having a baby. They say it's the war—just *thinking* about it. I mean, with the insecurity and all, not knowing when a man might have to go off somewhere. A girl would want to get married as soon as they could. It's only natural she'd leave college—*any*body would."

"I suppose she would. But I don't think it would be very wise. What if the man is killed in the war and the girl is stuck with just the honeymoon and the baby?"

"Oh, Ben," she moaned. "You just don't understand the way a woman feels. You don't understand at all."

"Well, I know it's crazy to rush into anything as serious and permanent as marriage just long enough for a taste. That would really put a strain on a person, wouldn't it now? Just supposing a couple who have been seeing each other a lot got married hastily."

"I don't mean hastily."

"All right—but get married *sooner* because they think the war is going to keep them from it later, and then the guy goes off to China for six years while she sits home every night wondering if he's all right, instead of leading a normal life, seeing people. I mean, she can *wait* for him to come back, and she will if she really cares about him, whether she's married or not."

"She can't, though."

"And the man off in China has the added anxiety of wondering if she really *is* sitting home."

"Well, it wouldn't be a very good marriage if you couldn't trust someone . . ."

"Oh, Angie—six years? Who would you trust for six years?"

"Wouldn't you trust me?" Waiting for my reply, the little furrow deepened over her nose.

Smiling, I said, "Of course not."

"Why?" She was not going to be put off with joking.

"Because you're ingenuous. You see harm in nothing. You take what people say at face value." Now *I* was in earnest. "I think that's admirable, mind you. You're just not suspicious of people and their motives. It comes from your protected childhood. Nobody ever took your candy away or called you dirty names. Now wait, let me finish. And because there'd be lots of opportunity. You love pleasure. You're sexy. You radiate it, send it out in waves, and men come flocking around, like Cates up there in the bar car, drooling over you."

"I can't help that."

"Perhaps. But I saw you provoke him. I saw you—right here, you tempted him. You're a flirt. You keep trying out your appeal to see if it still works."

She laughed, pleased. "What's wrong with that? Testing—that's all."

"It wouldn't be all if I were off somewhere in the desert."

"Why wouldn't it? Why are you so suspicious? You're so sure of yourself and so unsure of me—like a child, not to be trusted. Oh, damn you anyway. You're so stupid about women. Your lack of trust could make a girl go prove you right."

"And then it would be *my* fault? Oh, Angie, what specious reasoning. If that's really the way a girl thinks . . ."

"It is."

" . . . then she's a fool. There's nothing innocent about flirting. That's where the trouble starts. It was your flirting with Tony Cates . . ."

"Do you really, for one minute, think I was attracted to him?"

"If you don't mean it—it's dishonest."

"But were you really jealous of him? Could you imagine that I would rather be with him than you?"

"With Pierce, then. You *are* attracted to Pierce. Come on, don't deny it. His trying to kiss you was as much your fault as his, wasn't it? You were signaling him somehow, even if you were unconscious of it. I wouldn't know about that. You were signaling with your eyes and hands, your whole body. Maybe you don't even know it, but it's plain to anyone else. The first time I ever saw you, you were doing it. I was in agony, did you know that?"

"Why? You had no claim on me."

"It was like watching you being prepared for some sacrifice and I was supposed to save you, only I was powerless."

"You still don't, you know."

"I don't what?"

"Have any claim on me at all, Ben. Not really. You've never even asked for it."

"Then why did you stop Pierce? Or did you? You told me first he hadn't tried, that you talked about me all night, and then that he had. I don't know what to believe. Did he really kiss you? Tell me truly."

"No," she said and spun her head to and fro, sending her

hair flying as though she were again fighting him off. "No, no. He didn't. Not then."

"But sometime. When, Angie? Did he come down again last week?"

"A long time ago. That's all I'm going to tell you. I don't have to tell you any more than that."

"And what else did he do? Fondle you? Did he feel you up, the way he does every girl?"

"Oh, shut up. I don't want to talk about it."

"When was it? You have to tell me now. You can't leave me here imagining. When, Angie?"

"Last summer. In Paris."

"Paris? You saw him in Paris?"

She nodded.

"How did he find you?"

"Through one of the other girls. He picked her up in the Brasserie Lipp."

"He found out from her? Why did she tell him you were there?"

"Oh, he knew. He knew I was on the trip with these girls from school."

"Ah—in a letter? You wrote him you were going to be there?"

"He knew before we even left." Her voice cooled. "I didn't write anyone but you last summer."

"He called you at the hotel?"

"I think it was a message or something. I couldn't understand anyone on the phone. The French phones terrified me. Oh, I *do* remember." She smiled. "It was a message, a little telegram sort of thing they send around Paris in an underground tube—a *pneumatique,* that's what they call them."

"Saying what?"

"Asking if I could have dinner."

"How did you answer? Where was he staying?"

"The Ritz."

"Oh, of course. I suppose he had a big suite or something, right?"

Her eyes searched mine, then turned to look into the night,
where a streaming mudbank reflected our car's image and its
rectangles of trembling submarine light.

"He came for you in a cab?"

"Oh, shut up."

"I know all about Pierce's summer. He'd cracked up the
Bugatti, so he took you in a cab or you walked. Was he still
banged up? I know his arm was in a sling then, but I doubt it
cramped his style. Did it, Angela? I do think it's funny neither of you has mentioned going out together before this moment. How come? Were you . . . Yes, of course you were.
You were the girl he took to the *exhibition,* weren't you?"

Still staring through the window, she said, "I didn't know.
I hadn't any idea where we were going."

"You must have."

"Pierce didn't intend to. It just happened, really." She
turned, spreading her hands on her lap. "I'll tell you whatever you want to know, Ben."

"Tell me everything you did."

She took a deep breath. "We went to the Bal Tabarin to
laugh at all the people on the Paris-by-Night tours, busloads
of them paying New York prices for champagne and ogling
the bird in the gilded cage—a girl, you know, with feathers
on her hair and ankles. It was dreadful. Then when we got
out in the street a boy, a nice-looking boy in a seersucker
jacket, came up and spoke to Pierce. I thought he was a
friend. He had a crew cut and he looked American. We
walked down the street with him to where it forked around a
tiny flatiron building which had a café that was the whole
ground floor. The bar was flatiron-shaped too, with mostly
girls sitting around it, some of them quite pretty, and while
the boy was talking to them, moving from one to the other,
Pierce told me he was going to take us to a show not on the
American Express circuit—something we'd never see again
and was it okay with me."

"And you said of course it was. It never occurred to you to

say anything else. I mean, you could see the girls, what kind they were. You didn't really expect it was going to be folk dancing?"

"I didn't *know*. I didn't know anything. But they were all . . . well, friendly. They didn't look *evil*."

"Be honest, Angela. Don't say that when you stood with Pierce in this bar full of whores and watched a pimp round up the cast, you didn't know what kind of a performance you were going to see. You knew damned well—and you *wanted* to."

"I can remember being scared—but not scared enough to say uncle."

"And being with Pierce—Pierce arranging the obscenities for you—made it all the more exciting and irresistible."

"No, no. It wasn't like that. Pierce made me feel safe, that it was just funny. Can't you see? He was laughing and joking about them."

"Who?"

"There were three of them. The boy and two girls. A tall blonde and a colored one. When we followed them back up the street, Pierce was inventing all kinds of crazy things about their relationships and about what they did on their days off and about the union they belonged to. And we even thought about sneaking off and leaving them, only we didn't because he thought it would disappoint them. Yes, *them*."

"Go on. What next?"

"Everything? You want to know each detail?"

"Everything you can remember."

"Well, we followed them into a little hotel, I don't remember the name. It was very white and freshly painted, with deep carpets, and we waited at the desk while Pierce paid a round auntie-looking woman and she led us upstairs and into a large bedroom. It was clean and tidy, with cheerful blue curtains, and I told Pierce it was a bigger, nicer room than mine at the France et Choiseul, and he said I should recommend it to Miss Baldweg for next summer. The bed was huge, with a mirror for a headboard, and on the other side was a bidet, not screened off or anything. And we sat, just Pierce and me, at a little round table, though there were several, all with chairs as though sometimes they had an audience of a dozen. Pierce ordered champagne, a bottle for us and one for them, and they loved that. Nobody ever did that." Angela covered her face with her hands. "No, I can't. I can't tell you any more."

"Why?"

"Because it wasn't disgusting then, but it is now. As I start to tell you, I feel absolutely coated in filth."

"So long as you don't, it will be between us—filth and all. I want you to tell me everything. Go on. Don't leave anything out."

"Well, they undressed, except the blond girl got only as far as her bra and pants. She was best at English, she said, and was going to be our narrator. She turned down the bed and leaned against the wall and spoke in a monotone as though it was a play that never varied, and while the colored girl washed herself at the bidet, the blond girl said they would demonstrate how *it* was done in many different ways. First the little boy, the young man, sat on the edge of the bed and tried to"—Angela closed her eyes—"tried to excite himself, but he must have been tired or he'd done it so many times that day . . . So the colored girl came over to cover for him and they got in different positions—'This is the way the Greeks . . . This is the way the Chinese . . .' Writhing and groaning and pretending that something was happening . . ." Angela shook her head. "Oh no. No more."

She sat with her back straight, hands folded primly in her lap, her face colorless and translucent in the dim night light. Eighty fellow passengers cramped in their reclining seats, a few open-mouthed, snoring, filled the air with a moist, fusty smell of stale food and coffee and the souring of their uncomfortable bodies.

Her lips seemed to stitch together, and then she was

quickly on her feet, shoving past me into the aisle and weaving forward, fending herself off the metal trim of the seats, and disappearing into the ladies' lavatory.

When she emerged a quarter of an hour later she found a seat in the smoking section at the head of the car, and there, for a while, she watched a cold moon flirt through the pine scrub of the Carolinas and then she dozed, her head drooping to her shoulder.

At some small hour of the morning I crept forward to Angela. She opened her eyes at my touch and I thought she had not been asleep at all. "Come back," I said. "It's foolish to stay up here. No. No more. I won't ask any more."

She followed me back to our seat, where we folded our arms and shivered, and finding some slight warmth in our misery, drew it around us and watched for a sign of the dawn. But it seemed that this morning it lay forgotten on the other side of the world.

Because I could not help myself I said, "One more thing I have to know, Angela. And you must tell me. Afterwards— did you go to bed with him?"

"No."

"But you were aroused by the performance—by watching the rutting, naked bodies on that bed. How could you help it?"

"It wasn't that way."

"And Pierce. After that he wouldn't have let you off. No. Where did he take you? Did he take you back to the Ritz?"

"No. We didn't. We didn't. We didn't, I told you." She began to weep softly.

"What did you do?"

"He kissed me. I let him kiss me in the courtyard at the hotel."

"I wish I could believe that, Angela. I'm sorry, but I can't."

The gray light of a Georgia morning had at last begun to creep across a streaked sky, revealing a low fog hugging the swamps and bathing the sleeping figures around us in mortu-

ary light. Angela's face was colorless, eyes streaked, hair un-
combed and mouth bruised as though from a night of love-
making.

"No," she said woodenly in a voice that sounded oddly like
her mother's. "I suppose you can't. But then—what are we
going to do?"

"I haven't any idea. I don't see how we can go on to Del
Ray. I don't see how we can go stay with Pierce. Jesus."

"No, I guess we can't do that." She seemed not to care
about it. "I'm sorry. You wanted so much to go, didn't you?
Why don't you? You go on and I'll go home. I can get sick."
She laughed helplessly and passed a hand across her forehead,
through her tousled hair. "And it's true. God, I feel awful."

In spiritless rationalizing I tried to repair the damage we
had done, tried to see if somehow we could not bind things up
and save some of the promise of our holiday. Some good
times, I said, might provide the healing we sought. But as
we slowed for Jacksonville, Angela, combed and resolute,
dragged her valise and tennis racket out of the luggage rack,
and with the help of a stranger, carried them up the aisle.

The train had already stopped when on sudden impulse I
seized my own belongings and clambered off. The long silver
cars began to move again on the final leg of their trip, and we
stood together watching the last car, leaking wisps of steam as
though it were as tired as we, until it disappeared down the
track to the south.

The morning was clear, and though still cool, there was an
unfamiliar gentleness to it and at the same time the unmistakable breath of tragedy. When the northbound train came
through at noon, we boarded it and dozed the whole way to
New York, aching with fatigue and disappointment, speaking
only when necessary and sustained by a hope that when we
were back where we started, this hideous journey could be
erased.

We took a taxi from Penn Station, and riding uptown I
looked out on nighttime crowds as they waltzed along East

Side streets, then a fellow hugging a girl in a doorway, and I felt no envy of him, only my emptiness.

Angela's voice emerging from her dark, opposite corner was withered. "How does it end? Tell me, Ben. What do we become, now? Enemies? Old buddies? Do we wave if we should meet, as if we'd been to some camp together?"

"I don't know," I said. "I'm too tired to think."

8

Angela and I unable to come was all my telegram had said, leaving so many questions unanswered that I expected to find Pierce fretting with curiosity. But as we reconvened for spring term, he did not even mention the collapse of our vacation plans.

In that first week I avoided him—by night drawing up heroic confrontations, and by day abandoning them as impossible. I think he guessed from my sulkiness precisely what had occurred between Angela and me, and I needed no further proof of her faithlessness nor his own shocking callousness.

But then he sought me out. Bristling with enterprise, he settled on the edge of my bed to ask, "Interested in watching Tap Day?"

"They won't let us in. Just juniors."

"I know how to get by the campus cops, and there's a room at the west end of the court that's not used."

Our Tap Day was a year off, but I was already anxious and Pierce's old knowledgeableness prevailed. "Yes, I'd like to see it," I said and thus buried my lively grievance between us.

Concern over senior societies was a part of the uneasiness we all knew in that last term of sophomore year. I saw quite clearly the nimbus which cloaked the knighted. The simplest act of those fortunate upperclassmen was cloaked in assurance. I recognized each as a member of his band, as though he wore a cockade. It was the ritual concealment, denying a thundering conspicuousness, that lent the societies their mystic awesomeness.

The elections—the fifteen now-distinguished names which each of the six societies had chosen, appended with hometowns and the name of the senior who had given the accolade —would be published on the Friday following Tap Day. They would appear on page one of the *News*, and on page three of the New York papers. The son of a Yale man lived with a foreboding of his father's opening the *Tribune* to the lists, there to search vainly for his name. My own father's not knowing, at least not enough to care deeply, was, in this case, a consolation. It was ample pride for him that I was at Yale.

In passing the eyeless tombs—Skull and Bones' mossy Greek temple on High Street, Scroll and Key's Romanesque basilica on College and Wolf's Head's steep-walled cloister on York—I would quail, as though eyes watched through a chink in the masonry. It was on the border of farce, and we knew it, made clandestine jokes about societies among ourselves, yet our desire to be chosen was profound. We knew its significance precisely. It was the dubbing, the true touch of the broadsword.

On the afternoon of Thursday, May 8, Pierce and I, with six of our classmates, clustered about a narrow window in Branford. We kept it closed so as not to draw attention, and the only sound was of our breathing as we watched the juniors arriving. They took positions on the grass below—hands in pockets, bunching for comfort, each figure stiff with aloneness. Pierce, with a pair of binoculars and rare solemnity, identified them for us. High in the south wall, behind the casements, faces like moons were appearing, to locate and point out candidates.

"Bones in the center. They always have the center suite. Eastlake—see him in the dark suit? See—with the old guy? I think they're locating Bailey. Do you see Bailey down there? Yes—right by the tree. Beezee and Snake over the entry. Keys and Wolf's Head either side. Big banker there, up from Wall Street for the day. I bet it's a sluggish market."

The afternoon itself had been a glorious golden one, with moist, rooty smells rising from the earth to stir and tantalize us with that melancholy restlessness of spring. But below, a thousand men readied for the solemnities of investiture and a hush of pure awe was lowering upon Branford Court. Long shadows crept across determined patches of grass, through the field of juniors who huddled, whispering, not daring to look up for fear of thunderbolts.

As Harkness' melancholy bells, in elaborate lacelike couplets, tolled the terrible hour, the casements of all six societies flew wide to reveal the juries. Intent on lists in hand, they pointed, watched their black-suited couriers in the court below, circling, circling, spotting their man, singling him out, then standing off, waiting, watching the throng as it crushed out its last trembling cigarettes and listened to the last five strokes roll away like huge cartwheels.

In the woolly stillness came the first slap, a crack like a pistol shot, then the others in a volley, four at once. Pale faces turned to confront the couriers, to glance at the gold pin, worn this once on the knot of a black tie, then, releasing an agony of pressure, the shrill cry, "Go to your room!"

As the tapped ran from the field, a flutter of applause trailed them until it was stifled by another crack, another piercing cry, now one upon the other so fast that the eye could not follow, and I wondered how, in the bedlam, the men at the windows and their circling couriers could keep it all straight. Who might be left that they wanted, where was he, and if in their zeal they might take more than their quota of fifteen.

A window slammed, and Pierce said, "There goes Keys. Keys is finished. And look—Wolf's Head too." Though not ten minutes had passed, though the crowd in the court below seemed scarcely decimated, the windows were closing, firmly and forever, on the Class of 1941. "And Bones," he announced sternly. I looked at the Bones window and saw a man with a steep bald forehead look for a moment at the crowd. You could hear a murmuring from the juniors, rising like a flight of little birds, as their eyes looked to see if some final window, some recess for their hopes, remained. It was the last glance of a man leaving a hotel room, to be sure he had left nothing of value behind. He turned away and pulled the window firmly shut.

The Westminster quarter chimes, four aerialists afloat above the multitude of heads still in Branford Court, announced that the ceremony was complete, that the hours, and life, had resumed. Ninety men had been chosen from eight hundred to ascend Olympus.

We watched the culls depart. There was no laughter, only a maundering like that of a chastened congregation leaving church.

"How dismal it must be," I said to Pierce as we walked along Elm Street, "to want that badly and not get it. I suppose a lot of them just come to look, must know they don't have a prayer—but some surely think they do, and don't."

"I can't speak for the class," he said, "but I wouldn't go out there without a damned good idea of my chances. I'd find that very damned depressing, to walk out of Branford Court with a virginal back. Yes, I think I'd be sore enough to go burn something down."

*   *   *

Beyond these real, local anxieties lay the intangible one. Still remote, still easy to thrust away, yet insistent, it was a crack that had been no wider than a hair but now could take your finger, and it was threatening the order of our affairs.

The fall of Norway and Denmark, the surrender of Holland and Belgium, the invasion of France, the grim resolve that seemed all that was left of Britain had a numbing effect on most of us, but thoughts of war exhilarated Pierce, winding him up so that I expected some rashness. He was collecting service information, the requirements for Army, Navy and Marine air forces, like a boy at a boat show, and I thought he might, any day, walk down to one of the recruiting offices and enlist.

"Goddam," he said one afternoon just prior to the end of spring term, "they won't take me in the ambulance corps. I had an idea I could get to Europe and see some war. Boy, wouldn't *that* be something to write about—but they won't take me, not just for the summer, and shit, I don't want to drive an ambulance any longer than that. But I'd sure like to see something." He looked at the letter from the ambulance service and tossed it into the wastebasket. "What are you going to do, Mose?"

"Back to Providence," I confessed. "I have a job, same as last year."

I too was uneasy and dissatisfied, but in a very different way from Pierce. It seemed that time was running out, that in six months or a year we would be in uniform, and I wanted some return on life's investment now.

At times I felt purposeless and hollow and my thoughts would drift irresistibly to Angela, luring me with the thought we had made a mistake, misread our directions and lost our way. But in the act of writing or calling her I was stayed by the disciplining certainty that my provocation was weakness; that Angela and I were forever obliged to walk the same path, one whose forkings and byways were simply illusion, marvels of trompe l'oeil—for the path was high-walled and led only to places, like the platform of the Jacksonville station, where we had been.

My loss ached constantly. It was made more painful by having to disguise it, for melancholia was as abhorrent to the extrovert world in which I lived as uncleanliness or a profusion of hair. So I went about my affairs; classes; a couple of hours at the Student Agency's office, reconciling the week's collections with our books and writing stern notes to the flagrant delinquents; a drink and dinner at Fence; and studying in the now long warm evenings, the window wide to voices and foot-steps quickening toward pleasures, wondering how I would find a new girl.

I knew that she existed, someone as suitable as Angela was not; hardier, independent . . . yet dependent too. And her hair—curiously, I could see that quite clearly—was brownish, arranged naturally, as though it got scant attention beyond soap and brush. Though I could not make them out, I knew her features were strong. She was, as yet, faceless, like those uncompleted portraits the limners carried in search of a sub-ject.

While I imagined making love to her, it was not sex that spurred my need but a feeling that a girl ought to be no bur-den, no great sack of animal comforts shouldered against the cold nights and deserted bivouacs, but someone to admire and perform for, not a sea anchor but a sail for my mast.

I went about finding her methodically, writing to girls I had met in New Haven or New York, one leading to another across the latitude of dormitories. I traveled to Poughkeepsie, Northampton, Bennington, and in those gloomy taverns, Ra-har's and the Dutch, I sipped doggedly at copper-flavored beer that filled but never exhilarated me and I sang "We'll Build a Bungalow" and "When You Wore a Tulip" and be-wildered myself and the girls. They failed to please me or found me wanting—or, more precisely, they sensed the check-list in my hand, the grim insistence in my courtship. Kate, Barbara, Molly, Deedee, Janet, Helen. I went through the motions of unbuttoning them (mostly figuratively, once lit-erally), only to find to our mutual dismay that I lacked the will to proceed.

*　　　　*　　　　*

I went home to an ebbing, retrogressive summer of law-clerking and getting a foretaste of war time, learning that like other kinds of time it can be read from clocks, but when the huge hands of Big Ben would finally jump one minute's space, whole months of one's own life had ticked away, quite empty. It was my first glimpse of the enormity of human waste that is the very heart of war.

German troops were in Holland and Belgium, and General Gamelin's order to the remains of his army was to hold position, to face death rather than withdraw, and it was clear a German victory was imminent. Westbrook Pegler said there was a fifth column in every city in America. In Washington, they were drafting the Selective Service Act; and in the back office at Littlefield and Sullivan, it seemed time was too scarce to occupy it with title clearances, yet there was not enough for anything I really wanted to do. The girls I knew in Providence seemed so plain there was no joy even in impressing them. I learned from one that I was now regarded as stuck up. The irony tickled me, but I wasn't troubled by the advice. I was indifferent to their opinion.

*   *   *

Late in June, Pierce ransomed me with an invitation to Newport, and I found Bellerive as grand as I had anticipated. I had never seen a house so elaborately equipped to please the senses—a sweeping *allée* of lindens down to the sea, massive gracefully arched walls of soft ochreous limestone, and garden paths which surprised me at every turning with a bower, a new glimpse of Bellerive's chimneys or the slate-blue sea. There was an awesome stillness. Servants on urgent errands, with a freshly ironed pillow slip or a tiny tray, moved as though in stockinged feet, in fear of waking those who slept. There was only the whispering of leaves and the conversation of birds, and sea sounds, a mournful whistling buoy rocking in the swell off Brenton Reef. There were cool eucalyptus smells, peculiar to different rooms and different parts of the grounds, all strange to me and yet evoking some bittersweet recollection out of dreams.

Pierce, stimulated by my appreciative wonder, displayed Newport's possibilities for pleasure with a mixture of pride in their antiquity and contempt for their folly. We did the Casino and the Beach and a pair of cocktail parties, and went back to Bellerive to dress for a dinner-dance that was to take place in the huge white house of a steel manufacturer with three beautiful daughters.

But Pierce's joy, and thus mine, in all this was curbed by his concern for his mother. From our claim-stake on the beach, he pointed out a tall, beaked man who with European assurance was making his good-mornings among the ladies.

"What would you say about a creep like that? I mean, you can tell from here, can't you, Ben? You don't need binoculars and the handbook to tell that kind of bird. They send us a new shipment about this time every year. Son-of-a-bitch is trying to marry the old lady. Imagine. You'd think she could see what's perfectly plain to everybody else, that he's a predatory bastard whose sole purpose is to get at her dough. Well, you know Ma. She's pretty soft upstairs."

"I can understand how you feel, Pierce—but I don't expect, if she likes him, there's much you can do about it."

"Actually, there's a lot I can do about it. I've told Ma what I think of him. That's the first step."

"And?"

"Oh well, she thinks I'm wrong. She thinks I'll come around to like him. God." Pierce sifted sand from fist to fist. "Look at him there—he thinks he's a peacock. I had a detective agency check up on him, and it turns out, of course, he has no money and no means of support, that he's a professional sponge, moving around from one poshy tub to another, just waiting . . . until he can move into my old man's house."

His eyes followed the horizon, where a merchant ship moving imperceptibly eastward was a momentary reminder of the peril at sea. Pierce got up and strolled down to the water's edge to kick at the festoons of red kelp. I joined him, and we walked along the hard wet sand, avoiding where we could the pellets of oil so common along the seaboard that summer, supposedly the ugly residue of submarine warfare now moved right to our own coast.

At the end of Bailey's Beach a great hump of brown rock lay awash like a beached whale, and we sat on a ledge of it, sunning ourselves, tossing pebbles into the tide pools and scraping with a clamshell at the coins of oil that clung so tenaciously to our feet.

"He claims to be a political refugee. From France. Now I ask you, what does that mean—coward, right? Can you imagine being here in a place like this while your country was being licked by the German army? Wouldn't that sicken you, Mose? He claims to be a widower and I doubt the hell out of that, but they couldn't find he'd been married more than once." Pierce made a sound of disgust. "It was an expensive inquiry but not very thorough. He looks like a regular Bluebeard to me, but they found nothing beyond that he's a vagrant with expensive tastes. I *knew* that." He looked up to where the luncheon crowd could be seen gathering on the terrace. "He's the kind of fellow must have been involved in some scandal. It sticks out all over him. Just in the phony way he talks you can tell he's been up to something—only my dumb detectives can't find out what it is. You know, I was just thinking of inventing something. Suppose, Ben. Just suppose that while you're swimming your wallet gets stolen from the cabaña, and you report it to the office. And then it should turn up. One of the beachboys might find it in de Villepin's bathhouse."

"Pierce." I laughed. "You're not serious?"

"Every season there's stealing at the club." He frowned at a smooth stone in his hand as he flipped it over. "Somebody's money or jewelry gets stolen and people talk of nothing else for a month—about who did it, you know. It's just the sort of thing they like best up there."

"But I couldn't do that, Pierce. It's a wild idea."

"You couldn't, uh?" He shrugged, threw the stone away. "Maybe. Maybe it is. I'll think of something." He jumped up, and brooding, led the way up toward the cafeteria.

When, a few hours later, I met Victor de Villepin, he did not seem as unpleasant as Pierce had made him out. Despite

Pierce's brutal rudeness, he maintained a good-natured politeness to me, Melissa Jay and to Pierce himself. But for the rest of the weekend Pierce was preoccupied with schemes to discredit Victor de Villepin. In departing, I promised to return for the Fourth of July celebrations, but three days later Pierce called to rescind his invitation. He had changed his mind about sticking around for the summer. He was on his way to California. The weather was more certain there and you could fly every day. Come September he would see me in New Haven and take me up for a spin. A week later I read of Melissa Jay's wedding in Newport to Victor de Villepin.

*   *   *

Pierce turned up for the opening of college, directly from Santa Barbara, tanned but wan-looking from a summer of excesses that I would soon hear about in loving, lascivious detail. He registered for Sam Bemis' Diplomatic History, Spykman's International Politics, Coker's History of Political Ideas, quarreled with Miss Lugg at the Dean's office for not permitting him Rudin's European Diplomacy and Imperialism or Arnold Wolfers' Contemporary Problems in International Relations, and staggered from the Co-op with an armful of crisp, gleaming texts.

I found something absurd and implausible about his hugging these recondite books as though he might acquire their wisdom by osmosis. He had taken to wearing glasses, hornrims, which gave him an industrious look I could not help thinking was spurious—yet he had found his way to the stacks of Sterling Library and spent half the night there preparing for a class. It seemed to me that his academic obsession was part real, part calculated. At one moment I was persuaded that by an act of will he was making himself over into a scholar, that just as he claimed, he could master anything he chose—and in the next he was an impostor out to hoodwink the learned world, and I laughed aloud at him.

The comedy in his posture was never lost upon Pierce. "Books, not bullets, Ben," he said. "That's how we'll solve the world's dilemma. Why not trade in those tiresome French and sociology courses for some of these dandy realpolitik ones, and we'll chart the new order together?"

"I'd choke on all that government. I need variety."

"But it's an *age* of specialization. Come to think of it, the people at the Dean's office are as behind the times as you, still arranging our study like a balanced meal, a little of this and a little of that. The Dean's a dietician. Might be a column in that."

*   *   *

During the fall term the senior officers of the *News* would choose from among the twenty-one of us on the junior board a new management to succeed them at midyears. So it was a comfort to be in evidence and we haunted the *News* building even when not required.

Sprawling around the scarred yellow-oak desks on the second floor, we rewrote the next day's stories with the vast casualness of old hands, ragged the heelers and offered advice to Doc Bellinger, the incumbent managing editor, who, in assuming Bailey's mantle, held to his indulgent, humanistic view of the world and of Pierce Jay in particular.

But it was not entirely this crisis of ambition which drew us here. With its array of city dailies and news magazines, it was a listening post to the world outside. We could usually find an argument going—over Willkie's chances against FDR, or over Churchill, who had just replaced pathetic old Neville Chamberlain and prescribed a victory diet of gall and wormwood. We were newly interested that fall. Across the smooth surface of our beloved indifference had fallen the buzzard-shadow of Selective Service.

On October 10 each of us who had passed his twenty-first birthday sat down to one of those offensive government forms and filled it with irrelevant facts about ourselves—place and date of birth, citizenry, color of skin, eyes and hair, state of mind and body, record of crimes. Yet we found no space to tell how generous nature had been to us with her gifts, no way to indicate how distinct we were from your garden variety of conscript. We could feel the mechanical fingers of draft-board machinery plucking at us. The war was no longer on the moon or across the sea. Its cries and cordite smell were creeping onto the campus.

"They're the real heroes," I said of Alter, a student in the Divinity School, and Swift, head of Dwight Hall, who had made page one with their refusal to register for the draft. "To actually stand on your belief when everybody, me for one, who's been talking about doing it goes off like sheep and signs up. I've been thinking I was a conscientious objector for two years, but when it came right down to it, I didn't have the guts. I'm ashamed of myself."

"Twaddle," said Pierce. "They're going to prison for a year, like those holy Joes at Union Seminary. A year in the federal pen, Mose. Only some oddball would want to do that. Come on—if there really *is* a war, you don't want to be in jail for it."

"I might."

"Oh no you don't. Alter and Swift are absolutely wrong, of course, but they believe in it, so that makes it okay. Only *you* don't believe in it. Anyway, it's too late for the gestures. We're at war now. You can go on talking all you like, but isolation is dead. There's an illusion around here that it's still alive because the great American bourgeoisie is running scared and playing right into Hitler's hands. The clerks, the people with tidy, godly little minds always want to play it safe and not antagonize anybody. Listen . . ." From his drawstring bag he fished a book of Saint Exupéry's and flipped the pages. "It's about an old clerk he sees in the airport just as he takes off in a squall. Listen to this: 'You who built your peace by blocking every cranny through which light would pierce, making a wall of genteel security in routine, stifling conventions . . . raising a modest rampart against the winds and tides and stars . . . having trouble enough to forget your fate as man . . . You are not the dweller on an errant planet and you don't ask yourself questions to which there are no answers. You are a petty bourgeois. Now the clay has dried and naught within you will ever waken the sleeping musician, the poet-astronomer, that possibly inhabited you in the beginning.' There's our villain, Mose—the clerk, the man whose imagination has atrophied in keeping his books. The bookkeepers have taken over America and they absolutely cannot comprehend the enormous ruthlessness of Hitler's ambition. Precisely what happened in France. It was individual apathy that licked the French—that and looking out for themselves. They aren't cowards but they won't make any sacrifice together. They'll go die for France any day but they're suspicious of their neighbor—you know, that he'll drink his wine or make love to his wife while he's gone. Poor buggers drowned in their own material comfort."

Pierce groaned over each *News* editorial. They were the work of Sturm, the sober, self-absorbed chairman from Keene, New Hampshire, who had succeeded Butterfield, and as so often happened with *News* officers, he had come to resemble him in manner. Yet we sensed he was a lesser fellow, defensive in everything he did. He took his views on international developments from Senator Taft, who, he predicted, would be our next President.

Pierce's view was surely a minority one, and he had despaired of converting me, but Morton Wolfe, invariably fragmented and defensive in his convictions, as though he saw a threat to his person in every group loyalty, surprised Pierce one night with an opinion resembling his own.

"I'm astounded at the effect Sturm's editorials are having even on the A.S.U. boys. I thought they were smarter than that. They come back from their humbug meetings and try to persuade each other Stalin *didn't* make this deal with Germany. It's like an echo of the *News*. The privileged youth around here is so busy defending its privileges, it won't believe what's in front of its eyes."

"What's all this, Wolfie," I asked. "You want to get your head shot off? You been reading Emporia Bill?"

"I've been reading my aunt."

"Who?"

"My father's sister in Danzig. She used to write and tell us about the joys of being back in the Fatherland—the restrictions, you know, how she had to dress and where she could go and where she couldn't. But we don't hear any more."

"They censor her?"

"She doesn't write at all. Nothing—in three months. It makes you wonder."

We were all three silent a moment—Pierce smoking, stretched on our sofa, one hand behind his head, and Wolfie staring out the window, looking ashamed, as though he wished he had not admitted us to such private thoughts.

"Why don't you write a letter to the editor, Wolfie?" Pierce asked. "I've been wanting to, only I'm sucking up to him this week. Why not write and tell him what you think of his crummy editorials?"

"Me?" He laughed. "Shit—I couldn't write a decent letter." He reflected, though, intrigued, before adding, "Even if I could, they wouldn't print it—not from me."

"Reading our rag," Pierce went on, "you'd think we all agree the war is like a mediocre movie we're watching at the Poli—however it comes out doesn't matter. If it turns out well, that's fine—if badly, the stupid bastards deserve it. You know what I mean? But it *does* concern us—right? It concerns you, for one."

"Who reads letters?" Wolfe argued. "You're only talking to yourself, maybe a couple of guys who already agree with you . . ."

"You've got to, Wolfie," Pierce said. He was up, rummaging in a drawer for paper and pencil. "I'll help. I'll tell you what to say. I'll write the fucking thing . . ."

"That'll be your letter," Wolfe said.

"Oh, Wolfie—if you're going to boggle at a little misrepresentation, we aren't going any place." Pierce turned to face him. "All right, yes. Let me borrow your name long enough to tell these guys what we think." Walking to Wolfe, he leaned a fist on his knee. "Listen, I *know* what I'm asking you . . ."

"You'll get caught," I said. "Somebody's going to figure it out. And I don't think Sturm will think it's so funny."

"Funny?" Pierce braked his excitement to glare at me. "But I don't think it's funny either. Do you, Wolfie? You're missing the point, Ben. If you don't have any better suggestions than that, why not keep 'em to yourself?"

"They know you, Pierce. They know your fine Italian hand. At first suspicion they'll be on to you. You're going to screw yourself at the *News*."

"What does that sound like to you, Wolfie? You know chickenshit when you hear it?"

Wolfe looked at me and slowly smiled, luxuriating for a moment in the sweet collusion between them. "Okay, Pierce, let's see what you're going to put in the letter."

*   *   *

Sometime in mid-October, Sturm published an editorial critical of Roosevelt's promise to Churchill of arms and the ships to deliver them through the U-boat blockade, and that same day the first of the Morton Wolfe letters appeared in the office. It took issue with the editorial's contention, that we could afford to let Britain lose the war, and ridiculed its theme, that we had repudiated the European conflict, with all its hatreds and prejudices, a hundred and fifty years ago.

Perry Sturm declared the Wolfe letter irresponsible and declined to run it, but Pierce argued for it so persistently that Doc Bellinger came around to agree with him and, finally, to change Sturm's mind. The letter ran prominently beneath an editorial of stiffening resistance to it.

Thus encouraged to feel like regular contributors, Pierce and Mort produced a second Wolfe letter, one in response to Sturm's editorial on Thomas Mann. Mann had told an audience in Pierson College Commons that though he despised Hitler and was a refugee from his Germany, the Nazi movement was but one aspect of the German character, in many ways a noble one. With this for his text, Sturm explored the familiar path of Hitler's being a necessary instrument for restoring the national pride, but inside Germany there was growing opposition to him and all we need do was bide our time and the *Herrenvolk* would set matters right.

Ridiculous, retorted the Wolfe letter. *The Germans are not like us—good or bad depending on circumstances.* It itemized the broken promises, the twelve nations already crushed. *They are monsters and they are carving up the world. They will destroy everybody.*

Anne Morrow Lindbergh had just published a book called *The Wave of the Future,* and Sturm described it as obligatory reading for all who would understand the meaning of the horror abroad and summarized it in the editorial columns. *You had to realize,* he paraphrased Mrs. Lindbergh, *that the war abroad was the birth pang of a new order. It was the struggle between the totalitarianism of the future and the democracy of the past. And the wave, like that of the French Revolution of 1789, was so vast it was futile to breast it. And what must we do? We must defend our American dream. And where? In America first.* He concluded his editorial by pointing out there was far more to the noninterventionist argument than reason alone. As so ably illustrated in *The Wave,* it was simple faith.

A third Wolfe letter went after Mrs. Lindbergh, asserting that women should not be permitted to grow mustaches or hold political opinions, then proceeding to chide her book for its mysticism. *What do you mean,* the letter asked, *that we're so close we can't see what's happened in Russia, Germany and Italy, and how can you be so sure the "evils of totalitarianism" are not themselves the future rather than the* scum *on the wave of the future, and what is the American dream you subscribe to? Is it the totalitarianism you find so irresistible?*

This, the most telling of them all, brought Morton Wolfe a modest celebrity that he did not appear to enjoy. I was at a table near his in T.D. Commons when two of the Political

Union seniors tried to get him onto a team for the lend-lease debate, and he excused himself brusquely on the grounds he did not speak well.

It was clear that the council of seniors was nearing a judgment on our board, and those of us with hopes leaped to oblige them as though we were heelers once more, and when asked an opinion, tended to give ponderous ones—weighing our words, quoting Edgar Ansel Mowrer or Philip LaFollette.

Since I was to head the Student Agency and would be well paid for it, I had renounced, publicly at least, all *News* board ambitions, but Pierce was frank about his aspiration to the chairman's office. He made a point of getting in to see Perry Sturm daily for a few minutes, or "sucking around," as he put it—never actually complimenting Sturm on an editorial but finding ways to draw him out and become an eager listener.

"I hate myself for it," Pierce told me. "I *think* I've got it made. It stands to reason. I'm not all that hot, but who else *is* there?" He ticked off the candidates for chairman along with a sound motive for vetoing each one. "Doc Bellinger will go to the mat for me. I'm his boy. But Perry Sturm doesn't like me any better than I like him. Sometimes when I'm talking to him and I'm thinking how I detest him, he smells it. He's a fake, Sturm. Underneath the smuggery and Dean's List condescension, he's a timid grocer. He has a contempt for his heart. He doesn't trust it until he can check it out with his slide rule. You know, I suspect all those guys who hide behind curve-stem pipes—Wickersham, Butterfield, Sturm. You notice how much alike Sturm and Butterfield are—aloof, snotty, as though they typecast the chairman."

"Maybe they do."

"How do you mean? That Butterfield chooses Sturm in his own image?" Pierce asked. "If that's the way it works I'm a goner."

"No, they don't have anything to say about it. The *News* casts them. It *makes* them into the kind of person it needs. You too. You'll see." Pierce laughed, but I pursued this idea, which became more persuasive the more I considered it. "Seriously, it's like a play in which a man is molded, made over by his part. He becomes that character. It's the Power Play. Man is subject to power, like filings in a gravity field. Power transforms him to its needs. And come to think of it, it isn't Sturm you dislike, nor Bellinger you like—it's the machine itself you're reacting to. Sturm you believe is standing in your way, and Bellinger helping you to the controls. But that's illusion. The machine itself is encouraging you with one head and discouraging you with another. Sturm and Bellinger are two heads of the same beast."

"Oh, what crap!" he cried delightedly. "What have you been smoking, Mose? I'm not filings, I'm Pierce Jay, and no force on earth can make me into something else. Oh no, my dislike for Sturm is for his shopkeeper's mentality and what it's done to the *News*. That's what gives me acute pain in the butt. Oh brother, will there be changes around here. Will there ever be an editorial policy that leads student opinion on national issues instead of trailing it. That's what an editorial page ought to be, Mose, a sharp nose and a long neck that can reach into tomorrow for an idea that will startle or shock, you know, but get the boobs shook up, make them cry out in rage maybe, but make them think. Next year, if I'm in there, campus complacency is going to have a real enemy."

*   *   *

Our tall, shy boyhood hero was also back in the news. He had been making a series of broadcasts—"coast-to-coast" and "on both hookups"—and he announced his intention of making an October appearance in Woolsey Hall. Before he arrived, the *News* published a resolution signed by fourteen faculty members, making known their admiration for his character and the belief that his point of view deserved full hearing.

Pierce had conflicting emotions about his visit. "He's a flier and he was a big buddy of my old man's and he wrote me introductions when I went to Germany summer before last, and it pains me to knock him, but he's been got to." He had been writing subheads on Fred Rodell's outcry against the

colonel which the *News* was to run next day and he held up
the proofs like a proclamation. "He's very proud of that Nazi
decoration—a real prodigal son of the Reich, that's what.
He's been suggesting a white coalition against the barbaric
hordes of Asia and Africa. The superior race, see—right from
Goebbels. And in these broadcasts he's been saying it doesn't
make any difference who wins the war. Doesn't to *whom?* To
the people who're paying for the broadcasts? That's what we
want to know—who's paying for the broadcasts—and who's
writing 'em?"

Pierce did come along on Colonel Lindbergh Night at
Woolsey and lurked in the back, wearing a distasteful expression, pacing about nervously as the tall aviator spoke in a
thin, mild voice about how misguided our country was in vac-
illating between neutrality and idealism. He told the solemn,
mature audience (undergraduates were still staying away
from public meetings) that we were totally unprepared for
war and had antagonized the great military powers of Europe
and Asia, that invasion of our hemisphere was impossible and
that we must keep out of the European war entirely or participate in European politics permanently.

Lindy—there was a hero's mantle on him yet and he wore
it modestly and well. He was magnetically appealing, and to
me, at least, persuasive. I thought I would see Pierce go up to
the platform for a word with him, but at the close, Pierce had
disappeared from the hall. I could only imagine that he had
headed for some sanctuary where he composed his Wolfe letters.

Doc Bellinger emerged from the dissolving crowd, shaking
off a limpet with hopes for the sports desk who had been his
shadow for a week. He nudged me along High Street, talking
of the colonel's speech and the coverage he would be giving it,
halting once to pay me a compliment. "By the way, we're assuming you have your hands full at the Student Agency."

"Yes," I said. "I keep busy over there on Chapel Street."

"So you wouldn't be tempted by a *News* office?"

"As manager I'm getting twelve hundred bucks a year. It's paying the freight—and then some."

Bellinger nodded. "You're wise, Ben. And not on account of the money, either. You won't need to worry about that, whatever you do. But in the big scheme, the important one at Yale . . . You know what I mean?"

"Yes," I said devoutly.

"The Agency managership carries as much weight as any position on this campus. You know that, don't you?"

"I guess that's true."

But he had something else on his mind. He ambled along in silence, on the point of it, yet constrained. I knew what it was and waited with kindling eagerness.

Pausing in front of the library, he said, "Look, Ben. I'm not asking for any advice. We're perfectly able to make up our minds, but I'd like to know what you think about the elections."

"Jay—you mean?"

Bellinger looked uncomfortable. He frowned at his watch, at some approaching pedestrians, and then, touching my elbow, moved further into the shadows by the entrance to the library. "Jay's a close friend. I don't expect you to be totally objective about him. I like him too—but what do you really think he'll do? Would the ideas come. A wide range of them? How would he be on university policy, say? There's going to be lots of that stuff next year—what the university is doing to meet the challenge of the war. Could Jay handle that, Ben?"

A sweet, heady warmth settled around me like fur. Every sense quickened. There was a humming in my ears and I recognized that hush which precedes an important event. Bellinger had laid the instrument in my hand and I had only to speak, tell what I knew, to change the expected order of events—or be still and permit them. I remember teetering, hefting the scepter Bellinger had given me, and thinking of Pierce, wondering if he wasn't, as always, beyond range, if he wasn't always free of the restrictions placed on the rest of us.

He studied, or not, as he chose and emerged with a record as creditable as mine. He helped himself to whatever he fancied, knowing he could pay for it when the bill came—or *whom-ever*, for that matter, me or even Angela Rice. The night it-self became still. Vines of smoky light crept down stone trunks from the lantern in the peak of Sterling's entrance. All about me—branch, buttress, the luminous sky itself—stood forth in electric clarity as I sensed what I was about to do.

"I think he'll make a very aggressive chairman."

Bellinger nodded, groped for a cigarette, offered me one. "Right. He has flare and excitement. We need that. When we have it the *OCD* is a better paper than the *Crimson*. You could be certain of one thing—it would never be dull around the *News*. And he's matured in the last couple of years. The Bronson stunt was a real lesson to him, I'm sure of that. By God, he's getting to be a good writer, too. If you have the intent, the skills come along. It's remarkable."

"What are you worried about, then?"

"I'm not. Oh, there's some thought he's all flash, that he doesn't have"—Bellinger tapped his head—"you know, the background. Remember the kind of thing Jackson used to do?"

"A few months ago I might have agreed with that. He doesn't have the tradition of curiosity and concern in the way of the really first-rate writers like Bundy and Noyes and Jack-son. Jay's father may have known a lot about the banana re-publics but he wasn't a reflective sort of man. He was a doer. No, Jay's not a born intellectual by any stretch, and it's hard to believe that anyone could make himself over into one—bang, just like that—but he's remarkable, Jay is. He once told me he could do anything he wanted to. I don't know if he believes that, but I'm beginning to. I could tell you some-thing that would hearten you about him—maybe convince you, as it has me, that he has real editorial ability."

"Go ahead."

"It may raise more questions than it answers—not in your mind so much as in Sturm's."

"What questions?"

"Jay writes the Wolfe letters." I puffed at my cigarette and watched Bellinger's eyebrows rise.

He looked at me for a second before he said, "The loony bastard."

*　　　*　　　*

One more Wolfe letter arrived. I presume it was on the subject of Colonel Lindbergh but I don't know, for I never read it. Unlike its predecessors, it never appeared.

Then, on a night in early December—it was late and I was in bed, just turning out the light—Doc Bellinger knocked and came into my room, his benign good humor under a cloud of anxiousness.

"I want you to come down and talk to Jay with me," he said. "We're giving him a column. He can write anything he wants there. Will you, for God's sake, come down and help me persuade him, Ben? It's important or I wouldn't be bothering you, damn it. I've been trying to tell him it's important for the *News* and for *him,* that he take it."

"Chairman?"

Bellinger shook his head. "Blodgett."

"Oh no . . ." I got halfway out of bed and reached for a robe. "Blodgett, for God's sake . . ." I could not believe it. I was stunned, as though the disappointment were now mine, and I felt a chill of self-knowledge and an awe of consequence. From some cranny of recollection I brought forth an incident of my childhood. We were living in an old yellow house on Garfield Street in Providence, next to the family of a policeman named Rouse. There was a boy, Bobby, and though he was about my own age, he was ugly as his father, and I didn't like him. Still, like the other children of the neighborhood, I was fascinated by his father's roaring motorcycle and we would stand at the curb and brave his anger just to touch its shiny plumbing. What I was remembering now, as I sat on the edge of my bed staring at my slippers, was that I had hurled a rock one afternoon and with uncanny accuracy struck Bobby Rouse in the eye. Terrified, I hid behind the garage till nightfall, crying, shivering and repeating the family grace, until my mother, not Officer Rouse, found me.

"You can't be serious, Doc," I said.

He gave a helpless shrug. "It's a sensitive spot. If you have to err in a chairman, it had better be on the side of prudence."

We went down the stairs together, me trailing, for I was dreading the sight of him, to Pierce's room—but he had already gone.

*   *   *

Next day I missed Pierce at the *News,* and when he failed to turn up at Fence for dinner I looked in at his room, where Aldrich reported that Pierce's suitcase and toilet kit were gone, without explanation.

I grew so apprehensive at his disappearance that I could not concentrate on any work. I imagined him in some dramatic act of self-destruction. I was sure he was in New York, anesthetizing himself in a marathon binge, then hurtling down dark highways that would blur before him. I tried unsuccessfully to reach him. I needed to see him. I yearned to have him once more in sight and kept searching the crowds of undergraduates for that lope of his that I could recognize at a quarter-mile, the shaggy head, the big hands working restlessly in the air about him. I longed to reassure him, and thus myself, that life was more substantial than at this moment it seemed. In my heart I felt that if events could be so easily turned, they could as easily be channeled back where they belonged.

On the third day of his disappearance, I found his car, a Buick that year, parked on Wall Street, a fresh swath of bare metal running down its right side, and went at a jog to T.D. Aldrich was out and the entry was still, but Pierce was there on the long couch, smoking—pale and vacant-eyed as though he had not slept in days.

"Morosely?" he asked. "What are you doing here at this hour? Don't you have a class?"

"We've been worried. Where were you? I had no idea where you'd gone."

"Little vacation. Everybody needs a vacation now and then. New faces, new ideas."

"I can imagine how you feel. What a shitty deal."

He licked the underside of his lip. "Yeah."

"But for God's sake, you mustn't quit, Pierce. It didn't work out quite the way you planned. Okay—but don't bring down the whole china closet."

He stared out the window, puffing slowly on his crook, and said wearily, "Why not?"

"Because everybody, seniors included, has his eye on you. Whatever satisfaction you get out of telling them to shove it is only going to be temporary, and you'll blow everything. Besides, there's no point in taking it out on the whole organization for what one or two guys have done. You have a lot of friends there."

"Doc Bellinger?" Pierce laughed.

"He likes you. He wanted you. He was outvoted."

"It doesn't matter." Pierce tucked an arm behind his head and stared at the ceiling, and after a moment's thought he seemed to regain some of his insouciance. "You know, the *OCD* isn't that good. It's just another student paper. There's this illusion that it's part of the *Time-Life* synod, another one of the Luce orders. The heelers believe it. Notice how they try to write that backasswards, gerundive style? But what a gyp. It's a lackluster performance and I for one have had enough of those frightened, bank-teller's editorials. The only reason I stuck around this long was the belief that when it came our turn, Mose, we'd show 'em how. But it seems they want small-mindedness, not only in their term, but in ours as well. So fuck 'em."

"All right. That's all true. I agree. And you could show them with a column."

"It wasn't a *Views* they had in mind for me—more of a *Straws*."

"Take it, Pierce. Take it and write whatever you please— politics, the war, the university. Hell, write about the *News* itself if you want. Satire is the sharpest instrument, Pierce, and you're good friends with it. Take the column. You can show everybody."

"I'm not a professional jester. If I really wanted to be a clown, Mose, I'd have joined the circus. Oh, sometimes I put on the cap and bells, but only when it suits me, my boy, not on call to tumble from the wings in a pratfall between the serious acts. You know me better than that. I'm in earnest and any man who mistakes me is my enemy." He asked sharply, "You understand?"

I nodded.

"Okay then, shut up about the *News*."

*　　　*　　　*

So Pierce Jay's name was struck from the masthead and he never again entered the Britton-Hadden Building that had been our real home at Yale—the site of our trying-out and achievement, our clubhouse and gazebo. On his way to Fence, he would walk all the way around the immense, high-walled Wolf's Head enclosure to avoid the *News'* front door.

But in early December, I was relieved about him, for he seemed to shake off his bitterness and to plunge with characteristic totality into new interests. He was flying five times a week at Wallingford. He told about the new Taylorcrafts in which the student sat alongside his instructor, a big advantage over the JL-3 Pipers. He was building toward the thirty-five hours he needed to be eligible for his private license and working earnestly at the other aspects of the C.A.A. course, the ground school, the classes in civil air regulations, navigation and meteorology. He was in the first twelve of the forty in the program to solo and at the Fence bar he retold the day's adventures entertainingly, demonstrating with his hands the afternoon's spirals and sideslips.

One grimly cold day he drove me out to Wallingford, Lufberry Field, named, he told me on the way, after the Sid Lufberry who had been his father's friend, one of the World War I aces who after downing thirty-two German planes had been killed in action.

Pierce explained that it was sharply against regulations to take me up, and I watched from the edge of the field as he took the little airship off the ground, circled and landed with loving facility. I sat in the instructor's seat while he pointed out the controls, and then, looking to see if we were observed and believing we weren't, he said, "Come on, Mose. Fasten your belt. We'll go for a little spin. No one's looking."

"No thanks," I said, hopping to the dirt. "I have enough thrills riding in a car with you."

"It's safer than a car—much."

"Nope."

"You don't trust me?" He was laughing at my reluctance.

"No, it's not that. I've seen you fly. You're good. But there's no purpose to my going up."

"You've never been up in a small plane. Aren't you curious?"

"It can wait until I have to." I walked away wondering why I had declined, for I *was* curious about flight, and then it occurred to me that I was indeed frightened of going up with him. For all his control and restored humor, I could feel in Pierce, now, a fresh-honed recklessness.

When he was not flying I might find him in the library, where he was enjoying a puzzling infatuation with some contemporary novelists. Sinclair Lewis was followed by a prolonged reading of Thomas Wolfe. He sat up all one night to finish *Look Homeward, Angel*. Then there was Faulkner, who I suspected was beyond Pierce as gratification but satisfied his need for some posture, both a view of himself as free spirit—soaring, yet with a flight plan—and as a protest against all the Babbittry he had newly rejected.

Otherwise he could be most likely found at the Fence bar. Not drunk—he never seemed to get drunk—but drinking persistently and developing a raw edge to his tongue. It was not turned on me, but I could feel its work on the periphery of the crowd—little lashings of scorn for campus propriety and decorum and all those in awe of it. He would stop conversation with a joke about senior societies and he was capable of cruelty to the vulnerable. Ugliness, weakness, stupidity, all brought forth his malicious jests.

Although in his manner there was little dramatic evidence of Pierce's disappointment, during the winter term, his erratic, though sometimes quite promising, academic trajectory went into steep decline. Most of his courses were small, intimate ones which he could not cut discreetly, yet he would idle in their last rows, turning the pages of a newspaper or staring out a window, deploring the waste of clear sky.

Most of Pierce's instructors overlooked his behavior, but Selden Agnew, who taught the nineteenth-century European history course I shared, had a more elementary indignation. When he found Pierce ignoring the discussion, he would ask his opinion of it. Often Pierce's improvisations would redeem him, but when he turned up for class, which was at nine, still in evening clothes and giving off a miasma of bar and bedroom, Professor Agnew assigned him a paper on the influence of Metternich, massive as a senior thesis, to be written before Pierce left for spring vacation, and dismissed him.

Pierce had asked me to come to Florida again this year, and when I inquired if his Metternichean research, which should have confined him to the library for three weeks, wouldn't interfere with our plans, Pierce assured me blandly, "It's all taken care of. I've commissioned the Blue Ghost of Riverside Drive—the guy who advertises he'll write anything. Metternich turns out to be right up his street and he's already at work on it. I'm expecting it any day."

*   *   *

Then, just ten days short of the end of term, I got a curious telephone call from New York.

"My name is Choate Waterhouse, Class of 1920, Mr. Moseley." It was a mature, buttery voice. "I expect to be in New Haven tomorrow and I wonder if you're free for lunch."

My first thought was of a confidence game or an insurance salesman's last resort, but there was authority in the Waterhouse tone that suggested other possibilities, and I felt my way. "Could you give me some idea what it's about?"

"Of course. I'm what you might call an interested alumnus. I try to keep in touch with what the undergraduates are thinking, and your name was given me as one of the most interesting men in your class." He laughed with first evidence of anxiousness. "I'd simply like to see if all the good reports of you are true."

"That's all?"

"Perhaps I can tell you a little more across a luncheon table."

Later that evening I stopped in at the *News* to look him up. He had prepared at St. Marks. He stood tall and shy in the back row of the varsity hockey picture, peering out from under a clump of thick black hair. He was Psi U and Book and Snake, currently a vice-president of The Guaranty Trust Company, and he belonged to a parade of clubs.

The following noon a reassuringly distinguished-looking man smiled and waved to me from a table in the Taft dining room. He evidently had access to a more recent photograph of me than I of him. Balding, elliptical and barbered smooth, Choate Waterhouse sipped his whiskey and revealed an accurate knowledge of my accomplishments and precisely what they meant for someone of my high school background. He told me a little about himself, that he lived on Long Island and to his regret had produced two daughters and thus, in all likelihood, would not have a son at Yale.

When the dessert plates had been cleared away and we were drinking our coffee in an increasingly uncomfortable silence, he went abruptly to the question he had come to ask.

"Do you have any plans for Tap Day, Ben?"

"Plans? I'm sorry. I don't know what you mean, Mr. Waterhouse."

"I'm a member of one of the societies, and while my position is quite an unofficial one, I like to be helpful where I can—take some of the anguish out of the ceremony. That's a help, I think."

"Yes, sir. From what I've seen, there's room for that."

"I don't know what you've heard about the tapping out there in Branford Court and how it's actually accomplished, but it's not exactly as it seems. Certain arrangements are made beforehand. By the way, did you look me up?"

"Yes, sir."

He smiled approval. "Good. Then I needn't mention the name. It's simply—The Hall. Okay? Now, for the moment all I want to know is your inclination. Have you formed any ideas of the societies and do you have a preference among them. In return I'll try to answer any questions of a general nature."

"I'm not committing myself?"

"Neither of us. We're two strangers who have met as we might on a train somewhere and we're exchanging information that could be useful to one or the other—or both."

"Well, yours seems a very . . . genial group," I began carefully. "I know it mostly through the seniors there now. Do you call it a delegation?" He didn't reply but he was listening carefully. "They're not so intense as the Bones people. I sometimes wonder how *they* get along at all. Not so locker-room as Keys, nor so aloof as Wolf's Head, and yet well represented everywhere. Yes, I have the highest opinion of . . . The Hall."

"It's always good to hear that from someone in your shoes. Have you been approached by any of the others?"

"No, sir."

"You may be. Though not by Bones. I suspect they'll come to it soon enough, but up to now they haven't made prior commitments. Would any of them, Bones included, have stronger appeal to you than The Hall?"

"If I were to answer no to that, it would be a commitment, wouldn't it?"

He laughed, pleased. "Perhaps it would. Go ahead then. It's your turn now." He spoke as an equal. I liked the man. "Want to ask a question?"

"Yes. What's the purpose of . . . The Hall?" That euphemism was coming awkwardly. "Or, for that matter, any of the societies?"

"That's easy enough. The purpose is Yale." With a smile he acknowledged this to be more riddle than answer and flattered me by what seemed a fresh appraisal. "I don't know why they were begun. I suppose, like any fraternal group, they sprang from the most primitive urgings to band together and then to persuade the men within that they were better than the men outside. But they wouldn't flourish long in so sophisticated a place as the Yale of today, wouldn't be the bedrock on which the university rests—yes, really, that's true, Ben—if they weren't a great deal more than that. You'll get any number of explanations of the influence of the societies, but here's mine. Let's see, your father was not a Yale man, was he? No. Even so I suspect you already know what Yale means to most of us." Here I must have revealed some apprehension that I was in for a dose of old Blueism, for he read it instantly. "Oh, you needn't be concerned, Ben. I'm not a sentimental man. But still, you must be aware of the unusually deep and lasting loyalty we older fellows have. I often wonder about it. Perhaps it's that the four years here are the purest part of most men's lives. Friendships are made whole—know what I mean? Not for business' sake or because your wife likes to entertain. And however you occupy yourself here, you have a sense of purpose which, as you serve it well—as you've just demonstrated, Ben—increases you. It's the way life should be and it works rather better here under the elm trees than elsewhere.

"For that reason I like to come back to New Haven from time to time. It's a refreshing experience to walk the Old Campus paths and to look in at my old room in Connecticut Hall and find things not much changed from twenty years ago. But of course, like everything else, the place is getting big, so busy and preoccupied with day-to-day existence there's not much place for an alumnus to take any continuing nourishment." He raised his cup and drained it. "That's where the societies come into their own, Ben, in making Yale lifelong for all of us, giving us old guys a chance to keep in touch with living Yale, with the exalting experience you fellows are enjoying, the exploration of one another and the loyalty that develops from it. That's why I'm here today, why I come up once or twice a month to The Hall and see my friends there. At the same time there is a benefit . . ." He smiled. "I think you can see that, Ben—to a young man, his being able to call on the experience and resources of generations of Yale graduates . . ."

"Yes. I can see how—in peacetime—it would be most helpful."

Mr. Waterhouse widened his eyes. "And in wartime. People in The Hall manage to turn up in positions of authority throughout the services." He let me think of that for a moment, and then asked, "If you were invited, would you accept the commitment now? Are you sure enough so you wouldn't be swayed by subsequent interest from other societies? We'd have to be certain of that."

"Sir, could I know who some of the others will be—who will make up the delegation?"

"The only honest answer I can make is that in each of the six societies there is a list of the ninety most desirable men in your class. They have been arrived at separately, but the names will be the same. Each night they are being rearranged in order of desirability, and making allowances for legacies and some individual tastes, the order will be roughly the same on each list. Remarkable how similar our standards. At this early stage of the game it's impossible to tell which of our first fifteen men will accept our tap. You might know more about that than we, and if you were to commit yourself, you could be of some use to us among your classmates."

"Do I stand among your first fifteen?"

"I'll tell you when you answer my question."

"Does Jay? Pierce Jay?"

Mr. Waterhouse sucked his cigar, then gave a brief shake of his smooth, polished head. "I can't tell you that either. His father was Bones. He'd be a Bones legacy. A particular friend?" When I nodded, he plucked a small notebook from a vest pocket, thumbed some pages, replaced it without response.

"Must I reply now? I'd like a few hours to think about it, sir."

"Well," he said, smiling, leaning back, "I don't *enjoy* leaving my proposition open. I wouldn't want it to become general knowledge in the class that you had been approached—if you *weren't* to accept. You can understand that."

"It won't," I said. "You can rely on that."

"How's ten o'clock tonight? I can make it a point to be in my room upstairs."

*   *   *

I spent much of that afternoon poring over old *Banners,* looking at the faces, recalling names and persuading myself in favor of Book and Snake—and then went looking for Pierce. I found him upstairs at Fence, winning a game of billiards, but got him down into the main-floor lavatory, searched it, blocked the door with my back and reported what had happened.

"Oh, Mose, that's great." Pumping my hand, he glowed with a joy for me that I had been unable to muster for myself.

"You'd take it—now?"

"Want to go someplace else?"

"No. But I'd like to know who's coming with me."

"You'll be the pivot, Mose. You'll know. You can even lean on 'em a bit. Come along and let me raise my cup to you."

On the tide of Pierce's approval I was at last elated in my good fortune. I dogged down to the crowded barroom after him, and as I reached for the drink he had bought, he clapped me square between the shoulders. The report, for it was getting to be the season, stopped conversation all around us. "Oh, Mose boy," he bubbled with pleasure. "I told you so— remember?"

*   *   *

A few hours later, in Choate Waterhouse's room at the Taft, I tried to make Pierce Jay a condition of my acceptance.

"No," he said. "Nothing doing. Jay's not in our first fifteen. He's in the first forty, though. I'll tell you that and you'll see that he can move up very easily as soon as commitments are known. But isn't Jay something of a wild man? That was an odd thing, his bringing a Negro girl to the Junior Prom. What was the point of that?"

"It was the kind of thing he does—a joke. He introduced her as an African princess—M'Bu."

"But it was unpleasant for her, wasn't it? What's funny about that?"

"He was very careful of her, watched her all the time to see she was with someone. He protected her."

"But other people? The Southerners here—the Southern girls? Wasn't there a fight?"

"Someone—a senior in Deke—tried to keep them out of the dance there. He said the word *nigger* so that Pierce overheard. Yes. It drew a good crowd, even at two in the morning —bloody noses, torn shirts, campus cops. Jay came off the victor, though."

Mr. Waterhouse nodded, though his expression was still questioning. "I don't quite understand. Something to do with equality, some moral principle, bringing her?"

"Remotely—the intellectual excuse, you know what I mean? But no, he doesn't have much sense of social injustice. Nothing like that. Surely no bleeding hearts in his background. No, it was to provoke some reaction. To get a rise out of people. Show them up for what they really are. That's his thing. He's against complacency. That's the purpose really— and of course he liked the fight."

Still puzzled, Mr. Waterhouse said, "I'm not surprised.

Chip off the block. Pierce Jay was well before my time but they were still telling stories about him." He looked longingly at the maroon bedspread and sank down on it. "Your man sounds an individual all right."

"And much more."

He nodded. "I'll see what I can do."

And the venerative *The Hall* began to slip more easily, comfortably across my tongue.

*   *   *

Next day at noon I found Pierce coming out of Yale Station, bearing his bundle from the Blue Ghost, and as we walked along he unwrapped it, producing an inch-thick typescript bound in red leatherette.

"Here we are, in plenty of time. You thought he was going to fail us and stand in the way of our well-deserved vacation. No faith at all." As he flipped the pages the bill with its itemized charges flew up from between them. "Ah, good. Glad to discover that. Mistake to pass it on to Professor Agnew. Might be a more substantial reckoning. I was thinking of dropping it off on the way, but maybe I'd better have a look so I'll know what I wrote."

"I would." I took it from him, and as we walked I skimmed the pages. I had expected it would be hackish in flavor, and a few samples did nothing to surprise me.

"How's the old pipeline into mausoleum row?" he asked. "Pumping nicely?"

"Now listen, Pierce"—I glanced over my shoulder—"it's absolutely top secret. I've broken my word by telling you. I shouldn't have. So for Christ's sake, shut up about it."

He laughed richly. "Tut, tut, Mose. There you go getting self-important, as though you were the only plugged-in junior around."

We had been walking along Elm Street, skirting the Green, where the university gave way to the city, and now with a clue from his puckering, sportive look, I jumped at his meaning. "You? Do you know anything?" At the corner of Temple

Street, where the traffic, a cavalcade of groaning trucks, afforded as much privacy as we were likely to find, I braked him. "Bones? Have you heard something? Come on, Pierce. Has someone spoken to you?"

But the teasing smile faded and he shook his head. "No. As you well know, any naturalized Chinaman has a better chance."

"But you know something. I'm sure of it."

He shrugged. "It's just Bellinger."

"He's keeping you posted?"

"No. Of course not. Not really. But I can read him." Pierce put an arm through mine, and turning me into Temple Street, we strolled along toward T.D. "His hello—it's transparent. I catch him every day coming into Yale Station after his Berdan class. Those big, gentle eyes of his, they wobble, you know, with self-reproach about the *News* and I see a promise there of making it up to me somehow, hopefully where it counts, in Branford Court, but that he's bucking Sturm and those guys again. It's all there, like a bulletin from the Bones council chamber. He gives me that game smile. I see the small amiable flicker and I know the battle isn't over yet."

In Pierce's room, I watched him thumb through the typescript, presumably skimming it against the possible interrogations of Selden Agnew, but pausing to read portions with puzzled concern.

"What does adumbrate mean?" he asked suddenly. "My God, Ben," he said, looking up, "whatever made me think I could put my name on this crap?" He weighed the several pounds of it in one hand and sent it flying into the wastebasket. We eyed its protruding red ears and I could feel the tension building up in him.

"If there's anything I detest it's graduate school pedantry," he muttered. He started around the room, erratically, kicking at a sweater on the floor, then straightening, like a tidy housewife, the ashtrays and a bowl of matches on the table. He glanced at the bill which he still held in his hand, and then, frowning, slipped into the chair at his desk, pulled a check-book from the center drawer and began to fill in a blank.

"His facts are probably sound enough. You can fix it. You could run it through the wringer in a couple of days and it would come out all right. Vacation doesn't begin until Wednesday."

He tore the check out, thrust it in an envelope and addressed it. "Never fear. The Florida Special is going to leave on time."

"How?"

"I'm not turning in the paper at all."

"He'll get you, Pierce, sure as there's a Dean's other list. Agnew's a vindictive man. Let's retrieve this thing before we have to go crawling over the dump with a flashlight after it."

As I reached, he snatched it from under my outstretched fingers. "To make sure I don't fall in with your evil suggestion." And to my horror he ripped the typescript in half, then quarters, and when he could bisect it no further, he began to feed it into the fireplace, where he touched the heap of it with the flame of his gold Dunhill lighter.

*　　　　　*　　　　　*

I had already begun my clandestine missions for The Hall, moving under cover of the class preoccupation with an imminent Tap Day and the back-room huddling over it. I became bird dog to an efficient intelligence apparatus, reporting at specified hours to a telephone I presumed was answered within The Hall itself.

"Hadley," I would announce as I peered warily from my drugstore booth. "Keys has got to him all right. But he's holding out. He wants to go with Lawrence and Oliensis."

It was exhilarating, this covert manipulation of my classmates' destinies, and I was swelling a bit with the knowledge that I was a valued instrument for an organization by which, though uninitiate, I was now properly awed.

On the third day of my informing I was rewarded by the cold, half-familiar voice of my monitor. "Pierce Jay next," it instructed me. "Tell us what you can tomorrow night."

"He's up? First fifteen?"

There was a doubtful hesitation, then, "Yes, for the moment. I can't say how long he'll stay there."

*   *   *

Pierce's room churned with activity. Aldrich, it seemed, had something up and was entertaining mysterious callers. I lured Pierce outside and then, for the purpose of our talk, got him to drive up to East Rock, a trysting place at the summit of a red stone outcrop overlooking New Haven. There, in the darkness, peeping at the neckers in adjoining cars, Pierce listened, with an air of distraction, to the Book and Snake invitation. When I finished, he responded, disappointingly enough, with a silence which I attributed to his being fast in his old dilemma.

"I don't know anything about Bones," I said. "Nobody knows about Bones. Maybe you'll get it—maybe you won't. But this is certainty. If you really have your doubts . . ."

"No doubts, Ben," he replied crisply. "None at all. I got a poor reading off of Bellinger this morning. Right at the bottom of the steps there, you know—and *nothing*. He just looked away."

"Good. Can you scrub it now?"

"Oh *yes*," he said fervently. "I can. I really can. Not hard, not hard at all for me to be as happy as you are about the prospect of Book and Snake. No, no, Mose. I know there are great guys. McMullen, a guy I knew at school, was there, and Caulkins and Windy Slocum—and way back, Gus Plimpton, who was a friend of the old man's. No—I'd be proud to go there, Mose."

"But what?"

"But nothing. If you've got this thing straight and they really do want me, I'm damn happy about it. It's good to know you're going someplace they want you. That's a good feeling. Who would want to go someplace where you weren't wanted?" He regarded me thoughtfully. "Thanks."

So here on East Rock the damage, if not wholly repaired, was at least atoned for. Yet as I leaned back to savor the moment, my satisfaction was not entire. Pierce's acknowledgment, that "Thanks," so alien to him, though sincere enough, disturbed me, made me question if it wouldn't have been wiser for someone else to approach him. I said, "It's no thanks to me, for God's sake."

"Oh, Mose . . ." He began to laugh and emotion bubbled up in his eyes. It was as though he was having to use force in containing it. He reached out for my arm and gave it a powerful squeeze. "I know. I know all about it. Let me say it this once. I won't again. Gratitude doesn't come all that easy to me."

Driving soberly back to T.D., Pierce began to reflect, sanely enough, on his jeopardy in History 205, and as we turned into the entry he announced he would write the Metternich paper, after all—right from scratch. He'd put in the three weeks in the library and make it a bleeding masterpiece. There went Florida—and he was contrite over that, urging me to go down without him. But alone it wouldn't have been fun, and my disappointment was outweighed by the satisfaction I now took in the salvaging.

At the first meeting of Agnew's class after vacation I saw that he had Pierce's plump thesis on his desk during the lecture and that he glanced at it, even touched it, as though it was on his mind as he talked. Afterward, as I waited for Pierce in the doorway, I heard him tell Pierce, with an irony more caustic than amused, "You surprise me, Jay. I've been around here long enough so I don't expect students to surprise me. But this thing"—he reached behind him for the binder, riffled its pages—"is a pretty creditable piece of work. Damn it all—an indifferent student like you has no right to pass my course."

*　　　　*　　　　*

Pierce Jay was not my only Book and Snake charge. I had been given four classmates to prospect, persuade and, with increasing assurances, certify for the delegation, and in the week just prior to Tap Day, I was fully absorbed with these affairs. It was a trying time. Individuals, pairs, whole groups swayed back and forth in their intent, so that on Monday as we were tasting the serenity of being fully subscribed—we lost four men to Keys. In the midst of these anxieties I had been counting Pierce and myself as certain.

I did notice, but attached no importance to, an exceptional comradeliness in the community of our entry. Once, finding Pierce's door closed, I opened it on a circle which included our outcasts—Wolfe, Sudermann and Chwast. They looked up, startled, and Pierce, who was leaning against the mantel, closed the book from which he had been reading aloud. "Ah, Ben, come in, come in," he said, and there was a burst of laughter from the others, as though I had found them at some naughtiness.

My presence dispersed them, and as I glanced at the book which Pierce had dropped on the table, I saw it was from his growing collection of esoterica, a moldy volume about Pachacuti, the Inca emperor, and the communal civilization he had established in Peru. "What was all that about?" I asked.

"They were interested," he said blandly. "The thirst for knowledge is very strong, you'll notice, now our course is nearly run." He pushed the door shut and leaned against it. "Mose, would it be terribly tough on you if I were to relinquish my place at Snake. Because I think I must." I had become inured to all sorts of last-minute reversals but I was quite unprepared for this particular defection, with its cord of personal and public betrayal, and the impact must have shone starkly on me. "Yes, it's awful for you—and them— isn't it? I'm sorry. But how can I, Ben? How can I do it and at the same time let them know how grateful I am but that I feel unworthy?"

"You're kidding, aren't you?"

"No."

"Well, it's a lot of shit then. I won't let you, goddam it. I've been counting on you. What happened?"

"Nothing. Or if anything has, I can't tell you about it."

"Bones. You think you're getting Bones now." I nodded and slumped into an end of the sofa with overwhelming disappointment. "Well, of course, it's not strange. If one society wants you, it follows the others do. Either Bellinger didn't know or they changed their mind. No"—I sighed—"I can't blame you. You're not really under any obligation to Snake."

"But that's not it at all, Ben. I *am* under obligation and I wish there were some way I could tell them how bad I feel about it."

"Pierce, I don't know what Bones has told you, but it's never certain, is it? I mean, it's true, isn't it, that they never promise, that you don't really know?"

"They've told me nothing."

"All right. Let me ask Snake if they'll wait—wait and see. Let me ask if they'll tap you last, so if there's some mistake you'll be covered."

"No—I'd feel bad about that. I don't want to keep somebody deserving on the fence."

"Well, at least let me see. Let me see what they say. Goddam it, Pierce, I don't want to lose you. I'm not going to enjoy it there without you. That was the whole point—the idea we were going together."

Pierce's eyes filled. "I know, Mose. I'd like that. You don't know how you tempt me. You really do." And to my surprise he embraced me, a huge, crushing hug that startled me and made me laugh with embarrassment. "But you see," he said intensely, "I have an obligation."

"I understand."

He shook his head.

*   *   *

At noon on Tap Day itself, I went looking for Pierce, hoping we could spend the next few hours together, but found him already at a small table in T.D. Commons, lunching with

Wolfe, Sudermann and Chwast. Watching them from the long table, I thought they were behaving unusually, heads together, talking as though they feared to be overheard, and while I knew it was unlikely the other three were Bones candidates, I felt he must be under some special instructions, and I was envious.

In the end I went alone to the ceremony, joining the swelling stream of juniors that moved solemnly along the walk west of J.E. and turned into Branford Gate. No one spoke. There was only the augmenting sound of hundreds of shoes treading stone.

I joined a grave circle which included Blodgett and Ames, and as we stood facing each other, I felt as alone as those about me whose tap was not assured. There was a chill of stage fright in my stomach, a dryness of mouth and such unsteadiness of jaw I thought my teeth might set up a clatter. We were mostly here now, five hundred of us. Just overhead, the faces were appearing at the windows, and high up Harkness tower, the cumbrous hand held us from five o'clock by a few unendurable minutes.

Then there was a nervous sound, a tittering—alarmed and surprised. It skipped through the crowd in advance of four latecomers, who emerged from the gate, marching two by two in the grave, preoccupied, self-important way the societies themselves marched their members home from meetings. They wore black clinging hoods with oblong slits for eyes and mouth, which gave the four figures the look of hangmen on their way to a gallows.

They halted, and then, as if by carefully prepared plan, moved off in different directions to take positions behind astonished members of the class. All around there was a craning of necks, a little surf of whispering, a standing on tiptoe. Overhead, puzzled faces peered down through the windows.

The tallest of the hooded figures approached our circle, and aghast, as though I had witnessed the dropping of a trap door in the turf on which we stood, a vast chasm yawning below, I recognized that swinging lope. It was Pierce Jay.

I watched him take a position behind Baron Blodgett, directly opposite me, and I looked into the slits, right into Pierce's black eyes. They gleamed with some fever of the moment but there was no slightest sign of recognition. Blodgett had frozen with bewilderment. Someone was hovering over him and he could feel it, see its reflection in our eyes. The color left his face. Then Pierce's arm rose high in the air and came crashing down on the Baron's back in a blow that came near felling him. Still buckling at the knees, he turned to confront Pierce, whose other hand now held forth, directly under Blodgett's nose, a shriveled, hairy bull's ear.

Just beyond us another of the hooded figures cracked a small bespectacled classmate between the shoulders, and he, in turning, in confronting the black mask and bull's ear, turned pale and sank to the grass.

With eyes wide, as though stunned permanently open, Blodgett turned his back on Jay, who promptly trotted off, all business, on further errands. I followed his appalling progress as he sought out the eminences of our class, to tap them solemnly and by each in turn be spurned. As the mockery was recognized, he performed briefly to bursts of laughter, but the crowd's preoccupation was not to be diverted for long and the laughter faded as quickly as it had begun.

The chimes, the majestic quatrains and the five full-throated notes of the hour, floated down to put an end to the mocking prologue. The society windows flew open, and at once I sensed a presence behind me. Then, in the first volley, I felt the sweet relief of the smiting square between my shoulders.

Turning, I looked into the sober, gentle face of Harold Pickett, his eyes round with the weight of the moment. He caught my hesitation. "Do you accept?"

I heard other slaps, the thud of feet on sod all around, and knew it for the moment of action it was, and yet I whispered, "It's Jay in the mask. The tall one."

Pickett's eyes ranged the field quickly. "Okay."

"Can you tap him?"

"I don't know. I'll see."

I bobbed my head. "I accept."

"Go to your room!" he cried, and as I ran off, Pickett trailing, I heard the applause for me—wondered at the sound and felt the sweet prickling of pride.

We paused in the shadows of the gateway and he began to give me instructions—that I should go directly to my room, where I was to admit no one until I heard the knocks—three, a pause, then two more—and the word *Zoroaster*.

"Can I stay and watch for a minute? I want to see about Jay."

Pickett seemed dubious, but he was an amiable fellow and he said, "All right. But stay here in the shadow where nobody sees you. Don't speak. And go in five minutes, no matter what."

Peering through the gate, I saw that with the real tapping now at its height, the four hooded figures were being ignored amid the cries and running feet. But they had reassembled and were conducting a disheveled close-order drill. Pierce gave commands in mock German while the others responded with random left and right facings and salutes.

Then I saw Pickett emerge from the entry door under the Book and Snake windows, and to my relief he circled the field, paused as though for a deep breath of courage and plunged toward Pierce Jay's side show. I noted that in the windows overhead, charts-in-hand were being neglected to follow this part of the drama.

Before his troops, Pierce was performing the arms manual, unaware that Pickett had taken a position behind him. It was Wolfe who called his attention to it, jumping up and down like an excited child and pointing. Pierce paused, brought his imaginary rifle to the ground and peered over his left shoulder.

At that moment he was tapped, and it seemed that all the tumult, indeed the breathing, in Branford Court had ceased. Pierce turned, looked at Pickett, examined the pin gleaming on the knot of his black tie. I was waiting, as I'm sure every other beholder was, for Pierce's nod. Although I recognized the flicker of his indecision, I was certain of his assent.

Then someone laughed, shrill as a steam whistle, and Pierce's arms shot out from his sides to clap Pickett on both shoulders. Jay's voice rang out, echoing hollowly against stone walls, "Go to *your* room!"

Pickett, as though contaminated by the touch of Jay's hands, backed off crabwise, and immediately Pierce formed up his troop. Together the masked foursome marched from the field. They went in orderly fashion, counting cadence— one, two, three, four—left-right, left-right—their voices sounding in the tunneled passage before they were lost, gradually, in the distance beyond.

*   *   *

It was, of course, a parting for Pierce and me. The rigid disciplines of the societies required that. We gathered in the great tombs at seven each Thursday and Saturday, walking, stiff with importance, across campus in our black suits and ties, our grave, purposeful faces provoking awe in the uninitiate. And close to midnight we would be returned in marching columns to our own doors. It was made clear to us that our final year was scant enough time to learn the traditions of our venerable brotherhood, to extract its benefits and, in company with fourteen elect, though diverse, spirits, to replenish it.

This was clarified for the rest of the community by an injunction against communicating with it at certain hours. On Thursday and Saturday nights we could speak only among ourselves from seven o'clock in the evening until the following daybreak.

On one of my first meeting nights Pierce must have heard the tramping in the courtyard as the procession released me in a ritual like a mounting-of-the-guard, then my own footsteps, on his landing, then climbing the stairs to the floor above and finally the prescribed closing and bolting of my door.

In a moment he followed me up and knocked. I paused in the midst of taking off a shoe, hoping he would go away after a try.

"Open up," he said. "What have you been doing up there —circle jerking? It's all right. The other spooks have gone away." After a moment he said, "Come on. You can't hide from me, you mumbo-jumbo Mose. I know you're in there and I'm going to smoke you out." He laughed, banged on the door, and this time I got up and opened it.

He walked in, grinning and looking about as though he expected to see an array of masks and ceremonial vessels. "I've been waiting for you. Can you come down a minute?"

I put a finger across my lips and made a helpless gesture.

"Oh, for Christ's sake."

I found a pad and wrote *Can't it wait until morning?*

He smiled in a pained, stung way and shook his head. "No. Too bad." Then he laughed at me and went back down the steps two at a time.

From that moment on, Pierce avoided me. When we approached on campus paths he was preoccupied, and if I hailed him he would respond with a nod—and walk on.

He had made some gallant efforts for Selden Agnew early in spring term, taking notes with diligence and offering comment, but it was little more than manners and he soon fell into old habits. When the midterm marks came out he was flunking two courses and put on probation. This seemed not to bother him, for he announced his intention to leave college the moment the R.C.A.F. would enlist him, and in the middle of May, drove up to Toronto for his physical. I would see him of a morning in Yale Station, peering into his box, hopeful his call would come before the end of the academic year.

Meantime, after lunch each day, he would set out for Lufberry Field with a good humor that was unshakable, except when bad weather threatened to interfere. And then there was drinking. He went about it earnestly now. Five-thirty found him in the Fence bar, double bourbon in hand, beaming as though he were rewarding himself for a good day's work. He kept at it steadily through the evening so long as there was company. Moreover, he was losing his immunity to it. A third drink would slur his speech and slow his reflexes. One midnight as I marched toward T.D. I had a glimpse of him, alone in the middle of a deserted campus. He swayed, a slim tree in the wind, as he urinated defiantly in the middle of Elm Street.

Then, in late May, came the accident. I learned about it in a humiliatingly indirect way, pausing on Temple Street at the sight of Aldrich as he stuffed Pierce's valise into the Packard and prepared to drive off.

"Oh? You haven't heard about Jay?" In Aldrich's manner I detected that old freshman-year aloofness, no longer painful but still irritating. "Yes, he's in the hospital. He cracked up one of the planes." He raced the engine meaningfully while I clung to the door. "No, sorry, Moseley. No visitors. Not allowed to see anybody. Just dropping his stuff off. Yes, I'll let you know when he can . . . No, don't know how it happened. No one around, for some reason."

As Aldrich edged the car into the street, I walked along beside it with the infuriating feeling that information was being kept from me deliberately.

"What's wrong with him, for God's sake, Aldrich? Don't you know anything?"

"He was crushed—his back. Skull fractured. Maybe an eye. The doctors themselves don't know yet."

"But he's going to get well?"

"I expect so. I don't really know." And the car pulled free of my grasp.

Later, at the Fence bar, I learned more from John Huggins. "Mr. Jay came back in from Hamden about three." There was a tremor in John's rich Bahama voice. "Told me they'd called off the flying on account of the thunderstorms. He sat there by the window, watching the sky all along, and had his drinks." John held up a hand, five fingers extended. "Then—must have been about four-thirty—he say, 'John, it's clearing. I must be flying now,' and he run off up the stairs as if it was somebody after him." John wagged his dark, majestic head. "What I hear—he got out there to Hamden and they wasn't nobody there but he went flying anyhow. Been feeling bad about it."

"It's no fault of yours, John."

Wiping his cloth across the polished bar, he said, "It's hard to know . . . with you boys."

Later I learned more about the accident from Morton Wolfe. "Yes, that's right," he told me, confirming John Huggins' account. "When Pierce got back to Hamden the weather had cleared, and even though there was nobody around, he slipped the anchors on one of the planes and took it up. Some farmer heard him coming through the trees and found him at the edge of the field, the nose of the plane buried in his potato patch. I've been out to the hospital," he added. "I met his mother out there this afternoon. It's his back, you know. His back's broken."

That evening I found Melissa and Victor de Villepin at the Taft. They had been thoroughly frightened but were comforted by recent conferences with Pierce's doctor. We met in the bar, and I remember that Melissa was buoyant with relief. Pierce's back was indeed broken, but in spite of the anticipated long convalescence, upward of four months in a body cast, there was no longer any doubt that he would recover. There was still doubt about one eye. But he could see.

She did not reveal any awareness of the change in climate between Pierce and me, and I asked her if she would see I got onto the visitor's list as soon as it was permitted. On one of the first days of June, I had a note from her saying I could see him at the next visiting hours.

Sitting in the waiting room at Grace Hospital, I was wondering if there was anything I might have done to alter the events that had brought Pierce here, the fraying of his hopes in recent months. Once more I thought about that moment on the library steps, wondering if I had really influenced Sturm or Bellinger, if it wasn't Pierce's own violence and self-destructiveness that had delivered him here. It seemed to me he had been courting this all along. Even so I wished, with the urgency of a prayer, that I had it to do again.

I found Pierce in a breastplate of plaster from which his head and shoulders protruded turtlelike. One eye was bandaged, and as he turned to regard me with the other, he seemed a frail, threatened fellow, as though old entrails had been replaced with new wires and pulleys which pressed painfully into his flesh. I had hardly settled myself in the chair facing him, when I became aware of the palpable awkwardness, a sense of old tackle, between us, hanging damaged and useless.

On the table at his elbow a tiny radio had been playing, and he looked at it twice before he shut it off, as though he might introduce us first, or as though he might prefer its company to mine if he were free to choose. Then, abruptly, he spoke of Colonel Lindbergh. We were new strangers, feeling among general topics for a channel. Had I been following it —how FDR had compared him to the Civil War Congressman, Clement Vallandigham, who was arrested for treasonable utterances, and how the estimable Lindy—you had to hand it to him, really, for knowing when he'd had it—had resigned his commission. Now how about *that* for telling us the score?

"The only difference is that we aren't at war."

"Oh, the hell we aren't." Into his lusterless eye came something of the old snap. "That's a Philadelphia lawyer's argument. We're already losing our classmates. Butcher, for Christ's sake—he's gone down on the *Zamzam.*"

"Butcher's safe. He was just reported safe somewhere in German-occupied territory. Don't you get the *News?*"

"Oh sure. Aldrich brings me out the *News,* and it mostly gives me a pain." He winced, presumably at a real jab somewhere inside his carapace, and laughed. "Christ—those editorials of Sturm's. Can you imagine him writing that thing today—that open letter from a future member of the A.E.F.? Where the hell is it?" Squirming, he plucked it out from beneath a book and read: " 'Mr. President, are you really contemplating invasion of a bastion three thousand miles away that has been years in preparing for war while we have been isolationist? Let's not confuse recklessness with courage . . .' Not even you would say a chickenshit thing like that, would you?"

"Well, Sturm is howling in the wilderness now," I admitted. "And he knows it himself. He's just stubborn. There's no choice any more—except which service. Maybe not much of that if we don't act fast."

"So—what are you choosing?"

"I don't know. The Marines are very big this week. If you live through the three months in Quantico they make you a second looey. They took twelve seniors out of the fifty who applied. That Candidate's Course is harder to get into . . . than Fence."

"Would you fly?"

"I went around and listened to the Navy last night. Ever hear of a Commander Gardner?"

"Sure, he was Yale Unit. He's at Floyd Bennett. He persuade you?"

"They showed a film that makes it look pretty glamorous— silver wings, our boys in blue, 'Anchor's Aweigh.' I'm afraid that corny stuff does get to you, after all. I don't imagine it's much like *that,* though. They didn't show the mistakes."

A nurse entered, bearing a glass of dark liquid, and stood over him trying, with good-natured severity, to make him swallow it. She left us on condition he do so the moment she had gone. Pierce then asked me to pour it down the sink, and when I protested, he was sharply angry with me. I yielded, and with improved relations thus established between us and his medicine down the drain, he folded his hands on his shell and told me about the intercollegiate air meet in Turner's Falls he had missed over last weekend.

Even without him, Yale had taken second place with its excellence in spot landings and bomb drop. No one, it seemed, was indispensable. Still, they had failed in the spectacular events—the paper-strafing and 360 landings in which he excelled. They had canceled the aerial scavenger hunt and, since only one aviatrix had appeared, the bangar dance, a misprint he laughed over until some edge of his plaster sobered him.

Then he began to talk of his own accident. There had been no excuse for it, he admitted. He'd had twenty hours in the Taylorcrafts and knew their capacity well enough, though in preparation for the meet he had flown the Kittyhawk and the Morocco, both more powerful ships.

"After the rain it was suddenly such a damned beautiful day. I was feeling so great—all that field and sky to myself. When I came in for what I meant to be the last time, I just couldn't bear being down—you know? No, you wouldn't know about it, but it's like coming back to school after vacation and it's like when you suspect you've had one drink too many but somebody says let's have one more. I figured I could go around again, and I gunned it, but the little two-bit engine didn't have it and I sideslipped and clipped a big oak at the edge of the field and folded a wing back. I still had quite a bit of power on, you know, trying to get out, and I went in so hard I damned near came out the other side. There was nothing left of the ship"—he looked down at his body—"and fucking little of me."

"Well," I said after a bit, "you're the first war casualty I know. That must be some consolation."

He smiled ruefully, then tried to push himself higher against the pillows at his back. "Hey, listen. What do you think about this Hess guy? Why would a crazy Nazi bastard fly an ME 110 from Augsburg to Glasgow? Did he have a fight with Hitler?"

"I haven't the least idea," I said. "There's talk, you know, that it's a peace mission—that Hitler sent him with terms."

"Oh *no*—how could that be?" He squirmed in new discomfort against the cast, like a man in a tight collar. "Goddam it though—wouldn't it be just my luck."

 9

Seven months, the summer and fall of 1941, passed without
my seeing or hearing from Pierce Jay, and in the growing mo-
mentum of senior year—New Haven was wholly ours now
and there was not time enough for its last round of pleasures
—he left my thoughts.

As my final *News* assignment I was watching preparations
for the Christmas tour of the Dramat show, files of boys in
shirt sleeves and determined frowns grappling with chorus
steps to the addictive vamping of the pit piano, when I heard
the first of that dreadful news. It drifted in like a balloon set
loose from a madhouse, to lurch across the sprawled figures in
the orchestra and onto the stage. Voices crackled from the
Bakelite radio telling of devastation half a world away, but we
could not comprehend it or grasp its effect upon our lives.
None of us had a clear idea where Pearl Harbor was. Someone
thought it was Orson Welles again, far more likely the Mar-
tians than those comic-opera fellows from *The Mikado*. It had
all the flavor of a Pierce Jay prank, and I looked around the
circle of bewildered faces, half expecting to find his—grinning.

Gradually it became clear, though our ears could not credit

it, this was the call we had been expecting. And now, what was important? The still unfinished weekend assignments? The show, whose perfection, until this bizarre intrusion, had been the demanding, unquestioned master of us all? Or some larger loyalty?

On the premise that it was a substantial contribution to the national morale, *The Waterbury Tales* opened its Christmas tour on schedule at the Waldorf in the first week of vacation, and it was there, in the sea of Yale relatives and best girls, all a bit overwrought at the sight of some beloved youth on stage, that I was seized by an exuberant Pierce, arrayed in the uniform of ensign in the United States Navy. He gave a massive hug to my shoulders, and not only was there no sign of old rancors in his eyes, they seemed joyous at this reunion.

The war was still such an infant that uniforms were not yet commonplace, and the sight of one on a friend woke all sorts of slumbering emotions, caused young men to glance down at the very latest in herringbones and find it shamingly out of fashion, and young women to stare and color as though they were remembering what they might give for their countrymen.

Pierce's gleaming brass and Navy blue drew eyes all around, and he was bathing in the attention. At the same time there was something virginal about his particular outfit. Lacking wings and service ribbons and that verdigris hue of gilt, evidence of exposure to salt water, it looked right out of the tailor's box. So that I first guessed he was fresh from his commissioning—but then, taking account of his deep color, decided he had just come from tropical duty where summer uniforms were all he'd had occasion for.

"I was thinking you couldn't possibly be here, and yet I came in the hope you would be. I felt something in my war-weary bones," he was saying. "I swear it. Didn't I say so, Deirdre?" He turned for an instant to a girl beside him. "I said we just might find Moseley here, and by golly, here you are."

"You look absolutely great—are you stationed here?"

"Here? Hell no. I've got orders." He banged his breast as

though he carried them there—the threat and armor of his heart. "Proceed orders. Celebrating orders. I'm off in the morning and tonight we're recruiting a party. Come on now. And bring your bag, there's plenty of room. Who else's here?" He was looking up on the stage, where the performers and their guests were now mingling. "Let's get Killy and Borden Whitmarsh. We're all going to my place."

He bundled five of us, including two girls he had picked up in the lobby, into a cab, and as we crept across town I tried to discover where he had been and where he was bound, but he seemed reluctant to talk about it. He would only say that he had forsaken the fleet air arm for the sea itself.

"Flying's for the birds," he announced from underneath Deirdre. "That's what those frigging veterinarians have persuaded me. It's a conspiracy, Ben. Every time I'd let 'em catch me in sick bay they'd imagine a new fault in my fine white body. When it wasn't my eye—I can see everything with that eye, it works fine. I can fly every plane the Navy's got, but those quacks . . . Next day the eye would check out but they'd discover some equally spurious lack of clarity in my urine. Who cares—it's not for drinking, is it? I got caught"— he chuckled richly—"switching samples on the buggers. Ah— here we are."

The apartment which I recalled so vividly from freshman year for its perch safely out of reach of the city's seven million envious, larcenous and ill-tempered citizens had lost some of its toploftiness. In the living room, furniture had been swept aside and the rug peeled back and several couples were dancing to the music of a trio on the exposed parquet. It was clear that Victor and Melissa de Villepin were still in Florida.

I recognized some of the guests as Pierce's old friends, New Yorkers and Newporters, with the sated, *jeunesse dorée* look about them. In the center of the floor, rapturously absorbed in the symmetry of their step, were Sandy and Dilys Given, such mirror images of each other's delicate Northern fairness, I thought of them as twins rather than as a young man and his wife. All Pierce Jay's kind and caste they were, and though he loved to scorn them for their vanities and clannishness, it was to them he returned—a ship to harbor.

Pierce sized up his party, liked the look of it and waded in. A blonde, no longer Deirdre, clung to him as he made the rounds—taking a tribute of embraces, waltzing a few steps with a girl who had just come in and still wore her fur coat, exchanging the empty glasses of a pair of his guests for full ones. Although he wasn't drinking himself, he was boisterously, excessively enjoying his own party. He was hero, host and master of the revels.

A remarkable change had taken place in him. Seven months earlier, in mid-May, he had been haggard with disappointment and failure. All his supply of bravado and all the whiskey behind the Fence bar could not disguise his terrible disappointment with himself. Now, loping about, he seemed in radiant health and spirit. Whatever the truth of his story about the Navy doctors, Pierce flourished.

I watched him descend upon a couple who wore the anxious look of the uninvited and I thought for a moment he was turning them out, but instead he was introducing himself and then waving them grandly on to the dining room. He was all gesture tonight, his father's son, and it struck me sharply how odd and ironic it was that the war which I had abhorred and dreaded for so long was already proving—just as he had hoped—Pierce's salvation.

It occurred to me that Angela's number would still be high in his directory of tractable maidens. The likelihood that she was here, or on her way, made me apprehensive, and yet when I had wandered through four rooms without finding her I was disappointed. An observer of the party, I sulked at the bar where a man in hotel livery was serving French 75s, an ambrosial and, I supposed, lethal, mixture of brandy and champagne, and kept an eye on the door.

The table where I had sat down to Sunday lunch three years before was a gastronome's dream. The morning papers had featured a rationing program for luxury foods and there was growing evidence of shortages in the city, yet here rose an

Everest of roast birds and beasts, racks of smoked salmon, tiers of plump shellfish bedded in ice and a silver bowl the size of a derby hat heaped with gleaming black caviar.

From the summit of this embankment grew, appropriately enough, a Christmas tree. But it was such a maimed one— wads of medical cotton and shattered ornaments clinging to its charred limbs—that it stood a preposterously sinister Jay-like warning on the heap of plenty. I was imagining Pierce, between phone calls this afternoon, gleefully distressing a perfectly good balsam in order to remind us that this was a very special Yule—when I recognized the back of Angela's golden head.

My heart, a great dark fish, turned in my chest and I gazed at the edge of her profile, letting the emotions play across me —a quailing as though I were seeing her for the first time, utterly desirable and beyond reach, and then, as a band of erotic recollections skittered through the woods of my memory, I felt a rush of possessiveness. It was aggravated by her unconsciousness of me. She was listening to the man beside her, leaning to him, touching him, looking up into his face with the intimacy that arouses my jealousy even of people I don't know. It was as telling as an embrace, persuading me that they were lovers, and some old anguish machinery started up in my loins.

He was an agreeable-looking fellow, and though I could not recall ever having seen him before, he was tantalizingly familiar. Something in my unconscious was touched—some irony I could not name. He was square-faced, more plain than most men here, and dressed for the campus. He wore his tweed jacket badgelike, as though he felt he might be excluded from choosy parties without it. Across the room I sensed he was an acquiescer, a dabbler in protective coloration—the least bit spurious. And whether this was perception or wish I didn't know or care, for the exhilarating wave of it bore me toward them.

Angela was charmingly flustered. Her blush and nervous laughter as she presented me to Harry Cowles told me how matters stood—that whatever she was to Harry, there was still joy for her in beholding me. She had an opulence now, a soft, ripe look, as though she had turned from girl to woman in the almost two years past. She had lost something in clarity and freshness, but not in appeal. The thought that she was attached to this man pained me as though I still had some claim upon her. She was so lovely and desirable to me at this moment that I felt a sense of outrage at the restraints which had kept me from having her.

For half an hour we three clung together, bound by strong cords, as the tide of the party rose noisily about us. We eyed each other and spoke only of the irrelevant things that chanced into our heads—of Harry's acquaintances at Yale, of college tailors, of our draft status (my 1-A stayed by a promise to the Navy's V-5 program, his 4-F). Cowles blinked as he was reminded of his precious eyes. "Afraid I can't see across the street."

I was unable to wrench my own from Angela's mouth. My lips ached to touch it and the little soft place where the smoothness of her neck flared to meet her chin. I was wondering what would cause Cowles to leave us alone, even for a moment, and realized that he could read my mind—that nothing short of an ox team would do.

"Where do all these people *come* from?" Angela was asking, and over her bare shoulder I noted that Pierce's party had swollen in an unhealthy way. I recognized the sharky wariness of marauders. On the dance floor the squeeze-and-stretch, country-club style was giving way to the lindy, and on girls' faces, the "natural" artifices to chorine masks of pancake. Greed stalked the buffet, reached to heap plates and snatch glasses from the waiter's tray. From the living room came the sound of a crash, as of a lamp or bowl shattering. There was a hush and then laughter.

Pierce emerged from the throng, unrecognized but unruffled. He was still smiling as he pushed his way toward us.

"We're being infiltrated," I said. "It's the fifth column."

He considered the spectacle. "I suppose it's my own fault. I told some people to spread the word. I didn't mean in the subway."

"They don't seem to know. They think it's a convention. Who sent you?" I called at the vanguard. "Do you have any idea where you are—what we're celebrating here?" One man looked at me pleasantly but as though he hadn't understood a word, and seizing a spoon from the buffet, I rang on my glass. A few paused in midassault on the collation, and in this moment of opportunity I raised the glass and cried, "I want you to join me in a toast. I'm proposing a toast here . . . would everyone please shut up for just a minute. I see a few strangers here, who may not"— a burst of laughter drowned me— "may not know this is a party for Ensign Jay, who's going off in the morning . . . to war!"

Those nearest smiled indulgently, as though they thought me an amusing drunk. Beyond, the party seethed and boiled like a sea indifferent to my cries. I was powerless to capture an audience and my frustration was increased by Pierce's amusement.

"You're outshouted and outsung," he said, thumping me on the back. "Very game spirit there, Moseley, but you're licked. We're going to have to throw 'em out. Or sell some war bonds. Hey, that would clear the place in a hurry, wouldn't it? Where can we get some war bonds to sell the bastards?"

At the corner of the buffet a sharp-looking fellow, sharp in feature and clothing, was refilling his plate. Pierce studied his narrow, almost pretty, oval face with its V of mouth, and then, as the man withdrew his fully laden plate, Pierce took it from his hand. "Sorry," he said. "Only one to a customer."

The man's nose and mouth twitched twice as he turned to size up Pierce. The slender red-headed girl beside him closed the mouth which had been open to receive a chunk of lobster and pressed her arm against his. "Why?"

"There's a war on, didn't you know?"

"Where you fighting it, 90 Church Street?"

Weighing the plate, Pierce took a step toward him.

The man's sharp eyes flicked from Pierce to the girl. "Okay, come on, let's go," he said to her and backed away.

Watching them leave I said to Pierce, "Where *have* you been?"

He smiled, and avoiding the subject, put an arm around me and nodded at Harry Cowles. "Eerie, isn't it?" he whispered. "I thought it was you coming in with her."

"Who?"

"Him. The one Angela brought. Cowles. Don't you realize he looks enough like you to be your brother?"

To my astonishment it was so, and the solution to the puzzle of Cowles. My first thought was of coincidence, but my next told me that it was not—that in Cowles, Angela had paid me the excessive compliment of choosing a successor in my image. There was a sobering realization of my effect on her, one I could never fully credit, and then the irony, the ludicrousness of it overwhelmed me.

"How long since you've seen her?" Pierce asked.

"Not since the spring of sophomore year."

"How does she look?"

"Better than ever—I'm afraid."

He gave me a satyrish look. "You're not going to let that imitation Moseley monopolize her while the original is around?"

"I can't think of a way . . ."

"Oh, Harry . . ." Pierce turned in time to catch them as they were stealing off to dance. "Harry, would you help me with some of the undesirables? That unpleasant fellow over there is next. Just stand beside me and flex your muscles. I'll do the rest. You wouldn't mind, surely?"

With a churlish eye lingering on me, Cowles moved off at Pierce's side.

"When he comes back," I said, taking her hand, "we'll try to think of something else for him to do."

Angela shook her head. "Why?"

She resisted as I pulled her along, but her hand was soft and pliant to my touch. "No . . ." she protested as I pushed at a door onto the terrace, admitting a blast of chilling air. "It's freezing out there." But I drew her, protesting, into the wind and darkness, then into a corner where there was some shelter. When I put my arms around her she came easily against me, but when I tried to kiss her she turned away.

"Don't, please. I'm a little drunk, that's all. I'm not crazy."

"I want to kiss you."

"I don't understand." She spread her fingers across my lips and the very tenderness of their obstruction made me tear them away and pull her mouth to mine. There was an instant's surrender and then she broke away and ran toward the terrace door.

I found her inside, leaning against the piano, hugging herself. Under the voluptuous curve of their lids, her eyes were smoky with pique. "Will you dance with me?" I asked.

She didn't reply, for she had found Cowles now. He had seen us and was bearing down.

"I was wondering where you'd gone." He had a sullenness for me and a glare of accusation for Angela as he joined us, and I enjoyed that hugely. It was my first taste of the up-end of jealousy's teeter-totter and it was heady there.

"We were looking for a cigarette," she said.

"There's lots around."

"No Parliaments." Then, to my surprise, she coolly asked, "Would you, Harry? Would you be a dear?"

"Oh, for God's sake, Angie."

"They must have some down in the lobby. Please."

He looked me over as refusal crossed his mind but he could feel my strength and he bent before it. He set off on his errand, head thrust forward as though he could feel, upon it, the humiliating sprouts.

I danced Angela halfway around the floor before I led her away. She came obediently, following me down the hall, past a girl who stood under the dangling mistletoe kissing a boy hungrily as he kneaded her buttocks. The door to Melissa Jay's room had been posted with a sign, crudely lettered Seduction Chamber. Pushing the door open I found two men and two girls sitting sedately enough on her wide bed.

"Sorry," I said, and they laughed.

Opening the door to another room I found it dark within, but the light from behind us fell upon a couple who lay across a spread of fur coats. I could see the white skin of the girl's thigh and her face with its smeared rouge and tangled hair as she rose on an elbow to say, "No . . . don't come in . . ."

I tried another door, which gave, to my surprise, on the little storage room. The contraption, the barber chair Pierce's father had brought from Honduras, stood in its center exactly as I remembered it, the brass and mahogany freshly polished. There were signs of packing around it, some rough lumber, a partially completed platform and a heap of excelsior. The extraordinary thought occurred to me that Jay was planning to take it with him to the war.

"What's that?" Angela asked.

"A magic barber chair." She looked at me doubtfully. "All right, I'll show you," I said, climbing into its seat. I struggled with the lever, tilted it back and closed my eyes. "It's very restful, you see. Pierce's father used to think expansive thoughts in it. Pierce, too, sometimes. Want to try it?"

"Yes."

I caught Angela's hand and pulled her roughly and clumsily down on top of me, and after a moment's laughter our lips met and the kiss became earnest, endless, our tongues entwining and struggling as though each would pluck the other from its roots.

"Why?" she pleaded as we paused for breath. "Tell me why we're doing this?"

"Because it's like coming home. Oh, how I want to make love to you, Angela. I've never wanted anything so much. I've tried to put you out, Angie, but you won't stay. No one else has even come close."

"Truly?" Her nose, uptilted, touched my chin. "You didn't get another girl? It's funny. I was sure you had. I used to think about her."

"Is Harry Cowles my replacement?" She didn't reply. "Or is he just one of many?" Her shoulders moved slightly in the cups of my hands as though to question what business it was of mine. "Is he permanent or temporary?" She laid her head to rest on the pillow of my chest, and then I pulled her fully on top of me and kissed her hard. We searched each other greedily. Her fingers tried the softness of an earlobe and scuttled through my hair. Mine found the slope of her neck and felt for the zipper at her collar.

"No, no, no," she moaned against my mouth.

"Yes, please, Angie."

"Not here. Please, not here."

She held me away, with the tips of her fingers felt my mouth and eyes, and then to my joy, took my hand, slid off me and led me from the room. On the alert for Cowles, she skipped ahead of me down the hall. Seeing him, she gave a little cry of terror and doubled back. Then, gleeful as a child in our deception, she led the way through the pantry and out through the kitchen door. Coatless, hatless, we took the service elevator to the street.

*   *   *

Although Angela's mother and father were in California, she asked me to wait in the library while she ran off to her room. I flipped through a *House and Garden* with mounting impatience and went to look for her. I found the door to her bathroom closed, and from behind it, the sound of running water. I moved about Angela's silky preserve—once mine, now reclaimed—like a landlord in the wake of departed tenants. There was a gap in the festoon of snapshots around her dressing table, giving the impression some had been barely snatched away. The bed had a trespassed look about it. Perhaps it was just the new spread, but I readily envisioned in-

truders there, rough, hairy fellows, and I walked around it
sniffing suspiciously, an eager hound after a corroborating
scent.

Angela came from the bathroom, combed and freshly made
up, wearing a dark blue flannel wrapper like a boy's. She
looked at me, her head a bit to one side, and then walked
tentatively, shyly, slightly sidewise, as though to protect herself, into my arms.

"Done this much?" I asked.

She waited, thinking, listening to my heart, then looked up
with a teasing smile. "I've been pretty good."

She loosened my tie. Then, slowly and deliberately, her
fingers moved from button to button. My clothes fell away to
make pools about our feet—as did old, inhibiting concerns
for Angela's innocence. I was wondering where she kept her
diaphragm: in her medicine cabinet, where her mother or the
maid might come upon it? Or in some secret shoe box? Or
with her, in her purse, always handy now for an emergency of
passion? The thought that she had become so adept and familiar with the mechanics of love—stung, chafed away, swelling the soaring tower of my desire which had begun to sway
above us. It was like some giant sequoia reaching a thousand
feet into the night sky, but groaning with age and weight,
beginning to pop and crack, threatening at any moment to
come crashing down upon us.

Naked, clinging to crush the tiniest air pocket in some neglected hollow between us, we staggered toward the light
switch, and with one hand, cloaked ourselves in darkness.
And then, mouth devouring mouth, we fell upon the bed,
and Angela gasped—gave a great, grateful suspiration of relief—as I entered, glided gloriously, and at last, into her.

And then, even as the real world reasserted itself around
me, with some nighttime city glow from the window at play
on the bedspread and Angela's fingers still pressing, like
bonds, into my back, she said, "I've wanted this so much—
for so long." The words were drugged with sadness. "If we'd
only done it then—way back then."

"Yes. We should have." I raised myself against her resisting hands and lay on my back beside her.

"Didn't you ever feel like calling?"

"Many times. I'd get all the way to the phone booth—the change out and ready."

"Did you have any idea—any tiny little idea—of how much I wanted you to? No . . . you didn't, of course."

"I can't believe you've been all that lonely."

"Oh, Ben, what do you mean? I go out. Of course I go out. What did you expect. It's been a long, long time since that horrid train trip." She laughed. "Oh *God*." Then she raised herself on an elbow and in languor her fingers touched a tumbling length of hair back over an ear, then reached out tentatively for my chest. "Do you really think I could go out and have a good time with somebody else? Don't you see that was the worst, to be with someone who wasn't you?" Her fingers trailed along my ribs. "I do wish I understood whether it's that you don't know how you've messed me up. I'm not much use to anyone—really, I'm not. Or that you don't care. I don't suppose you'd know that, would you?"

"Neither."

"Then why did you just get the change out? Why didn't you call? What kept you?"

"I didn't want to start it up again unless I was sure—and I was never sure."

"Of who? Of me? You're frightened of me, aren't you? Yes —I always have the feeling you mistrust me, and that's so totally insane because at the same time you know I'll always do anything you want me to—anything." After a moment she asked, "How does that feel, knowing there's someone you own, someone who'll do whatever you want?"

The sweat of our love-making was chilling. Salty, animal smells prevailed over perfume and the room seemed close, as though air were being pumped out of it and there was some danger of suffocating here. I felt a yearning for the cold street outside and its biting wind, for people who didn't care for me, for people who didn't even know of my existence.

"Well, you know, Angie, it *isn't* a good feeling. Did you think it would be?"

"I wouldn't know."

"You exaggerate, of course. You aren't that dependent on me. But it is true that you have this urgent need for *some*one. You aren't as self-reliant . . ."

". . . as I should be."

"Well, I think most girls do have some *thing* they care about. They like music or horses or social work, I don't know what. It can be any superficial, crazy thing, but it sustains them, keeps them from . . . But you aren't interested in *any*thing. You don't even read."

"Oh *no*—not the knitting."

"Well, it's silly, I know, but that's what we always come around to, that you don't *have* anything to do, that there's so little to occupy your thoughts. It's as though they were hungry all the time, and when I'm not around, when I'm off somewhere, I worry about that. Anybody with so little to do is just naturally discontent."

"But that isn't true," she wailed. "You think of all these things that I might do, or might have done, and they're just not true. You're always imagining. You make them up, don't you see? They're just your suspicions."

We lay side by side, stiffening. In the building across the street a window lighted up and a young woman, yawning, appeared and drew the shade.

"I was just thinking about poor Harry Cowles," I said, "I was wondering how he must be feeling now. Jesus."

Angela began to laugh in short, helpless gasps. She rolled over on her stomach, smothering her face in her baby pillow, and the laughter became sobbing. Her buttocks rose and fell with it, and when, gradually, the sounds subsided, her shoulders still shook in spasms. Then, quite suddenly, she leaped from the bed, snatched up her robe from the floor and disappeared again into the bathroom.

*   *   *

"I'm sorry," I said as we awaited an elevator that seemed abandoned for the night. "I shouldn't have said that at all. I don't seem able to help myself."

Angela rang the bell again and shook her head as though to say *Stop—don't say any more, you only make it worse.* Yet I went on as though if I did I would find the words to make the truth about us clear.

"Sometimes I think it's my being such a hick. I have an awe and fear of sophisticated morality. I always think I'm getting lost in it."

There was a heartening whine in the shaftway, telling of release from our cave, the refuge we had sought so single-mindedly, and presently we were riding down behind an elevator man with yellowed white hair. His dickey askew, he yawned and scratched himself under Angela's sullen gaze.

It was three, and Sutton Place had been left to whirling wisps of steam. Ghostly ballerinas, they swayed and reeled in the center of the pavement. Blown flat by a gust of icy night wind, they rose to dance again. Angela had taken a cloth coat, but I had only a jacket to clutch against my throat. Across the street a parked car started. Its swinging headlights caught us, held us for a moment, before the car completed its turn and sped off uptown.

"That was Harry," Angela said indifferently, and, curiously, it didn't seem to matter; perhaps not even to Cowles, who might, at some other time or place, have stopped long enough on his way home to fight with me or scream some obsenity at Angela. But he had clearly come to accept the perfidy of his women and was simply confirming, without a sign of indignation, his maggoty view of the world.

I saw a cab turn the Fifty-seventh Street corner, hesitate and then move uncertainly uptown. "There!" I cried and whistled. The cab paused, and grasping Angela's hand I tried to run toward it. She held back, pulling against me, and I remember thinking that this was the way it always was—my dragging a resisting, unwilling Angela. Still running, I released her. I heard her heels strike twice on the pavement and then her cry of terror.

I turned to see her sprawled and slowly gathering herself. "Oh God, I'm sorry," I said. As I bent to help her up she yanked her arm from mine and rose alone. Angela stared down at scuffed knees poking through two great gaping holes in her stockings. The cab tooted and I waved for it to wait.

"Go on," Angela said. "I'm not coming."

"I *am* sorry. But it's late and we're both tired. I didn't mean any of that." I heard the cab's motor race and turned to watch it drive off.

"You did, though. You always mean it. It's what we always quarrel about. You make such a big thing of being reasonable and yet you distrust me. What right have you ever had to distrust me? It's like a disease with you." The high threshold of her indignation was reached. She was a smoking, sputtering arsenal, and even in my cold exhaustion it was appealing, her vitality unexpectedly laid bare. "I hate your condescension. You make me feel like some kind of retarded child. You're giving me an examination all the time just to prove to yourself that I'm lacking here and lacking there and that I'll have to pull myself up if I ever expect to ride with you. And you know what? I think you're scared—of being blackballed or something—through someone you love. It's leaving yourself open—isn't that it, Ben? Aren't you scared that I won't be pretty enough or social enough or bright enough or rich enough to please the guys who count? Isn't that it? Oh, if I can just keep remembering that . . . Dear God, let me keep remembering that!"

As I reached toward her, Angela backed away. "Come on," I said. "Peace feeler—really." Confidently, I stepped close and reached around her waist, and as I leaned down to kiss her, Angela's fist shot out and caught me hard and painfully in the socket of my left eye.

Through a shower of sparks, touching my cheek and feeling blood sprout from a tear her ring had made, I watched Angela admitted to her house.

*   *   *

The cab stank. It held the stubs and stale fumes of a thousand cheap cigars, an infinity of early-morning assignations. I lowered the window and took deep drafts of the dank air as we shot along empty streets, and I clung to the idea that I was still intact in spite of a city that seemed bent on dividing me. In the dark, my hand touched a wadded handkerchief on the seat, and as I flicked it to the floor I saw it was stained. There was a mean taste in my mouth and my stomach roiled.

*   *   *

On the thirty-second floor of the Savoy, I opened the door into Melissa de Villepin's apartment and found it brightly lighted but still. The music stands, the bar, the ravaged buffet had vanished, and the only evidence that a party had been in full boil a few hours ago were the fragments of blue vase carefully assembled on the mantel and a sprawled figure, one of the boys from *The Waterbury Tales,* fast asleep on a sofa.

The transience seemed another of the city's threats. The previous day I had seen a suicide on the pavement outside the Yale Club, a lumpy bundle under a blanket from which a bloody rivulet trickled toward the gutter. Passing the corner again, my furtive, morbid eye found only a stain, not much greater than the discs of chewing gum around it, to mark the place where, within the hour, a man had taken his own life, and even as I looked, that was fading under hurrying heels.

I moved down the hall, drawn by the sound of Pierce's voice. His door was open and I pushed it wider, to find him already retired. In blue silk pajamas, his knees propping the morning paper, he was reading a dispatch from Chungking, where the American Volunteer Group under Colonel Chennault had had its first clash with Japanese planes and shot down four.

From the bathroom beyond, I heard female sounds, a murmur, a soft jingling of bracelets, and before I could move away, she had appeared in the doorway, her head tilted as she

tugged, with one of Pierce's silver-backed brushes, at her un-
commonly long coppery hair. I could not have been more appalled to find a nun emerging from that bathroom—than
Dilys Given.

I had admired her as I might admire an exceptional painting hung in a public place, without coveting. It had never
occurred to me that the swift, handsome twins, the metropolitan tribute to slow, old matrimony, might be unyoked. Confronting the evidence that it could—that nothing in this field
was impossible to Pierce—my disgust with my times was complete.

It was Dilys who saw me, caused me to mumble, "Excuse
me . . ." and start off.

"Oh, come on in. I'm just going." She laughed with a trace
of self-consciousness. She was dressed but lacked lipstick.
Without it she seemed a child, and Pierce the more reprehen-
sible. "I was just turning down your bed." And to be sure, the
other bed was turned down and my valise was open on the
rack beside it.

Pierce beckoned.

"I'm going to look in the kitchen. Is there any milk?"

"Look around," he said, returning to the paper.

A few minutes later I was at the kitchen table, taking gulps
of cold water, when Pierce appeared, barefoot.

"Bless me," he said, smiling. "You want something for that
eye?"

"It'll wait. There's nothing in the refrigerator but champagne."

"Harry was a bit put out when he found you'd left without
him, but I didn't think him capable of decorating you like
that."

"He didn't."

"Angela?" That amused him and he laughed sporadically
as he padded along the hall to the bedroom. "Well, one thing
is clear to me," he said, getting into bed again. "We certainly
failed in disposing of the thing, whatever it is, between you
and Angela. You ought to have seen yourself in the act of

abduction. Oh my—you're still stuck on that girl, Mose. What happened?"

"I'd as soon not talk about it." I sagged into a chair and plucked at my shoelaces. Pierce shrugged and picked up the newspaper again. His valise lay open, piled with neckband shirts and blue serge. "Are you going to tell me where you've been?"

He nodded. He seemed to ponder the answer as though there were some mystery. "Oh, I've been harassing the foe, I guess—in my way." Then, bristling, "Enough so I get pissed-off at chiselers and slackers. Come to think of it, why does the university let the Dramat cart that silly show around? Didn't they get the word up there? The Japs are landing an army in the Philippines, and our people are getting creamed out there at Mindanao. You read about Colin Kelly pranging two transports off Luzon and then taking a last dive into the *Haruna?* Jesus. And yet our gallant college boys still have *debutantes* on the mind—debutantes and the big crew race and senior societies. It's enough to make you puke. When you write it up I hope you'll note that one observer was not amused. Book and Snake! Book and Snake!" He pointed at me and brayed, "You flinched! All right, what *do* you do in New Haven now? Business as usual? Guys digging out some hot stuff on Metternich? Gunning up to Northampton to sing with the girls? Playing the pinball machine in George and Harry's? Marching off to spook meetings? Say, tell me one thing if you can. Now don't get in an uproar—nothing specific—but when you got to the final inner mystery, when the last of the thirty-seven secret veils were drawn aside, was there anything there? Honestly now."

"It's hard to say."

"Didn't you want to laugh at the huge joke on everyone? When you peel away the layers of brotherhood horseshit you come to absolutely nothing—right?"

"It's possible. I'm not being evasive, Pierce. I just don't know."

"What about you? Ever get a little itchy reading the paper?

Listening to the news? Do you wonder what the draft board is doing with your number? Question what you're doing in New Haven?"

"No, the dirty old place is becoming very dear to me—and there's nothing more I can do about the war."

"You could go down and enlist tomorrow morning. Lots of people are doing it—twelve thousand in the last week. You'd get your degree."

"Oh, I'm signed up. I'll be going in June, right after graduation. I'm in the Navy—the V-5."

Jay squinted as though his heart had faltered. "You *fly?*" He threw the paper on the floor. "You're joking. I thought you didn't like it."

"I didn't. You talked me into it."

He studied me, the V deepening in his forehead, and then he leaned against the pillows and laughed. "Oh Christ—now wouldn't that have been something, if you'd turned up in Pensacola as a cadet. That would have tied it—the trade-school boys and fleet veterans at the mess table and you in the front row of my class. That's what I've been doing, if you want to know—instructing down there. Training films—parallax, bracketing the target, tracers, the principles of radar—all that crap. From the window I could watch the flight line, see them, hear them taking off all day, everybody in the place flying, and know that with this frigging eye I was never going to take up one of those lovely Hellcats. So just yesterday I wangled a forty-eight-hour pass and hitched a ride to Washington. There's a guy there in Bupers who used to fly the Bluejays. He's only a two-striper and he doesn't run the Navy, but he told me I could have all the action I wanted, eye and all, in the surface force. A piece of cake, Mose. He took my card from one file and put it in another, and presto: Orders! Norfolk. Further training. Maybe even command. Get that—maybe even *command.*"

"What kind of ship—subchasers?"

"New kind. Amphibious, built to carry troops and matériel and deliver them right to the beach." He sank back onto his bed, and as I went into the bathroom he began to tell about the training program and the huge ships which were planned.

When he paused, I called in to him, "I was wondering what kind of comfort you were expecting. I notice you're taking your father's barber chair."

In the mirror, I saw him smile and wag his head. "It's going to storage. I don't like to leave it around here, you know what I mean? There's always a good chance Ma will cut back on the Arab's allowance and he'll sell it on me for pocket money. It's been troubling me what to do with the old man's chair. I don't like the idea of it lying in some cell of the Manhattan Warehouse and getting auctioned off the way they do with stuff that nobody comes for. It winds up under a pile of old Victrola records in a thriftshop on First Avenue. I'm paying five years, which ought to do for even a long war, but if I don't come for it, how about you, Mose? Would you like it? Would it mean anything to you?"

I came to the door and found him sitting cross-legged in the center of his bed, altogether earnest. "You want to *leave* it to me?"

"Why not—if you want it? Sometimes I can see this guy in some Mitsubishi factory turning a piece of steel for me—so real I can see his fat face intent on the lathe and the little curlicues of metal peeling away. You ever think of that—that in some pretty forest, there's a tree growing, right along with you, to make your coffin?"

"No."

"There, you see. Your tree isn't even a sprout or you'd feel it. You're going to live to be a hundred, Mose, live to be a bigshot lawyer. Judge Moseley. You'll settle down in Armonk and make a home for my chair—you and Angela . . ." He padded to the desk and groped in the drawer for a sheet of stationery. "How do you make out a will?"

Dictating legal-sounding phrases—*my last will and testament . . . do hereby give and bequeath*—I watched him at the desk, writing away with a wild intensity that was altogether genuine—the idea that I should succeed to his father's chair really possessed him—and yet with the self-mockery and burlesque that always saved him from total self-absorption. At the window, the sky was graying into a grim backdrop for the Plaza's battlements, opening on an awful sense of real, impending tragedy. With a clarity distilled of my weariness I could see the erratic trajectory of Pierce Jay's aspiring life against that portentous sky and at the same time I sensed his anticipation of doom was more wish than prescience—that he found a fitting end for himself in the kind of rocket burst, the scattering of bright particles in public display, that a war provides.

Wondering if indeed he *was* marked and if he would find the heroic death he sought, I saw the great central lure of war for men—the cauterizing of their disappointments, the sluicing away of the foulness they had made about them and could no longer endure.

Then, astonishingly, I felt indignation at such easy apotheosis—at Jay's ledger cleared. He wouldn't have to pay at all. My vision of him as a truly tragic figure melted, to re-emerge as that of a fellow who would steal calamity's cloak.

"You know, I don't believe you're going to die, Pierce," I said. "I don't even believe you believe it. It's *phony* fatalism, isn't it? It's license for anything you want to do."

"What do you mean?" He turned, examined me. "Like what?"

"Oh—like Dilys Given."

"Dilly? Lovely Dilly? You'd deny me Dilly on my last night in town? It must be that hair shirt making you miserable again—confusing you about chastity and virtue in a woman. They're not the same, Mose. Chastity *isn't* virtue in a woman. It's frigidity and timidness, fear and stinginess, a lack of appetite at the feast and joy at being alive."

"Or might it be wisdom and discipline."

"Have it your way. I prefer mine."

"And Sandy? What about him?"

He made a slight concession, a rueful cocking of his head.

"I thought Sandy Given was a friend of yours."

"I always assume that if a girl is willing, she has all that stuff in hand—that either Sandy doesn't care, or it doesn't matter if he does."

"That's ducking it, Pierce. You can't take a girl into bed with you and have it wholly her responsibility. It's at least half yours."

"Oh come on, Ben. Every desirable girl has been staked out by somebody from the time she was six. If you worry about trespassing, you might as well forget the pleasure to be had from women—and given them. You spoil the sport of life, the adventure of it. Why would you want to do a dumb thing like that?" He laughed. "Anyway, of the two, Dilly is the closer friend. After all, it's the friendliest of acts."

"Just as it was with Angela?"

"Ah. That's who we're really talking about?"

I nodded. "Your friendly act was the original drop of poison between Angela and me. From it, of course, we've distilled quarts and gallons all by ourselves. But just face up to that once, will you, Pierce? Angela told me on the train going down to Florida. Did you know that? It was why we never arrived. I couldn't come and stay in the same house with you and Angela—knowing she'd slept with you. I mean, you *do* understand that, don't you?"

He nodded. "Yes, I'll face up to that, and while I do, here's something for you. You're attached, you and Angela. She's deeply in love with you and you're equally in love with her. No kidding, I believe that now. I think you're just as strongly attached to her as she is to you. You didn't plan it that way but there it is, the nature of things. In spite of all your analysis and talk, down in the subsurface your roots have grown together inextricably. You're like a couple that's been married for years and gets as much pleasure from fighting as loving. Only, your inhibitions and your mean, prudish Calvinist ideas on behavior have absolutely paralyzed you—keep you from any courage. You've held against Angela that one episode that she was honest enough to tell you about and I stupid enough to confirm, threatened her with it, made her miserable with it for almost two years. Talk about being a shit. Do you remember when we talked about her being too dumb for you, or not innocent enough, or something? My God, she's all innocence. It's you that's not—can't you see that? It gives me a pain in the ass—your feeling you're too good for her. You aren't, buddy. Your trouble is you don't know if you're man enough for her. Yes. You doubt you can keep her happy, keep her in the clothes she likes, keep her in an apartment where she'd want to live, keep her satiated enough with love so she wouldn't be filling in with part-timers. That's it, isn't it? You think about that for a while, Mose—that if there's a heel in Angie's life, if there's a guy who's failed her—well, let's not get confused about who he is. Okay?" He reached for the button of the lamp beside him and turned off the light.

*   *   *

At eight in the morning the immensity of Pennsylvania Station concourse had all the awesomeness of a medieval cathedral. Overhead, fingers of pale, spiritual light probed the sooty reaches. Dwarfed, resigned travelers stood about in clusters of their pitiful belongings, listening to the echoing chanting of departures—the litany of some priest to whom the words were rote.

I stood with Pierce at the gate of the Washington train, watching the farewells. A sergeant with a clipboard was lining up his ragtag file of conscripts, prying them determinedly from the girls they were leaving behind.

Pierce and I clasped hands silently. He picked up his valise and swung it. "So long, Mose." He started, then turned back to say, "Go call her. Take her to the Plaza for lunch. Let her have a look at that eye."

"All right—maybe I will."

"You'll need someone to see *you* off."

He paused in the gateway to show his ticket to the trainman, waved, and then he was gone, eagerly, loping down the iron stairs, then swallowed by the crypt.

Watching him go, I felt some eagerness for the war and its

cleansing, the scrubbing out of the past that was ready for us, ready to start us fresh. It was a buoyant, new feeling and I stood for a while savoring it, leaning against the door of an empty phone booth before I went over to the window and bought my ticket for New Haven.

PART TWO

Newport

1948

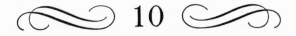 10

I recall the years immediately following the war with more poignance than the war itself, which has become lost to me in the very commonness of the experience. They were years of reluctance to commitment. Few of us even looked for jobs. We drank. I could find half a dozen classmates at the Yale Club bar in midmorning. We talked about values. And there were weddings. Marriage was an event that would not be put off—my own among them.

Someone said Pierce Jay was in the West and it was not until the spring of 1948 that I saw him again. At a wedding in Dedham, that of a classmate of Nancy's, he came bounding through wet bushes bordering the canopy, crying, "Morosely, you old goat! Where have you been?"

Tracking mud across the temporary floor, ignoring my spirited red-headed wife, he embraced me. "What are you doing here? What are you up to?"

"I'm at the Law School. I couldn't resist the G.I. bill, and it puts off the decision for a couple of years."

"But it doesn't. It's all made. And of course you'll be a splendid counselor. You've been one all along, now I think of it. Judge? Judge Moseley?" As he frowned, considering, I thought he looked thin, tired about the eyes, as though he still punished himself with excess. "Yes, of course. Congratulations, Mose. How do I reach you?" He was peeling back the cover of a matchbook, fetching a pencil from his vest pocket. "Still enjoying dormitory life?"

"No. They wouldn't let me in with a girl. This is Nancy, Pierce."

"The effigy!" Nancy cried. "The Hitler effigy! But you never told me he was at*tractive*—or at least you didn't tell me enough."

He took her in unwillingly, glanced at her left hand, where my diamond shone, a distant star. "But you couldn't. You're not really married, are you? How could you, Mose—without me?"

I apologized with a clumsy joke about necessary haste, and though Nancy laughed and put her hands across her flat stomach, Pierce was not to be thawed. He was shaking his head, making me aware of my perfidy.

The truth was that even the simple ceremony and sparse reception at the faintly moldy clubhouse in Tuxedo had been beyond the Converses' present means. But Pierce could not conceive of that, and I realized his injury was the deeper for thinking it was the senior society business again—that I had had my Snakes for ushers.

"Will you come and see us, Pierce?" Nancy asked. "We're in an apartment on Kirkland Avenue. It's compact, but not as squalid as Ben pretends. And I cook. I really do. I make a very passable casserole."

This touched him and he laughed, suddenly delighted with her. He took her shoulders in his big hands and kissed her, a massive smack, square on the mouth and wheeled me around so he could embrace us, one in either arm.

"You two," he said, grinning, looking back and forth, eyes brimming in overwhelming approval. "You two. I'll be damned. Now tell me about it. Tell me where you met. Tell me what you were doing."

"It was a beach party in Cohasset," I said, "one of those ice-breakers they give for the first-year law students. I was in agony being an audience for a fellow from the U. of Tennessee when this girl with freckles and bare feet stepped up and asked us where we came from. I could hardly wait to tell her."

"You're at the Law School?" Pierce asked her.

"Me? Oh Lord, no. I was just up from New York. I crashed. I used to be a professional weekend guest and party crasher. I was visiting a friend who lived down the beach from this law-school professor. When we saw young men stirring and looking lost, it seemed such a waste."

"Only partly true," I said. "You *were* invited."

"But what did she *say* to you?" Pierce insisted. "What did she *do?* I want to know what you remember."

"That she could read a map," I said. "We went looking for a boatyard later and Nancy found the way—in the dark, mind you, lighting matches. I'd never met a girl before who could make any sense out of a map."

"You beast." She laughed. "The awful part is he *means* that."

"What do *you* remember, Nancy?"

"Nothing complimentary, not after that."

"Come, come. I want the truth."

"Oh . . ." She gave in easily to his earnestness. "That he had a nice, comfortable smile and an old Shetland sweater that was raveled at the cuffs. He was actually listening while the others talked. He was the only one I saw that wasn't trying to impress. He wasn't so interested in what they were saying as he was in sizing them up, as though he was confident enough and there was time enough so he didn't have to run the race tonight."

"Oh, that's good. That's our Ben," he cried. "Where were *you*, Nancy? Where were you in college?"

She shook her head. "I wasn't. I quit college."

"So did I."

The bride, a tall, dark-haired girl named Millicent Handy,

just become a Mrs. Fish, waltzed by, smiling self-consciously, in the arms of her father, and we joined in the approving patter.

"Nan was St. Tim's," I announced—not that Pierce could have been confused about Nancy. For a party like this she wore her silks—the careless manner, capricious thoughts in durable metaphor—and you could scarcely see the starch, the good horse sense that some teen-age adversity had given her.

"I heard you were in California and might never come back," I said.

"I liked San Francisco. It's as self-possessed as New York and the only other place in this country where you feel you aren't missing it. The girls are good-looking and proud and I never ran across a stingy one. I thought I might find something to keep me in that agreeable climate . . ."

"Someone?" Nancy asked.

He waggled a hand indifferently. "A reason. Any reason. But there was none—and so I came home, to see if that was it. I was encouraged, you know. Newport isn't too bad in the winter. I stayed in the garage and got myself a job on the *Register*. Reporter—remember?" Pierce laughed. "They let me have all the big stories because they could see right away I could handle them—the lively meeting at the Elks', the debate about the new ferry schedule, and the funeral of Toby Macario, former water commissioner. I managed just two months of it, but meanwhile I had gotten the idea I'd like politics and where better to start than right in the old hometown. To my surprise—and you know I've seen everything, Nancy, I really have, Mose'll tell you—I lacked the stomach. Oh, everybody knows about greed and stupidity, but you have to see it for yourself, really see them with their big, rubbery jowls and little glinty eyes, to understand about pigs at the trough, pushing and shoving for the trickle of patronage. So—in March—I bought a half-interest in the town airport, along with a Bonanza that does taxi service to Providence and some charter business. I fly it myself, sometimes. It's pretty good fun."

As Pierce described the future of this latest venture and the likelihood of scheduled flights, Nancy drifted away. It surprised, and just slightly annoyed, me that she had found Pierce's struggle with The Readjustment Problem optional. I saw her across the tent, moving expertly from one clump of wedding guests to another, an efficient bee on a pollenizing round.

"Your Nancy's all right, Mose," he said. "She's raveled up that old sweater for you, hasn't she? I can read it on your creamy face. You thrive on those casseroles of hers. No more of that nighttime urge to prowl, right? Oh, you are a lucky son-of-a-bitch. Yes, I have the feeling, and very rare it is too, particularly with somebody I've just met, that girl is absolutely right for you."

"I think that *is* true. We do something important for one another." I laughed at his rolling eyes. "No, honestly, Pierce. You're right. We're many times stronger together than just the sum of the parts. You know what I mean?"

"Ahh. That's what marriage is said to be. I've always been suspicious it was propaganda. You wouldn't deceive an old buddy, would you?" His concupiscent eye trailed a pair of swinging buttocks around the dance floor. "You know, I saw Angela about a year ago. She was in a restaurant in San Francisco with other people. One of them was Kidder—remember Adam Kidder?"

"Vaguely."

"They were married, he and Angela. They'd been married a few months." He grinned. "She looked beautiful, radiant, you know, the way she always did when she was embarrassed or surprised."

"That's fine. Of course I'm glad. What did you expect?" I said. "Kidder—I can't connect it with a face."

Pierce had tugged some thread of discontent that went a-winding backward through half a dozen years. I seemed to recall Kidder as unimposing, a church-schooler—St. Mark's? —who brought stunning girls up to New Haven and made us question what they saw in him—one of those quiet, sexy fellows. Imagine, Angela happy. I could see her stretched full-length at the edge of a pool, one hand dipping idly into vivid blue water, all our anguish of a few years ago dispelled in California sunshine. I wondered what circumstance could have made Angela Rice my wife, if that was as near a thing as it had seemed and if it was chance prevented it, or wisdom, or war or some larger force I could not name.

Nancy came winding toward us through the crowd. She was bringing with her one of the bridesmaids, who wore the chaste garnet velvet that had given the bridal party a Victorian look. Hair the color of October oak leaves fell to the girl's shoulders and she had an air of innocence, a schoolgirl exuberance still about her. It was the clear complexion perhaps, a kind I associate with fortunate British girls. Her eyes were alert, appraising us openly as she approached. They were the light blue of Southern seas.

Nancy introduced her classmate, Lily Parsons, and as the murmurs died, Lily spoke up, in a voice cool as spring water, as though she liked the taste of words, "Are you *the* Jay? The Jay Line Jay?"

It struck me as girlish candor even before she explained—not smarty, as Pierce must have thought, for he took noticeable offense. Without looking at her, he glowed hostility and shook his head.

"Oh?" She glanced at Nancy as though she'd been misled, but was undaunted by the gulf of silence. "Sorry. I thought you must be. Have I said something wrong?"

Just audibly, over the music, a sullen Pierce replied, "It was my father."

"Oh well, that's what I meant. You don't look old enough for a founder. We flew to Lima on the Jay Line when I was eight, but I remember it perfectly. The pilot took my sister and me into the cockpit and let us hold some knobs and persuaded us we were flying the plane . . ." She sipped from a punch cup of champagne. "You don't like flying? Mr. Jay?"

He was not appeased, and for a moment I thought he was going to be fierce and foul, but Lily smiled at him blandly, as though she didn't care, and Pierce replied, just civilly, "The lines are too big now. They're like the service, and we're all trying to get as far from that as we can. You understand?"

"I've heard about that."

"Anyway, the Jay Line doesn't exist. It was absorbed by Pan Am after *the* Jay died."

A curtain of silence fell upon us until Pierce asked Nancy to dance. Lily Parsons and I watched their departure, and though I could easily have turned her loose into the sea of wedding guests, I hesitated. I felt no obligation. She was too self-sufficient for that. It was not physical. I had no wish to touch her. There was grace and a charged vitality in her long-limbed body, but a tension, too, that I took as a warning, to admire as I might a frisky horse in a paddock but not get too close.

I liked her nerve. I had never seen a girl provoke Pierce. Instinctively she had touched his vulnerableness and revealed him. And I was relieved she had gotten off without some eruption from the smoldering Pierce. She had come within a whisker of unpleasantness. Yes, that was it. She had evoked a response customarily dormant on short acquaintance, my protectiveness.

"You're in college?" I asked.

"Radcliffe." But she shook her head, indicating there was no need for perfunctory politeness when she wanted to question me. "Why did you choose Harvard? Why not Yale? Yale's Law School is just as good, isn't it?"

"A change, I suppose. I've seen New Haven."

"Is that all—really?" She was a sharp inquisitor, spiking a frivolous reply.

"Well, no, actually Yale has a think-big notion about teaching the law. They're very strong on theory, the social forces behind it, as though they expected a second coming of the New Deal and everyone must be prepared for an appointment to the Supreme Court. Harvard is hard-nosed. It assumes we're going to take the Bars and go into practice."

"And you are?"

"I expect so. For us poor fellows that's the expedient thing."

"But that isn't why at all. You like it. You find it satisfying, don't you? I mean the law itself, the neat way it categorizes human behavior and accepts the worst a man can do, along with his best. The cynical legal eye?"

"Maybe. Maybe I do."

She looked unhappy that I had no more to tell her. Oblivious of the chatter and bobbing heads around us, she was unreasonably absorbed in what I was doing. I felt I was disappointing her. "Tell me something else. Do you like being married? I don't mean to Nancy. Of course you like that. I mean do you like the *state?* Do you miss any of the bachelor freedoms?"

"I never made much use of them."

"Unlike your friend?" She found Pierce, still dancing with Nancy. "What's the matter with him, anyway? Did I step on something?"

"He's odd, Pierce is. I wouldn't worry about it."

"Oh." She laughed as though that were not likely. "I certainly won't."

"Like to dance?"

She reflected, then said, "No—no thanks." She folded her hands behind her back and sauntered away, saying over her shoulder, "Good-bye, Ben Moseley."

A quarter of an hour later, dancing with Nancy, I said, "That girl. She's not Pierce's kind. Did you imagine she was? Was that the purpose of bringing her over? He's joyboy, don't you remember my telling you?"

"Why," she asked, "why *not* his kind?"

"Because she's a nice girl is why. That's perfectly obvious." We danced on, vaguely irritated with each other's obtuseness. "She's at Radcliffe. She's a perceptive, a very intelligent girl."

"Oh sure, she's intelligent. Yes, I think the world of Lily. Do you think she's good-looking?"

"Not especially. She has a *clean* look. I suppose it's that determined virginity—" Nancy interrupted with a delighted giggle. "What are you laughing at? Come on, what's the joke?" But Nancy shook her head, still smiling. "Well, it's plain enough. And personally, I find that appealing, but Pierce's taste is for tarts. Isn't that apparent? He's a bird of prey with a bloody eye for the pigeons. Let's see where he's got to now."

While I was searching for his lair, Pierce touched my shoulder. "Oh, Ben," he said, "what are you two doing over the weekend?" As he came alongside I saw that his arm encircled Lily Parsons' narrow waist. "I'm trying to talk Lily into coming to Newport."

*   *   *

Oh, I was glad to be along all right, glad Nancy had prevailed over my doubts. Lately I had been so immersed in the gray novitiate of study, with its budgeting of time and energy, its forgoing of present joys against the promise of tomorrow, that I had forgotten how to respond to this kind of escapade. We were short on pleasure, Nancy and I, short on the sort of experience worthy of gluing into the pages of our recollection.

My pleasure was the least bit clouded by the thought that Pierce had so easily persuaded Lily to come along. Her casual acquiescence had surprised me. I had the impression she would have agreed even if we had not. She sat beside him now, in the forward seat of his Bonanza, looking out at the quilted countryside, buttoned here and there with a house or barn.

From the afterseats, Nancy and I watched Pierce giving Lily instruction. He pointed out the controls, banking gently to the right and left in demonstration, and then he let her take the wheel.

Her eye went to the compass, then the turn and bank indicator, getting the sense of it, and I could feel the steadiness of her hand and foot. There was competence in the set of her mouth. She was aware of the seriousness of what she was doing, and I relaxed. We were at three thousand feet, heading southwest, and Pierce, realizing she liked it, let Lily fly on.

"This is lovely," she said. "I think I like flying enough to learn. How long does it take?"

"A week," Pierce said indifferently. "You could solo in a week."

"At Pierce's field you might," I said. "At Logan they'd want you to do about thirty hours with an instructor. I think three weeks is more like it. In my day, at Pensacola, they thought we oughtn't to be allowed up alone with government property until we had fifty hours, and ten of them on instruments."

"You were a Navy pilot?" Lily asked. Her attention went from the instrument panel to the air space ahead.

"Marine corps."

"But you flew?"

"A little."

"Don't be coy," Pierce said irritably. "He flew in the Battle of the Philippines."

"That's true." Nancy seized the explanation. "Ben has the Air Medal and a D.F.C. And he dislikes flying. Isn't that funny?"

"What were they for?" Lily asked.

"A Zeke," I said. "I got a wounded one limping home. It wasn't very exciting, actually."

"Anyone would have done the same in your place, right?" Pierce said. "Oh, that boyish modesty looks good on you, Ben. Why, you're one of our few authentic war heroes. Don't deny us."

"You saw far more than I," I said. "You saw the real war."

He squinted at the hazy horizon for a moment and then he said, "Oh yes, I sure did."

"Oh, Pierce," Nancy said. "Ben tells me you were in the Normandy landings. What *did* you do in the war?"

Abruptly he said to Lily, "Okay, I'll take it now."

Releasing the controls to him, she said, "Thanks for letting me fly."

"Well, Ben certainly dislikes flying," Nancy said. "He's that much hero. He'll always take a train or drive when he can. You know, I've never flown in a small plane before and I *adore* it." She reached across the seat back and patted Pierce's shoulder. "Show me how sometime?"

"Oh, any time." He looked around and grinned at her, then leaned on the wheel and rudder, putting the Bonanza into a steep bank. Through my window I watched the starboard wing dip straight toward blue water, and in the windshield the Portsmouth shore spun by like a carrousel.

Eel-like vertigo slithered through my entrails, and I cried out, "Pierce, for Christ's sake . . ."

"It's okay, Ben." Pierce pointed ahead to the towers of the Mt. Hope Bridge. "It's dead low tide."

"Don't be childish . . ."

Nancy was looking at me apprehensively. "It's all right," she said with a gesture toward Pierce, meant to reassure me of his competence, even as he demonstrated he should be grounded. He had brought the Bonanza into a nose-down approach to the center span. We were at a thousand feet and losing altitude abruptly. Two men in brown uniforms emerged from the tollbooth at the Bristol side to watch us.

Pierce unlatched the small window, admitting a blast of air into which he shouted, "One of our engines is shot away and the tail gunner is dead, but we're coming in on a wing and a prayer . . . Look out belo-o-ow!"

When we were even with the bridge roadbed, he leveled off, but not, I thought, soon enough. From the high-water mark on the pilings I could see that it was not low tide and there were less than fifty feet under the span. Through my window the whitecaps grew as we dropped toward them, and I braced my feet, anticipating the lurch as we struck the choppy surface and cartwheeled into Narragansett Bay.

I closed my eyes, clamped my teeth together and began to count. I was stopped when I reached twelve by Pierce's delighted laughter. "Look at him, will you? Look how white. Oh, Ben . . ." I felt his hand clap onto my knee. "Oh, Ben . . . you can open your eyes now. We've come through."

I did, to see his great beak flushed with pleasure. Beyond, I found we were climbing into a clear sky. When he turned to attend to his flying, I took a deep, convalescent breath. My fingers were still sunk in the leather armrests.

It was Lily who gave me first comfort. "I don't blame you for not liking that," she said quietly. "I don't know if it's really dangerous or just looks that way, but I'm shaking. I really am."

"Are you going to be all right?" Nancy asked.

I glared at the back of Pierce's head, loathing every vain black hair that curled so insolently over his collar and around his ears.

"Shall we do it again?" Pierce asked.

"No!" Lily cried out. "Really, no more acrobatics. Not with me."

"And I don't think Ben wants to either," Nancy said.

"Okay, okay. We'll go in," Pierce conceded. "For kicks tonight I know where I can line up some rocking chairs."

He circled his Newport field and landed with textbook precision. When he had blocked the ship and unloaded our luggage, he led us across the field, past a dozen private planes, and into the hangar, presenting us gravely to a man in overalls.

"A month ago you wouldn't have kept cows in here," Pierce told us. "No watchman. Kids from town would come out and help themselves to parts. There was water in the gas —the tank leaked—and the mechanic couldn't fix the windshield wiper on his car. When it rained you could see it scraping away at the hood. Yes, we might even make a profit someday—eh, Bernie?"

He was making amends, but the more I tried to disguise my irritation, the more rigid it became. It was a presence, a fifth passenger in the car driving into Newport, and although Nancy and Lily chattered nervously, filling the silence, I could not speak. I wanted to be left alone.

In one of Bellerive's huge guest rooms, I stretched out on the bed and watched Nancy unpack.

"Well, it was wicked of him," she ventured. "He really *is* a bad boy, isn't he? But that's no surprise to you, surely?" A few moments later she ducked out of the closet, saying, "Oh come on, Ben. Don't sulk about it. We needn't fly with him again. We can take the bus back tomorrow."

"You don't screw around in an airplane just for the hell of it—not unless you're really eager to die. He's cracked up before, you know. He's nearly killed himself any number of times—damned near lost his eye the time in New Haven."

"Oh, I know, Ben. I know it isn't funny." She sat on the edge of the bed, folding her hands. "I was terrified. And worse, I had the feeling I had brought it on. It was my fault for bragging about you. I didn't realize . . ."

"No. It's an old game. It's Say Uncle. He likes to play that with me."

"Oh? Are you sure? I had the notion it was about your showing up better than him. He didn't like that, not in front of Lily he didn't. It was an exercise in envy."

"No. He's had his war. He was at Omaha, the toughest of it. He *couldn't* fly, you know. His vision was damaged." I watched her fingers trace the delicate carving, some pointed leaves and fruit in bas-relief, in the oak frame of the footboard, then the thick, lustrous fabric of the bedcover. "No—Pierce Jay isn't envious of anyone, Nancy."

"I suppose you'd know. Still . . . I wonder . . ." She rose from the bed and walked toward the double windows, to admire the hedged garden, where now, with approaching dusk, swallows with last-minute errands sailed back and forth like arrows. I saw her approve the twin pillows, carefully plumped and smoothed, the box of cigarettes, carafe, the Kleenex discreetly encased in embroidery, the Roman-looking bath in view behind a mirrored door. She took a brush from the table, and as she passed it through her short coppery hair, it seemed to glow with reflected affluence. Her compact, sinewy body had a silken, pampered look that did not appear in Cambridge, and I felt a surge of pleasure for her enjoyment. "Anyway, he's clearly devoted to you," she said. "He's doing all this for us. Why spoil it?"

Lying there, sorting out my thoughts, my sulk ebbed. I did not attach real importance to Nancy's theory, nevertheless the thought that Pierce's foolishness of the afternoon might be rooted less in scorn for me than in envy *was* a comfort. That was what Nancy had intended. How good she was for me.

I was thinking of our courtship, how she had come to Boston twice that fall and each time we had met for carefully budgeted evenings and talked endlessly about ourselves. She could make me laugh with her sharp, satiric observations of the salesgirls and customers in her shop and be equally entertaining about her other life—that of her friends, to which she slipped away of a Friday night.

We scarcely touched. We seemed too good friends to be lovers. On the steps of the handsome house where she was staying in Louisburg Square, I leaned to kiss her a chaste goodnight, and she permitted so slight a brush of her lips, it was less ardent than a clasp of hands.

Then, in the middle of the fall term, I went to New York and arranged to pick her up at her aunt's house on Park Avenue. She met me at the door, eager not to have me beyond the vestibule, explaining that her aunt was entertaining.

"Nice as it is," she told me on our way downtown, "I'd prefer an apartment of my own, but Mother feels it's unsafe, you know—for a girl alone."

Over dinner in an inexpensive French restaurant Nancy had chosen, I asked about her own family. She hesitated, watching me seriously, before she said, "Well, we were very pampered little girls, my sister and I. We had an English nanny and a house on Sixty-first Street and summers we went to a big house in Tuxedo. But every year since I was a child, it seems something was lost—the pony cart and Timothy the chauffeur, whom I loved, and then the house itself. The annual erosion." As she spoke she drew furrows in the cloth with her fork, and though she smiled, her voice grew soft, so that I had to strain to hear it. "When I was nineteen I couldn't have a party. I came out at a tea with three other girls. When I was a freshman at college I found out my uncle

was paying for my tuition. I quit in the middle of the year
and went to work. My father, you see, is a totally, wickedly
charming man without the least capacity for business, and the
more, poor dear, he realizes it, the more he's bent on disaster.
A variety of it."

"Your mother?"

"They're in Tuxedo. In a rented cottage that used to be
our gardener's."

This confession left Nancy drained, and I was moved by it,
well aware she had drawn aside some curtain and allowed me
a rare glimpse backstage. It had a warming effect on me and I
urged her to tell me more, but she would not. I tried to speak
of other things, but her own tight-sprung tongue was still and
at an early hour she asked to be taken home.

We walked listlessly through the Indian summer night.
Somewhere in the park, about halfway between the zoo and
the Seventy-second Street exit, there is a hill, a hump of black
rock worn smooth by children's running feet during the day
and at night by lovers' backs. We found ourselves ascending
it, walking silently round and round its spiral path, hearing
murmurs in the dark, glimpsing a shirt sleeve, a leg, bone-
white, to a summit where we looked out over an enchanted
velvet lake in the steep crater of the city. There was a sweet
musky smell all around, and when I touched her hand, Nancy
came hard against me with a suddenness that so surprised me
I laughed.

But it was no mistake. We sank there where we stood into a
soft fold of the hilltop where worn grass lay matted, and a passion I could not believe in this cool, freckled girl burst from
her and overwhelmed me.

Thereafter I was regularly included in Nancy's plans. At
the end of a visit to friends of hers in Connecticut, we were
coming into New York on the train and I watched her eyes
leave the magazine in her lap to stare into the windows of
tenements that hem the New Haven tracks before they
plunge under the city. There were flashes of milk cartons on
oilcloth and bodies in underwear.

"You know, Ben," she said, "there are worse things than being without money, and yet it's so ugly, isn't it? It hasn't any charm at all, though if it's remote enough, it seems to. I can't imagine anyone so strong or noble it wouldn't hurt them. Just owing"—she glanced at her valise in the rack overhead—"is a miserable feeling. You know, someday I'd like to have a house"—she put a finger on an advertisement showing a canopied bed—"where a thing like that wouldn't be obtrusive. And I'd like to go to Europe. I've never been."

"Nor have I," I said, and in that instant recognized we were adjoining parts of the puzzle, my moderation and plugging dependability mortising with her rather dynamic ambitions. I was on the point of a proposal.

I had expected some practical advantages of marriage—ridding myself of that wasteful anxiousness, the nighttime need to prowl that Pierce had indicated, along with companionship, of course, and having my meals and laundry looked after. But now, after a full year of it, my marriage had brought far more. Life was better than comfortable. Though we were still in preparation, Nancy and I, making do, displaying the silver frames on thinly disguised orange crates in our one and a half pea-green rooms, we had begun well. Watching Nancy ply her iron around the buttons of my shirt to thwart the dour Chinese, washing dishes in the bathtub during the sink-drain crisis, the simple acts of eating and waking had significance. We had joined a stream of such strong currents that there was no doubt of our destination, and all those things which we had imagined unattainable now lay in reach, immediately or in the course before us.

Angela Rice swam back into my thoughts. I saw her clearly, with that flush of surprise Pierce had described, laughing, tossing back a strand of her soft blond hair. Supposing it had been Angela, not Nancy. Good God. Still, it was not difficult to recall how strongly I had been drawn to her at the time. Was it a youthful obtuseness, a taste for sweets that had to be outgrown? Or was it, conceivably, that I had imagined her as Pierce's, his *kind,* if not his belonging. With a warm, rather gratifying amusement, I wondered if that might account for Lily Parsons' growing appeal. Standing on the steps of Bellerive half an hour ago, I had found her newly lovely.

My musing had refreshed me and I rose to bathe and dress with some eagerness. Putting on my dinner coat, I looked in on Nancy and discovered her still supine in the steamy bath water. "I'm going down and try to scare up a drink," I said.

"All right." She spoke from the depths of her drowsiness. "I'll be along pretty soon."

*   *   *

The elliptical well of Bellerive's main staircase widened into the entrance hall, now shadowy and chapel-like in the last hour of daylight. It was here I found Lily. She looked scrubbed and shining in a white blouse with shoestring shoulder straps and a long blue skirt.

She had been looking up at the huge portrait of Pierce's father and she turned as she heard my tread on the carpet, smiled and reached to touch a switch at the frame's edge. A hooded light at the top brought the elder Pierce Jay to life. In World War I tunic, hands thrust into the pockets of his breeches, he stared down at us from deep-set black eyes. The proud aquiline nose and the palisade of a brow were part of his son's legacy, but not the chin, which was flared and undershot as though he were used to leading with it. There was, in this image of the man, something so robust and indestructible, it was hard to reconcile with the fact.

"He must have died hard," Lily said, reading my thought. "He must have taken a chunk of the Andes with him. Those *eyes . . .*"

"Very quick—aren't they?—quick to see the joke."

"Yes, but hardly amiable—not necessarily amiable. Equally quick to anger—rather like Pierce's. Slow only at forgetting. He looks the kind of man who never forgets a friend."

"Nor forgives one?"

She nodded. "I think he's telling us something."

"Reminding us that we're enjoying his hospitality."

"That's it exactly." She bobbed politely to Pierce Jay Senior. "Thank you, sir. I'll keep it very much in mind."

"Would you like a drink? I'm sure we can find one."

"Not unless you do."

I shook my head.

Lily pointed through a pair of doors which were open only a few inches but admitted a view of the wide terrace. "What I'd like to do is go out there and sit on the wall and look at everything. Do you suppose we could do that?"

"I'm certain of it."

We passed up some metal chairs for the low wall at the terrace edge and from there we admired the face of Bellerive. Little fingers of soft salmon-colored sunlight filtered through the lindens to the westward and played along the crests of the steep gray-slated dormers. Below, the roof was already wearing its somber shadows and thus the house as a whole had a brooding, grave expression. On this side there were still no lights within and the tall doors and windows reflected bits of tree and sky like black mirrors.

"I'm puzzled about you," I said.

"Why?"

"Why did you come?"

"What a funny question. Because I wanted to, of course."

"Because there was to be a party and because it was Newport? Yes. Everyone ought to see Newport in full blaze. You never can tell when it will go out for good and carry along the shades of August Belmont and Mrs. Cornelius Vanderbilt. It's something to tell your grandchildren about."

Lily tugged at her school ring, working it up the finger. "But that's not it at all. I don't like parties, not big social ones where I don't know anyone and the people don't really talk to one another. I get tense and miserable at them. I came because of Pierce. He seemed to want me to come."

"I don't quite understand. Why did you want to please Pierce, Lily? Do you go out of your way to do things like that? A girl as pretty and as intelligent as you must be besieged." I looked at her closely, wondering if she could be unaware of her beauty. "You must have a dozen admirers—and a very heavy beau. Won't you have to explain to him what you're doing here?"

"On the contrary."

"No? Tell me some things about you."

"Which?"

"Where do you live?"

"Prides. It's out on the North Shore."

"What does your father do?"

"I suppose he's a banker." Her ring came free of its finger, the second of her right hand, and she slipped it onto her little finger, where she turned it slowly. "I was thinking that father feels about his business—which is making people rich and keeping them that way—much as you do about flying. He's good at it but he detests it. And every now and then he goes off and does something else for years at a time. When I was little we lived in Italy while he studied church architecture, and later we went to public school for a couple of years while he worked for the Friends. When we went to Lima it was a plan of his to help the Good Neighbor program."

"He's home now? In Prides?"

"In Boston. Father and Mother are separated."

"I see. You'll be going to Prides for the summer?"

"I'm going to Ireland on a dig. The Agassiz. They're uncovering some bones. Nice old ones, they hope."

"Are you really interested in old bones?"

"Well, I *am*. Discovering something new about the past is as exciting as discovering something new about the future. And it's a great deal more certain."

"Still—there must be a man going."

She gave me a sidelong look. "Of course—four of them. Four archeologists."

"One of them a particularly likable archeologist?"

"Yes. One of them is a young, dedicated man who wants to excavate and write and teach . . . yes, he's extremely likable. He's also married, devoted—and it's impossible."

"I'm sorry."

"No need to be—but what *is* all this?"

"You said you came along because Pierce wanted you. I was just wondering."

"Why, Uncle Ben." She laughed. "What makes you think I can't take care of myself?"

"I suppose you can. You girls are always more durable than you look." My eyes followed the lofty ridgepole of Bellerive, skirting the clustered chimneys, and along the green copper ribbon that was its spine, now just blurring against a hazy mauve sky.

"Have you known Pierce long?"

"Since college. I used to come and stay here." I pointed out an upper window. "In that room right up there under the eaves. It's still magnificent to me, but imagine what it must have seemed then—to a doctor's kid from Providence."

"Very grand." Lily smiled and her upper lip arched over her front teeth. They were white, square and even. "You like that?"

"Yes. Is that so strange?"

"Is that what you're warning me about?"

"No. You don't strike me as impressionable in that way. But you don't know him. You could be so easily misled. I thought I could save you some time. He's been spoiled by women all his life. He moves from one girl to another— nightly. It's the experiment that interests him. A girl's appeal vanishes for him the moment she becomes familiar. He's told me that. No woman is ever going to satisfy him. It's true, really. Isn't it apparent?"

"No."

"Well, for God's sake, Lily. What *do* you make of him?"

"Oh, dear Uncle Ben," she said and unexpectedly thrust her arm through mine. "You'll never understand what attracts a girl to a man."

"You *are?*" I said. "You are attracted to Pierce?"

"I'm curious."

"But he's crazy—spoiled and crazy."

"Maybe he'll get over it."

"Oh, Lily!"

She sighed grandly. "You know, you're part of the conspiracy against us. Under the guise of keeping us pure for motherhood or some such rot, we're meant to stick to our embroidery while the boys are finding out what life is really like. It's all a dreadful scheme to humiliate us and make us feel inferior so we'll put up with a dull, boring life without complaint. It's perfectly all right with you for boys to carry around condoms in their watch pockets, isn't it? Just in case? Good sense. Never can tell, right? Well, what about a girl who gets a diaphragm fitted and carries it in her purse? Why should that be any different?"

"The danger is greater for you."

"But it isn't. That's a myth . . . and I wish you'd stop looking at me like that—as though I were turning into a toad."

"Don't you want to get married?"

"As a matter of fact I don't. Remember, I asked you yesterday whether you missed any of the freedoms. I suppose I'll feel differently in a few years, but right now . . . No, really, I'm serious. I put the highest value on being able to go as I please and not be responsible to anyone—to go off on my dig, or spend three days in the library as I did last week, or to pile the skis on my little car and go to Vermont, or take it into my head to go down to the Keys bonefishing with a couple of Greek boys as I did at Easter. That's part of my education, isn't it? Why can't you understand that, Ben? Why do you suppose a girl would care less about her freedom? I love being able to try anything I want . . . or any*one,* anyone who appeals to me. Oh yes, I *do* that. I take up with some of the damnedest people. Oh"—she laughed—"if you only . . ."

"You're trying to shock me."

Lily shook her head, smiling. "Oh, poor Ben, no. No, I'm not." And as she put a hand reassuringly on mine, I seemed to be falling—a long, slow plunge from an immensely tall cliff.

*   *   *

Light, passing through some frosted-glass panels behind the bar, cast a diffuse, submarine light on Nancy's fair face and it seemed that her eyes had gone a deeper blue. "Oh, it's true," she was admitting. "It's the way women see things. We want to link the world to us in a chain of hearts. When we get it put together, then anything is possible. Anything. Just tell me what it is."

Through the open door, in the darkness beyond the terrace, I saw Pierce and Lily, still as statuary on the lawn. Lily's blouse, Pierce's jacket drew some luminousness from the night and they were so close I thought he must be holding her. She was small beside him—her head, tilted backward, came only to his chin. Then I heard his laugh. It was low, and sure of her.

"What's wrong with that, anyway?" Nancy went on. "Men are always trying to get things done with such blunt instruments. Everybody knows that reason doesn't work, but you go on bashing away with it until you get discouraged, and then you try to buy it, and if you can't buy it you bring up the dynamite. Women are more practical. They know the way to their desires is through affection—or more accurately, through getting people into bed with one another."

"Oh, for Christ's sake, what do you hope to accomplish in this? To bring us into Pierce's orbit? Would you really like to spend every weekend here?"

She replied with a coy shrug.

"Harlot. Can't you see that being a friend of Pierce Jay's is no hobby? It's a full-time occupation."

"Yes, I suppose it is. Still—he's a nice change from the tutorial types on Kirkland Street."

"Do you like him?"

I'd surprised her. She was the least bit embarrassed, but the smile with which she recovered was charged with mischief. "Well, you know there is something challenging in all that steam of his just going to waste. Yes, it's the waste."

"But you're deceived. Pierce isn't going to be made a useful citizen by the likes of you girls."

There were sounds outside the door, and then Lily came in, swiftly, looking pale and the least bit frightened. Pierce followed, hands clasped behind, the end of a cigar tucked into the corner of his mouth. They didn't look like lovers, not even quarreling ones, and I enjoyed the moment of relief a parent knows on hearing his child's return from dark city streets. Nonetheless, they had brought something new with them—a palpable tension.

"Your mother and Victor went on to dinner," Nancy said with her own flavor of irony. "She said we children should have a good time. Now isn't that terrific to be *children—and* told to have a good time. Nothing about going to bed by ten-thirty or getting our homework done first—just have a good time. And then—sleep as late as we like in the morning. That's what I thought heaven was like."

Lily murmured a distracted agreement. There was a moment's silence before she proposed, "Well, if *we're* going . . ."

"Yes, we'll need to comb our hair." Nancy slipped out from the table and the two girls left us quickly, as though they couldn't wait to get away. I could hear Nancy's voice, muffled yet urgent, questioning Lily as they climbed the stairs.

"It's getting along, you know," I said. "It's quarter past eight. What time are we due at the Bledsoes'?"

Pierce gave me a baleful look that left no doubt of his sullenness, but it had not yet occurred to me that I was its object.

"It doesn't matter." Pierce turned his back and picked a glass off the bar shelf. He studied it as though he thought it might be dirty and then poured himself an inch of whiskey.

"They really don't care what time we get there?"

When he turned to face me now, Pierce's mobile features, always a mirror of his restless thoughts, had thickened into a mask, the corners of his mouth stiff and white. His dark deepset eyes were glossy with truculence and the point of his tongue licked dry lips. It seemed that he was trying to speak, but couldn't. He raised the glass to his lips, took a gulp of whiskey, and as it settled into his throat Pierce found his voice.

"You son-of-a-bitch." His voice was thick and furry.

"What?" I asked. "What are you talking about?"

"What did you tell her? What did you say to Lily?"

And then, with a collapsing sensation, I grasped Lily's perfidy and the folly of my own loose tongue. Accused—I could not efficiently recall the confidences I had shared with Lily on the wall. What had I said? That he was inconstant and predatory. That he was spoiled by women. That his joy was change and experiment. That he was only interested in . . . Jesus, would she have repeated that? Was she such a fool as to imagine my friendship with Pierce impervious? Or could she conceivably *want* to . . . Yes. Now that had a fine, feminine logic to it. She was adroitly dismantling my interference with her courtship. Would I never learn to keep my mouth shut?

I nodded Pierce my penance. "Okay. I told her to be careful. And I want to give you the same advice."

He shook his head quickly, unwilling to be diverted. "You told her I'm a tail hound—right?"

"But you are, Pierce." The sound of my own voice—whining and high-pitched—disgusted me. "I was only thinking of you both. I don't want you to make one another miserable."

"That's nothing but shit." He finished the whiskey without taking his eyes from my face. "What the hell do you know about it? What the hell do you know about me?"

I sat mutely, listening to his breathing for several minutes and then, hoping to break the spell of Pierce's vindictiveness, climbed out from behind the table.

"All right," I said. "I apologize. I shouldn't have opened my stupid trap. It's funny, you know—I was telling Nancy that people are seldom thanked for taking a hand in their friends' affairs. All the same, I haven't changed my mind." I put my hands in my pockets and smiled at him. "Now, either we're going on to the party or we aren't. If we are, I'm going to take a leak."

Pierce's great hand reached out and seized a piece of my lapel and shirt front and I was pushed off balance and slammed with force against the door. Pierce's flushed face was an inch from mine. His breath, fumed with the whiskey, came hotly into my nostrils and I was frightened. Surprise and his superior weight drained my strength and I went limp.

"When I want any help from you—with this girl or any girl—I'll ask for it. Understand?"

I didn't reply. Upstairs in the now silent house there was a sound of a door opening and closing—and then I felt a reserve of animal strength coming to rescue my dignity. On a surging of blood I gave a great heave, pushing Pierce from me, moving us to the middle of the doorway and locking us in an embrace. We teetered thus, clumsily, for a moment before his strength bore me forcibly and with a clatter back to the door.

The preposterousness of this, how I must look lurching about this huge Newport villa locked in Pierce Jay's arms and now about to be surprised by my wife and her pretty classmate who were making their way down the stairs, was too much for me. I began to laugh.

"Pierce, for Christ's sake, stop, will you?" I struggled against him, trying with all my might to free myself, but I could not budge. I gave up the effort and felt his grip tighten suspiciously against my passiveness. "All right, Pierce," I said. "Whatever you want. Do you want us to go? If you want Nancy and me to pack and go, if you want us to get the hell out of here right now, I'll be overjoyed. I really will. But I'm not going to wrestle with you—you frigging great idiot. Stop it. Take your . . ."

He did. He let go and stepped back, still staring at me. The beety pitilessness drained from his face and he became Pierce, my friend, smiling at me. It was an astonishing performance. His hand reached to set my lapel straight and gave the front of my jacket a solicitous tug into place.

Now the girls' voices came to us clearly from the stairs, and

Nancy called, "How about it, Pierce? Are we going? Are you taking us off to this fabulous bacon-heiress' party?"

"Right away," he called cheerfully, and reaching out, gathered up his glass from the counter behind me. "We're just having one more"—he winked at me—"for the road."

*   *   *

The Bledsoes' house was called Greenfields. I saw the name chiseled into the stone capital of the gate as Pierce bowled through it and up the drive, threshing crushed bluestone against the fenders, toward one of those great dark piles—all porches and curiously impractical ramblings of scalloped shingle, spiked here and there with a lightning rod—so unpretentious that it must be a retort to the neighboring châteaux and palazzi.

As Pierce guided us up the steps and into the bustle of the party, it seemed that his rancor toward me had dissolved. I was puzzled by the instantaneous change, punctuated by that ridiculous wink, which had taken place before my eyes, like an actor slipping from one costume to another. Pierce took my arm affectionately to introduce me to the manservant who had opened the front door for us. It was droll, demented behavior, yet not unkind, for he knew the man and it was all accomplished in high spirits.

But my own spitefulness was not so magically dispelled. I had not had a word for anyone between our departure from Bellerive and my how-do-you-dos at Greenfields. I carried a great lump of acrimony for all and I was preparing for a good long sulk.

We were the last to arrive, and I had only to look at the guests—I judged there were thirty or so—to feel new waves of resentment. There were pretty ones, boys and girls alike, displaying that wilted posture and languid gesture that suggest indolence or arrogance or both. Most of them were so very young-looking, perhaps a decade younger than Pierce and me, and all of them were at home here, busy with their drinks and conversation or gathered around a grand piano where an entertainer was playing *Kiss Me, Kate* songs and chatting with his audience. They would know him by his first name, I thought, for he played all the parties, just as the magician had a few years earlier.

The scene summoned up an intense feeling of not-belonging. I didn't envy these children any more. Honestly, no envy. I even felt a first twinge of compassion for them in the deserts of boredom I anticipated for most of them. But I was separated from these people. They would not laugh at what I thought funny or be touched by what I found touching or find interest in what I found interesting. And now I had some pride of my own—enough to keep the distance there. I wasn't going to make an effort. I could feel myself looking for the dark corner. I wanted to go unnoticed.

Nancy, of course, sought the main currents. She was clearly delighted by our hostess, who indeed proved as unassuming as her house. She was a tall, healthy-looking girl and she repeated my name as though she meant to remember it and good-naturedly endured an elaborate greeting from Pierce which ended in a patting of her satin-encased bottom. It was this sort of outrageous behavior that made me doubt Pierce's quickly donned benevolence. I was uncomfortable now in his presence.

I found the library empty, and I settled into a big sofa with my drink to listen to the babbling and the music from the room beyond and to brood there undisturbed for half an hour. It was Lily who came looking for me and to tell me they were now serving dinner.

"Don't want any," I said, all petulant child.

"What's the matter?" She didn't seem to comprehend the black accusation in my glare and rather gaily sat down beside me.

"You," I said. "You're the matter. Don't you know a confidence when you hear one?"

"Oh dear," she said with a smile. "Is that what you were talking about while Nancy and I were upstairs?"

"Why in God's name did you tell him?"

"Why shouldn't I? Wasn't it true?"

"Don't be evasive, Lily. I'm a traitor now in Pierce's eyes. We had a fight back in the bar. It isn't funny."

Her eyes sparkled. "Well, he's just as angry with me. He deserted me the moment we walked in the door."

I glanced down at my wrinkled shirt front. "I thought he was going to do me some real damage."

"I *am* sorry. Honestly, I didn't mean . . ."

"What did you mean to do? I wish you'd explain that."

"He told me he wanted to make love to me." She made a helpless gesture. "What you had said about him seemed pertinent. It was on my mind and what's on my mind generally gets said. Everybody is so frank around here, it never occurred to me any particular subject was taboo."

"There was no need for it," I grumbled. "Well—at least you're beginning to see what I mean about him, aren't you?"

She nodded. "He's capable of unkindness—needless unkindness. I can't bear that." She smiled as though to say, *See, we think alike, you and I. We're agreed.* "I love your worrying about me." Her hand reached, touched mine and returned to her lap. "But there's no need." Then she leaned back in the sofa and looked up at the tongue-and-groove ceiling. "It's charming, this house. It's big, but it's a summer cottage—a real summer cottage."

I watched her, allowing myself to be enchanted, particularly by a lustrous coil of her hair; and, by upturned blue eyes, persuaded of her innocence. So—by the time Nancy arrived with her first conquest, a tall, effeminate-looking boy called Gordon Grimes, I was well on the way to forgiving Lily her perfidy.

Then, with the serving of dinner, our library retreat lost its privacy. Waitresses scurried in to set up little folding tables and to bring us plates of lobster Newburg from the buffet and trays of full wine goblets. Two young couples who were strange to us came in, and barely glancing at us, took over the area in front of the fireplace. There were chairs enough but they ignored them and sat on the floor to dine Indian-fashion.

Pierce arrived alone but with a glass of whiskey in hand and settled himself on the arm of the sofa next to Nancy, who was giving full concentration to the beguiling of Gordon Grimes. Pierce began to fidget at once and promptly startled me by shucking off the blue batik dinner jacket, revealing fireman-red suspenders. It was not particularly warm in the room and it struck me as an arbitrary act of nonconformity.

Despite that good-time grin I was not deceived. Pierce's eyes were pink and glossy. There were other things on his mind. Behind the cheerful façade, the pressures were at work. In his presence I sensed the kind of oppressiveness that precedes a summer storm. The deterioration of the evening, I suspected, had scarcely begun. Irritations budded all around. I was even put out with Nancy for having such a good time.

Oblivious to all, she was chatting with Grimes about Capote's novel *Other Voices, Other Rooms,* which had been published that year. It seemed to me she was enjoying the attention and feeling her own introduction to Newport was a success. She later denied it, claiming she knew what all of us were enduring and had a particular awareness of the intensity of Pierce's frustration with Lily. She maintained that her frivolous behavior was only an effort to distract him from some mayhem. She tried to draw Pierce into the discussion by asking him if he'd read the book, and he promptly replied that he had but hadn't liked it, whereupon he got up and moved unsteadily toward an elaborate record player opposite us. From the living room, the piano could be heard clearly. Nonetheless he selected some records, stacked them on the spindle and experimented with a cluster of buttons until a blast of dance music poured forth and filled the room.

He grinned at us happily and did not acknowledge a protesting "Hey!" from the four young people sprawled conversationally at the hearth. He returned to his perch on the sofa arm, took a long swig from his drink and then, as though he could only talk about books with a full orchestra for background, said, "You know what's wrong with a book like that? It may be well written. I wouldn't know about that. I never finished college, you know. But it snivels. You know what I mean? It doesn't have any guts to it. What the hell's wrong with this big busting country now, that we have to read about decadence? This is the land of hope, not homosexuality." Here he looked significantly at Gordon Grimes, who smiled back blandly. "Christ, where are our new Hemingways and Wolfes? Tell me that."

Reaching up, Nancy put the point of her finger on Pierce's red suspender. "You. Why don't you write?"

Though clearly pleased at this thought, Pierce shook his head. "No, I'm not smart enough, Nancy. I'm a playboy. Haven't you heard, I'm just interested in girls. All kinds of girls."

"My kind?" she asked.

At that moment one of the boys from the fireside passed in front of us on his way to the record player. We watched him examine the controls and then turn down the volume. He made no apology, nor did he look at us, and Pierce watched him casually until he had rejoined the others and sat down with them. Their empty plates were stacked on the hearth. One of the two girls, a pretty blonde in a pale green dress, had stretched out her legs and was resting her head and elbow on a zebra-skin rug, waving her wineglass as she talked.

"My kind?" Nancy asked again.

"What?"

"My kind of girl? Do you like my kind?"

"Oh *yes*." Pierce said. Putting down his drink, he leaped up, grasped Nancy's hand and pulled her to her feet. Delighted, she laughed as he clownishly gathered her into his arms and danced her around the sofa.

Gordon Grimes, Lily and I watched them go round and round us and then approach the record player, where, I was certain, Pierce would turn up the volume. We could hear the piano outside arguing with the record Pierce had selected, and the result was unpleasant cacophony. But Pierce danced on without touching the machine. He had stopped his clowning and they were dancing in earnest. They even paused to kick off their slippers, since stockinged feet glided more easily across the carpet.

Pierce was listening attentively to Nancy, who I presumed was telling him what a good dancer he was and what a good time we were having. Once when they came close I heard her ask if he wasn't hungry and suggest that he have some dinner before we went on to the dance—or didn't he ever eat any dinner?

This, it turned out, was Nancy's objective and presently she attained it. They stopped before us and made a mock bow to one another and then to us. As she toed her way back into her slippers, Nancy explained, "I'm going with Pierce while he gets some of that heavenly lobster."

Pierce, more quickly shod, had a preoccupied look, as though he meant to leave without her. Indeed, he now began to edge around the sofa, and Nancy said to him, "Wait, Pierce. Your jacket. You can't eat lobster Newburg without a jacket."

Jacketless, hands in his pockets, he was walking toward the two couples on the floor. They were so occupied with their conversation they didn't notice him until he stood over them, Nancy behind, holding his blue jacket for him.

With the toe of his evening slipper Pierce hooked the hem of the blond girl's long evening skirt and held it high, permitting a glimpse of thighs and elastic underwear. Her startled reaction was instant. She doubled her knees, bringing the skirt chastely around her legs.

Into the upturned face of the boy opposite her, Pierce said, "Prettiest crotch I've ever seen." He laughed, turned to an aghast Nancy and took his jacket from her. He put it over his arm and walked with her from the room.

Gordon Grimes arose and glided silently away, leaving Lily and me alone on the sofa. In Lily's eyes I read dismay. They were round with it. Neither of us had dared look toward the fireside, but our four neighbors had gotten over their surprise and their first outraged grumblings could be heard.

"What happened?" one of the boys asked excitedly. "I

didn't even see him. What did he do? What did he do to you, Sally?"

I searched Lily's face for a sign of disappointment or disgust, looking for some indication as to whether we too shouldn't decamp—if we hadn't reached the moment of total renunciation of Pierce, of gathering up our selves and our belongings and getting the hell out. I found no such signs. There was some fresh color in her fair cheeks and a stirring in her full underlip that at first I mistook for a smile, then saw was a determined pout. I guessed we'd stay.

"Who's that? Who is he?" Standing over us now was a bland-looking boy. Ovoid features—they lacked a finishing touch—were accentuated by a short crew cut and his face was pale with mounting emotion. "Who's your friend?"

"Where are you from?" I asked.

He looked to Lily, then back to me. "Why?"

"I wondered. I didn't think anyone who lived here would ask."

"Narragansett."

"His name is Jay. Pierce Jay."

The other boy, one with a sallow, fleshy face, stepped up as reinforcement. He looked younger and no more formidable. Behind us, the two girls had got up off the floor. They sat whispering side by side on a love seat and keeping apprehensive watch.

"Is he crazy?" the crew-cut boy asked. "Is he crazy or something?"

"I don't know, but I think he has a license to do unusual things."

"What?"

"Everybody lets him."

The two boys glared at us and turned away. They stood in the library door looking into the rooms beyond, where the party, now laden with food and familiarity, had lost some of its effervescence. "Jake!" the blond girl called, and instantly they disappeared through the door, deaf to the cautionary cries which pursued them.

The offended blonde in light green and her small, earnest companion fled after them, and Lily and I followed, expecting to find commotion in the Bledsoes' living room. But the pianist was still playing, idly now, talking to one girl. A waitress was clearing away dishes from a coffee table and the guests had gathered into protective encampments where the habitual monopolists had taken over the talking. The plateau was attained. I saw a girl yawn. A boy looked at his wristwatch. All over the room thoughts were running on to what was next. There wasn't a sign of Pierce's row.

Nancy came toward us alone, smiling and shaking her head in wonder. "He's quite difficult, your friend. He's still not having any supper, but he's having a good time—I guess."

"We're forecasting a fight," I said. "Where is he?"

"Out there." Nancy pointed through a window, where, sure enough, Pierce could be seen perched on a porch railing talking to a blond girl—drink in hand. "I got him a beautiful big plate of lobster and he dropped it into the bushes." Nancy laughed. "But as yet, no fight."

"Well, I promise you one. And really, I don't feel equal to it. Look—do you suppose we can get him out of here quickly?"

Nancy appeared crestfallen, as though I were a stern governess come to take her home.

"Yes," Lily said. "I think we'd better try."

They moved off together to their task and presently reappeared with Pierce. Grinning and docile, he made his thanks to Tootie Bledsoe, and when we had all gotten out the front door without a glimpse of the party from Narragansett, I was beginning to believe the blond girl had convinced her escort that her honor was intact enough and there was no need for the shedding of blood.

But as we started down the driveway toward the car, Pierce leading, an arm through Nancy's, and singing, " 'It was just one of those things—just one of those ca-razy things,' " in a high, carefree voice, we heard the sound of running behind us and I knew who it was. He had only been waiting for us to leave.

We stopped, just short of the car, and turned, all four of us in a row, to confront him. While Jake, still breathing deeply, glared at him, Pierce went on singing. It was a curious spectacle—the big house in the background, lit up like some great cruise ship, the guests in party clothes moving along the porches and the piano music trickling out to us on the darkness, our five faces pale as moons and alone in our private unpleasantness.

Pierce stopped singing, and Jake said to him, "What the hell did you do that for? Are you insane?"

"Do what?" Pierce asked amiably.

"Kick her dress up." His frightened face looked from one to the other of us, expecting we might deny it and confuse his outrage further. "I didn't see it. My back was turned. But everybody else did. What the hell did you mean by that?"

The sallow friend approached. He came quickly—crunch, crunch, crunch—along the driveway and stood once more behind Jake, legs apart, a little to one side, like a second, as though he knew the rules for this kind of thing.

"I was admiring your girl," Pierce said easily. "That's the way I do it. That's the way I admire girls."

Jake's mouth trembled, open and closed, open and closed—speechless but taking thin sips of the night air. "It's my wife," he said.

"I was admiring your wife, then. You're a lucky fellow to have a wife like that. Very pretty." Grinning, Pierce put his hands in his pockets.

"Hit him." It was a boy's voice from just beyond the circle in which we stood. I saw several people there and more drifting toward us. I heard someone back toward the house call, "There's a fight!"

"Go ahead and hit him, Jake," the voice insisted.

I saw Jake lean into his humiliation warily, feeling for its trigger. Then, clearly through the night, came a girl's voice, strained and plaintive. "Jake, don't!" I saw her, the blond girl in the green dress, running toward us across the lawn. "Don't be foolish, Jake. Don't dirty yourself."

For another minute Jake didn't take his eyes from Pierce and the menace in his jaw grew more pronounced, but I sensed the wilting of his spirit.

"Jesus!" he said and wheeled away. He walked to his wife and they turned their backs on us and moved off.

I suppose they went to their car and thence, silently, to Narragansett, where they railed the night away at Pierce, his friends and Newport and assured each other Jake had done the right and sensible thing. But he was shamed, and I knew that for the rest of his life he would be thinking about it, wishing he could have it to do once more.

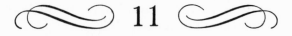

On the way to the Beach, Nancy, Lily and I silently contemplated our cowardice and the curious perversion of loyalty and civility that had made us accomplices to Pierce's arrogance.

To our anxiety about the emotional wreckage we were strewing about us, Pierce was adding the physical. His drunkenness was now apparent and he was driving too fast for his irresolute command of the big car. Turning sharply into Ocean Avenue, he veered into the ditch on our left side. We lurched heavily onto the lower wheels and I thought for a moment we were turning over, but instead of braking, Pierce accelerated and we emerged, miraculously, onto the road.

Pierce did not slacken speed. Indeed, he seemed to feel our preservation was a further sign of his favor under the natural laws, and so emboldened, he began to explain.

"Well, it was all inexcusable, of course, and I apologize to you. I'm a disgrace. I know that. Yes—the poor boy should have hit me or laughed or done *something*. But look, you mustn't waste any pity on him. In fact, he may have learned something useful." Pierce's curly head bobbed up and down reassuringly.

"Useful?" Lily asked. "How?"

"If he suspects he's a coward, maybe he can do something about it." She didn't reply, and he said, "All right. Maybe not. Then he is contemptible and doesn't, as I say, deserve . . ."

"But surely he's sensitive," Lily said.

"I'm not so sure. I'm not so sure a fellow like that is really sensitive at all. It's like worrying over how a lobster feels when you put him in the boiling water. They don't feel at all, you know that?"

"How do you know?" Nancy asked.

"Well, I don't, but I know the world is full of unfeeling people, full of brutes and beasts, vicious, stupid people on whom kindness is wasted every day. Christ, you can't go around worrying about hurting people's feelings all the time. What kind of a life would that be? There are more important things than hurting the feelings of creeps."

"For instance?" Lily asked.

"Some kind of courage. Not measuring out your life in coffee spoons. You know that? 'The Love Song of Prufrock'?"

"Yes," Lily said. "What has it to do with kicking up the girl's skirt? I haven't seen that done since the year I was in public school."

"It's a very courageous act. Maybe not in public school—but around here—Boy!" He laughed briefly and alone.

Pierce turned into the parking lot and I looked with foreboding at the clubhouse, so brightly lit in welcome. There was a striped canopy stretched on the terrace and I could see some lanterns, haloed in fog, and hear the reedy phrases of a Meyer Davis band.

Pierce avoided the policemen who tried to direct him into a rank of parked cars and drove into the darkened area near the tennis courts. He shut off the engine and leaned forward on the wheel, grasping it, head lowered as though in pain.

"I didn't like them," he said. "I'd never seen them before and I didn't like them turning down the damn music. I didn't like the way he did it—without saying anything. That's rude. Isn't it rude?"

"Well, I suppose the boy thought *he* was provoked," I said, "by your putting the music so loud in the first place."

"All right. I didn't like him. I didn't like any of them. I didn't like the way they looked. I detested that one with the crew cut and the weak, self-satisfied face from the moment I saw him. I could feel him a block away—really. The whole thing, from when I walked into the library, was all arranged."

None of us spoke, and presently he got out of the car and briskly, as though he had washed out all that had passed, said, "Come on, you clods. Let's go to the dance."

The table he had reserved was one of the few small ones on the terrace. We were flanked by big parties whose guests were still arriving. Older people, ruddy with certainty, predominated. Framed in narrow shoulder straps were yards of aromatic skin, perennially tanned, dimpled and slack over soft flesh. At a great distance I had a glimpse of Melissa and Victor de Villepin.

Once we were seated, Pierce doubled his efforts to reunite our spirits. He ordered us each a stinger, insisting we would find it irresistible, while he had a whiskey himself. He took a long pull on it, folded his hands around his glass and then hunched his shoulders as though to draw us into intimacy, here at the edge of the revels. A lock of his rich, dark hair had fallen with theatrical boyishness across his forehead, nearly to his eyebrow. His long face, its color deepened by whiskey, had a demanding, dynamic attractiveness. The deep brown eyes moved restlessly from me to Nancy to Lily, glistening. The strong arched nose twitched over the beginnings of a smile. But we remained an inert party, our tongues still weighted with shame.

"I know you were in the Normandy landings," I said to him. "It was in the class notes Blodgett sent in." I watched him tilt back, look at a passing girl. "Weren't you at Utah Beach?"

"Yes. I was there," he said. "Though not quite. I missed Utah itself. The picket boat took us by way of a minefield. We hit a steel tripod with a charge on it that blew my bow off and we settled down in easy range of the shore guns. They welcomed the boys pair by pair. Only three got to set foot on France and they weren't there long enough to enjoy it. They came across some jumping clams. You step on 'em and they pop up about two feet and explode at the genital level. No, I'm all right, thanks. Just fine down there. I swam away. Captain doesn't go down with his ship any more. What's the point?

"It was disgusting and boring—but I wouldn't have missed it, not one lousy minute. From the midst of the blood and shit you get quite a view, especially when you're swimming through floating chunks of what were shipmates. It makes you wonder about the importance of winning the war—even of making a pile of money and having everybody suck around."

"Does anything seem worthwhile, then?" Lily asked.

"Yes. One thing—your own precious life. No—you don't understand. I'm not talking about survival. The hell with that. But what you do is, you make yourself a promise that if you're spared, you'll never waste it, the way you were going to. You won't piss it away at stupid things."

"Like what?" she asked.

"Like these idiots here . . . No, you'll do something useful and important with it. Something new and different. Something nobody's ever done before. There are new ideas around. A whole new kind of man is going to run this country. Not these people . . ." He glared around him. "You ought to hear them in the bar every afternoon telling Harry Truman off. They don't know they're as extinct as dodo birds, and they can go on contributing to the Republican party forever and they'll never get Bob Taft elected President. They don't have one tenth the influence of some shop steward in Providence, some Polack they wouldn't pee on. You know what their influence is? One vote."

"I'm sure there's a lunatic bunch in the bar every afternoon," I said, "but all these people can't be stupid and in-
effectual."

"Oh, can't they, though." He nodded at the next table.
"They think all they have to do to keep Grandpa's place in
the world is to hang onto his dough, and so they've blown
their real inheritance and they don't even know it. The future of this country isn't in the hands of these sunny, self-
satisfied old farts who haven't done a day's work in their lives.
No, goddam it, the hope of this country is in the unwashed,
the kids who had to scrap to stay alive, the people with the
funny names. They've got the guts and the wits. I'm all for
'em. Let 'em in. Let's let 'em in here if they want to come."
He frowned. "God knows why they would, come to think of
it, but I'd like to see the place swarming with Jews. And Ne-
groes next. Why the hell not?"

"If you feel so strongly," Lily said, "why don't you do
something about it?"

"I will." He returned her gaze unsteadily. "I find a nice
Negro girl I'll damn well bring her right the hell in here."

"Or—if you dislike it so much here—why do you stay?"

"I don't dislike it," he said, slurring the words. "It's these
people. And I don't see too much of them. I'm busy out at the
field."

"I wanted to ask about that too," Lily said. She looked very
serious as she rearranged the flowers at the center of the table.
"How does that help? Isn't that just fun for you?"

"Is there anything wrong with that?"

"No . . . I was just remembering what you said about
your swim."

Someone passing bumped against his chair, breaking the
spell, and Pierce looked up angrily at a woman who paused to
excuse herself.

"It's all right." Furrowing his brow, Pierce arose, knocking
over the chair as he did so. He looked at it as though he expected it to rise of itself, then leaned to pick it up and tilted it
whimsically against the table.

"Dance?" he asked Lily. "That's what we're here for."

"No," she said, her hand still among the flowers. "No thanks."

In the same instant Pierce asked Nancy, who got to her feet immediately, and they went off together toward the dance floor.

"Do you want to dance?" I asked.

"No, really." She shook her head thoughtfully. "I think it's going to be peaceful with him gone and I want to enjoy a moment of that. He's really quite a strain, isn't he—for friend and foe alike."

I nodded and we turned to watch the dancing. The younger couples were appearing—supple, agile things with shocks of blond hair and long white dresses that swished and swung, and black-bowed slippers quick and easy to the drumbeat. They butterflied about their stolid elders steadfastly plying the currents. Nancy's green dress caught my eye and I thought she was having a good time as she did at a dance. She was amusing Pierce, but as I watched I saw he was toiling. He was making sprints, forceful forays into the mass of dancers, but in between I noted the unsteadiness in his feet and the weight in his eyelids.

"He's fairly drunk," I said. "If you do dance with him, be prepared to have your toes stepped on."

"Thanks." She was watching Pierce with curiosity. "I think I'll avoid that altogether."

"You *can* dance?"

"A little." She smiled. "But I think we'd better not."

"A walk, then?" Looking along the seaward side of the pavilion, I saw an exit to the terrace and, beyond, a glimpse of the restorative infiniteness of early-summer night.

"Yes. That's a nice idea."

As we left she turned, but Nancy and Pierce were not to be seen and she followed me outside. The sound of the sea, the soft burst of a wave reminded us we were in the real world, but we could not see the surf. Like a ghostly army, the fog was encamped upon the ocean surface, sending scouts and patrols up the beach to brush by us as they crept off on their missions.

We strolled the sea wall until we found steps leading onto the beach. On the lowest, Lily took off her shoes to run her toes through the damp sand. Overhead the stars emerged and disappeared.

In the certainty that whatever interest she had had in Pierce was now largely clinical, I said, "The trouble is I'm torn between apologizing to you for him—he really is something tonight—and scolding you for bringing out his blackest side."

Lily kicked some sand into the mists. "Well, you needn't do either. Lord knows you gave me enough warning. If I were having a most miserable time, and I'm not at all sure that I am"—she laughed and embraced her knees—"I'd have no one to blame but myself. Surely that's clear, isn't it?"

"Yes."

"Hasn't he always been like this?"

"He's always worked at his reputation for being wild and crazy. I can remember having the hell scared out of me driving down to New York from New Haven at a hundred miles an hour and trying not to show it, because I knew he was doing it for my benefit. He wanted me to go back and tell everybody and keep the legend alive, but also he wanted to prove he *could* scare me, you know, to prove to both of us it was he who had the courage and me that lacked it."

"But fun."

"He was always capable of arrogance," I began doubtfully, "and inexcusable behavior. But no, no viciousness. The war . . ."

"He's older. He lacks the excuse for making a public nuisance . . ." Lily raised her face to look at me, and in the reflection of an unveiled chandelier of stars, she looked fresh and true and painfully desirable. "Is that *all* about him?"

"Oh no. That was only a part of it. I can't explain to you what an effect Pierce had at college. He was a real legend. Freshmen and sophomores studied him—ran to buy pink shirts and black ties like his and affected that loping walk. For me, he opened a whole world of possibility. He antagonized and then captivated me. I had to be around him for fear of missing out on the excitement. Even now. Even now, even with the dark side, the one exposed tonight—oh sure, an embarrassment to all—still, I'm doubly alive when I'm around him. I gather some of his intensity, a sense of the way life ought to be. Do you feel any of that?"

"Well, I see—and that it's getting strangled by bitterness and a conspiracy of inertia. The ringing name. That wiry little man in the breeches has been dead for ten years but he still lives with Pierce—don't you imagine?—still opens all these doors for him, so easily, just with his name."

"And his money."

"Yes, of course, the money." Lily was braiding a lock of hair ruminatively. "But just think of coming down that flight of stairs with your hangover, passing the portrait and sitting down to breakfast across from Victor de Villepin. Wouldn't that be something? And to go to a party right here in your own realm and find someone who didn't even know a prince when he saw one. That and a taste for booze and those girls. You spoke of the ones who spoil him so. Well, they aren't in a class with his mother. Do you suppose he can do anything about it?"

I was thinking that I hadn't the least notion, that I took Pierce Jay at his own value and could not even guess what was to become of him, when I realized I believed in him. Perhaps it was the wish to seem perceptive now, but as I spoke I persuaded myself. "He told me—it was some time ago—that he could do anything he chose, that he never doubted his own ability to do anything another man could, whether it was carrying a football or making a girl or even . . . intellectually . . ."

"But you don't believe that, surely—or believe *he* believes it?"

"I know it sounds unlikely, but I *do*. I've seen him, overnight, turn himself into a decent scholar. He very rarely achieves . . . but he's never content with halfway. Oh yes, tonight—if I didn't know him, I'd say he was destroying himself and that it would take a miracle to stop him, but you know the odd thing about Pierce is that miraculous things do so often happen around him. He makes them happen. He has a talent for it. I haven't written him off."

But I did not seem to have been persuasive, for Lily brushed some sand from her hands and stood up. "I think we'd better go back."

We walked silently until we stood again on the threshold of the party, peering in. Our table was still empty but there was no sign of Pierce and Nancy on the floor.

As we stepped gingerly back into the light and noise, pausing for an instant, both of us feeling an impulse to turn back to the kinder darkness behind, my right arm was caught in a painful clutch. Pierce's fingers sank into my flesh like talons. He had come up swiftly alongside and was laughing wickedly at my pained surprise. Just behind, Nancy watched us with an expression of tried patience, as though she had had enough of adolescence.

"Ho, ho, ho!" Pierce's hollow stage laugh boomed in my ear. His eyes shone with a disconcerting glee and one eye closed in a broad wink. "By golly, you do all right for an old married man. I admire that. Yes, sir. You may be married but you ain't dead, eh?" He looked knowingly at Lily and then back at me, sizzling like a fuse.

"Oh, stop, Pierce, for Christ's sake." I wrenched my arm free of his grasp. "We went for a walk."

Instantly Pierce turned to Nancy, and putting an arm around her waist, drew her up beside him. "Right?" he said to Nancy. "I'll bet you have to keep an eye on the old dog here every minute, don't you?"

"I wouldn't think of it," Nancy said and leaned flirtatiously against Pierce's shoulder. "Let's *us* go outside. It's a lovely night."

"Time for a change." Releasing Nancy, Pierce turned away too soon for a glimpse of her humiliation—naked for one split second before being clothed, hastily, in indifference, as he said to Lily, "Come for a walk with me?"

Lily looked over her shoulder at the opening through which we had just returned and then, with a shudder, folded and rubbed her arms. "It's awfully damp out there," she said and added the flourish of a frivolous smile.

Pierce took an unsteady step toward Lily. "A dance, then?" He held out a hand for hers, and although he still maintained that air of contentious high spirit, that it was all terribly funny, there was a raw intensity in his manner and I felt that when Lily refused him, we would have some real unpleasantness.

"Yes," Lily said, putting her hand in his, "I'd like that." With relief I watched them move off, Lily leading him toward the dance floor.

From the table we watched their progress among the others. It was an uneasy spectacle. I saw them lurch into a couple and stumble, and I suspected Lily's gameness and agility were losing out to her embarrassment. Pierce seemed unaware of his clumsiness. He was licking his lips as though they were dry and he wore the beady, self-confident expression of a man who is beginning to feel part goat.

"He's really too drunk," I told Nancy. "I think I ought to cut in and bring them back, don't you?"

"Lily can manage. You'll only get Pierce madder at you. That was dumb taking her outside. Whatever possessed you to do that?"

"Why shouldn't I? We just went for a walk. It seemed a pleasant thing to do. What are you suggesting?"

Resting her chin in her hand, she looked into my eyes. "That it would make Pierce angry—that's all. No . . ." She laughed. "No, I don't think you *did* anything out there, you idiot. And I don't suppose Pierce does either, but you do meet less resistance than he does and I think it burns him up." She glanced up, taking my attention along, to find Lily returning to us alone.

Her fair skin had taken on a high color and she was smiling. Where another girl might weep, Lily smiled, and sometimes, as now, the tip of her tongue emerged from the corner of her mouth.

On my feet, I pulled a chair back for her, but she shook her head. "No thanks. I'm going to go. I don't know quite how but I'm going. Do you suppose I could steal a car?"

"Where is he?"

"I don't know." Lily was gathering her purse and the white sweater she had worn as a wrap.

"What did he do? Was it something he said?"

"Let's all go," Nancy said and arose, gathering her own things and looking toward the door. "Ben, do you suppose there's a taxi? Maybe they know at the office."

"Yes, of course. We'll all go now." I took Nancy's elbow, touched Lily reassuringly on the arm and nodded them ahead of me toward the clubhouse entrance. I followed like a nervous shepherd, looking right and left for Pierce. I was certain of ambush and hoped it would not be in too public a place, for I knew that with all the will and self-righteousness on my side and Pierce stumbling drunk, he could still beat hell out of me.

At the club office, a severe woman grudgingly phoned for a taxi, and I went to wait for Nancy and Lily outside the ladies' room. I planned to lead them swiftly outside. I was trying to imagine what particular outrageousness Pierce had turned on Lily—our visit to the beach, as Nancy had suggested, exaggerating it in the crude obscenity that was his specialty. No doubt he was in the bar now, tamping down his remorse and stoking up his courage for more.

Seeing us in flight would tie it. I knew that. The blood which he had twice been denied tonight would be let. To my relief, Nancy and Lily emerged now, spirits visibly redeemed by fresh make-up and shared confidence.

"Come on, the taxi's probably here," I said, and they followed me to the door where a station wagon was unloading latecomers.

When I inquired at the office, the woman frowned, letting us know we were not members, any of us. "Well, I haven't any notion how long it will take. Sometimes they come right away. Other times they're busy. It depends, you know."

"I see." Looking apprehensively over my shoulder, I found we were discovered. Pierce was separating himself from a cluster of people at the mouth of the corridor. Steady and determined, eyes wide, staring at us, whether in surprise or anger I could not tell, he was making his way in our direction. He held two full highball glasses in front of him and the liquor sloshed over his knuckles.

"Hey, what the hell? What the hell *is* this? What are you doing out here?" He came up between Nancy and me, teetered toward Lily as, with difficulty, he focused on her. With a free finger he flicked Nancy's jacket. "You look like you're going."

"We are," I announced. "That's what we're doing."

"I was in the bar"—he leaned close to me, so that I felt the heat and smelled the whiskey, deep yellow layers of it, in his breath—"getting this." He held up one tall glass, a monumental stinger. "It's for all of you." His eyes, the whites so pink they looked painful, moved to each of us in turn as he offered it and was refused.

"We're all tired," I said. "We want to go home. I've just called a taxi."

"What do you want with a taxi?"

"We want to go home in it. Don't worry about us, Pierce. We can take care of ourselves."

"Now wait. You haven't given this joint a chance. If you stick around another hour you'll really *see* something." He looked over his shoulder. "Like Harry Chase—see there on the floor? The big guy with the bald spot, practically copulating with the pigeon in blue? Well, as every clacking tongue out there is telling every willing ear, that's Harry's doxy. He keeps her in a cage on Beekman Place, and what the hell is she doing here, at the same table with Harry and his wife— see her, Grace her name is—observing as though she has reason to think the plumbing is backing up? Well, something exciting is going to happen there. I'll guarantee it. And if it doesn't, by golly, we've got a dozen other acts waiting, any number of jailed spirits awaiting the turnkey . . ." He winked broadly at Nancy and laughed, a fake, wild laugh at his banality, then raised the glass for his own gulp of delivery. Smacking his lips, he said, "No sir, this thing hasn't even got warmed up yet. It'll go on till two or three."

"Not with me," Lily said. "Ben and Nancy are going to take me home."

"No-o." He waggled his head like a big animal trying to rid himself of pests. "We don't want to go yet, goddam it." Thrusting his chin forward, Pierce held his glass against my chest. "Do we?"

I didn't answer, and he blinked slowly, grasping the resoluteness of our mutiny. His face, like a child's, went grave at denial, and stiffly, truculently, his lips seaming, he said, "Okay. If that's how. I just thought you wanted to *see*, that's all. If you're not having a good time—Christ." He turned to Lily and said, "But if anybody takes you home, it's going to be me."

"I prefer Ben and Nancy."

"Why?"

"You're drunk," Lily said in her cool, precise voice, "and disagreeable."

Pierce smiled at her, rocked—heel to toe, heel to toe—as the color left his face. "No-o." It was a groan, the sound of a man wounded and yet ringing with defiance. "You're coming with *me*."

Lily started for the entrance and after a moment's hesitation Nancy followed her. As they left us to pass through the door and out onto the porch beyond, I blocked Pierce and said, "Look, it'll all be fine in the morning. Why don't you go back and have a good time?"

"Don't," he warned me. His eyes looked into my own, and I had the curious impression that in this instant the mists of his drunkenness were lifting, that he had been stunned into sobriety. Without emotion, like an officer who expects to be obeyed, he said, "Don't stand in my way, Ben."

Behind me I heard voices of young people arriving. A girl, in passing, said, "Hi, Pierce," but he didn't acknowledge it. I stepped aside and let him by.

I followed him out onto the terrace where they waited. Nancy, gripping the railing and peering into Ocean Avenue, ignored us as she told Lily that a pair of distant headlights were surely coming for us. Lily, backed against a pillar, watched Pierce's approach. I saw her straighten and cover her apprehension with that same façade of a smile.

Pierce had lost all awareness of Nancy and me. He looked at Lily as though they were alone and with an abjectness that for him was a totally unexpected humiliation—so much so, I felt I should turn from the sight. They looked at one another silently as Lily felt the extraordinary change in Pierce's manner.

He looked down at the glasses he was holding, puzzled to find them there, and tossed the tall stinger over the rail into the bushes. "Yes, yes, you're right. I'm despicable," he said. "I know that, Lily. Oh Christ, don't think I'm unable to grieve over that, over every stupid thing I do, over provoking that boy at the Bledsoes', over what I said to you. Lily, I despise myself even more than you do." He paused, looking into the glass of whiskey in his right hand. "And this stuff isn't any use, is it? It makes the truth so ugly. Look, if you let me drive you home, Lily, I'll quit. I won't drink again tonight." With a pitch that miraculously left us dry, he sent the glass sailing to shatter against the brick wall of the clubhouse. "Or tomorrow either."

Lily had become equally oblivious of us. All suspicion of Pierce appeared to have left her. She looked stunned. Her lips parted. Her face reflected a sense of wonder—at herself, I suppose, at her power as much as at this extraordinary transformation.

"All right, Pierce," she said in a gentle, moved voice. "If you get the car, we'll be here."

"Come *with* me."

Obediently she took his hand and they walked away from us without a word. We watched as they went down the steps and crossed the parking lot and became lost in the darkness.

*   *   *

Actually, Pierce and Lily arrived at Bellerive as I was paying our driver, and the few minutes since we had parted seemed to have restored the familiar lanes of our relationship. The great green car had hardly braked behind us when he was alongside, returning my money and paying the fare.

"You idiots, why didn't you wait?" he wanted to know. "We were on our way to get you."

"I was terrified of that woman in the office," I said, looking him over warily. "I'm sure she would have come after us and *made* us take the taxi. She reminds me of a piano teacher I used to have."

Pierce laughed. "She's pretty bad, particularly when you get to know her." He gave the fender of the departing taxi a whack, as though it were the flank of a mare he'd sent to the stables, and looked up the steps of Bellerive, where Lily stood watching us. "Well—let's go in. Myself—I'm not drinking, but I can offer you all a nightcap."

We followed Pierce up the steps and waited in the hall, like tourists for their guide, while he closed the heavy door behind us.

"No drink for me," Lily said pleasantly.

"I am *tired.*" Nancy looked to me. "I think I'll go on up."

"That's a good example, particularly if we're going to get an early start in the morning." I looked to Lily and she nodded. "Goodnight," I said.

Pierce watched the three of us edge toward the stairs. "Okay," he called after us. "Goodnight, all." But when we were halfway up, he said, "Lily?" and we all stopped to peer down to the bottom of the stairwell. He stood with his legs apart, hands clasped behind him, in a striking reflection of the portrait above him. "Come down and have a glass of something with me—a Coke?"

She looked at her watch.

"It's not late."

"All right." Lily went by me lightly, back down the stairs to him.

*   *   *

The paneled bedroom door clicked firmly behind us, shutting, I hoped, like a portcullis on the evening's furies. I did feel very tired, and peeling off my dinner jacket, I sank into a little armchair and with relief pried off my evening pumps.

"Well, it may not be the most agreeable Saturday night we've ever spent," I said, "but it was different from playing bridge with the Motts. You've got to give Newport that. Plenty of rare birds to look at—and music. It's been a long time since we've been to a party with a band."

"I'm not complaining." She skinned out of her dress and gathered up her nightgown from where it had been laid out on her bed.

Nancy closed the bathroom door, leaving me with my thoughts, until they were penetrated by the sound of a girl's laughter—brief and distant, but unmistakably Lily's. It touched off some mischievous stirrings in me and brought me quickly to the door, my ear to it, hoping to discover she was coming upstairs now, that her laugh had been a farewell. I heard nothing and cautiously opened the door on an empty corridor. The lights in the wall sconces and the big chandelier over the stairwell also awaited them, but with a pale, infinite patience. The house was still.

Closing the door, I crossed to the window and saw that pools of light fell onto the dark lawn below. In one I found my own shadow, and waved. At intervals, on either side, I identified the illumination from Pierce's room and what was either Lily's or the De Villepins' to the westward—all unshaded, for this was the seaside. Below, closer to the house and on the stones of the terrace, lay an oblong of light from the bar. I found no moving shadows, and after a moment I leaned from our window, hoping to catch some sound that would tell me what Pierce and Lily were doing.

Over the sound of the surf and the stirring of leaves in the lindens, I was at last rewarded by the noise of ice being shaken against the side of a glass. It was followed by muffled words. It was Pierce's voice but I could not catch the sense. I thought he said, "I'm going to enter the carrot wheel."

As I leaned out farther, trying to hear what Lily would reply, I sensed Nancy behind me. "Hey, snoopy," she said, "be careful you don't fall out."

I brought my head back quickly, scraping an ear on the casement, and confronted my wife, already in nightgown and blue flannel robe. "All right," I said. "I *am* curious. I heard Lily laugh and I just leaned out to see."

"See what?"

"I can't believe she's been sucked in by Pierce. I know him, for God's sake. It's all part of a campaign to get Lily into bed."

Nancy smiled. "Oh? Do you think so?" She held a hand to her ear. "Some creeping about the halls tonight? Well, why don't you get a flashlight and go on sentry duty?"

"Honestly, Nancy, I do feel some responsibility."

"You behave as if Lily were just out of a convent and you the mother superior. Lily's not a child. She can deal with it by herself and she'd prefer it." Nancy admired the covers of one of the twin beds, so invitingly turned down and folded. "She doesn't want you butting in."

"She's got too much sense."

Nancy sat on the edge of her bed to take off the worn ballet slippers, and placed them side by side. "You just cannot accept the fact that she finds him attractive, can you? Well, she does, Ben." She took off her robe and flung it on the window seat. Then, climbing into her bed, she pulled the covers blissfully around her. "Aren't you going to get undressed?"

"No. Tell me—what's she like? She was trying to persuade me she was an adventuress—imagine, a girl who looks like that. I didn't believe it for a minute. Do you really know her?"

"Well, Lily has heart. She really does do things most girls just think about. She was the first girl I knew who actually had an affair with a boy. Yes, while she was still in school. She pretended to go home but instead went to Cambridge and stayed all one night in a dormitory. I remember it vividly because she'd borrowed a skirt of mine and she said it was the first thing she saw when she woke up. It was hanging over the back of a chair and she laughed. It struck her funny, it being *my* skirt—not that I was a prude, but I was very cautious. I wouldn't have *dreamed* . . ."

"Do girls do that—brag about exploits? I thought just boys."

"No—she wasn't bragging, not at all. It was just interesting, about the skirt, that it now had a history. I thought of it when you told me about Lily's virginal look at the wedding."

I tugged at the bow of my tie and stared into the mirror on the bureau top at my reflection. It was disheveled and unattractive—mouth raw, hair mussed, eyes red from unaccustomed indulgences.

"Oh, Ben, of course she wants to be down there with him." She spoke sleepily, as though she was already drifting off. "I mean, he's devastating." She smiled up from her pillow. "Anyone that looks like that, anyone with all that spark. But most of all, it's the terrific power of self-destruction. Any girl with . . . oh, you know. She'd want to touch that."

"What do you mean *touch* it? Why? I don't understand."

Nancy sighed. "Oh, I suppose in the belief she could turn it—bend it in some way."

"You don't believe that, do you?"

"That Pierce is attractive? But I *do.*"

"To *you?*"

Nancy looked at me playfully. "Sure."

This simple piece of information was shattering. I was that self-centered, that absorbed in my tasks, that in the short year since my marriage it had never crossed my mind that Nancy might be attracted to someone other than myself.

"I'm sorry," I said. "I just don't believe that—not to somebody who drinks himself insensible and is capable of consistent rudeness whenever he's not being just plain cruel."

"They aren't enticing, either of those . . . uh, symptoms." Twisting around, Nancy plumped her two pillows against the headboard and leaned into them, half sitting. "They tend to make others uncomfortable and even to break up a perfectly good party. But a man who has that much courage . . ."

"Courage . . ."

". . . to not give a damn what people think. Viciousness, meanness, violence and all—are exciting to a girl. They do all sorts of things to her."

"You're teasing me, Nancy. You're teasing, aren't you?" I perched on the edge of her bed and she made me room. "It might be true of some overindulged, emotionally starved teenager, like those pretty things at the party tonight. They were surfeited, did you notice? You could see it in their eyes. I can see how they might go for Pierce, that he might have some spurious, romantic appeal. But my God, Nancy, I simply cannot believe that anyone as sensible as you . . ."

She yawned and her eyes closed in drowsy contentment.

"Nancy—you *are*."

"Are what?"

"Drawn to him." I started to get up, but as I did, she caught my shirt sleeve between her fingers. With a smile and a tug she drew me back to her side.

"Don't look so cross," Nancy said. "I'm not going to leave you—not even when Pierce comes to ask me." She slipped a hand under my shirt, then rose on an elbow to whisper into my ear. "They're a terrible hardship, these single beds—but I think that if I make myself very small, you can just squeeze in here."

*   *   *

Awaiting me at the breakfast table I found a tall glass of orange juice and Pierce. In Basque shirt and yellowing flannels, he was swallowing coffee and making a turbulent way through the Sunday papers. These he shoved aside, and while magnificently poached eggs on thin slices of toast were placed before me, he began to tell about the sloop *Bluejay*.

She had been his father's, designed and built at the Hereshoff yard in Bristol. She had followed her owner to the West Indies and as far south as Ecuador on each of the last winters of his life. But now, with his mother's indifference to sailing and Victor's—well, Victor could not even see the beauty of *Bluejay*. In the one season they had kept her, she proved the core of their triangular contentions. So she had been sold, on most generous terms, to her skipper, who now made a living from her charter. *Bluejay* was available today, if anyone cared to go sailing.

Lily, looking rested and fresh as a child, hesitated on the threshold of the dining room, awaiting an invitation to join us. She had caught in her eyes some of the young spring sun and the smoky landscape beyond the tall windows.

Pierce waved idly. "Want some chow?"

"I do." She advanced toward the place between us, with a smile for me as well as for Pierce, and I had a whiff of her, sweet but not perfumed. "I'm ravenous."

I rose awkwardly and sank again, watching for some sign as to how it stood with them.

Pierce spread some marmalade on a piece of toast. "I was telling Lily about college last night." He popped the toast into his mouth and chewed it with pleasure, watching Lily all the while.

"Oh—that's what kept you up?"

Lily looked to Pierce for an answer, but he only smiled back at her with a sly privacy.

"He was telling me what Yale was like." Lily watched a melon slice arrive and then gave me a penetrating look as though at last we were getting to something interesting. "I've only been to New Haven once, for a Yale—a *Harvard* game, but I've always had the idea it's highly organized."

"Conformist? More so than Harvard?" I asked. "I don't remember conforming much, but maybe that's what I was doing."

She nodded and put chin in hand to give me some amused study. "Pierce says you were a big wheel. Is that right, Ben? Were you a BMOC?"

"No," I replied, "that's not right at all. A lot of people majored in that. But it takes a great deal of time and I didn't have it. I had to work too hard."

"Oh come on, Ben," Pierce said. "You were the best of all. Even then you had the mark of success on you. You were good at everything without trying." To Lily, he added, gleefully, "Ben could have been Bones, you know. But instead he went Snake."

"I was a poor boy," I said. "They had one in every class to maintain the democratic tradition. It made everybody, including me, feel good. But, Lily, it was Pierce who was a major campus figure."

Lily laughed. "I *do* wish I had known you then."

"I'm glad you didn't," Pierce said. "I'm glad you didn't know me."

Lily brought her napkin to the corner of her mouth with a tinkling of the gold charms on her bracelet. I had not noticed this girlish piece of jewelry before and I think it was the first time she'd worn it.

Pierce's attention had also been caught by it, and as his hand reached out to touch the several charms, Lily dropped the napkin into her lap, and with her elbow resting on the table, inclined her wrist toward him so he could inspect them one by one. She tilted her head toward him, too, so that her short, straight hair, the color of ripe wheat, fell beguilingly across her cheek.

It was a thoroughly intimate pose, the two of them so preoccupied with themselves, heads together, Pierce's dark curls nearly brushing her shoulder, his long, rather delicate fingers exploring the veined, sensitive underside of her wrist. Their very unconsciousness of me made watching them embarrassing.

"What is it?" I asked. "What's so interesting?"

"There's everything here," Pierce said without looking up. "There's a fish, a many-jointed fish. That's for fertility."

It was the teasing of familiars and she laughed, eager party to it. "Oh, it isn't, Pierce. It isn't for anything of the sort. It's for good luck."

"And some mad money folded up in a little box that says For Emergency Use Only," he went on. "My God, that's small. Is that really a dollar in there?"

"It is," she said. "I know because I had to use it once."

"How did you get it back in again?"

"There's a jeweler on Boylston Street who can fold them into a tiny little block like that. I don't know how he does it—in a vise, I suppose."

"Was it really mad money? Some guy made you walk home?"

"No, he didn't make me walk. He was a taxi driver who took me to the North Station, where I found I had just a quarter."

"He was a mean son-of-a-bitch to make you open it."

Lily nodded. "Not like Davey."

"Davey?" I asked. "Who's Davey?"

"Davey Gilles," Pierce said. "You remember Davey, for Christ's sake, Ben."

"I don't think so."

Lily looked up now. "The crap game?" she asked me. "The crap game in a locker room at Madison Square Garden?" I shook my head, and she went on to explain. "Pierce's father played crap against a taxi driver named Davey Gilles and won everything he had—including the cab. And then gave it back to him. Davey was so grateful that whenever Mr. Jay was in New York, Davey drove him. He wouldn't take any other passengers while Mr. Jay was in town."

"Yes, I guess I do remember, come to think of it. He waited for him everywhere, like a faithful dog." I pushed my chair back and made ready to rise. "Which reminds me, I must call about the bus. There's nothing I'd rather do than stay on, Pierce—you know that. I'd love to go sailing and have a glorious day in the sun—and I know the girls feel the same only more so—but I've *got* to get back. I'm long overdue at the library."

"Right now?" Lily asked.

"Well . . . in about half an hour." I watched her nod acquiescence but her disappointment was plain.

"Now goddam it, Ben," Pierce said. "You know you don't mean that. It's your frigging Puritan ancestors getting to you again, and spoiling the sport. He was like this in college, Lily. Just when the party was getting good, he'd spook and say it was time to go home. He could be talked out of it, I'm glad to say, and next morning he was always grateful that he hadn't missed the fun."

Light footsteps, resonant as castanets, sounded on the marble floor of the hallway and Nancy appeared in a gay print dress that looked like a costume for church and luncheon at the beach rather than a bus ride to Cambridge.

"Good *morning*, Pierce," she said, taking her place at the table, and it was with such an exuberance that she looked around, smiling at Lily, sensing the new harmony that prevailed and dispensing some of her own, that I knew an early departure was far from her mind. She was planning to see some more of Newport.

"Put it right here, would you, Thomas?" Pierce said, and seizing the pot, he leaned across the table to fill Lily's cup. "Ben?"

"No thanks."

Filling his own cup, Pierce said, "Well now, here's the plan, Nancy. It's such a sailing kind of day that I think we might take the *Bluejay* out on the bay for a couple of hours. Would you like that? Are you any kind of a sailor?"

"I'd adore that, Pierce."

"Nancy dear," I said. "I dislike being the kill-joy but we do have to go home. I know how agonizing it is on such a morning—and just when you've fallen for Newport."

"Have I?" Nancy asked.

"I think you'd gladly send for your trunk and stay on forever."

"Well, it *is* beautiful. I don't know about staying forever but it's a stunning place. I didn't realize there would be such a feeling of being surrounded by deep sea, of being on an island with all these dazzling houses. Aren't they glorious? The carved stone soars on endlessly and the sight of it really does something quite marvelous to me. The men who built these houses could *really* be conspicuous, couldn't they? They showed their affluence and didn't feel guilty about it the way we do now."

"Oh? Do you really think the rich feel any guilt about it now?" I asked. "Don't you think it's more that rich men's taste has improved in the last fifty years? I mean, the money's been in the family for a couple of generations now and they've got themselves educated in how to create envy. You don't put up a copy of a French or an Italian palace any more to impress your neighbors."

"I don't care if they are copies," Nancy said sharply. "I like them. I like this house. I think Bellerive is absolutely lovely."

"I didn't mean Bellerive. I meant The Breakers and Ochre Court—the big places along Cliff Walk."

"No, I *don't* think they're in bad taste—if that's vulgarity, I'm all for it."

I scowled at Nancy. She was prone to this kind of blunt response, derailing abstract traffic before it could leave the station. "Look, Nancy," I said. "Rich men spend a great deal of money on their houses today—nearly as much as they did here in the last century. But the money doesn't go into ornamentation. You can't import whole villages of stonecutters from Tuscany, but they wouldn't be wanted anyway, because the money goes into utility and comfort. Simplicity is the goal. Maybe we're getting back to a Greek idea of beauty."

"I disagree," Lily said firmly. "It isn't a matter of taste at all. You don't see better taste in a place where rich people are building houses now. The houses are plain, to be sure. They're unembellished and standardized, but for the most part they're sterile—and you know what I think? I think it reflects the lack of grandness in businessmen today. They're punched out from a pattern, and by God, they like to look that way—for fear the government or the unions or somebody will come and take their stock options away."

"Oh, that's delightful, Lily." I laughed. "Where in the world did you get such romantic notions of nineteenth-century American businessmen. They weren't appealing fellows. They were still peddlers at heart and you'd have looked all day to find a trace of imagination or conscience—to say nothing of taste—among them. They were made by their times and there was nothing admirable about them unless you admire acquisitiveness for its own sake. You must be as happy as I that that era has passed into history, that you can't amass that kind of wealth in this country any more."

Pierce had sunk low in his big chair at the head of the table. He covered his mouth with one hand, over which he was regarding us sourly. "You're crazy. You can get richer than ever in America today. I know all about how you get rich today and beat the taxes. I know a guy who's made a fortune out of a trucking company, all in the last two years. There was a guy in the bar last night who made a million bucks in cosmetics. Honeychile, it's called. You buy it in the five-and-ten. Can you beat that? Making a fortune out of high-school girls? And there's another fellow who made it out of a copy machine. You know, the laziness and incompetence of secretaries today. It isn't the big stuff any more. Steel and banking and airlines are all worked out. You've got to have a gimmick—a *new* idea"—he made a shaping gesture in the air—"about how it's going to be."

"That interests you? Making money? I thought, from what you were saying last night . . ."

"No, it isn't the money. That's too easy, just getting rich."

Scowling at me, Pierce took his coffee into his lap. "I don't even think about money. If you think about the money, you're through. You think about the idea. That's my business philosophy, if you want to know. If you've really got it—the imagination to dream and plan and the guts to back it up— then the money comes. You don't ever have to worry about it."

"What *will* you worry about?"

"You'll see." He gave me a big wink. "Now, before we go any further here today I want to say that everybody has a job to do—and yours, Nancy, is to shanghai this no-good son-of-a-bitch." Pointing his finger across the table at me, Pierce grinned. "He talks like a mutineer."

"Pierce, I'd like to stay," I said. "I can't imagine anything I'd rather do than go for a sail on the bay, and I don't want to spoil the party, really. But you know I can't. I'm a law student and I have an exam on Wednesday. The guys I'm up against weren't out dancing and drinking last night. They were in Langdell, reading their Con law, and if they went home for a few hours' sleep, they're back there now, reading the Tax Code."

"It's plain to all of us, Ben. That they need you worse than you need them," Pierce said. "I'm not worried about those poor bastards sweating away in the stacks, except for how far behind you're going to leave them. No, the only thing you have to fear is overtraining."

"Oh, do say you'll stay, Ben," Nancy put in. "We could start back for Cambridge as soon as we come in from the sail." She turned to him and asked, "What time would that be, Pierce?"

"Three. We'll be in by three."

"There, you see, if we left at three, wouldn't that be time enough? You could stay up a little later."

Lily, who had been regarding me with a gratifying earnestness, suddenly said, "No, we mustn't urge him any more. It's just a sail. It's just fun and Ben's exams are serious."

"Oh, I *know*—" Nancy said.

I peered at Lily, who, of course, had found the only access to my tractableness, wondering if she had done so out of sincerity, truly putting my welfare before her own desires, or from cleverness, sensing that my resistance thrived on opposition and wasted away without it. I thought I might guess the answer from her expression, but now as I looked for that reassurance—that signal light of understanding I was sure I had seen in her eyes a moment ago—it was gone.

Thomas laid Nancy's breakfast before her, and with a magician's flourish, removed the steaming glass bell which had covered her eggs. "Oh, how lovely," Nancy said.

When I stared at Lily, insisting she look at me, she did so with an impatient toss of her head, her blue eyes mirrors.

"You're very generous, Lily," I said. "I know you want to go. You're fond of sailing, aren't you?"

"Yes, but it doesn't matter, really." She looked away.

"I'll see when there's a bus," I said grimly. "If you'll excuse me . . ." Nancy and Pierce watched me fold my napkin carefully and put it beside my plate. Lily did not. "I'll be ready to go in half an hour."

"To Cambridge?" Nancy asked.

"Cambridge via Boston, if that's where Lily wants to go." I rose from the table and started for the doorway to the hall.

"Hey, wait," Pierce said. "Are you absolutely set on this?"

"Set."

"No way of talking you out?"

"None."

"Well, there's no need for Lily to go." He turned to her. "You don't have to go off with them. I'll fly you up to Logan after the sail."

She did not hesitate a moment. With a cool fluttering of lashes, she said, "Sure," and then to Nancy, "I'm sorry you won't be coming."

"Nancy can come too," Pierce said. "She doesn't have to study for exams."

Brightening, Nancy looked at me for a reaction. I gave it in a shrug and left the dining room with a final glare of disapproval.

*   *   *

As I was shaving, I saw Nancy in the mirror. She had come into the room without speaking, and now I heard the sound of opening drawers and the ring of hangers from the closet, whereupon she appeared in the doorway to the bathroom, her nightgown folded across her arm.

"Ben, would you really mind if I stayed and came up this afternoon with Lily? She has a car at the airport and could drive me home."

I rinsed my razor and dried it. "You do what you want," I said. "Do whatever you want. What *do* you want?"

"Well, it's been an eternity since I've been out on the water and it does sound like such a lovely boat. I'm not likely to get another chance soon, you know. Of course I don't like going without you."

"Sure. Go ahead. Have a good time."

She looked at me brightly. "Well, if you really don't mind my staying . . ."

When I looked into the mirror again, she had gone.

*   *   *

Dressed, I put my belongings into the one valise we had brought, and leaving it behind for Nancy, I went in search of Pierce. Re-entering his room, I was pleased to find it little changed by the passage of eight such eventful years. Still in place, forming the headboard to twin beds, was a veteran wooden propeller. The model of a DC-3 with Jay Line markings still soared on its silver plinth over shelves of faded boyhood adventure.

I recalled the wonder with which I first beheld all this, the cherry-striped wardrobe there, with its abundance of shirts and pajamas, each painstakingly laundered, awaiting his careless choice. But I was amused that now this room, like the rest of Bellerive, seemed far less imposing than I remembered it.

Pierce sat on one of the beds, loading a sixteen-millimeter moving picture camera.

"I guess you know what you're doing," he said, squinting up as though wary of my reaction, "leaving me with two pretty girls. But it seems a rash act for a reasonable fellow like you."

"I'm sure I'll regret it," I said amiably. "But you really will bring Nancy up in the afternoon? I mean, no fooling. I'm not much of a cook and I get hungry around six-thirty."

Pierce snapped the camera's lid shut, and setting it on the bedspread, arose to give my shoulder a great comradely squeeze. He was looking directly into my face, eyes dancing with amusement at, I suppose, my sense of obligation which had left him the day's victory. But there was admiration too—and an affection which left me embarrassed. "Don't worry, there'll be no interruption of your routine. I promise."

"It's been a fine, diverting weekend, Pierce." We pumped hands. "Good for both Nancy and me. Very grateful."

"God, it was good seeing you." Pierce kneaded my shoulder some more and I could swear his eyes were filling. "We'll do it again soon. Would you and Nancy come down again?"

"Sometime. We'd love to."

"Maybe over the Fourth?"

"Maybe," I said. I took a backward step and looked at the door. "Will you say good-bye and thanks to your mother?"

"Want to say it yourself?"

"Wouldn't she be asleep?"

He shook his head and beckoned me to follow. We went along the hall, past prints of old ships, I breathless, tiptoe, for the house was hushed as a holy place. But Pierce rapped confidently at his mother's door, and presently she called, *"Entrez, entrez!"*

Melissa de Villepin was in bed. Her breakfast tray, a great wicker affair sprouting a yellow rose, bridged her knees, while combed, powdered and bed-jacketed, she was nested in little pillows.

"Oh, you're not going so early, Ben," she said and tossed a newspaper to the floor in a display of disappointment.

"I'm afraid I must," I said. "But it's been a wonderful time for Nancy and me."

"Oh, wasn't it a lovely party last night," she purred. "Victor and I enjoyed ourselves. Did you and Nancy? Really? Oh good, I'm so glad. Yes, there are such nice young people here this year. But you must have left the Beach early. We didn't see you at *all*. So you see, you can't go, really. There are all these things I wanted to talk to you about. Oh, Pierce darling, do run along for an instant and let me talk to Ben—would you? Thank you, angel."

Pierce rolled his eyes comically and marched from the room.

"I do want to ask you about Pierce." Her voice lowered to a conspiratorial whisper. "How you think he is—how he's behaving, you know? And your sweet wife, that Nancy. I'd hoped to get to know her and now you're taking her away."

"Actually I'm not, Mrs. de Villepin. She's elected to stay for a sail. Pierce is taking the girls out on the *Bluejay* and flying them up this afternoon."

"Oh?" Melissa raised her eyebrows. "How are you getting home?"

"The bus . . . No, no—I don't mind. I have some work to do."

She smiled. "But you're not altogether pleased."

"Not altogether. It's all right, though."

"Oh good." She plumped a couple of pillows at her back and leaned into them luxuriously. "Ben, do sit down for just an instant—right there, please. I'm dying to know what you think about my poor darling boy. Is he all right?"

"I don't know." I sat on the edge of the chaise longue as she had directed. "He seems fine to me."

"I do hope he's not going to be one of those men who take forever to settle down. Don't you think it's just a matter of the right circumstances coming along? The flying field seems to absorb him—still, I wonder if it's enough, if he won't find that disappointing after . . ." She groped about for a Kleenex, with which she dabbed at the corners of her mouth. "Did he talk to you at all? Do you think he's serious about any particular girl?"

"Well, you never can tell with Pierce, and he's known her less than two days, but he does seem taken with Lily . . ." She seemed bewildered by this, and I added, "Lily Parsons, the girl who's staying here."

"Yes. Yes, I know. But do you really think . . ." For the moment that she contemplated these possibilities, various lines sprouted around her mouth and eyes, aging her a decade, then vanished magically in a brightening smile. "Now *why* doesn't that please me, Ben? She's a pretty girl, isn't she?"

"Yes."

"Well, I mean not a *great* beauty, but attractive. There's nothing cheap or flashy— Oh, Ben, if you could see some of the girls Pierce has brought home to frighten me. It's a wonder I haven't turned white." Melissa's hand rose to her short, carefully tended pink-blond hair. "No, it's because she's *so* serious. I should rejoice, shouldn't I, at the thought of his being interested in a clever, serious girl, someone who'd keep him from overdoing the drink and all the foolish things he's capable of. But somehow I think a girl like Lily Parsons might ask too much of Pierce, and you know, he couldn't bear that."

"I think you're right."

"He's a darling, of course, and filled with courage and imagination and all kinds of wonderful ideas, just like his father, but he's only happy when he's running things, you know. He has to be in charge." Melissa heaved a long sigh as though to say that was the end of that and we must proceed to happier aspects. "She must see that too. She's an intelligent girl. She wouldn't have set her cap . . ."

"She might have."

"Oh? Well, dear Ben. I do hope you can be of help to him. Sometimes I feel I'm not any at all. Just be*cause* I love him so much and understand—oh, all too well—what he's going through. Try as I will to help him find his way among all the doubts and uncertainties about himself . . ."

"Doubts?"

"Oh *yes,* Ben. And he trusts you, you know. He has from the very beginning. I knew. From the time he brought you to Sunday lunch."

There was a tapping at the open door and I looked up to find Nancy there asking if she could join us. I was pleased, and not so terribly surprised, to find her now dressed for the bus trip to Cambridge.

"Well, my dear." Melissa held out a hand to Nancy. "I'm miserable to think of you going off like this, but it is a good idea not to let Ben go alone. That's how men get into the worst kind of trouble—when you leave them by themselves for too long, poor things. And that old boat isn't as glorious as Pierce would have you believe. I've been deathly ill on it." Hopefully she asked, "How did you persuade Lily to go back with you?"

"Oh, but I didn't," Nancy replied. "Lily's staying. I think Pierce is bringing her up this afternoon."

"Ah—" Melissa said. "I wonder. You don't imagine she's planning a longer stay?" She looked from Nancy to me, eager to be reassured.

"Oh, I don't think she'll be staying over," Nancy said. "She has to be back in Boston first thing tomorrow. She has to be at the Agassiz at nine-thirty."

"I see," Melissa said, her mind not fully set to rest, recalling, I suppose, any number of house guests who in enjoying themselves too fully had failed to depart on schedule. "Well, she must, I'm afraid. One of the servants is ill and has gone off to Providence for some shock treatments and there are guests for dinner. It wouldn't be convenient at all. Are they planning to go out in the boat alone—just the two of them? Oh, I do wish they wouldn't."

The cloud of her concern hung oppressively over the leave-taking. And even with the smile and squeeze of hands, the invitation to come again, she seemed to be adding some new responsibility to my baggage.

"You won't forget, Ben," she said, waving. "You won't forget our little talk?"

Descending that grand curving staircase (for the last time, as it turned out), I noted the picnic basket plump with luncheon for four and a wicker-covered ice bucket from which protruded the slim green necks of two bottles of Moselle.

*　　　　*　　　　*

About a year later—it was early summer of 1949—we had a cable from Paris: *Revolutionary celebrations here culminate in our wedding July 14 say you'll come. Lily and Pierce.*

It had all the marks of a spoof. I decided they had met accidentally and composed it of one part cognac and two of mischief. We never considered going, but when Nancy discovered a notice of the marriage in the *Tribune,* I wrote Pierce, wishing him happiness and proposing a party for their return.

I had an abrupt reply, a postcard with a view of the café Aux Deux Magots. I deciphered the scrawled, unsigned message as, *Now it's sanctioned by church and state, in each of seven wonders we'll fornicate. Might never come back. Adieu.*

PART THREE

Cambridge

1951

 **12**

The winter of 1951 was a bleak one for Utopians. It began in even contest—the visionaries howling over the pillorying of Alger Hiss, while the hard-nosed demanded the Bomb be dropped on Moscow without delay.

Just before Christmas we suffered a humiliating rout in Korea. In six months of undeclared war the U.N.—or U.S., depending on your persuasion—had suffered forty-six thousand casualties and now MacArthur had abandoned Seoul and was retreating toward Pusan, looking much like a man about to be pushed into the sea. Harry Truman's hair had turned white in the past year and an oppressive odor of doom hung over all endeavor.

Then, with the year still young, there was a tidal change. The Eighth Army began to push the Communists back up the peninsula. And this was attributed less to the brilliance of its new commander, General Ridgway, than to the amazing vitality of American industry. Under "Engine Charlie" Wilson, Detroit was going to win the war. So the winter ended in a sunburst of self-confidence and a clear decision for the practical businessmen. The belief flourished that our only vulnerableness lay in the wide and undiscerning eyes of the pinkos, in our tolerating the likes of William Remington (misguided, Ivy League, Red) or in sparing the likes of Julius and Ethel Rosenberg (obdurate, villainous, City College, traitors).

One afternoon in late March of that year, the secretary I shared with two other probationists at Black, Baer & Aspinwall, reported she had a man on the phone who wanted to speak to me but refused to give his name. When asked his business, he said he was treasurer of the Chelsea Communist Party chapter, that he had been suspended from his job at the naval shipyard following an accident on a destroyer and needed counsel.

A moment later she came back to say the man was insistent, he wouldn't be put off. I came truculently onto the line. "We're extremely busy here at this season and we aren't soliciting new business," I told him, "but even if that were not so, we would not be interested in representing anonymous clients. I'm sure there are firms here in Boston who feel otherwise."

In my receiver I heard a voice strangling in its own laughter. "Oh my," it gasped as the man gained some control of himself, "spoken like a loyal citizen." It was Pierce, absolutely stricken with delight. "We're doing a spot check down here at the State House, making sure you fellows are coming up with the right answers."

"You dreadful bastard, Jay! Where are you? Is Lily with you? Is the endless honeymoon over at last?"

"Scarcely begun, but we're told our country needs us, and so, rich in old-world wisdom, we're here . . . What? Oh, absolutely, Mose, all seven. Well, no, I must confess it didn't work out entirely to our satisfaction. Rhodes was all right. It's a decent enough place, and we managed under the Colossus in broad daylight, not a soul around. But some of the others— I mean it's *cold* on top of a pyramid at night. A fellow could freeze his dingbat off, and it's one hell of a walk up there. You know, it turns out I was mistaken on the tower and the Taj. Too new. Weren't even built when they made up the list, I guess. Most of them are in Turkey and Egypt, and the Arabs don't give a damn for their antiquities. The Hanging Gardens of Babylon, Christ, it's in Iraq, and a mile away they never heard of it. I don't blame them either, because it's the town dump, rusty cans and evil-smelling carcasses strewn all over. Oh, we made it all right. Lily's nothing if not determined, but it was not up to the lovely promise of that name. It may surprise you to learn, Mose, that one of the best places I know for screwing is right here at the Ritz, no kidding. I'll never wander too far from a sound flush toilet in good working order again and I advise you to do the same. Oh—that's what I called about. We've found a house in Cambridge, a Victorian monster on Linnaean Street and Lily loves it. I want you to buy it for us—really. Title search, pass papers, closing, all that legal foolishness. Can you do that for us? Oh, positively, yes, I mean it. We're going to finish our education. Lily can get her master's in a year— No, anthropology. She's really something, you know. Every place we went she'd poke around the museums and then sit on the edge of a rubble pile, staring at it with a boozy expression, putting the things back up—temple, marketplace, steam baths, whorehouse and all, people coming and going. She never minds the bedbugs or the lousy food so long as there's another heap of rocks to see. Puts me to shame. Oh, right—when *do* we get together. We've been back since last month, you know, but we've waited until now so we'd have all our slides to show you. The whole show takes a hair under seven hours and I know you don't want to miss a minute of it—when's good for you?"

*   *   *

They came to our little apartment on Chestnut Street later in the week. It was the ground floor and garden of one of the old Federal houses and you entered it through a long brick-arched tunnel that was supposed to have passed cows down to graze in the Common. I can recall the stunning sight Lily made in emerging from it, laughing at Nancy and me on the doorstep with our open arms, Pierce looming behind and loping toward us in outsize strides with a great, hungry grin. She wore a short, comically shaggy coat, the pelt of an unpronounceable Himalayan animal, and there were a few flecks of snow glistening in it and in her hair, which she had cut short, like a boy's. It was a new "poodle" style that was becoming to her and she looked more self-contained than ever, as though she had been brushed by that certainty and knowledge of well-bred European girls.

There was a kiss for me, full, square and warm with emotion, a curious kind of kiss that was generous, without any holding back, yet asked for nothing in return. Beneath the curly coat, Lily wore a dress of heavy saffron-colored material, so simply cut that even I, who know nothing of fashion, recognized its perfection.

As I made the drinks I could hear Nancy, whose interest in clothes was absolute, cross-examining Lily about its source, while Lily, whose slim, boyish figure and panther grace absorbed beautiful clothes and made them part of her, was vague and perfunctory about them. The dress came from someplace in Athens, she thought. Yes, it had spoken to her from a window but now she had to pull the collar around for a glimpse of the label before recalling its name.

We sat around the fire with our drinks, listening to her account of the balance of their journey. In contrast to Pierce, she had found the Seven Wonders more gratifying than even she had anticipated. The pyramids bathed in moonlight, with the surrounding desert stretching like a milky sea into the past, were exalting. The sight lifted you right from your shoes to send you soaring like a Daedalus.

I was comparing their versions, wondering which was the more accurate, and then, how the act was accomplished, whether with joy and abandon and laughter—or resolutely, like an explorer planting the flag on a mountain peak. I wondered if they brought a blanket and disrobed or if she simply snatched up her skirt and they went about their coition in some shadowed corner, like slum kids in a tenement doorway.

Come to think of it, watching her in the firelight, so very

young, so slight, it seemed no coarsening had spoiled Lily's face or figure during the nearly two years of her marriage. She'd kept that virginal look. Remarkable. So often marriage, sometimes overnight, turned a swift runner of a girl into a sow, as though nature had snatched away the bright buttons of allure to put them somewhere needed, leaving the poor creature stunned, dull of eye, to waddle about her drudgeries without even a memory of beauty.

I made the masochistic effort of imagining them naked together, Lily's lovely hams spreading to receive a huge Pierce, her great eyes dazing, their lids fluttering together in transport—and mercifully, I could not. Here beside me she was far too civilized, too independent, too animated, her small blunt hands busy in the air as she described the Zeus at Olympia. It was this unquenched enthusiasm of hers that for an instant led me to think Lily Parsons had not been wholly attained, surely not domesticated—that in her heart lodged a tiny splinter of discontent.

As I filled the Jays' glasses with my coldest, clearest martini, he said, "It's funny what's happened to us since Paris. I thought we might never come back, you know—that there was so much to see and learn there, so much that has stood the test of time and makes everything here flimsy by comparison, that it would take a lifetime to absorb a meaningful part of it and that we might settle down someplace in Paris or Rome or maybe in one of the million beautiful places in between. There must be a hundred paradises strung along the Mediterranean shore and across the islands of the Aegean, Mose, each more beguiling than the last—and yet I'd always have the feeling we'd been in one too long, or not long enough, to feel comfortable—you know what I mean?"

"Maybe because you lacked something to do. If you'd had some project—"

"Here, here." Lily said as though my obvious suggestion was a cudgel of her own. "A man did offer him a job, you know."

Pierce laughed. "Coca-Cola, for God's sake. Bringing the

fruits of our great culture to the heathen. There's a crusade
for you."

"Well, no, you wouldn't have cinched a Nobel prize," Lily
said, "but it might have been fun. It was operating a bottling
plant in Rabat and it paid a huge salary, really. The Arabs
can't drink alcohol but they love sitting in cafés and they positively dote on Coke. A big house overlooking the sea went
with the deal. I thought he ought to take it. How would you
know whether you liked doing a thing like that until you
tried it?"

Pierce shook his head firmly. "I can find better things to do
with my time any day." Reaching across the arm of the sofa,
he clutched my forearm with such affection, a wringing of my
flesh, that I laughed in pain. And recalling this familiar exuberance of Pierce's, I found it hard to remember where we
were in time. For an instant it seemed we were still eighteen,
that a decade had not passed, that we had not divided and
subdivided ourselves as in fact we had.

"No, that wasn't the problem," he was saying. "I could always find ways to occupy myself. Only idiots need some task
—busywork to keep their minds off their bowels and their
penises and their death. I met a man, an Englishman, in
Capri who had never worked in all his life. He had read
everything and traveled the world and he seemed to me one
of the wisest, wittiest men I'd ever met. I used to go to this
café in the square every day to sit and drink with him."

"He was charming," Lily said, "but an old faker. I don't
think he was a good influence on you at *all*."

" 'Any idiot can hold a job,' he'd say. 'Any fool can fill his
days in shuffling papers about. He'll be praised for it, paid for
it and thus he'll feel useful and important because of it. His
wife approves, for it keeps him out of the brothels and bar-
rooms' "—Pierce cast Lily a provocative glance—" 'but to
defy the custom of simply occupying yourself with these insig-
nificant tasks and thus be able to enjoy the world—to look at
people and really see them, not as customers, but reflections
of yourself, to read the best they have written, to search out

beauty in nature and art, to listen to music and the sound of the wind and the sea, to feel the sun—that takes a real artist at living.' That's what really puts the demands on a man, Mose —to live beautifully and fully without, in the eyes of your fellows, doing a damned thing."

"Not everyone can afford it," I said.

I awaited his tart response, but instead, the barb I had thrown so haphazardly found its way, stuck, like a banderilla in bull withers, irritating and distracting him. We watched him swirl the last of his martini in the bottom of the glass and toss it off. A shadow of humility spread across those haughty eyes. Then he shook his massive head, and flinging aside the pesky pricking there, got on with it.

Holding his glass out to the shaker's spout, Pierce said, "I'd had enough of being away. It was sudden. We were sitting on the terrace of a hotel in Tangier, eavesdropping on some Americans, consular people, talking about politics at home, and I looked down at my disguise, the sandals and sailor shirt, and it displeased me. I saw the fraud. The wine and peculiar cooking which had so beguiled me now stuck in my throat."

"It's true," Lily said. "Homesickness hit him hard."

He smiled but a glance flicked her a warning. "It was the whole idea of expatriate existence. It disgusted me. And I suppose it was some kind of call, as though I were being summoned—you know what I mean? As though it were really important that I return. You understand, Ben?"

"I don't quite. Some mission here? What *are* you going to do?"

"I'm going to *learn*." Pierce's eyes swept around the circle we made. They danced, as always, suggesting he might be making fun of himself, and yet his face had gone brick-hard with conviction. "I'm going to make up for the years I wasted when I should have been getting an education. I'm going to be my own G.I. bill."

"A degree?" I asked.

"No, no. No tags. Pure curiosity. Except, of course, at the back of my mind is the idea there's no better way of turning up my—whatever it is I'm meant to be doing—my métier."

"You see," Lily said, "he cannot bring himself to say *job.*"

"I've had a job," he said, "and I didn't like it enough to take one away from anybody."

"You *did?*" Nancy asked.

"I was a reporter."

"Oh, of course. On the Newport paper. I *do* remember."

Lily smiled blandly and then turned to me. "Don't you think you have to have a job—not necessarily a big job; not the chairman of the board or anything like that, but maybe a paper route—before you're entitled to opinions?"

"To an *audience* for them . . ." But as I answered her I was losing mine to my son, who was also unemployed, who had awakened crossly in our bedroom. He could now be heard working up his indignation and in no time he had arrived at a trembling rage at the world's indifference to him. It was a sound that even after four months unnerved me, and Jay, who had never been at close quarters with an infant, did not hide his dismay.

"What's the matter with the baby?" he asked. "Is it sick?"

"It's the rattle of the ice cubes," Nancy explained. "He's a temperance nut and he hates the cocktail hour. He complains about it every evening."

Pierce looked at Lily. "That would drive me up the wall— a noise like that."

"They're supposed to get over it eventually," Nancy said.

"That's interesting, your reaction to a baby crying," Lily said. "Do you think it wants something of you?"

Pierce shook his head. "It's the terror. Listen . . . are you sure . . ."

"It's not all milk and rattles," Lily said. "When you wake up you're never sure they haven't gone off and left you." She was looking coolly at her husband. "If we should have one it'll sound like that." She put her glass on the coffee table and stood up. "Can we go see him?"

Nancy, eagerly on her feet at Lily's suggestion, laughed at Jay's anguish. "Don't worry. You won't have to hold him."

"Why not?" Lily asked.

"He'll stop crying if you leave him alone," I said. "If you bring him out here we won't be able to talk, for God's sake." I looked at Jay helplessly as Lily and Nancy left. "I agree with you. They're a pain in the ass. I haven't a notion what women see in them."

"You get up at three? Give him his bottle? That kind of thing?"

"I have. I've read somewhere that over the years there's a reward. We'll see. When he's old enough to ride a horse or carry on an intelligent conversation, I'll have him brought to me."

"But you don't get any big charge out of him? You don't look at him and feel immortal."

"No. Oh, there was a sort of awe and wonder when I first saw him. I couldn't believe I had sired a child. It's the closest I expect to get to taking part in a miracle. But it's lost now— lost on one of those midwatches—like part of a dream. No, I don't have any particular response to him. He's not interested in me—just his stomach. We share a woman, and at times he seems to be getting better than his share."

Through the door I heard the clang of the diaper can.

"Well, it can wait," he said. "It's fine to have them when you know what you're about, as you do—but having kids would be a disaster for us. We've got to be free for a while, to work out the essentials." He looked up apprehensively as Nancy returned, bearing Ben, blanketed, red-faced, and still ticking with reserves of wrath.

Lily followed and sat down between Nancy and me and became wholly absorbed in the baby's reactions. After looking around the room, it fastened on Pierce, exchanged glares and instantly began to cry again.

"Go on," I said to Pierce. "We mustn't let him take over. He will, you know. You were telling about your G.I. bill." I poured more drinks. "What kind of course will you take?"

He gave my squalling son a wary look and set out to ignore him. "Astronomy," he said, "so I can learn how really puny and laughable our endeavors are—so I can learn how brief our lifetime is, and so be sure never to waste a second of it in some nonsense—in things that aren't important."

We realized simultaneously that the crying had stopped and looked to see that Lily now held young Ben. He had quietly inserted his thumb in his mouth and nestled an ear against her breast. As she cradled my son in her arms, Lily's expression was blissful as his and I was moved—sweetly, erotically and with great force.

"And either Russian or Chinese," Pierce was saying, "so I can learn at first hand what the other guys are saying about us, so I can try to make some single path of understanding between us, even if it's only between me and one other person. That's the main thing, Ben, before we blow our whole civilization to bits. Don't you agree?"

We began to talk in general terms now, about what we believed, and after a few minutes of it I realized we were sparring, touching little raw places and then skirting them, finding that we really disagreed, that, astonishingly, Pierce had developed one of those proudly liberal attitudes which in that era people bore like the cross, but in fact were flimsy things built of emotionalism and nailed together with ideas about the way humans should, rather than the way they do, behave. It was a point of view which I was beginning to find not just irritating, but irresponsible.

"Well, I don't suppose we'd better get on to Hiss, had we," Pierce said at last, "but if you want to know what I think, it's this. He's sincere. He really believes in whatever he's done, whether it's foolish or wise. If he's a fool, he's one on the grand scale, and I believe this country is big enough and strong enough to allow for that, for everybody to believe what they want. That's the basic idea here, isn't it? That's what freedom means—to believe in what*ever* kind of god or form of government your reason leads you to."

"Oh come on, Pierce. You're not so naïve as to believe the C.P. is a political faith, or a native third party out to help the poor. You *know* what it is."

And that became the bone on which Pierce and I gnawed for the balance of the evening—growling, backing off at Nancy and Lily's insistence, yet returning grimly, without hoping to persuade the other but because we could not accept this really fundamental disagreement in someone close. And intimacy had prevailed tonight. Occasionally a familiar feeling had crept over me, that Pierce "had been around," as we used to say, was a kind of elder brother with a greater wisdom of the world. Yet I was convinced that liberalism, in a man of his background, was a borrowing from shipboard acquaintance and the rootless life he had been leading, rather than true conviction.

The evening, which had begun as joyous reunion, ended in constraint and discord.

*   *   *

"I feel sorry for that poor girl," I said to Nancy as we went to bed. "That's a precarious arrangement. I'll give it another six months."

"Oh, really? Isn't that funny. I didn't have that reaction at all. I thought they were getting along fairly well. He's taking this exploratory voyage, which I don't propose to understand but I don't see any harm in it. He can afford it. You want him to be doing what *you* do, and he'd be lousy at it."

"What about the drinking? Lily had to help him going up the steps—you notice that? She must put him to bed every other night. And oh God, as if that weren't enough, he's gone parlor pink."

"I didn't take that seriously. He was just showing off, trying to get your goat."

"Listen, I know *Pierce*. He's serious, all right. I had the feeling he'd go marching off to Moscow in the morning if he could only find the way. It's not easy to find if you've inherited three million bucks."

Nancy laughed. "I think you can count on that."

"I wonder." I turned out the light. Outside, a small car labored up the hill, its lights passing through the window curtains. Beside me Nancy lay, stiff. "He isn't going to come up with any formula, for God's sake. For a man it's work. That's the only answer. He thinks there's something else. It's funny —both of you swallowing all that crap of his like a couple of schoolgirls. You're bewitched by him."

"Well, of course I am, even more so now. Oh, you needn't feel you've inflicted any punishment on Lily. I mean, it's no mystery to *me* she's attracted to him. And the jeopardy itself makes him exciting, and the waywardness—oh sure, the re-forming urge in every woman—the taming of wild loco animals."

"I never can understand that. Something physical?"

"Sure." Then, at my groan, Nancy laughed, touched my arm. "Oh no, not like you, dearie. I'd never feel comfortable and protected and looked after with Pierce. No danger of my slipping off with him some dark night—even if he'd have me."

"They're quarreling," I said. "They were on the edge of several open wounds tonight—the baby, the job."

"Not convincing evidence, sir. We quarrel regularly and I think we're happy. It might be more alarming, given Pierce and Lily, if they didn't."

"They aren't committed. They're still a couple traveling together, and watching to see if it's going to take."

"Well, they're neither of them domestic types. Lily's a maverick in her own right. She'll probably never make a conventional wife. She's not an intellectual—at least, not what I think of as one—but a natural bohemian. She doesn't think about how it looks, she just is. She's sure of her heart, and it leads her. So long as she cares—I'm not worried about them." There was a very long silence in which I thought she was drifting into sleep, and then she said slowly, "Would you like to sleep with Lily?"

"No, for God's sake." I pulled Nancy to me. "Too skinny. I like a lot of woman."

*　　　　*　　　　*

I had scarcely arrived at the office next day when Pierce rang. His voice, clear as a spring morning, without a trace of last night's rancors or ill effects of my hospitality, dispelled my own lingering disappointment and cheerfully insisted we meet to inspect the house in Cambridge.

It was a monstrous, ugly place, built in the nineties as a rectory and parish house for St. Crystosom's Church. Even in the postwar housing shortage, it had stood idle, gathering cobwebs in its narrow Gothic windows and sinking slowly into its thicket of syringa. The effluvia of bean suppers and ancient plumbing which persisted in the corridors was so alien to the Pierce Jay I had known that I tried to dissuade him.

"Why not look at one of those new towers along the Charles, or near us on Beacon Hill. This place is too big. What do you want with a sixteen-room house? You must be planning a family, a huge one, to consider an ark like this."

"Not at all," he said, forcing open a door to a room at the back of the house. "We're going to need plenty of space for work. Lily's taking the study and this is going to be my office, with a desk looking down into the garden."

Peering out, I saw a jungle of dried stalks and branches poking up through the slush. "Wait," he said. "The Rector was a magician in the garden. That's wisteria on the arbor—a pair of plums. And the box is a maze. A little pruning and it'll be a Versailles down there. See the building?" I did—a stable with a precarious lean and a ravaged cupola. "That's ours too. Make a fine studio."

"What about that great barn of a meeting room? Absolutely useless and impossible to heat."

"Parties. We'll give everyone fur coats."

I walked into the bathroom, where spots of color from the stained-glass window played in a long, narrow tub whose ball-and-claw legs were planted on the brown linoleum amid pools of flaking paint. "I thought you were never going to separate yourself again from functional plumbing."

"It functions. They don't build stuff like that any more."

A chain fell from the oaken box which clung to the wall overhead, threatening the toilet bowl, and when I gave it a tug, a faint sigh floated down to us—but no water.

"It's turned off."

"How much are they asking? No—let me guess. Eighty-five hundred—and they're holding their breath."

"Not quite. Seventeen thousand. If you think you can get it for less—fine. But don't risk losing it."

"All right—but let me get something straight. This is Lily's idea?"

He looked offended. "She likes the house—but no more than I."

*   *   *

Later that afternoon I bought the St. Crystosom's rectory for the Jays at fifteen thousand—and my wonder increased as they promptly put twice that sum into its refurbishing. Outside, the house became pale gray and lilac, accentuating the Gothic sorceries and giving it the appearance, on that sober street, of stage scenery. Inside, it became a museum, with mementos of their travels and signs of their hopes displayed as though for guided tours.

The entrance hall was an Algiers street corner. Ocher pots, ample enough to conceal a two-hundred-pound genie, sprouted blue-tasseled elephant grass. On whitewashed walls, Lily had splashed shop fronts, the keyhole windows of a brothel with a glimpse of a veiled face. A functional flower box sprouted fresh anemones, and the last house was marked by a real sign, lettered in Arabic and French, Rue des Cambistes.

Pierce was proudest of his office, where he had had built a semicircular desk that resembled the organ consoles one used to see at giant metropolitan movie houses. It contained files, dictaphone, electric typewriter, telephone and tier on tier of pigeonholes. The center of the console was cut away to allow a view of the now flourishing garden.

"What do you do here?" I was looking at the reference

books, the *Editor and Publisher,* a journalism directory, *Who's Who.*

"Two hours of Chinese every day. I found a summer course. The astronomy begins in September."

Fixed to the wall with pushpins were a dozen matted enlargements, and while I recalled that in college Pierce had owned a pair of expensive cameras with which he took snapshots, I realized these rather arty studies in light and shade were clearly his. There were some fishing boats nestled on still water, an old man ascending a narrow, twisting flight of steps toward a bright patch, and one which hypnotized me. At the foot of a thick, fluted column, pitted like blue cheese, lay Lily, nude, kitten-curled, eyes closed as though in sleep.

"Any more of these?"

"Yes—but you can't see them, you old goat." He crossed the room and regarded a long table. "Come look at this." It was a display of magazines: *Time, Newsweek, Current Affairs,* and a fourth, strange to me, called *Colonnade.* I flipped some pages and found it a weekly which drew on already-published newspaper columns to present current issues in both sides of their controversy. The question of review boards and the firing of government employees on reasonable doubt of their loyalty was one I happened on, with Westbrook Pegler on the one side and Drew Pearson on the other. The reader, presumably, was left free to draw his own conclusion.

"It's a magazine of opinion, you see," Pierce explained. "The others are of fact, or rather they pretend to be. They make opinion seem like fact. This is opinion properly handled. What do you think of it?"

"I haven't seen it before. Is it new?"

"Very. Not even on the stands yet." He pointed to the price, twenty cents. "It cost me more. It's a dummy."

Turning to the masthead, I found his name buried in its midst as an associate publisher. While I did not reveal my doubts then, it did occur to me that though it was clever and might intrigue intelligent readers, most of us avoid dilemmas where we can, that the appeal of the columnists, like that of the news magazines, lay less in their perceptiveness than in their blinders.

*　　　　　*　　　　　*

Nancy and I had assumed we were going to integrate the Jays into *our* Boston. I had already described him to some of my friends in the State Street trust offices and brokerages. It seemed logical that if he were casting about with his money on ventures such as *Colonnade,* these alert contemporaries of mine would find him interesting and in turn could provide him with projects far more likely to sustain his interest than a course in Chinese.

And so Nancy, who was equally eager to display the splendorous Jays to her friends, arranged a dinner party. We selected our guests carefully and invited more of them than we had ever entertained in our small apartment.

"There are some people coming tonight I think you'll enjoy," I told Pierce as I poured him a preliminary drink. "Most of them are Harvard types, but intelligent, you know, not obsessed with the market the way they are in New York. That's what I like about it here. We meet for lunch, some of us, at the University or the Racquet Club, a couple of times a week, and we're as likely to be talking about new books as business. If you'd like to join us, come along any time. Just let me know . . ." I had an eye on the door, where Nancy was welcoming a group of four. "By the way, how is the *Colonnade* thing working out?"

"It folded."

"Oh, too bad. Well, I had my doubts. I didn't want to say anything at the time. You didn't have much money in it, did you?"

"Enough."

"What a shame," I said. "Ah—there's Gordon, striped tie. He's the live wire at Grimm and Fuller, with all kinds of bright ideas. He's working on some oil leases you'll probably hear about."

Pierce gave me a curious, amused look.

As I listened to the icebreaking conversations, I thought we had arranged it well. I was taking pride in the brightness of our party. Even the wives, who tended to flock and compare formulas, were chatting with other people's husbands and making comment that was beyond my expectations. The revelations of the Kefauver hearings on crime were a novelty on television and made the preliminaries, but soon gave way to the more sensitive issues, McCarthyism and the unruly Douglas MacArthur, whose threats of an attack on the China mainland had just caused Truman to fire him.

I had been keeping an eye on the Jays throughout, and while Lily moved easily about, listening earnestly, flattering our friends by remembering their names and displaying an almost hyperbolic interest in their jobs, Pierce was elusive. He ducked sullenly, as though bored, away from each group as it locked in discussion. I saw Jeff Gordon's amiable smile fade as Pierce left him abruptly to join the one unattached girl we had asked—largely for her decorativeness.

My disappointment with Pierce turned acute as I heard his voice rise out of the babble, loud as a horn and slurred, "No —you've got it wrong, my friend. What you probably don't know—very few people do—is that Styles Bridges and Mac-Arthur were both Communists back in the twenties." He was addressing two men who stood flanking the kitchen door. One of them laughed, but Pierce fended it, rebuked him with a haughty silence. There was a curl of nastiness to his mouth, which I recalled from years ago, and it was felt around the room.

"No need to believe me. It's all coming out next week, how the whole Chiang conspiracy, invasion of the mainland and all, is a Commie trick to suck the U.S. fleet into Hong Kong and make another Pearl Harbor of it. It's going to be the big stink of the year." He was talking directly to Gordon now, daring him to challenge.

I found Lily only mildly concerned. From a footstool at the edge of the fireplace, she was ignoring her husband. A glass cradled in her hands, she was looking indifferently around the room, noting reactions. When my eyes caught hers, she grinned as though to say, "You never know with Pierce, do you? But at least he's never dull." And thus reassured, I looked for some agreeable, high-spirited climax to Pierce's performance.

As I tried to divert attention I could hear him rejecting arguments, serious and facetious ones, skating on the edge of rudeness to these friends of ours who had gathered in his honor. Next, to my dismay, since it was scarcely ten, Pierce and Lily were emerging from the bedroom, coats in hand. Linking an arm with hers, he made a circuit of our astonished party, saying his goodnights in a formal way, and left.

My indignation eased with a suspicion that he had somehow taken offense—felt the pigeon here among the eager financiers—just as Nancy's did at the generous reaction of our other guests. No one appeared offended. There was a willingness to excuse him. I heard speculation about whether he had a worrisome obligation elsewhere or perhaps had been suffering a temporary illness. There was a lot of twenty-four-hour flu going around. Several people spoke of the curious sense of loss after the Jays had gone and Gordon assured me Pierce had intended no rudeness but rather wanted to communicate some message, an unusual if obscure—oh, *that,* all right—truth about ourselves and times.

Still, it was plain the Jays were not embracing our circle of friends, nor us, for that matter. After Lily's call thanking Nancy for the party, there was a seven-week silence. Knowing they were not hermits, we suffered from hurt and a curiosity about whom they *were* seeing.

Then, in mid-June, came Lily's invitation to dinner and a feeling of reprieve from banishment. Yes, precisely, for we had imagined that in the interim the Jays had been establishing court in Linnaean Street, gathering about them clever and attractive people from Lily's North Shore and from the cosmopolitan camp around Harvard and MIT.

We dressed with great care, Nancy trying on several dresses and discarding them as being too this or that for a party where we half expected to find President Conant or Cabot Lodge. But among the first guests I encountered on the Rue des Cambistes was a fellow with hair like wood shavings, dressed in dungarees and sneakers. He gave my dark suit and black shoes a disdainful glance as he moved into the big room, which was now decked with mechanistic sculpture and abstract paintings. At one end hung a huge tapestry portraying a purple earth shattering under a bright orange atomic burst.

Pierce himself was presiding unaided at the bar, asking new arrivals their preference in drink before presenting them with juleps which stood in a field before him. There was no residue of chilliness from the night of our party. He was effusively glad to see us, with a great hug for Nancy and an exuberant stuffing of my glass with mint sprigs, making a bouquet.

Then, leaving his post, he bobbed out from behind the bar, and seizing us by our arms, surveyed the sea of faces, every one strange to us. "Now let's see—who don't you know here . . ."

Spotting Lily, the center of a group in the corner, I moved in her direction.

"No, no," Pierce said and, in his high spirits, danced a little shuffle. "I want you to meet some of these people. Fascinating, some of them. That's the point. Here you go." And mumbling some nonsense about my interest in antiquities, he propelled us into a nearby foursome.

The circle proved intensely archeological. Our presence acknowledged, it got right on with its business, and for us it was an experience like smothering. We listened to the halibut-faced man, then the full-breasted woman in bangs, and as the sites—Kirkuk, Barda-Balka, Karim-Shahir—were multiplied by classifications—Kassite, Würm, Mesolithic—and then by the equally curious names of people in their department, I thought they had left off English entirely, and parting the foliage in my glass, I gratefully buried my nose.

Nancy's determined smile was an indication of her belief that there was no such thing as a party where she could not have a good time, but I felt a growing annoyance with Jay and cast about for recourse. Lily had vanished from her corner, replaced by a young Chinese wearing the other dark suit.

I eavesdropped hopefully on the group beside us, where a pair of girls made an audience for a square, owlish fellow in green corduroy. "All right, I'll tell you what we should do," he was saying, "one thing or the other. Either you live by the Torah, follow as closely as you can every ancient tradition and custom, without concern for how queer you look—or else you abandon Jewishness altogether. The Jewish religion is not the same as the Christian. A Jew must worship God in a temple and He cannot be barbered up to look like George Washington. Liebman is full of shit—you know that?"

I pulled Nancy back from the anthropological circle and it closed with a snap. "I don't believe this is accidental," I said, looking around. "Pierce's done this on purpose. It's vengeance."

"The party?" Nancy was amused at me. "Why do you say that—because there aren't any lawyers?"

"All right—you go talk to them."

She glanced around us, appraising one group after another. "Well, we can't just stand here talking to one another."

Lily's short hair bobbed provocatively across the room and, catching her eye, I waved our desperation. We moved toward her with hope rekindled, to find her listening so intently to a slender man that she seemed unaware of our hovering. He had a tousled, academic look, and in the warmth of the room, and of his own enthusiasm, was removing his jacket.

"At two and three in the morning," he was telling her in an accent I could not place, "crying like wolves and shattering glass as they go. Really, the light outside our front door fell to a scholar's hand only last night. No, no, no. Not out of rancor toward me. We are quite fond of one another by day, or at the very least—curious, you know, respectfully curious of one another. No, it is pure alcoholic exuberance."

"Well, I'm not defending it," Lily said, "but it *is* one of the

freedoms. I forget which. I mean, American boys are supposed to learn how to drink in college. It used to be the *only*
thing."

"I'm sorry. It may be part of a man's education, but not the
university's part. The father's? The mother's? I don't know
whose—but not mine!"

Still under the fellow's animated spell, Lily at last acknowledged and presented us to Julien Weiss. "Come on, all of
you. Come in the kitchen while I do something about the lob-
sters—but go on, Julie, how do German freshmen learn to
hold their schnapps?"

"In a bar, of course. A bar is the proper place for violence
and being sick—not the university."

"Hold on," Pierce said, catching us on the threshold of the
kitchen, where a pair of ladies, who might have been left over
from the last St. Crystosom's guild meeting, were arranging
platters. "I want you to meet some of the Poet's Theatre
people. They're doing wonderful things here. I don't know if
you saw the *Antigone* . . ." And before I could prevent him,
Pierce had again plunged us into a social nightmare.

I was examined, found wanting in interest and cast adrift
in a queer theatrical sea. To my further annoyance, Nancy's
optimism was rewarded. A well-tailored, civil young man was
paying her attention. I could hear them discovering each
other, launching on *Darkness at Noon* and leaving me trussed
like Gulliver.

"Help," I whispered to Nancy. "I've had enough. Can we
go now?"

"You mean leave?" She had a wary eye on her new friend.
"No. Not yet. Not until we've eaten, anyway."

"If you're worried about hurting their feelings—forget it."
I moved off angrily, determined to find Pierce and tell him
what I thought of his rudeness to our friends and his deliber-
ate torture of us here tonight. I felt the need of a proper apology before submitting to his hospitality or inviting him to my
house again.

But Lily appeared in my path, two plates in hand, thawing

my indignation and saying, "Pick up some wine from the table and come talk to me, will you, Ben?"

Miraculously, as it always was with Lily, a vacant love seat appeared before us and, kicking off her shoes, she curled up there and patted the seat beside her.

I sputtered out my displeasure with Pierce. "What's got into him, Lily? What's he trying to do to Nancy and me?"

"The night at your house, yes. He did behave oddly, didn't he? Well, you know, it's funny, Ben, I finally decided he was punishing *me*—for being nice to your friends. Yes—all of them forging ahead so uniformly at the bank. Oh sure, he has a contempt for the values. That's real enough, but they run up his anxiety just the same. He's very sensitive on the subject of accomplishment."

My complaints against her guests were stifled as she identified them with a word about what they did, why they had been asked and some observation of their nature. I began to see them through her eyes, and thus, this largely hostile force became a magical entertainment. The man with the wood-shavings hair was not a painter but a next-door neighbor, an elementary-school teacher, who wrote poetry and entertained (gentlemen exclusively) on weekends. It was, most likely, wonderful poetry, bearing so strong a resemblance to Dylan Thomas', but she was unable to comprehend a word. Besides, he was the only person who could start their lawn mower.

I was enslaved again. She could be both truthful and amusing about her odd bag of acquaintances, even the girl she thought an addict, without being unkind. It was the essence of Lily, this naïve delight in people, in their absurd obsessions and behavior. And it was exhilarating, being in the midst of the crowd yet having her to myself. She quickened me, brought me alive, as I had not been in years. I was afloat in a euphoric sea, the world at bay and I, Moseley, the only man in the world for Lily Jay.

It was the comfortable feeling I always had with her. There was no need to impress her: she was fascinated—though how, I was never quite sure. She intuitively knew some truth about me, not of my modest accomplishments, but of the essence, something that she alone seemed to recognize and cherish.

Hers was the eternal female spirit. She forgave every offensiveness but banality. There was no moral nonsense, at least, nobody else's. Whatever Lily's rules of acceptance, they were all hers, uninhibited, knocked together for the occasion, invariably serviceable and often wondrous. There was no one so bizarre he could not be embraced—and thus unlocked and mystery shared.

"Oh yes," she was saying, "I'm drawn to freaks—and they to me. They can tell my soft spot a mile off."

"Then why do you like me? I'm practically cubic, aren't I?"

"Your mouth . . ." She laughed, and reaching to touch it, traced its edges tantalizingly. "It's strange, with some men it's hands, other men, their eyes, but with you it's mouth. Very wide and strong, and yet so thirsty. Why is that? Oh no, don't . . . you wouldn't *know*." Her eyes left mine to roam the room and I feared she had become distracted or bored, but then she added, "You're such a long way from being what you imagine, Ben."

"What do you mean?"

"Oh, the rectitude is real enough, but there's nothing square about it. It serves you well, that's all. Inside, you're a regular cauldron of steamy desires, and *they* excite me. You're single-minded and you're a realist. That's where you're so different from Pierce, the polar opposite, really. With you, the important thing is getting there, not style. Your style can be earnestly plodding, that's your own image, or, when called upon, heroic, though of course modesty prevents your enjoying that for long, and on occasion"—her smile teased me but there were depths of cunning in her eyes—"malicious."

"Malicious? Oh come on, Lily."

"Wickedness is irresistible, you know. It's a regular magnet to a woman, particularly if it actually threatens her, those close to her. Oh yes, the blacker a man's heart, the fairer the girls drawn to him. True Iago-like villainy, rooted in jeal-

ousy, envy and covetousness, is immensely appealing, so long
as it's on the grand scale. Small-time stuff won't do. No back-
office spite for me, thanks. Beware."

"Oh, I *will*."

She frowned, as though she failed to understand something.
"And yet you're steadfast. No matter how I behave, you go on
liking me." Then, recalling what had eluded her, she tucked
her feet beneath her skirt. "When I was a little girl I fell in
love one summer with a boy who had freckles and red hair.
His name was Ned Mahan, and though we scarcely ever
spoke, he let me watch him fish and he taught me how to tie a
bowline and square knots every time, instead of grannys. The
next summer, when he was sixteen, he'd saved enough money
to buy a dory with a one-cylinder engine that went pop, pop,
pop. I can still hear it coming through the fog . . ." She
laughed and pulled her ankles closer, remembering. "He
spent all day tending his traps, but it didn't matter so much
because that summer I had fallen in love with a boy named
Curly Hinman, who was twenty and flew the air taxi to
Rockland. I learned a good deal of what I know about making love in the front seat of Curly's Ford that July—and of
course he told Ned about it. I knew because of the way Ned
looked at me now, as though I'd cut his mooring line. Then,
on Labor Day, I came down with appendicitis, and Ralph
Earl, the island doctor, decided I ought to go to the hospital
in Rockland, in spite of the fog. So Curly loaded us into his
little plane at the wharf and then, taxiing out the harbor in
thick fog, we hit a lobster car and it tore off one of the pon-
toons, so that a wing dipped into the water and the cabin
began to fill. The pain in my stomach was so sharp I didn't
think I could swim, and anyway, we couldn't see the shore.
We called and no sound came back. Dr. Earl crawled out on
the wing that was sticking up and tried to right us, but it was
no use. We were sinking. Then, through the fog, I heard the
pop, pop, pop, first far away and then stronger, and I knew it
was Ned coming. He came alongside just as the plane foun-
dered, and pulled us aboard. On the way to Rockland, I lay

up in the bow of the dory, bundled up, watching Ned at the tiller, his face, freckles and all, brave and tragic. He never spoke to me, but I was so excited, just looking at him, that I was numb. I couldn't feel the pain in my stomach at all, and I began to cry."

"Why?"

"Because I loved him, of course."

"And you'd been faithless?"

"Oh no—because there wasn't enough of me or enough summers, or enough of anything, to go around."

"Poor Ned—no reward?"

"The stitches were barely out and I was back in Curly's lap."

"And I'm Ned—in my lobster boat? Pop, pop, pop?"

"There's a difference." She smiled. "But there *should* be enough of me to go around, damn it. Sometimes I think of being the only girl in town when the fleet comes in, and it makes me feel grand—as though I could take on the whole world." She laughed, that deep, rich laugh. "Oh, don't scowl like that. You know what I mean, Ben. It's such a dirty gyp, monogamy, to feel a perfectly normal, healthy attraction to somebody and not be able to *do* anything about it. Why shouldn't a woman compartmentalize herself? It's physically possible. It doesn't alter my love for Pierce to love you. *Denying* love is what sours a woman. You have to find it, make it, celebrate it, every chance you get. Oh, I'm sure of that. The more there is, the more it multiplies, the better—and I don't really care what people think. I like being thought generous with myself. The belief that a woman mustn't be is an old slavery idea, that she's chattel. Some man owns *all* of her." Lily sighed. "But oh dear, practically, a wayward heart can do all sorts of damage, can't it, Ben? It can make wounds that never heal." She frowned into her glass and then drank the rest of her wine in a gulp. "I'm all for keeping promises too."

Looking up, she saw Pierce across the room, making chopping gestures in the air as he talked to Julien Weiss and his handsome Viennese wife. "Did I tell you we're going to have a baby?" she asked. "In time for Christmas if he's punctual, and I think he will be. So far he takes after my side of the family. I'm getting a front like Jane Russell's, you notice?" She glanced down at her bosom, which, in the candlelight, did appear to be burgeoning. "Like it? I do . . ."

"Pierce?" I asked. "Somehow I can't see him as Dad. Is he . . . ?"

She laughed and ran a hand languidly through her hair. "No, not entirely reconciled. Still, it's beside the point. He's wrong that having kids commits you. That's what he dreads, you know, committing himself before he's ready . . . Oh, but of *course* . . ." Her voice rose, a hedge around her husband. "Of course he will. No, not G.I. readjustment. Dear God, no. It's only that he has to beat the world as his father did—but in his own way. Finding that way is what's hard about it. But he can . . . and so he will."

"How?"

She thought a second, then said, "You know, I'm content wherever I am, while Pierce is generally itchy and wants to move on. That's really why he's always lumped work with contagious disease. It's not the pain he minds, but the confinement. When we were in Europe he could conceive of the most elaborate reasons for avoiding people he thought might offer him a job. And then the moment I'd get an affection for a place, find some interesting people, he'd start looking at the map. I suspected he was doing it to thwart me, that he saw new acquaintances as *my* friends, you know, and that some of the urgency about moving on was the male thing. I even thought, before we came here to Cambridge, we might be doomed to wander the earth forever. But here, on Linnaean Street, it's different . . . Oh, I'm sure, Ben—little roots going down. He does have a nose, you know, and he's on a scent here. Just look at him. With these people he's . . ."

"Finding his way, you mean?" I looked around the room, doubt shining from me like a beacon. "With *these* people?"

"Maybe. I don't know. With you perhaps?"

"Me, for God's sake?"

She shrugged. "Why not?"

As though she had summoned him, Pierce came bearing down on us, and in a farcical display of old Blue comradeliness, dragged me off. His encircling arm guided me along the shore of the party, up the stairs and along the corridor to his study. Fully furnished now, its bookcases held an assortment of esoterica with an unread look about it. The photographs had been replaced by abstract paintings and several three-dimensional objects which I took to be the new art. Beside the door a baked telephone oozed from its frame on the wall.

"Doesn't this place get to you, Mose? No, no, I mean Cambridge itself. The hub, the intellectual hub, of the world is what it is. Where else can you find so many people doing what they want."

"To be quite honest," I said, "the ones I've just been ignored by struck me as a bunch of phonies. It's been a long time since I've been made so uncomfortable. Those archeologists, for example. They were a real experience—not just pedantic and pretentious, but plain rude, not a hint of awareness all that crap of theirs might bore somebody else."

"You don't say? Well—you may have frightened them off. They probably thought you were from the Rockefellers, checking up on their grants."

"Who's the Chinese?"

"Mr. Sin? He's an architect. He built a supermarket in Lexington. His father still runs a laundry here. You liked him?"

"I didn't meet him. He was too busy feeling up the pretty blonde. But I did meet two girls enjoying themselves by castrating the fellow beside me. I realized he was *married* to one of them. It was frightening. What kind of man . . . ?"

"Oh come. You didn't give 'em a chance."

"Listen, Pierce." I sunk a fingertip in the thick raspberry silk of his tie. "I gave them far more than you gave my guests on Chestnut Street."

"What are you talking about, Mose?" He flicked my finger away. "I spoke *up*. I laid myself wide open to your State

Streeters and nobody took me on. Now why didn't you tell the girls to lay off that nice boy before they grew long beards and testicles. They'd have liked that. Or you could have told Mr. Sin he had no business messing around with one of your white women. That might have livened up your end of the room. You haven't learned to swing, man." He laughed and kneaded my shoulder. "Oh, Morosely, you haven't changed a bit."

Somewhat appeased by this old Pierce Jay trick of affectionate taunting, I watched him rummage in a midget refrigerator, opening, examining, rejecting boxes of cigars. He turned with the box he had selected and offered it. They were Corona Belvederes in glass tubes.

"Thanks," I said. "And by the way, congratulations. Lily tells me you've decided on a family, after all."

"Your example was an inspiration." He revealed from under nearly shuttered eyes a flitting amusement.

I was examining a collage of rusty machine parts and discovered with a start it was phallic.

"Like that?" he asked. "Take it. It would go well behind your desk instead of that Old North Church. Might interest some of your old ladies. An office needs an imaginative touch."

"Thanks, but . . . Oh, where's the chair?"

"Chair?"

"Your father's. The one you willed me."

Pierce frowned, lighting his cigar. "I didn't keep up the payments. I suppose it's gone."

*　　　　　　*　　　　　　*

Driving along a deserted Storrow Drive, Nancy was saying, "Isn't that funny you didn't? Even with the eternity you spent with Lily? I met a whole slew of perfectly nice people. And I had a lovely time with Pierce. Oh!" She clapped her hands. "And isn't it super about the baby? And you're wrong he doesn't want kids. He's wild about the idea. He's never been in better spirits . . . I think it's wonderful."

"What?"

"Well, I mean, I should think you'd be very proud of yourself. *I* am."

"For what? I don't understand."

"Oh really, Ben. What's wrong with you? They're rapturously happy, Lily and Pierce. They absolutely dote on all their crazy friends and they're about to have a baby. We *can* take some credit for that. Think what a precarious man Pierce was a couple of years ago. Remember how he was in Newport? Now he's found his climate. It's only a matter of time before he finds what he wants to do."

"Chinese maybe? Professor Jay—authority in oriental languages?"

"Why not? I think he's capable of anything he wants to do. He's brilliant."

"Oh, Nan, be reasonable. You don't mean that. He didn't even graduate from Yale. Think about what real scholarship requires—an aptitude and desire from the very beginning, from the second grade."

"You just can't accept that Pierce is growing up, but he is. He's casting about now—don't you see?—looking for a new way. That's plain to me. He was having such a good time with all those people."

"Only he wasn't. They were Lily's friends and they were there because of her, not him. She genuinely likes all those bohemians. Not Pierce. He doesn't really care for oddballs. He doesn't like them for themselves and he likes them even less because they're her crowd. He has to be boss-man, Pierce does. I'm certain, Nan. Oh, he makes a show. He's a good host. That's part of the aristocratic tradition. Once inside his door, no matter who he is, Chinaman, Jew, even *pansies* now, the law of hospitality prevails."

"There at the end, with the three physicists or whatever they were, he wasn't being polite. He was totally fascinated by them. You're just unwilling to admit he's capable or intelligent. You're so funny about Pierce. Why do you run him down?"

"Oh, he's intelligent and he's attracted to bright and amusing people. Sure he was enjoying the three Jews and their computers . . ." I began to laugh.

"What's so funny?"

"Come to think of it, he's made just such an alliance once before—in Branford Court . . . remember? It's the same, you see. He 'takes them up.' You know what I mean? Only he doesn't like them. He can't help being the rich dilettante and the least bit patronizing, and *they* detect it, all right. They know that for all his interest in what they're doing, for all his bounty with the German wine and Cuban cigars, in his heart he's intolerant of them and at the next pogrom it'll be Pierce saying, 'Step lively there,' and urging them into the stockade with his electric cattle prod."

"You don't really find him changed?"

I reflected. "I don't think people ever really change."

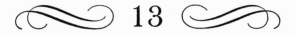 **13**

It was curious that Pierce and I could have settled within a couple of miles of each other, married to girls who had been close friends at school, and then conducted our lives as separately as we did when an ocean lay between us.

The four of us met but once in three years. Hoping to engage us in peace efforts, the Jays asked us to the Brattle Theatre for the showing of a Japanese film on Hiroshima. The portrait of an ordinary city, its citizens working and relaxing in their homes, their children at play in schoolyards, was followed by some newsreel footage, scientists in a laboratory, Truman at his desk, a bomb thrust into the belly of a B-29, a burst, and darkness. Then, to the dirge of a single stringed instrument, the camera moved slowly through the gutted city, pausing on every gruesomeness, entering the dressing stations to linger, caressingly, on the shriveled limbs and the maimed faces of Hiroshima's people.

In the midst of it I was aware of Lily's leaving the seat beside me, and when, after a few minutes, she didn't return, I leaned over to Pierce and proposed that since we had the idea, we might leave. He insisted on staying to the end.

As we passed through the lobby, there was no sign of Lily,

but on the pavement outside she appeared, shy and apologetic.

"Are you all right?" I asked.

She nodded but looked stricken, as though she might faint here on the street, and I put my arm around her.

"Couldn't take the gore?" Pierce asked.

In answer, Lily darted off, up Brattle Street, and Pierce went after her. Presently they reappeared, walking toward us slowly, and we all four went into the Window Shop for a drink. We sat around a table silently until Pierce, as though he couldn't resist the provocation yet hoped its outrageousness would set things right, said, "I wanted to get the total effect, and you know, after a hundred feet of stumps and twisted flesh you get a taste for them. A mixture of disgust and desire. I found it the least bit erotic."

Pierce laughed, but Lily, who had seemed in a trance, now said, "I'm sorry but I'm really not feeling very well . . ." She left us, hurrying down the steps into the night, and this time he let her go.

*   *   *

Our social worlds were not reconciled by the evening and I suspect we would have drifted apart entirely were it not that Pierce had me in mind, provisionally at least, as his local lawyer and a sort of devil's advocate. Every few months he would call, and resisting my invitation to the Union Club, take me to lunch at Locke-Ober's, where there would be wine to go with the crabs and hasps of cognac to hold the feast down. I would get back to my desk at three, sapped and guilty, excusing the waste of the afternoon with reassurances that one day I would have him as a client.

It was at one of these boozy lunches on a cold, bleak day early in 1952 that I heard of Julien Weiss again. "You remember? Black curly hair—narrow, ascetic-looking, but with a sense of humor."

"Of course, the computer fellow. He was the refugee."

"I've gotten to know him. These fellows, Mark Glauber

and David Blum are the other two, fool around with their electrical circuits and teach them to think—to play chess, for example. It's possible, you know, and the kind of idea they enjoy. I don't understand it, but it still intrigues me, the idea of a machine that *thinks.* That's the marvel of our times, Ben. That's what our age will be remembered for—if, of course, there is anyone around to remember it." He signaled the waiter for another round and I glanced at my watch. "They need a place to work, the three of them together, and I'm letting them have our stable. We weren't using it. I'll take you out sometime. I think it'll interest you."

*   *   *

"But I'm pleased they've come to me, for God's sake," Pierce assured me a couple of months later. "There are any number of places they could go get staked . . . No, not too much—a few thousand. The junk they putter around with is all fairly dear."

"And you don't have an agreement?"

"Not on paper—but we each have a quarter-share."

"I'm not at all sure you should put up a nickel, but if you do, you'll want more than a quarter-share. A half would be more like it, and you most certainly will want an agreement. You'll probably want to incorporate."

"Well . . ." he said doubtfully, "any kind of business talk puts them off—Weiss particularly. He's very jittery about what Harvard thinks, and Harvard doesn't think much of faculty moonlighting. It's a little bit different with the MIT guys—but even there . . ."

"If he wants to get staked, Pierce, he'll find a way around that."

*   *   *

The door in Dunster House was opened by Lotte Weiss. Her guardedness, primed for student invasions of Weiss privacy, melted into arpeggios of welcome.

"Pierce," she sang, reaching into the corridor for our hands

and towing us in, "and Ben. May I? Please sit down. Julie will
be with you in a moment. He's just correcting some papers,
and so he's been in a temper all the morning, but he must be
nearly finished. I'll tell him you're here."

The apartment itself was attractive—its paneled walls
painted white, its low windows giving on a Georgian courtyard. It was the kind of room that called for old chests and a
painting of a clipper ship, but the Weisses, whether from lack
of funds or taste, had fitted it out in veneer and strong autum-
nal colors from one of those stores that sells furniture in
"suites." The bookshelves held a hodgepodge of popular fare
—a few titles that even I considered trashy. A lamp made
from a miniature anchor crowned the television cabinet. It
was all supremely lower middle class, and yet Lotte Weiss,
producing glasses and vermouth with an urgent hospitality,
was so spirited and agreeable to look upon that the room,
echoing her throaty Valkyrie's laughter, was far from ordinary.

"Now . . ." She pulled a leather hassock to our knees and
settled upon it, tucking her skirt around her long legs. "I
know you plan to go to some marvelous restaurant and have
lovely things to eat and drink, but in hopes you would stay, I
have a quiche for you and a salad and Linzer tortes." Over
high cheekbones, dark, zealous eyes pleaded eloquently, first
with Pierce, then me. "It will save you time, you know. You
want to go to the stable and see what they are doing there,
and Ben, I'm sure, must go back to his office sometime. Do say
yes."

With her tawny skin and hair, she was leonine. She looked
Scandinavian. "The time *is* important," I said. "If you're sure
it's no trouble . . ."

Julien Weiss came to greet us, boyish, blinking, as though
emerging from darkness.

"Ah. All right." He had a feathery touch and an affectionate
smile for his wife. "So we shall stay here. It's not a mistake.
Lotte's good in the kitchen." Which of course made me think
she might excel in other rooms. She glowed with appetite. It

was disciplined but there was an excess of it. As she rose and stood beside her husband, she seemed too enveloping a woman for the slight, cerebral Julien. And yet there was such tangible, uninhibited devotion between them. I wondered what European experiences had brought them together. Dramatic ones, surely—if not persecution itself, then its imminence. That gentle touch on her shoulder revealed the whole cycle of tragedy they had inherited and renounced in their emigration. They knew at first hand about inhumanity and its compassionate antidotes, knew them with an intensity that shamed the country-club romances that were the rule among my countrymen and put me in awe of the Weisses.

Pierce, Weiss and I dined alone—Lotte Weiss setting a splendid lunch before us and then departing with a parody of a curtsy. In his charming, self-effacing manner Weiss talked of new developments. There was a budding in every gloomy carrel and laboratory along the Charles. There was a ferment, a true renaissance in the sciences. A mix-up in briefcases at the Faculty Club yesterday had caused the eminent Newberry Professor of Chemistry to dash with such heedlessness into Mt. Auburn Street, he had collided with a passing "Cliffie," toppling her from her bicycle.

Lunch completed, Weiss led us from Dunster House, through the Yard and along Cambridge walks, chatting amiably as we went. "There is such a profusion of new information being revealed in the academic ranges," he told us, "that the problem for the scientist is less one of attaining new peaks of discovery than in knowing where and how to apply what is already known, when to stop in his progress to single out this or that as of particular benefit to society, or"—and he laughed as he turned into the path leading from Linnaean Street to Pierce's stable—"to himself."

The stable was not prepossessing. License plates of the thirties and a dusty undertaker's calendar clung to stained tongue-and-groove walls. But at the far end, where wintry light filtered through filmed panes, a man bent over a new pine bench, working a soldering iron at a square of perforated board. I was introduced to Mark Glauber, and recalled him as the owlish fellow I had overheard instructing the girls in their faith.

Clearing a space among bright-colored bobbins, Weiss perched on a table. "If a man is working in some critical field," he resumed, "with the team at Minnesota, say, which is using ultrasonics to detect cancerous tissue . . ." In a spasm of enthusiasm, he tried to explain the test, a simulation of radio waves, emitted from a crystal and passed through a column of water into suspect tissue, the response indicated on the screen of a cathode-ray oscilloscope. Weiss smiled his apology for our bewilderment. "But no question, this must go directly to save what life it can, and yet it is a dilemma to the man responsible. Does he pause now to make certain it is properly and thoroughly reported to the world? Supposing a book will make it clearer, or a franchise to a company to perfect the instrument argues for better dissemination? Does he pause to celebrate and protect his discovery or does he get on with his business—the next experiment? It is a most personal question, embracing academic pride, which is good, and common greed, which is not. And of course, once you get into my field, where the applications are dizzying . . . We can tell you what is inside a tin can without opening it, or we can accurately forecast the weather. If a man keeps a careful watch over some useful product of his study and makes a fortune from it, he is no longer a scholar or teacher, but an entrepreneur, and if he does not—of course he is a fool. What a dilemma!"

"But there's nothing evil about money itself, Julie," Pierce said. "That's one of the big lies. There's nothing shameful about having it, so long as you aren't a pig about it and allow it to become the quarry itself. To use it as an instrument to good purpose, what could be more admirable? Why *not* a rich scholar? Money is freedom for the mind and spirit. It gives a creative man, a fellow with a contribution to make, the time to do the work he wants."

Weiss nodded, a slow, amused assent. "Ah, but it takes some getting used to, for us . . . virgins."

"Well, don't be deceived by the dowdiness in this town," Pierce said. "That's an old New England trick. It wouldn't surprise me to find a quarter of the faculty is rich—by any standards."

"Oh, I am well aware." From a bobbin, Weiss drew a strand of red filament, narrow as a hair. "And growing richer."

*   *   *

Walking toward the house, Pierce asked, "What do you think?"

"Making core-testers? No, I can't say I like it—not as an investment. Maybe as a charity."

He considered, unsmiling, and then he said, "What is there about you, you pussyfoot, that continues to appeal to me? You sound like a man of seventy-five with a safe-deposit box full of government bonds. There's no fun in that. I'm surprised you missed the point. It's Weiss. He's the thing."

"You've bumped into three bright boys, Pierce. I'm sure they're gifted, but you can stand in Harvard Square, spit in any direction, and hit three more like them. They don't even agree on what they're going to do."

"Weiss knows very well what he's going to do—and he's the smartest man I've ever met. Not just on his subject, but the *world*. History, art, politics. Not even a citizen yet and he talks about the Wisconsin primaries as if he *lived* there. He *feels* more intensely. I keep thinking if only we'd had him in college."

"Made us into physicists, you think?"

"Touched us, waked us. Not that that was easy." He led the way through a pair of French windows, directly into the hangar of a living room. "God, Mose, I shudder over what we thought was important then. But Julie Weiss could have made us realize why we were there. I think he could have made us aware there was a world of marvels so vast we hadn't time in our pitiful little lifetimes to explore but a corner, and we'd damned well better hurry."

"You've come a long way since 1939."

"How do you mean?"

"Ernest Bronson."

Pierce looked pained. "You mean because he was a Jew?" He shook his head. "That's not it. The night on the Old Campus, first time I set eyes on Bronson, I had the feeling, across fifty feet of grass, he was the real enemy. He was part of a kind of conspiracy of intellectual pricks—the pretentious, humorless bastards. He was out to break me. It was my ass—and yes, by God, Yale's, he was after. He wanted it in the name of grim, anonymous pedantry. He wanted to absorb it, splice it into some dreary academic chain of his, as if it were a department store." Pierce turned to me, as we reached the house, bristling suddenly. "But it had nothing to do with his being a Jew—you understand?"

"If you say so."

His storminess passed while he gazed at me. "I was as repelled by him as I'm drawn to these guys." He stood on the doorstep, putting his fingers slowly through the long curly hair. Then, abruptly, he called, "Lily? Lily?" There was no answer, and he loped off calling, then disappearing, down a dark hallway.

A moment later he reappeared, still somber, and went to the window, from where he could see the three of them, Weiss, Glauber and, now, David Blum, just emerging from the stable and straggling toward us across the lawn. "If they're still agreeable, I want you to draw an agreement. I'm grateful for your concern and your growing belief in my incompetence—but it's my money."

*   *   *

From that afternoon in the spring of 1953, when Microdom— a project that took ever larger amounts of my time and energy for seven years—was launched, I had misgivings that even

today I don't wholly understand. Of course, the whole program ran counter to Alexander Pope's advice, still as sound as
any I know for investors—*Be not the first by whom the new is
tried, nor yet the last to lay the old aside*—but even in the
early fifties State Street was cocking an eye across the Charles,
where the chem labs' new molecular linkages had converted
liquids into solids with remarkable properties and the din of
the plastics rush could be heard clearly enough to cause pros-
pector's fever at our door. Moreover, I believed Pierce had
unlimited resources and he was taking the responsibility,
overruling my caution.

No, it was more personal, rooted, I think, in Pierce's night
on Beacon Hill and his spurning of my offer of carefully selected, professional counsel. It pained me to have Pierce ignore my advice and set off so airily on his own amateur explorations without a guide. Yes, it's possible I sensed Weiss had,
as we used to say, a lot on the ball, and that I resented Pierce's
having discovered him and conceived Microdom with so little
help from me.

It took me the whole summer and part of the fall to draft
the Microdom pre-incorporation agreement, defining its purpose as development in electronics, its assets as the technical
knowledge of its staff, and then trying to protect the four
principals from the kind of plundering it was logical to expect if they were successful. I drew a noncompetition agreement, some reasonable terms of employment and a stock-
option plan that climbed with their success and corporate
longevity.

In the course of all this I got better acquainted with the
professors. I came to share Pierce's admiration for Weiss's
agile, imaginative mind, to enjoy Glauber's practical pessimism and to make an ally of Blum's shining aspiration. And
yet I was unprepared for the bewildering events which began
in October with Blum's suggestion they be paid nominal sala-
ries from the date of signature, then Glauber's that he hoped
his salary would be comparable to his university income.
When I wrote to persuade them that their demands were un-

realistic, they didn't answer my letters, but I guessed it was only their preoccupation with their work or perhaps a waning interest in the whole Microdom scheme. Then, in November, I received a letter from John Snyder, a grizzled, humorless attorney some twenty-five years my senior, with a wide reputation in contracts. The professors were engaging counsel. No offense, of course, but they were simple fellows, babes in the academic wood.

Pierce was surprised but not alarmed. "I don't blame them. It's just good sense on their part. They don't want to feel they're being exploited. They can get money any number of places. It's the knowledge and capability that's unique. No, actually, I'm glad about it. It means they're in earnest and have as much hope riding on Microdom as I do. We *should* share equally."

So I sent Snyder my draft, giving him a couple of weeks to familiarize himself with it, and then I went around to his office on Congress Street, where I found him in shirt sleeves, mopping his pursy neck, as truculent as reputation had him. "You're going to have to waive the invention clause," he told me. "There's no way to get around the MIT people. We've looked into that. And I see no reason why my clients can't look forward to a fairer share of assured income. No question you'll be able to afford it, is there? There's got to be some reasonable compensation for their time. Fellows like these are in enormous demand. They can write their ticket anywhere nowadays."

"But they're not being *hired,*" I said. "This is their company. They're getting stock at ten cents a share that Mr. Jay's paying seventy dollars for."

"Good," Snyder said. "I'm glad you brought that up about the stock. My clients will want access to twenty percent of it. Each of them."

"Well, that's out of the question. Surely you don't expect Mr. Jay is going to stake a company and then give away control of it?"

"Twenty percent isn't control." Snyder's gray eyes were

mirrors. He was not going to concede even a cynical under-standing between us. There was no point in talking.

"Absolutely not," I said.

He shrugged and nudged the agreement toward me.

*　　　　　*　　　　　*

Pierce decided the best approach was nonlegal, and so I awaited his report from the stable, knowing I wouldn't like it, whatever it was—and didn't. "Well, it seems we've bungled some," he told me next day. "They came over for dinner finally, just Julie and Lotte, and explained. To begin with, they expected a simpler agreement. They were awed by all that legal stuff. Come to think of it, why do you guys . . . ?"

"Awed? Do you be*lieve* that, Pierce?"

"It made them stop and think. The work contracts in par-ticular, committing them for years ahead. The pegged sala-ries. They hadn't thought about that and it put them on the defensive."

"It's an equable agreement—as standard as they come."

"Okay—but it scared them into getting their own lawyer. Snyder was Blum's idea, and of course he turns out to be the troublemaker. He saw them as hot prospects and turned up a man who wants to finance them. That's why he's being so difficult."

"I think you'd better get another lawyer. I'm out."

"Oh no you're not. It's not going to be hard to set this right. There's no real disagreement. They do want options on twenty percent of the stock but they don't want control. I have Julie's word. Isn't there a way to give them stock with-out control?"

"There's a way. We could put it in a voting trust and assure its not being used against us. That can be done. But, Pierce, are you sure you want *me?*"

"I wouldn't trade you for Joe Welch."

*　　　　　*　　　　　*

In the months that followed, Snyder and I were left to exchange the draft of the pre-incorporation agreement in one of those numbing, seesaw correspondences that erode a lawyer's patience and invariably gives the victory to the hornier tortoise. I doubted he had a moneyman as eager as Pierce, but I was so enjoined to see the negotiations successful I couldn't call him on it, and on the day in early 1953 when we all gathered in the board room at Black, Baer & Aspinwall for the signing, I looked at the stack of blue folios with the same distaste a carpenter must feel on closing up his toolbox and looking back at a bungled job.

I had arranged it so that Pierce, as treasurer, would vote all the stock, the professors' as well as his own, thus retaining control. Julien Weiss was to be nominal president, but along with the others, was bound by employment and noncompetition clauses to a perennial company loyalty. But Snyder had insisted on undermining my voting trust by subjecting it to revision in four years, when it would be possible for the professors to change their role from that of passive to active management.

Yet for all my dislike of the Microdom agreement, it had a bracing effect on Pierce, disciplining his fickle enthusiasms and making me wonder if the Pierce I knew—or thought I knew—had ceased to exist.

His absorption with the infant Microdom seemed total. He leased two floors of a loft building at 27 Otis Street, not far from Kendall Square, and on the first laid out a workroom with benches running around all four sides and a shipping room in the back. The second he divided into a pair of offices and a storeroom. He then made the rounds of the major New England laboratories after orders. They came in readily, and within a few months production, which could not be brought above two, or at most three, units a week, was lagging the demand.

The professors, always wary of strangers around their work, resisted help, grudgingly adding a single assistant to the payroll, a fellow who they agreed was too obtuse to be anything short of trustworthy.

One morning, early in the Otis Street era of Microdom, I found Pierce in his office listening to a spirited rebuttal from Weiss. "But we're not equipped for that, Pierce," he was pleading; "if we should make circuits for G.E. we may as well work there and get in on the vacations and retirement plan. Come—we can always take on the subcontract work, but why should we while we are paying the rent . . . and doing what we like?"

Jay regarded Weiss with mingled annoyance and affection. "You're a lazy fart—that's your problem."

Laughing, Weiss left us—while Pierce explained that he had just been offered a lucrative piece of a G.E. contract, but, as I had just seen, the professors were malingering down below.

"It's frustrating, Ben," he said, "this operating a company that wishes the customers would go away." He pointed to the workroom below. "I hound them so much they've agreed to my going on a long trip. Europe, anyway, and maybe around the world. I want to see what our market really is, see what else we might be doing. And . . . they can't wait to have me out of their hair. If I don't take any orders, they promise to be caught up by the time I get back."

Pierce was gone for three months, Lily joining him for the Asian part of the trip and some explorations of her own, and within a day of his return he arrived at my office, wearing a black homburg and affecting an international manner.

"A revelation," he told me eagerly. "Such possibilities everywhere I went. They're so far behind us and so eager to catch up—not just in Europe but in India, in Japan. In Tokyo alone I could have written a million bucks' worth of orders for special units. Oh, Ben, when I think of what we're sitting on . . ."

"You ought to drop in on Raytheon. They'd hire you today and you could go right back to Tokyo and sign these guys up."

He looked at me as though I were a backward child. "But I loathe sales. It's empty work. I could only sell for Microdom.

You can do things for yourself that you can't for anyone else. I was packing a unit for shipment this morning. If we had a truck I'd drive it. You can do these things when you run a place."

"But do you really run it, if it's not producing the way you want it to?"

"Give me a little time. David's as eager as I am. Mark too. He just wants to be sure it floats before he puts his full weight in."

"Weiss?"

"He doesn't want to be rushed. But there's only one of him —he'll come around."

*   *   *

Early in the summer of 1954 I made a preliminary audit of Microdom's books and reported to Pierce that in his first year of business there was to be no discernible profit. Nothing alarming in that. It was even reassuring, except that the core-tester units were aimed for a market they would soon saturate. I hardly expected my pessimism to have any effect on Pierce, but that evening Lily called from Manchester, where they had taken a house for the summer, and asked us for the weekend. It wasn't to be a business affair, she explained, except that they had asked the Weisses too, and Pierce hoped in the course of it to discover Julie's true feeling about their barely breaking even, and to see if he might not respond to a more aggressive plan. However, this was all secondary. The point was they wanted to see us before the baby—yes, they were expecting another in August, a boy, surely, this time.

*   *   *

The Jays' house was a white clapboard cottage with green shutters and a long porch overlooking a deserted beach. The water was forbiddingly cold, and Lotte Weiss alone braved it, hurling her body into the surf and swimming far out with a steady professional crawl. I keep a vivid recollection of her running toward us across the sand, dripping, still gasping from the shock of the sea, standing over us in a pale blue tank suit, skirtless and sheer as a silk stocking, that revealed her puckering nipples and the plump mound between her legs.

"Oh, I wish I could wear a suit like that," Lily said.

Lotte regarded Lily's maternity "dressmaker." "But yours is such a pretty one," and Lily laughed, helplessly, at the femaleness of it.

The main event was a sail on Saturday afternoon, and I was surprised to find the club launch bringing us alongside *Bluejay.* Confessing that he had only chartered the boat for three weeks and had forgotten whatever he knew about handling her, Pierce asked my help in hoisting sail, but once under way in a light breeze, the sea slippering along *Bluejay*'s gleaming sides, he gathered a reassuring skipper's manner.

In weathered canvas hat, one hand on the wheel, the other winching in the mainsheet, then reaching for the bourbon bottle to fill the glasses of his passengers, a cockpit full of us, it struck me that he was at last filling the role he most wanted— able master, bountiful host, with smiling, admiring, pretty women about, good friends, old and new, and a goal, Marblehead over there, its spires shining like Nineveh's through a summer haze.

Weiss, in an iridescent hula shirt, was clowning his unfamiliarity with seafaring, making us laugh with his landlubber names for nautical gear, but when Pierce persuaded him to relieve the helm, he steered so competently that Nancy asked if science was guiding his hand.

"What *about* automating the *Bluejay?*" Pierce asked with a pointedness that suggested he was getting around to it now, and made me question the moment, with our wives here multiplying the motives and persuasions, but I was equally sure it was calculated, that Pierce had chosen the situation, even prompted Nancy in some way to egg him on with "You couldn't, could you?"

"Of course. It wouldn't be difficult at all." Weiss warmed to it. "We would only have to give our computer/captain his destination and he would choose our course and correct it occasionally for tide and current." He squinted at the telltale on the masthead. "He would know from his experience how close he could sail to the wind vector, as well as how to set his sails most efficiently. With a Fathometer he will keep us out of the shallows and with a little radar attachment he will skirt these pretty islands and the more expensive boats. No, it could be done quite easily—and we will all go downstairs and have a nap until we get there."

"Pick up the mooring?" Nancy asked. "Tie up at the dock?"

"Refinements." Laughing, Weiss waved away all doubts. "We can work them out."

"He could, you know," Pierce said, distributing fresh ice cubes. "Julie could do all these wonderful things—*if* . . . Isn't that so, Julie?"

Weiss's gaiety clouded. He peered ahead at the clock tower on which he was steering.

"Make us all rich, you mean?" Nancy asked.

"But nobody wants an electronic yacht," Weiss said, his smile resurgent. "It defeats the purpose of pleasure boating, which is controlled hardship, making believe you are the ancient mariner, matching your wit and muscle against the mighty Poseidon."

"Watch him," Pierce cried in delight. "See how clever at dodging? That isn't what I asked at all."

"I know very well what you asked. Why am I opposed to making money?" His air of discomfort reappeared, and we sat, a silent audience, no one offering to relieve him of the need to reply. "But of course I'm not. You know what I'm opposed to—to losing my job."

"But you won't," Pierce replied. "There's no injunction at Harvard. You imagine it. Ben talked to someone . . ."

"The provost. He said there's no rule, written or unwritten."

"Call it what you want," Weiss said tartly. "Nothing should interfere with a man's profession—with teaching, scholarship." His eyes followed the opulent green shoreline. "For someone of my background—my father, you know, was a professor—the figure most abhorred, yes, pitied and feared, is the man who smells of money. Even as it draws us, that smell is what we Europeans distrust most about America. As you become older you become what you are most interested in, don't you think? You become more and more of what you do. It comes to possess you. You smell of it and look like it. The baker is bread and rolls, the actor is the audiences he has moved. You know what I mean? And the man who is only payrolls and securities . . ." Weiss shrugged. "No, I can't explain because I don't wholly understand myself."

"Oh, but *we* do," Lily cried. "We understand and admire you for it. If it weren't for that, Microdom wouldn't have drawn the six of us together and made us feel so strongly about it."

Weiss's eyes lingered on Lily—amused by the childlike devoutness yet aware of her real understanding.

"The only trouble is," Pierce said, shattering their warm, private colloquy, "that we haven't made any profit at all."

"We haven't?" Weiss seemed surprised but he rallied instantly. "Well, you got a trip around the world out of it."

"His trip wasn't expensive," I said. "It didn't amount to a third of any one of your three salaries."

"I don't mind," Pierce cut between our sparring. "I wouldn't mind if we were *losing* money. What I object to is playing at business. It's unprofessional and a waste of everybody's time. I remember hearing a storekeeper in a little town in Vermont explaining that he'd given up carrying raspberry twists because the kids liked them so much he couldn't keep them in stock. He'd managed to defy a business law, and so have we—for a year. You know, Julie, if I really wanted to make money I wouldn't be doing this. There are plenty of easier ways. Ben knows a dozen. I'm interested in Microdom for the same reason you are—but exploration is only half its commitment. The other half is to survive. I hope we can do both, but if we must decide between the two, survival comes first. We've got to grow to our capacity. Julie—I've found a place in Watertown. It's not going to be so convenient for you but there's more space. We'll be able to hire some people. I want to see continuous production next year and I want to take on subcontract work."

Weiss, reflective, unyielding, noticed he had drifted off course and swung the wheel to correct it. "Well, of course I'm opposed to doing someone else's work. I don't want to be part owner of a sweatshop. Work, yes, but it must be our own. And I'll tell you another thing I'm opposed to—failure. The idea makes me ill. It is unwise to suppose that commercial electronics is a sea full of fish awaiting our net. There are fishermen and shark enough. No, I don't like to put on an exhibition until I know I can do it well."

"But you can. We all know that. With your tiny filaments and cores and beads you can do anything. You're too modest, Julie. You know"—Pierce turned to the rest of us—"he's just built a luminescent panel, thin coats of photoconductive and electroconductive stuff, that glows to optical and electrical signals. It can make a readable image in an electronic system, one that could be used to control harbor or air traffic in a fog. He's Merlin—no question. And yet he keeps it on his bench."

"There must be a way for you to divide up," Lily suggested, "particularly now that you're going to have more space. They should leave you alone with your magic, Julie, while outside they have production humming. You could look out once a day to see they're doing it right."

"Perhaps it would be easier for you if you weren't president," I suggested. "If you want to step down, we could oblige at once. We're a quorum."

Weiss nodded agreeably, while beside him Lotte, alerted, watched him quizzically. She was like a benevolent older sister with her husband, neither awed nor impressed by him. She seemed to know even greater truths, timeless, lioness secrets, the kind that really turned the world.

"But, darling," she said. "I don't think you should do that —surely not without Mark or David here."

"No. You're right. I can't."

"Actually, it doesn't concern you at all, does it?" she asked. "Do you think of yourself as president while you shave?"

"No." Weiss shook his head, and after a moment he began to laugh. When Lily asked him why, he said, "The irony—of a Jew who is suspected of not wanting to grow rich."

*   *   *

At the dinner table that evening, there were five volunteers for a golf game in the morning, but when we assembled at the first tee on Sunday, there were but three of us—Pierce, Lotte Weiss and myself.

Lotte had no hesitation at being first to tee off. She smiled at us, and unfolding a long, flowing backswing, belted her ball straight down the fairway in a soaring two-hundred-yard flight that intimidated my own game at once. I was no match for her or Pierce and tagged after them with fives and sixes on every hole, fascinated by Lotte's powerful grace. She was a child turned loose in the country on the first day of spring. She strode along the course, every sinew in exuberant competition with Pierce. At the same time she entertained us with an account of her girlhood in Austria, how she had lived for sports and become an amateur swimming champion.

"Oh, but I *didn't* know Julie there," she told us. "We met here, in New York, just when he had arrived. I was working as typist in an importing firm, an associate of my father's house in Vienna. We met, you know, at a party, and while he was not in the least interested in my golf and only a little in my skiing, he could not ignore my cooking." She laughed and chipped from the edge of a sand trap, squarely onto the green. With an amateur's good humor and a professional's concentration, she continued with her game. On the eighteenth, with the slate roof of the clubhouse coming into view through a copse of tall pine, Pierce said to her, "Is Julie going to agree?"

"To what?"

"To our running a business."

"Oh." She smiled with an inward coquetry. "You mustn't

be misled by the vagueness or the playfulness. He is serious about everything he does. Yes, he is agreeable to moving to Watertown and to increased manufacturing. Did you really imagine he doesn't understand the value of money?"

In the locker room, Pierce was rejoicing. "You see, Lotte is the key, Lotte and the persuasive snip-snip of those lovely long legs. See how it works, Mose? Should we make her a director?"

"It's all very well to line everybody up on the side of expansion," I said, "but there isn't the money for it, you know. And you won't find it easy now, borrowing for a new place and a bigger payroll. If you want to know what *I* think, I think that with a company teetering, inching into the red, you've picked an awkward time to expand. Can't you wait until you show a profit?"

"No." He was squinting into the mirror, carefully parting the dark curly hair, thick as ever at the sides but, I noticed with a warming satisfaction, showing a first paleness of scalp at the crown. "We can't wait."

"Then you'll have to refinance."

"All right. We'll refinance."

*   *   *

The second round in Microdom's financing, wherein Pierce coolly forked out another hundred thousand dollars, moved it into more splendid quarters in Watertown.

The building had been a commercial bakery, and I visited it in early spring of 1955, just as they were settling in. Pierce showed off his own office with particular pride, for behind the desk stood an old acquaintance from Honduras—his father's barber chair. Brass gleaming, freshly waxed and polished, it put me in mind of a feudal throne. I watched him settle into it. "It was your suggestion," he said, fondling the knobbed armrest, "that put me on its trail. The warehouse traced it. They found it in New Orleans."

Through a large window we could observe the honeycomb

of benches on the main floor, where half a dozen girls peered through mounted lenses, forceping invisible objects.

"We're making ten units a week," Pierce explained, "and getting ready to start production on a circuit spinner."

"Are the orders coming in?" I asked.

"Well, it's been a little slow so far . . . Some sort of blight. Just missed the harvest time. We're competing with these massive reputations. That's what counts, whether they've heard of you. They will, you know, but it takes a while. Meantime I pin my hopes on the morning mail." He glanced at the top letter in the pile at his elbow.

Nonetheless, Microdom made little progress. When I finished the audit in June of 1956, the books showed a loss that was twice the fifty thousand dollars Pierce could write off under 1244, and for the rest of the year his difficulties multiplied. They produced some defective units, and as a result, lost their largest order. Hytron announced the marketing of a competitive core-tester. As the winter wore away, Weiss and Blum became diffident and elusive and no longer disguised the waning of their interest.

Then, in March of 1957, Weiss was offered a consultantship at Mitre, the new MIT spin-off, and he asked Pierce for a release in order to accept. David Blum applied for one too.

When Pierce called at the office for my advice, it was to let them go. "Think about it realistically," I told him. "Do you need any further evidence of how they're going to reward your faith in them?"

"Well, it's natural they're tempted by this offer," he argued. "You'd be too, Ben. But I need them. I've grown to depend on them in these last three years, and to admire them, by God." He grinned at my dourness, as though it was just what he'd come for, and went on with buoyant irrelevance. "What a *joy* they get out of life. I think they live more fully than you or I do. They're more sensitive to what's going on in the world. They excite me with their itch to know more, to keep putting the puzzle together. Everything they see or read or hear—a kid blowing bubble gum, a snatch of a new song, or an article in some out-of-the-way magazine—relates, adds to their knowledge. The only thing that bores them is a closed mind. Oh yes, Mose, we need these guys."

And so he left my office, filled with optimism, to go back to Watertown and work his stratagem.

At Pierce's request I came to his office at noon the next day for the meeting and found him tense and nervous, jumping up now and then to look into the street for Blum's Peugeot. His anxiousness seemed wasted over an outcome that was foregone. When they did arrive—Blum buoyant in London-tailored flannel and Weiss, though less elated, wearing his self-satisfaction visibly—to my mind it was over and I made ready to administer the last rites to Microdom.

Settling themselves, passing and lighting the cigarettes, Blum squirmed forward and cleared his throat.

Pierce restrained him with a raised hand. "I don't really want to know any more about what they've offered you." He had risen and perched on the window sill, one foot on the radiator. "I'm sure it's gratifying and that I should take some satisfaction in their confirming my own high opinion of you. You're worth more than whatever they've offered—surely more than you're drawing here. But the point is we agreed to take this adventure with my money and your time because, though we knew it might take a while, it was no gamble, that our confidence in one another was going to lead us to our full productiveness. Now what you're telling me is that you've lost that confidence in yourselves. What's come over you, Julie? You who were so reluctant to get into the scramble at all, yet now so eager for more, so quick to doubt your own sound ideas about selling yourself. And you've lost faith in me. Because I'm losing money you suspect I may not back up our compact. Well, you're wrong. To Ben's despair I'm going to go on backing you up until my money's gone, and at the rate we're spending it here that may take me another twenty years. But listen to me—

in just five, five years from this day, Microdom's going to be in a new place on 128 and each of you will have many concerns, but they won't be about money. You'll never worry about the means to do what you want to do again. That's not a prediction, you know; that's a promise."

There was a silence in which we all sat there, looking at our feet, listening to the sound of some laughter at the end of the corridor. Somone approached, hesitated outside the door and went away, and then Weiss said, "It's a very appealing picture, Pierce."

"But what?"

"But this won't interfere."

"I think it will. I think it would be a mistake for you to dilute yourself further. You haven't done effective work here for six months."

"Of course. I admit that. I'm in some swamp of the spirit. How can refusing this pull me out?"

"It will—if you believe in what I'm telling you. We're going to thrive here. We're going to thrive because I'm going to make it that way."

Pierce's passion echoed in the room, leaving Blum and Weiss confused. Their breeziness lost, they murmured between themselves. Presently they rose and left us and we could hear them talking in the corridor and then their voices drifted off, Weiss's door closing behind them.

When they returned it was with four Cokes from the machine on the floor below. These were passed, sipped from, and seats resumed. Then Weiss, smiling but shamed, a penitent schoolboy caught, spoke—they had decided not to accept Mitre's offer.

In surviving the crisis, all three professors paid Pierce fresh respect. There was no longer any question of his being the tolerated moneyman. He was boss.

But of what, it was not clear, for by midsummer Microdom's loss had doubled the previous year's and Pierce was paying his secretary's salary and his own travel expenses out of pocket. I failed to see how it could survive another year. But what I did not know was that halfway around the world the Russians were ready to send the first man-made satellite into space.

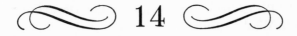 14

It is rare that a man can assess the swift stream of events of his own time, can observe them through his newspaper and distinguish between the historic and the merely sensational. But the fall of 1957 was marked by a crisis so dramatic that Americans like myself, men of ordinary perception, felt the earth tremble beneath their feet. On October 4 the Soviet Union, which most Americans regarded industrially and scientifically as a quarter-century behind, shot an earth satellite into outer space. Had it been armed with a nuclear warhead, it could have demolished Boston within eighteen minutes of its launching. In the time it took us to read and digest the first accounts, the downy bed of our complacency collapsed.

Pierce Jay saw the significance of Sputnik I, in light of his own and his country's ambitions, as a bold-faced summons, opportune as it was patriotic, to Washington.

He remained there for three days, and on his return, called to read me the fruit of his siege of the capital. It was a letter from a captain in the Bureau of Ships that sounded painfully formlike: "The Department is always interested in the encouragement of civilian enterprise which may someday contribute to the Navy's welfare . . ." It concluded with the politeness: "Please feel free to call on the Department if ever you are in Washington."

"That means no," I told him. "If they thought Microdom could help boost us into space, they'd have said so. He doesn't want any trouble with your Congressman. That's what he says. You can't read Pentagonese."

"We'll see," he replied. "I'm here just long enough to gather up my physicists. I'm going to accept the captain's invitation." I was reminded of the time he had gone down to Washington for the *News* and came back not entirely empty-handed; and I wondered if he could pull it off again.

But within a few days Pierce called from Washington to say that it hadn't gone particularly well. He refused, however, to give up. "I'm more than ever convinced this is our moment," he told me. "I'm doing what I can on the Hill and I've been out to see a friend of the old man's. He's retired but he knows everybody and he may be some help. Now what about you? You have a buddy in the Attorney General's office, don't you? Well, you never know. Sometimes the little guys have just the information you need. I'd like you down here anyway, Mose—if it's only to drink with."

*　　　　　*　　　　　*

This appeal brought me into the bar of the Mayflower late that same evening. I doubted there was a bona-fide big gun in the room but the assembly gurgled with talk. Urgent, long-suppressed information was spilling from a chain of lips—soft secretarial ones, curvy envious ones and the oyster shells of men who must have recalled McKinley's administration. I had the impression of a rite, an important twilight ceremony, in which workers in the vastness of the government, as well as tourists, told what they knew, and more, thus persuading themselves that despite the day's discontent, they were indeed here on the bank of the Potomac, taking its invigorating waters.

I found Pierce, freshly barbered and ruddy with big doings, just dispatching David Blum to infiltrate the Boeing group across the room. "No, Julie didn't come," he told me. Frowning, he rattled the ice in his glass and nodded to the barman, with whom he was already enjoying the instant understanding and fellowship of the big tipper. "He knows perfectly well how important this is, but he's in Cambridge. Got a class tomorrow. Oh sure, he'll come down. By appointment." He shook his head. "Well, I must admit he hasn't missed much so far. Dave and I spent all yesterday waiting in the wrong places. I believed a cab driver who thinks the Navy has moved into the Pentagon. Buships is just where it always was, on Constitution between Sixteenth and Seventeenth. By the time we got there, my captain had left. We waited for him about two hours, and when it looked like they'd lost my letter as well, I really blew my stack. Boy, Mose, you hang around here half a day and it's no surprise the Russians are one-up. I wonder we're a match for Uganda."

A waiter with a manner as comradely as the barman's brought a message which Pierce glanced at and stuffed away with the air of a commander receiving dispatches from the battlefield. "I got in, then, to see a j.g., who told us no. No program existed at present in which there was a place for us and he hoped the captain's letter hadn't put us to any extra trouble. He would keep us in mind for any change. But then, when I pinned him down about whether he was speaking for the President or just the Joint Chiefs, he admitted it was only Buships, for Christ's sake. *Navi*gating equipment. Projectiles are Buweaps. I ought to be used to this by now but it's always a surprise if you've been out of the service awhile . . ." He greeted a man who passed, guiding an Air Force colonel by the elbow. "So last night I got plastered and this morning I started from scratch. An hour out at Buweaps, waiting in a roomful of petitioners, convinced me we were going about it all wrong—psychologically. I came back here, Mose, and I'm staying here until they *ask* me to come and see them. Today I've harried our duly elected representatives some more and jiggled the wires . . ."

A red-headed hatcheck girl appeared with a flirtatious

summons to the phone, and a few minutes later I saw him returning, stopping to have a joke with her. Coming toward me again, he looked pleased with himself as he loped through the tables. He seemed to loom over the communicants, as bent heads, women's in particular, turned to look at this big, exuberant, easy-style fellow. Their eyes lingered on him, speculating. He seemed to own the place, much, I imagined, as his father had the bars and restaurants around the world from which he had run his business.

"Good news?" I asked.

"Not bad." He pulled a stool up beside mine. "The appointment's for nine tomorrow." He nodded to the barman's inquiring eye. "Yes, Harry, we'd better have a couple more."

*   *   *

Next morning, a Friday, I awoke with a hangover and an even meaner sense of waste—the kind of remorse I used to suffer after purposeless dissipation when I was young and foolish enough to venture it. But over breakfast, Pierce dismissed my eagerness to get home, and I was soon tagging along after him and David Blum, carrying one of the briefcases with drawings and descriptions of Microdom products and potential.

Pierce's urgency got us at 8:45 to a barren Navy Department waiting room, where I watched the hands of a big clock turn through an additional hour and a half and Pierce's mood turn resentful. We were received by an affable lieutenant commander who asked if Pierce was indeed the son of the man whose name he knew so well, and listened to a well-rehearsed presentation of Microdom's capability and its willingness to cooperate in well, say, the Navy's Atlas program.

The lieutenant commander thanked us, gathered up the drawings and Julien Weiss's articles from *The Journal of Applied Physics* and tucked them back into their envelope, which he returned to Pierce. Although he was polite, I got the impression he was amused at our presumption. At present there was nothing in the field of naval ordnance that required

Microdom's services. He would keep us in mind in case of any change, and meantime—with a glance at his watch—it was an extremely busy day.

We were a silent trio riding back to the Mayflower and I did what I could to restore Pierce's buoyancy by placing some calls myself. By noon I had reached a fellow on the White House staff, a friend of a friend, who assured me that no one could, or prudently would, do more than Pierce had already done in persuading the Navy Department to interest itself in a private enterprise.

Going home, Pierce seemed to have accepted this. He steered us into the bar in National Airport, and while we missed a plane, spoke of not being able "to win 'em all" in a fine display of resilience. But as I waved good-bye to him at Logan, he clung to the window and leaned in to say, "I'm going back to Washington on Monday, Mose. We're not through down there. This may sound preposterous for a two-bit outfit like ours, but whether it knows it or not, the country needs us—and goddam it, it's going to get us. There's the Army and the whole frigging wild blue yonder yet to go." He grinned and waved as my cab pulled away.

*   *   *

But Pierce did not get to Washington on Monday. Just before noon he came bursting into my office, trailing an exasperated receptionist. "Oh, you Morosely, you doubting, pessimistic Morosely!" he cried. "What a lesson in forbearance I have for you today." He danced around the desk, and as a horrified Miss Moller retreated, I wailed at an exuberant crushing of my knuckles. "Don't ask me how—you don't question things like this—but we did something right down there, because I've just had a visit from the inspector of Navy matériel at the Fargo Building. I took him around the plant and he talked to Weiss and Glauber and looked at what the girls were doing. Then he told us he'd been ordered—late Friday afternoon, mind you, while you and I were holding the wake in the airport bar—to clear us as a facility."

"For what?"

"To *talk* to them—so they can tell us what they want."

"It's incredible. Are you certain?"

"We're going back to Buweaps, Mose. This time to see Re 213, the Assistant Chief of Research for Guided Missiles. It's all classified stuff, so all four of us have to get clearances . . ." He produced the personal security questionnaires the inspector had left. "Now what do you make of all that?"

"I don't. There was surely nothing in what I saw to give the slightest hope . . ."

He alighted on the edge of my desk and banged it in joy. "But that's the thing about government. You don't seem to grasp it. All in reverse. Yes means no and no means yes and what's impossible on Friday is the likeliest thing to happen on Monday morning. Come on, Mose, get your umbrella. I'm buying you lunch at Locke's before you get to work on these things."

*   *   *

These things—the clearances—were arduous. A Republican administration was still tightening the vise which, in a careless youth, the New Deal had left so loose. We had just been involved in a civil rights case for which I had studied Jencks vs. United States and Yates vs. United States, and I was well aware that although Glauber had already been cleared for his A.E.C. team, Weiss, an immigrant, would require months of F.B.I. scrutiny and inquiries through our intelligence abroad.

I tried to guide Pierce about the investigations, explaining that they should give the fullest information on where they had lived, their education, travel and work—but to give as references people who not only thought favorably of them (references tend to air old grievances in confidence) but were circumspect themselves. An enthusiastic report from a man with the slightest shade of pink jeopardized the whole clearance.

But after his initial interview with Re 213, a Captain

Soames, Pierce heard no more from him nor from the inspecting officer in Boston, only hints from acquaintances, some of them slight indeed, that they were being questioned about him, and as the weeks of neglect continued, he became irritable. The delay and the pressure of being observed covertly had an abrasive effect on him.

One night in Christmas week Nancy and I were asked to Linnaean Street for supper with the Jays. The girls had been put to bed but their dolls and stuffed animals lay thick under a giant tree, and Lily, who was teaching a course for the first time and working toward her doctorate, looked wonderfully wholesome in brown tweed slacks and a tan turtleneck sweater. I remember that at Pierce's insistence she showed us, and then put away as though its opulence embarrassed her, the diamond and emerald bracelet he had given her.

It was cook's night out, and while Lily was preparing the meal, Pierce made more drinks and complained about the slowness of the clearances. "It's three months now. It's incredible," he said, eyes glinting with a kind of ironic amusement at his helplessness. "Really—while some watchdog of our security sleeps on Julie's file, the Russians put another satellite into orbit and announce the hydrogen bomb. We're so far behind in space, we'll never catch up. And you can be sure of this, that if Weiss were in the Soviet Union, there'd be no trouble about his doing government work. They'd have him up front. It's so fatally unimaginative."

"But realistically," I said, "they have a great deal to do, just looking into you. How do they know you're trustworthy? In 1939, his sophomore year, this fellow Jay incited a student riot with a Hitler demonstration. Yet in his junior year, he was writing incendiary letters, under a pseudonym, urging full participation in the war against Germany. Passionate and unstable, I'd say. Very fertile ground for seeding these 'isms,' right? And where was he after the war? Mysteriously knocking about Europe, talking to strangers in out-of-the-way places. Comes back and gets involved with these three scientists . . . Hell, man, I wouldn't trust you within a mile of classified material. It's a wonder they let you into the Mayflower."

But instead of making him laugh, or see the necessity of the delay, he turned gruff. "Is that what you told them, really? Did you go into all that *News* stuff?"

"Of course, why shouldn't I? Are you hiding something?"

"I'm hiding nothing, but that doesn't spare me the harassments of the witch-hunt. Each one of us is under attack by these vindictive, small minds, these arrogant, ignorant men down there who are intimidating every government department, every branch of the service, and turning us into a police state."

It was a parody of left-wing paranoia and I laughed.

"I mean it, Mose." He was revealing, just beneath the caricature, some conviction and live anger. "Whether you admit it or not, we live under a J. Edgar Hoover dictatorship. Just try to bring in some new ideas and *pow!*—you're the latest victim of the F.B.I.'s reactionary hysteria. I don't imagine this. It's real."

"What is?"

"That they're finding ways to spike us. Weiss, of course—because he's new here, because he's a Jew—he's a suspicious character. Oh sure. One malicious word is all they need. You told me that yourself. And now my own enemies are inventing stuff."

"Yours? Who are your enemies?"

"Oh, I *have* them," he replied mysteriously and ducked his nose in the glass.

"Who? Come on, tell us. I'd like to know."

But Lily appeared at that moment, summoning us to the dining room, and Pierce, rising, shepherding us before him, said, "The snoopers have been hanging around Brandeis this week, checking up through Lily. That gives me a swift pain, you know, asking about me, of all those queers she hangs out with, there in the anthropology department."

"Queers?"

"The furtive, phony intellectuals. I look at any one of 'em and I see Ernest Bronson."

Lily grinned, made a helpless gesture and passed a platter of huge, downy omelette.

Pierce was frowning at her from his place at the head of the table. "And you know, it wouldn't surprise me in the least if they were the ones making the trouble."

"But that's an inconsistency," I said. "You have one too many conspiracies. Both camps can't be against you."

"Why not? There's no monopoly on ignorance."

"Oh come on, Pierce," I said. "Nobody's out to get you. You're just sweating out a security clearance. You don't have anyone to be afraid of."

"I'm not afraid . . ."

"But you *are*. You've just told us that both the Justice Department and the OGPU are after you. Underneath all the fantasy you're nursing a political anxiety."

He shook his head. "I keep telling you I'm not interested in politics. I'm for intelligence and against stupidity. And I'm against anybody who's against me—I don't give a damn who he is."

"Shall I tell you what it is, Pierce? You *are* scared. And it's not that they'll find you're a subversive, but a good old Taft Republican, a chip off the old block. You're no progressive. You're miserable at it. That's Lily's act. I know you behind those false whiskers."

"That's crap. I never heard such crap."

"Not en*tire*ly," Lily cooed. "You do have your fantasies, darling." Turning to me, she said, "They're his personal hobgoblins—Hoover, the F.B.I., the Brandeis faculty, McCarthy's ghost, the Austrian ambassador—and they frolic nightly on the White House lawn to celebrate their foiling of him."

He spoke suddenly and angrily to her. "You'd like that though, wouldn't you, if somebody screwed it up for us? I don't think it would be beyond you to put some of your friends out there up to it."

"Oh, stop it, Pierce," I said. "You've lost your reason."

"It's all right, Ben." Lily, well able to fend for herself, gave an exaggerated sigh. "It's his reaction to red tape." She spoke wearily, as though this was oft-repeated and she did not expect to be heeded. "But what I don't see is why, if it annoys you, Pierce, you put up with it. When you work for the government, it's all you ever do—fill out forms and wait. But nobody's *making* you. There are other places to work and *I'd* prefer any one of them." Without pausing for a response, she rose to clear away our dishes.

Taking Nancy's and my own, I followed Lily into the kitchen, where she was rearranging fruit in a basket—silent, preoccupied, as though she was calming and disciplining herself by it and was unwilling to rejoin us until she had.

"I don't believe you can thwart him, Lily. Unless there's something I don't know about the professors, they'll get their clearances. And that's a determined husband of yours."

"Oh, I know . . . it isn't going to help."

"He doesn't always get what he wants but he invariably has his way." I laughed. "I'll never understand how he persuaded the Navy to get interested in Microdom."

"He never told you?" She looked up, amused, cradling a big yellow pear in her hand. "It was Julie Weiss. The same day you were in Washington, Julie was having lunch in the MIT cafeteria and one of the people at his table was Doc Foot. He asked Julie how Microdom was doing, and when Julie told him about David and Pierce going to Washington, he suggested they walk back to his office together. As they went, Doc Foot inquired about what kind of things Julie was doing out in Watertown—and that was it. Julie did it."

"Who's Foot?"

"Killian's friend. A government adviser."

"Pierce is aware of it?"

"Oh sure. He admits it was Julie. But he sees it as the normal irony. The way everything happens. He believes you have to push on the door to get in any place, and even if another door swings open, it was the push that caused it. Well, I believe in that too . . ." She frowned and her eyes drifted about, lighting at last on a potted pittosporum in the window. She plucked off some brown leaves, looked at the dining-room door from beyond which came the sound of their talking and then Nancy's flirtatious laughter. "But the other irony—that he might now be getting what he wishes for . . . You know what I mean, Ben? Now I'm dreading that."

"I wouldn't. No one ever gets what they want."

"Don't they, Ben? You mean, by the time they get it, it's what they used to want?"

"No . . ." I looked into her blue, unflinching eyes. "What people really want is always denied them."

She smiled and picked up the fruit bowl. "You might be surprised."

*   *   *

The clearances came through in late February, a record, to my knowledge, and meantime Weiss must have been given some direction by Soames as to what would be required from Microdom. In March, when my own clearance came through and I was permitted past the guard and the new wire gate at Watertown, I saw some of the components of the "Hound's Nose" which Weiss had devised.

Among the Navy's weapons programs was Regulus II, a missile intended to be guided from a ship at sea, rather like a pilotless bomber. Its range was to be well over a thousand miles, but the radar by which it was tracked was unreliable beyond three or four hundred miles.

What Julien Weiss imagined could be made to solve the problem of terminal accuracy was a device for giving the missile the target's "scent." It was in the shape of a radar receiver carried in the missile body, into which a chart with the marked target could be preset. In flight, the device would seek and match the actual terrain as it approached, correcting its course ever more accurately for its destination.

For the balance of the early spring Pierce shuttled to Washington weekly, sustaining himself on the rare drops of encouragement which fell to him in a nod of understanding or a welcoming rumble in the throat of the officer in charge of the Regulus II Project, Guided Missile Division, Bureau of Naval Weapons—the energetic, precise Captain Trumbull R. Soames, U.S.N., whom Pierce was never able to coerce onto a golf links or into a bar.

While Captain Soames might encourage him with a favorable comment on a difficulty surmounted—and Weiss provided these frequently—he would never allow Pierce and his delegation to leave his office without a reminder that there were four mammoth aeronautics companies seeking the principal contract and nearly a score of veteran smaller firms after the specialized work.

The Microdom specifications for its Hound's Nose went to the Navy in mid-April, but after the briefest acknowledgment, nothing more was heard, and again Pierce grew irritable.

To occupy himself, he decided it was important to be noticed at the National Service Industries meeting in Washington. On the eve of this convention, Pierce called me from the Shoreham to say he still had no word from the Bureau of Weapons, but the Microdom display at the meeting was going to be a knockout and they were giving a party in their suite before the dinner. His only disappointment was in Lily. She had refused to come down—no, not even for the dinner. "She might come for you, Ben. You have some weird control over her, and I want you to come anyway. But call Lily now, will you, Ben? Or go over and see her. Just get her to come down."

It was a perversely satisfying commission, giving me license to persuade Lily to do for me what she wouldn't do for him, and determined to make the most of it, I asked her to lunch at Henri IV, a little restaurant in a house on Mt. Auburn Street, run in a haphazard but agreeable way by a pair of French-women.

Lily came into the dining room a quarter of an hour late, wearing a white linen dress to match one of the first spring days and with a mischievousness lighting her great blue eyes that sensed and came to meet my own. For a while the dining room was ours. We were visited only by one of the proprietresses, who brought us wine and a delicious cold salmon.

We had not been alone, Lily and I, since Newport, and we slipped into an unexpected intimacy like some perfectly fitting old garment. I laughed, just at the sound of her voice, and we touched, even held hands. This easily explained rendezvous became the least bit wanton, exciting us both, I think, for I could feel the complex relationships falling away like old petals, leaving us in an unreal but no less blissful state that I can only describe as like new love.

"I'm going down to Washington sometime tomorrow. Will you come with me?"

"But I can't, Ben." Our bubble burst. She was a woman with responsibilities, frowning at her watch. "Mia, for one thing. She has one of those croupy coughs and it's made her insufferably cranky. I couldn't leave her."

"But all the more reason to go. She'll be perfectly well cared for and you'll be the fonder of each other for a couple of days' holiday. Honestly, Lily."

"Holiday?" She laughed. "A convention? I'd rather be locked up with a dozen croupy children. Oh no, Ben. I just couldn't be nice to all those stuffed admirals and important bullet manufacturers."

"But you always find someone who interests or amuses you, and these people aren't so bad, Lily. It's really quite exciting being around them—there's a great sense of urgency and importance. I think you'd find Captain Soames . . ."

"No I wouldn't," she said sharply. "No matter how charming he was I wouldn't like the idea of being charming back to him for business. It's a fraud to smile for money. It's whorish and I hate it."

We sat in silence and it seemed to me that she turned wistful—sorry as I that we'd lost the euphoria of our first moments together.

"I wouldn't mind going *some*place though," she said. "Just so long as it isn't Washington."

"With me?"

"Sure. Someplace with a lovely name." She held up her glass, swirled, and squinted into, the wine. "Castine, Westerly, Old Lyme . . . Oh yes, let's."

"Would you really?" She tried to laugh, but I insisted, regarding her steadily and seriously. I was remembering some bromide that *any* girl you wanted badly enough became yours in the end. Insistence alone made the most virtuous yield. "Would you?"

"Sometime."

"Not now?"

She shook her head.

"Then that's no, really. You have to be able to come with me now, not even going back for your toothbrush, to mean yes. Don't be a tease, Lily. I can't bear that."

"Oh, I'm not, Ben, never." And now it was with some kind of promise, real as coin, that she looked into my eyes. A warmth and expectancy enveloped me. I leaned across the table and her lips came to meet mine, and now they had found one another, our mouths were not content to part, even at the sound of others arriving, shuffling toward our room.

Stirring my coffee, I asked, "What's the trouble, Lily?" She raised her eyebrows, and I said, "Between you and Pierce? There's something. It isn't Mia's cough and it isn't the button with your name on it that's keeping you from Washington. What? Something very . . . personal?"

"No." She laughed. "It's not *that*."

"Tell me."

"I don't care what he does, Ben. He can go fishing all day and stargazing all night, whatever gives him pleasure. He doesn't have to prove himself for me—but he does for himself. He's haunted by the need to accomplish something. When he dwells on it, as he often does, it makes him ill, truly. What *is* that, Ben? There's such a guilt about being idle and rich, isn't there?"

"Why ask me?"

"But it's the male thing, too, isn't it? Even a man's virility is in question if he hasn't *done* something." She held the wineglass to her lips and sipped from it thoughtfully. "Now there's hope for Microdom, he's remarkably easy to live with, easier than any time since we've been married. So, you see, I mustn't spike it." Her eyes trailed away to the couple being seated across the room and it was a moment before she realized the girl was an acquaintance, nodding a greeting.

Lily acknowledged it, but then turned to me abruptly and spoke with a new fervor. "You know, I can understand killing if you're starving and that is the only way you can get food, or if someone you love is threatened, your child or your husband, but this sitting down around a drafting table to arrange the destruction of perfect strangers—it's hideous. Can you understand that?"

I nodded and remembered Lily's running out of the Hiroshima movie—how pale and cold she had seemed.

"The ways of killing people are efficient enough as they are. Oh, Ben, *why?* Why must they do that? There are a million other ways to make money."

"You're a picket?"

"Is that wrong, Ben? Tell me, please. Is it wickedly disloyal? What if Nancy did this to you? Could you forgive her?"

"If she believed in it as you do. Surely I don't need to tell you that."

She smiled, and with the point of a finger, drew a cross on the back of my hand.

*　　　　　*　　　　　*

One of the Shoreham's large halls had been given over to receiving the convening NSIA members, and beyond the reception desk there was a score of pens, each bearing its company name in funereal bronze, each with its grave man in dark suit presiding over a desk, some catalogs and a pair of plain secretaries.

As I made my way through, I found them widely neglected in favor of an entertainment at the far end. A crowd had gathered around a pit in which a tiny airplane attached to a wire was approaching the scale model of an aircraft carrier. Just off to the right, and curtained so that he could not see them, a man sat before mock-up controls and a screen which displayed some bars that had to be matched in order to bring the little plane safely onto the carrier's deck. The audience, middle-aged men, some in uniform, was calling out encouragement and laughing as the little aircraft closed, nearly missed, then set down on the foot-long flight deck. I was astonished to read the name of the exhibitor. It was Microdom, Inc., Watertown, Mass.

I found the door to 1704 standing open on a sitting room where a waiter was arranging bottles and several dozen glasses. There was nothing, no familiar face or article, to identify this as my destination, and I was reassuring myself by an inspection of one of the two bedrooms which lay beyond when Pierce came in from the corridor, a heavy squall, his eyebrows rolling downward. He was so engulfed by his fulminations at Weiss, who trailed him, that he was oblivious of me.

"Well, you saw him. You heard him. Now you know."

"No, I don't. I know nothing." Weiss waved to me and sank moodily into a chair. "I don't believe that."

"You don't believe what?"

"That his being unable to sit with us has any connection with any remark I could have made. It's the most natural thing that his wife should have accepted another invitation and he would feel bound by that. He could not make up an excuse like that on the moment."

"The naval mentality again?" Pierce looked at me for the first time, allowing his anger to deflate. "Oh good, you're here, Ben. Nancy?"

"Nancy too. We're on the fifteenth floor. On the other side. Very splendid."

He walked to the now fully prepared bar and made himself a drink. "Well, I'm grateful to you for coming down—though God knows it may all be in vain now. Soames, you know, was supposed to be at our table, he and his wife, but he caught us after the panel and begged off. He said his wife had accepted the Vought-Sikorsky invitation."

"Pierce reads into everything the man does, if he should sneeze, you know, or wave in an affable manner to the doorman, it is a sign that either we are—or we are not to have Regulus."

Pierce collapsed beside me and stared at Weiss. "You just can't grasp the idea that these guys have any real loyalty to the service. Well, believe me they do. They play the Army-Navy game every day. Touchy, very touchy. You're better off to make fun of a man's wife than his corps—but that's all beyond you, isn't it?"

"You're crazy, Pierce. You are obsessed with this Madison Avenue method of doing business—the backslapping and remembering names, the carnival display you have in the lobby. That nonsense will not have the slightest effect on the outcome of Regulus. It is what goes on the drawing board. They are not such fools as you think."

Lotte Weiss drifted into the room with a vase and a huge box of peonies. We watched her arrange them and then step back to admire her work. She wore a white cocktail dress and looked flushed, as though it was a true party she anticipated, and as she grew aware of the tension around her, she ignored it.

"Well, Pierce," Weiss said at last, "if you're so certain that we are croaked, there's no need to stay for the autopsy. I'm uncomfortable here and there are some things I could be doing in Watertown." He looked at his watch and raised his eyes to Lotte, who had turned her back on the flowers to perch on the arm of a chair.

"We have a table for fourteen," Pierce said. "Linahan hasn't canceled out yet." He glanced at the telephone as though expecting that in the next instant. "You really mean that? You're not sticking around for dinner?"

"Oh, Julie, do," Lotte coaxed. "Pierce is counting on you."

"On the contrary," Pierce said. "I'm not. I've learned."

Weiss seemed stung. "I hope you're not serious about that, Pierce. I've never let you down on anything important. Whether I am or not at a dinner table in a ballroom full of a thousand people isn't going to have any effect on anyone but me. The matter of Regulus is already decided. I think unfavorably for us or we would surely have some hint by now, but nothing we can do in the way of parades or circuses can change that—and it is of enormous importance to me not to go. You understand? No, you don't, you see. You don't understand me nearly as well as I understand you."

"Frankly I don't."

"At the dinner table you see only a waiter behind me with a dish of bright green peas, but actually it is Yahweh, Jehovah himself, with his long beard and terrifying eyes, breathing his fiery breath down my collar as he whispers fiercely into my ear that as I play the fool in the grand ballroom and listen, nodding gravely to fatuous remarks by General this and Senator that, the devil himself is writing *No Class Today* on the blackboard in 117 Lyman and slipping into my desk, mixing the papers hopelessly, muddling my computations with his long stick, making a shambles of the lab."

And Pierce laughed. Reaching out, he clapped Julien Weiss on his bony knee. "All right, Julie, go with Yahweh—but leave Lotte. We'll take Lotte for a hostage. Go on, boy. We'll miss you. Have a drink with us before you go."

*   *   *

Plainly, Nancy saw herself as Lily's surrogate and set forth at once to establish herself, reassuring Pierce and flattering him. "Oh, I don't care how it comes out. I just think it's wonderful you've come this far." She slipped a comradely arm through his. "I mean, just to *be* here, Pierce, I think it's marvelous—and it's all *you*, dear."

On the printed schedule the cocktail hour was designated as: 6 to 7 Informal Receptions—and then listed a dozen of them with room numbers. By six-thirty no guest had arrived, and we stood about, primed, anxious, occasionally peering into the corridor. But Nancy found some stationery and drew a seating arrangement for the dinner, putting Mrs. Linahan on Pierce's right and herself directly opposite with the Congressman on hers, checked to see there were enough cigarettes, that the barman had enough ice and a lemon peeler, moved Lotte's flowers to a different table and then settled between Pierce and me on the sofa.

"Well, I know how Lily feels," she said. "And I think it's wonderful that she's so independent—and you're man enough to want her to be."

"I don't mind her being independent," he said. "But of course she's crazy. I don't agree with her at all. I'm for peace too, for Christ's sake. Who isn't for peace? But if we don't prepare for war in the most efficient way we can, we'll be annihilated. We're a couple of castaways clinging to the butts of a waterlogged plank in a big sea and we can get a good deep breath only when we kick and get our end up a little, which of course puts the other guy's end under. But so long as we both keep doing that, we both float. If one of us gave up kicking, he'd sink. It's not the nature of us beasts to give up kicking. And anyway, technology is all too complex now to say what's munitions and what's not. Is a satellite a weapon? Is a defense against a weapon a weapon? And even if you decide it is, are you *not* going to explore it? Is the ability to strike the same as the will to strike?"

"Oh yes," Nancy said. "It's so terribly clear once you see it like that." She was warming to her role—binder of wounds, sharer of gladness, bountiful provider, the indispensable female on loan for the duration.

But Nancy had not reckoned on Lotte Weiss, who, in spite of her white silk dress whose borders plunged to her narrow swimmer's waist and laid bare the flawless colonnade of her back, now made a casual entrance. I had moved off to join Mark Glauber and his shy Louise in front of the television set, but I saw the glaze of boredom fall from Pierce's eyes as they followed the long-legged Lotte across the room, watched her replace the vase of peonies on the console table, touch a

bloom back into place, have an encouraging word for the barman and a moment's chat with us and then turn to the door
just in time to greet the first of our guests, an Air Force colonel and his wife who, it turned out, had come in error but
feeling the welcome so warm, stayed.

Nancy, who knows this game and plays hard, did not give
up so easily. When the others arrived, she was at everyone's
side, intercepting Congressman and Mrs. Linahan and taking
them around the room, never missing a name, bringing Louise Glauber together with the mouselike wife of the Consolidated-Vultee man in a triumph of adroitness, but she was losing and it was painfully apparent. Across the room you could
hear the joy around Lotte Weiss. Where she was, there was
laughter—and Pierce beside her, lighting up like a tall city
building in the first phase of evening. No—Nancy was no
match for Lotte Weiss, and I watched that brightness in her
eyes become humiliation, then repressed unforgiving fury as
Pierce ignored her.

It was Lotte, too, who had her antennae out when a fellow
from Vought-Sikorsky came in "just to look the Microdom
people over." Yes, he'd heard something about them at the
Bell party. He gave her a stagey wink. Hell, she *must* know
what he was talking about.

While we eyed him and wondered, Lotte went to attend to
the phone, which had been ringing unheeded in the babble.
She came from it to where Nancy and I stood talking with
some strangers and Pierce.

"It's he," she said, touching Pierce on the arm with a di-
rectness and simplicity that was intimate, letting him know of
the urgency, yet so delicately it was not a rudeness to us. "It's
Captain Soames," she said.

From where I stood I could see into the bedroom, and I
watched Pierce pick up the telephone, and saw Lotte, reflected in the mirror, leaning against the closet door, a senti-
nel. When Pierce hung up, they looked at each other for a
second, he seeming a bit dazed and Lotte watching him, trying to read his expression, and then he grinned. She put both

hands behind her, grasping the knob, and laughed, a hearty burst of exultation, and then they shook hands and he held hers while he told her, and both of them laughed now, and then she leaned forward and quickly, so I was scarcely sure of it, sowed a kiss on his cheek.

She skipped ahead of Pierce, coming back into the room to tell us—first David Blum, who was nearest, then, gathering him up, over to the Glaubers, and then all of them, arms linked like children coming down to Christmas, over to share the news with us.

"We have it," Pierce whispered to Nancy and me. "It's not official. We're not meant to know, but Soames just called to say it was leaking out and he didn't want us to hear it roundabout. We're specified as the subcontractor with Consolidated-Vultee. We're going to make the Hound's Nose. Oh, Mose baby"—he hugged us both—"we're in."

*　　　　　*　　　　　*

The grand ballroom was an anthill on swarming day. Neuters scuttled by with urgent last-minute errands in their mandibles. Stingless drones lumbered about, scraping acquaintance with alien queens. A triumphal parade bore in its captive. A corrupt and feeble old warrior was helped to his seat by slaves. Over by the door, I distinctly saw a worker milking an aphid, and in the rear corner, a predator lurking, watching a nervous bride-to-be as she was preened and comforted by her retinue —and even as he pounced, he was pounced upon, and so fled, paying out yards of silken lifeline as he lowered himself into the very center of a vengeful crowd.

But table 42, with the Microdom party assembling, was an island, reassuringly human. Nancy's face was especially so as she grasped that *some*one had been here before her to ring the table with place cards. Stuffing her own list back into her purse, where it was to smolder eternally, she took her assigned place between Mark Glauber and a Mr. Lovejoy from Lansing Tool.

Pierce was Papa. He had the exalted look of a man just

knighted. Beaming at us, he was listening, first to Mrs. Linahan, then to Louise Glauber, pleasing them both by his attention and a story about his naval training. Distributing a flurry
of currency, he transformed our apathetic waiters into streaks
of affable efficiency and commandeered the wine steward,
who soon turned table 42 into a garden of glassware.

Watching him, I was impressed by Pierce again, by his extraordinary growth in the past couple of years. I felt, with a
faint prickling, that his good mind had steadied at last and all
his vagrancies of the last decade had given him a breadth and
understanding well beyond my own.

I leaned across to say to him, "Congratulations, Pierce. It
must be a tremendous boot. I mean, you've really done it in
spite of all of us. My hat's off to you, old boy."

"Oh, Ben, that isn't so. *With* you. I'm just midwife, the
doctor—no more." He shook his head. "With everyone here."

"And some who aren't," I said.

"Oh, isn't it a shame Lily isn't here," Nancy said. "Did you
call?"

He didn't seem to hear, but Lotte Weiss said, "I reached
Julie. He refused to believe it, but he's very, very happy all
the same."

"What is this all about?" Linahan asked. "Do you have
some good news to share?"

"Well, it seems we do, Harry," Pierce said, "but it's not
official, and of course it would be bad luck to even—" Peeling
back several layers of tablecloth he found a piece of surprisingly desiccated wood to rap. "But I think I can say this
safely, that sitting here with you all tonight . . . My God"—
he laughed—"I think I feel a toast coming on."

"Go on, go on," Lotte Weiss cried, clapping, leaning
against Linahan, so that he too commenced to clap inanely.

"If I heard this coming from another table, I'd think it was
corny and embarrassing. Nevertheless I want to propose a
toast to a second-hand bakery on the seamy side of Watertown, Mass., which is really us—our spirit and intelligence,
the best we have to offer. We've seen it through some child-

hood diseases that seemed serious enough at the time, and I expect it will have some more, but tonight it seems bursting with health and promise—like a boy who knows he can't be licked and he's going to live forever." He looked around the table. "Can we all drink—from our seats, I think—to Microdom?" And we drank, solemnly.

Then, as the barrage of melon cup, fricassee, the predicted bright green peas and the ever-replenished wine passed over us, followed up by the fusillade from the speakers' table, Pierce's gaiety waned.

I was directed to the cause by Nancy's disciplining look, one which ordinarily means the children are misbehaving. I followed it and caught the signaling between Pierce and Lotte Weiss. A current ran between them, an eagerness that could be felt around the table. It became audible, seemed to drown the hollow sound of the speaking and made me intensely uncomfortable.

It didn't surprise me that before the cigars got to him, Pierce's chair was empty, nor, when I looked, that Lotte Weiss's was too.

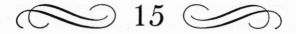 **15**

YOUNG BUSINESSMAN IN THE NEWS

A man who starts his career with a name as honored for achievement and leadership as that of Pierce Jay might be expected to drift along the safe waters already chartered for him, but not the dynamic, 37-year-old head of Microdom, Inc. His bouncing research and development firm, launched just five years ago in a Cambridge loft, last week announced the purchase of a 25-acre tract in Burlington, Mass., and its intention to construct there new quarters of a revolutionary design.

Microdom has in hand a Navy contract for a guidance system, and in the month since this announcement, has doubled its payroll. It is now engaged in the refinancing of a massive expansion program. Although immediate requirements call for upwards of three million dollars, Pierce Jay anticipates filling Microdom's needs for new capitalization privately.

I put the magazine down on my desk without comment but did not conceal my distaste.

"Why the long face?" Pierce asked. "What's the matter with you now, goddam it? This is something to celebrate. It's what I've been waiting for."

"All right, I do have a strong instinct against it. I think Microdom is too big now for a private recapitalization and I think it's a mistake to commit yourself to it. But I've been wrong before. I admit that and I won't urge caution on you. It seems I never can bring myself to think like a rich man. I'm always underestimating you—assuming limits. But, of course, you *can* afford it. And you must now, having said this." I put a finger on the page. "Having said you can raise that kind of dough out of pocket." Glancing up at him, I found Pierce still bristling but attentive. "You can, can't you? You and your mother can, with no great difficulty—because I can't, not in any substantial amount. And unless you do, of course, you're in jeopardy. Yes . . . I think they doubt you can. *I* would if I were them. And if they detect the smallest sign—a suspicion of lameness—the hounds will be on you."

"What do you mean, you can't get it for me?" he asked.

"Unfortunately, the people I must go to, the banks, are a cynical bunch. They don't believe anything they read and only half what they hear."

"Goddam. Must it always be this way—winning, by Jesus, and then coming home to hostile, doubting faces? I thought that would be over now."

"The banks? Why should you care?"

He stared at me for a few minutes, blinking, a hand covering his mouth. "Because I *don't* have that kind of money now."

"Well, if you don't . . ." I waited for an explanation and got none. "If you can't get it from your family . . ."

"Well, Ma's vague in the way of rich old ladies." Pierce leaned forward and folded his hands on my desk. "But not about what she believes is my little success explosion. Very alert about details. Most proud. So instead of being angry that she wouldn't stake me, I was touched. I could have, you know. I could have raised hell and made her give it to me. But I don't need any favors—least of all from Victor, who now fancies himself as her investment counselor. He's Machiavelli with the red eyes at the mention of money." Pierce frowned.

"So—instead I came back with a trunkful of the old man's memorabilia—not exactly the treasure I had in mind."

"That's too bad."

"No, not necessarily. As I looked over some of his stuff I had the feeling I'd come off with the real loot. What a guy! Not just him either, Mose. It was the whole lot of them, each with his certainty of the way the world ought to run and the guts to make it that way. Jesus. You know, I've been talking to Charlie Horne, my *Fortune* man, about it, and he thinks he can do a series, a biography really, focused on the old man but including the Yale Unit guys, right from college, through their war and what they did afterward. You've got to see this stuff, Mose." He frowned at his own picture on the *Fortune* page and reread a few lines of the piece. "Shit, we can get the money any place."

"However much it pleases you, that article is not going to help. They'll call your bluff. I wish you'd spoken to me before talking to this fellow."

"Listen." Pierce straightened, shaking off his euphoria. "If one bank doubts me, or two, get rid of 'em. Cross 'em off. There are a million banks."

"I've made the rounds, Pierce. They *all* want some assurance."

"Of what, for Christ's sake? What do they want now?"

"They've heard there's to be a new issue."

"You tell 'em it's bunk, don't you?"

"They've heard otherwise from Jack Snyder."

"We've had him before. Why don't you shut him up?"

"They can do it, Pierce. The moment the voting trust expires they can dilute your stock with a new issue. I think that's the plan. They'll do it unless you're a magician—and of course you are one."

Pierce was tilting back in his chair, studying the lustrous toe of his shoe propped on the edge of my desk. "I don't believe it," he said. "They don't want it. They've never wanted it."

"They've always wanted it, if it was worth wanting."

Pierce picked up the *Fortune* article and reread the first paragraph. "Isn't this the frigging irony, though? Think how happy it would have made me a while back, just knowing this was coming, that one day we'd be sitting here at your desk reading it. Now I'm reading it and getting a pain in the ass . . ." He tossed the magazine onto the desk. "What makes you think they want control?"

"Let me see if I can get Jack Snyder to tell you, Pierce. Let's see if he's in. You want to hear it from Jack?"

"You don't expect me to believe him?"

"Will you listen?"

"Where do I go?"

I led Pierce to Miss Moller's desk just outside my office, and while he listened on the extension I called Snyder and asked him if he was the source of the rumor about the Microdom issue.

"Well, Ben, we can't hold the clock on Microdom," he replied. "That's a hot little outfit and it's going to need more capital than one man can put up. Yes, we have in mind a placement, mostly institutional, for three quarters of a million shares of common stock."

When I inquired about the voting trust, he said, "No, I don't think my clients will want to retain the voting trust. I've never liked that."

Pierce returned, walking very erect, not visibly affected by Snyder's news, yet he did not speak as he wandered about, looking at the leather bindings of the law books on my shelves.

"Well, there you are," I said. "There's something substantial for a magician to work on. I don't know how you'll do it, but I imagine you'll find a way."

Then he turned to me, his triangular jaw shoveling forward, the black eyes sudden points of anger. "You're the magic. You're my lawyer. Aren't you, for Christ's sake? Or are you theirs?"

*   *   *

A few days later I found myself dressing for a dinner party at Linnaean Street and questioning Pierce's conviction that every dilemma could be solved by bringing the disputants together in a social situation—as though there were no real differences between men, only a lack of opportunity to drink together.

Nancy surprised me with the slenderest of reservations. Waiting for the car at the Charles Street garage, she was animated and expectant, glancing at her reflection in the glass, as though we were on our way to a conventional sort of party.

"Don't you find it a little strange," I asked as we got into the car, "joining in this particular Pierce Jay manipulation—Lotte, Lily and you around the table? Doesn't that make you feel the least bit crummy?"

"We don't *know* anything?"

"Oh, Nancy, what do you need, photographs? You know Pierce as well as I do. Does it surprise you? It wouldn't even occur to him there was anything unusual about this evening. I'm sure his father did precisely this—brought his girls home for dinner."

"His father had girls?"

"Oh, always, I gather."

"Well, I'm not excusing it or arguing it. Given Pierce and the circumstances—Lily's absence, the Austrian girl's presence"—she had been avoiding Lotte's name since the evening in Washington—"you're unquestionably right, but it isn't *our* problem."

"Isn't it? If Pierce brings us all together and rubs our nose in it—I mean, you're Lily's *friend*—don't we become parties to it? To a conspiracy against Lily?"

Nancy seemed puzzled. "But how could we possibly interfere? It isn't as though Pierce were some *stranger*."

"Of course he isn't. Oh, I'm fully aware of my loyalty to Pierce. That gets plenty of exercise, believe me. He assumes that. It's the whole predication of the party tonight. He expects loyalty from everyone—from every girl he sleeps with, along with his wife and her best friend—simultaneously!" I laughed. "And it never crosses his mind that in the very hoodwinking, he is lessening everyone—his wife the most of course, but the rest of us too, in our complicity. We're *all* clowns. I can't get it out of my head that there's something dishonest about permitting it."

"But what on earth could we do? Not go, you mean? I thought you *had* to go."

"I don't like the deception. Isn't there some way you could get that across to Lily?"

"You mean *tell* her?" Nancy's eyes glazed with astonishment. "But what an extraordinary idea. Of course I couldn't, Ben—couldn't and wouldn't. I wouldn't *dream* of meddling, in the tiniest way, with anyone's marriage, least of all that one. I feel very proprietary about the Jays, and so do you. They mean a great deal to both of us. But more important, they really need each other, desperately. I know they care for each other in a way that goes far beyond any foolish infidelity." She turned to the window and stared at a shell and its four oarsmen spidering across the glassy Charles. "Besides— she knows. Lily knows."

"Now what makes you say that?"

"Any girl with the least perception would know. I'd know."

"Would you now? How?"

"By the way you looked at me, the way you touched me, kissed me. It would be changed somehow, just the way I'd know if anyone had worn something of mine. Oh, I'd know all right."

"I wonder. It doesn't seem like Lily, to grin and bear anything."

"Sensible women do, Ben. Surely you're aware of that. Women who seem numb about their husbands' behavior aren't really. The ones who seem not to know or not to care just know how to wear their pride. Otherwise they'd be truant officers—and what an ugly, futile role *that* is. I mean, you never get a man back by running after him, but if you let him go"—she laughed—"even give him a little push, then he'll be back . . . If he loves you, he will."

I drove the rest of the way into Cambridge, not much convinced by Nancy's argument but rather puzzled at my rash proposal to her. I was wondering what had prompted it, if, rather than fair play, it wasn't some old jealousy that had spoken.

Indeed, the knowledge that Pierce had put his marriage in jeopardy now coupled in my mind with the discovery, earlier in the week, that he had run through the bulk of his three-million-dollar inheritance. And though I still believed in his magic so much that I could not have a real concern for Pierce, I felt faint, exhilarating pricklings, what I might feel in taking a seat for some exciting match—a championship.

*   *   *

We gathered on the raised deck, a sort of tree house Pierce had built in the lower branches of a big beech behind the Linnaean Street house. From it we could look down on the stable and its windows blurred with lantern light. Laced all around by the new-leafed boughs, hearing the faint stirrings and rustlings and smelling the juicy summeriness, I had a remarkable feeling of being in a nest. It was a bit of Pierce Jay legerdemain and led me to think there would be more.

He was perched on the arm of a bench beside Lotte Weiss, waving his cigar at the branches overhead, telling her about the Roman candles with which he had tried to dispossess the starlings and an indignant bird lover from across the street. Right under Julien Weiss's keen gaze (indeed, Weiss was beside his wife, smiling, with his weary but inexhaustible tolerance) Pierce was performing. Absolutely certain that any woman he had made love to would wear his touch, be an ally forever, he was unfurling the old charisma, letting it flutter around her to haze her eyes with recollection.

Across the deck, Lily sat in a forked limb, talking to Nancy about the nursery school where the girls would be going in the fall. She held a globe whose flame cast a shadowy, imperfect light upon her face, where I thought I saw the line of disappointment.

I could not see Pierce's face clearly, only hear the resonance in his voice. It was an exultation, as though he were on the point of laughter, and it was clear he was stimulated by having Lotte here with Lily. He was that sure of Lily's allegiance and his own dynamic maleness.

Pierce's voice broke through firmly, and across the deck Nancy and Lily paused in their chatting. "Come on, Lotte, it's time for a walk. Come down to earth with me." He grasped her hand. "You don't mind, Julie—for a moment?"

But Lotte declined. With a determined shaking of her head, she withdrew her hand.

"No?" Pierce asked. "But I want you to." He turned from Lotte to Julien Weiss and back. "What's the matter? Have I said something wrong?"

"It's comfortable here." She was sitting primly, hands folded in her lap. "I seldom get to sit in a tree."

"Well, you can come back. Now I want you to come and see my waxworks." Wheeling toward the house, he pointed out the lighted windows of his office. "It will give you a view of the past—the America you just missed. Come along, Lotte."

"Just me?"

Pierce hesitated, smiled, conceding. "All right. All of you." He waved his glass at Weiss, Nancy and Lily on their limb, and me. "Come on. We're going to see the exhibit. Bring your drinks."

*   *   *

Standing against the wall was the portrait of Pierce's father that had dominated the foyer at Bellerive. Perhaps it was the passing of nearly a decade, but the image of the man was less awesome than I recalled. There was a sensuality about the eyes I had missed, but the spirit—vital, boisterous, determined—was undiminished. It was obviously Pierce's intent that we feel in the presence of eminence, and I think we did. Genuflection came to mind.

"You like it?" He seemed to be addressing Lotte Weiss. "Well, I do. Oh, I know it's peculiar. We don't hang the old

man's portrait nowadays. Why *is* that? How come? Too strong
a reminder of obligations? Or just too old-fashioned to take
some pride in our inheritance? Afraid it will smack of Victo-
rianism? Snobbishness? Well, I'm different. I want to hang
the old man's portrait." He raised his glass to him and took a
gulp. Nancy and I followed his example, sheepishly, while
Lily and the Weisses did not. "Where, though? I'd like your
advice."

Lotte Weiss failed to respond, and I said, "Not here, surely.
Not with the melting phone and the whatchamacallit."

"I'm thinking of retiring all this junk. Still—no need to
keep him to myself. It's a big house."

"Who is the decorator here?" Lotte asked, turning amiably
to Lily. "Is this a family controversy? Perhaps we should hear
both sides."

Lily smiled coolly from the doorway. "No. It doesn't matter to me."

"There, you see," Pierce said unreasonably, "that's the
problem. It doesn't matter."

"I didn't mean that I didn't care. I do. Let's hang him in
the dining room, then. I've got some imposing forebears
somewhere. Can they come too? Or do you suppose they
mightn't get along?"

But Pierce did not seem to hear her conciliatory answer.
Preoccupied, he moved along to the trestle table where lay,
presumably for Charles Horne's inspection, most of Pierce's
Newport booty. He took a shotgun from its pigskin case,
broke it and looked through the twin barrels at us, then held
up for our inspection a canvas helmet, tattered fabric from
the fuselage of an airplane, a German flag, a silver flask, a
compass torn by a bullet. I began to poke through the exhibit
for myself and found a diary begun in 1927 in Montevideo
and kept sporadically for a year. It bulged with personal cards
scrawled with notes and greetings, snapshots of groups eternally celebrating in hotel bars and country clubs. There were
old photographs, one of the 1915 Yale football team and
many of fliers alongside their biplanes and drinking in the

courtyards of French inns. In each I found Pierce's father, radiating that characteristic heartiness. Here he was with fishermen and hunters and diplomats. There he was with good-looking women in the short skirts and boyishness of hair and figure that was the mark of their rebellion.

Pierce set his drink down to take up one of the photographs. "This is the first Yale Unit," he said, holding it up. "These are the guys that quit college in the fall of 1916 and went down to Peacock Point, Trubee Davison's place near Port Washington, to learn how to fly. They got some money from a man named Colonel Thompson and from Rodman Wanamaker and J. P. Morgan, and they bought some machines of their own." He held up another photograph. "This funny-looking crate is a Wright. One motor drove two propellers by chains and the elevators were out front, pilot and passenger suspended from the frame, right out in the air. And Don Pomeroy gave them this, the *Mary Anne,* the old flying boat they soloed in. Look at the thing, built like a speedboat, out of mahogany. The old man flew it across the Sound one rainy night, trying to get to a dance in Stamford. He got lost and had to fly it along the New Haven tracks and scared the engineer of a Boston train into pulling the emergency brake, and everybody in the diner had soup in their laps. It made the *Tribune.*" He pointed out a head. "This guy here is Hank Henriques. He was from Caracas, but aside from the way he looked and the way he handled women, he was just like the others. He was a natural hitter and he got two of the three runs that won the Harvard game in 1915. He went along to Peacock Point, absolutely certain that the U.S. Navy wouldn't keep out a Yale man even if he was Venezuelan. He was wrong, of course, but he flew in the Escadrille. And it was Hank who got the Jay Line its first franchise in Latin America. The old man didn't want any part of a local corporation with South American officers and South American capital and South American politics. If he couldn't do it his way, he wasn't going to go in at all. But Hank fixed it so everybody was happy—and made the pattern they used in Brazil and

Peru as they opened up the route south. Not for money—
Hank wasn't in the Jay Line. He wasn't even on retainer. It
was the way they were with one another." He held up the
picture in both hands. "They were his ushers. He had twelve
ushers at his wedding. There's a funny picture of Hank leer-
ing at the bridesmaids. And they all came back to Newport
for the funeral too. Ushers and pallbearers. They came from
all over both times. And they sang 'Mavourneen.' You know?
The old Yale song? After that gruesome rite at the cemetery, I
can remember these guys putting their arms around one another and singing 'Mavourneen.' " He put the photograph
down and picked up his drink again. "You'll forgive me. It's
not very modern—or scientific, is it, Julie?—to think favorably of your forebears."

"On the contrary," Weiss replied. "It's both modern and
scientific. Genes, genes, genes."

"Not genes," Pierce said irritably. "What a man *lives* by."
His large, handsome head swayed to and fro as he examined
the canvas again, appraising that arched nose with its flaring
nostrils, the steep forehead and the full, curving lower lip
that, with the years, were becoming his own. "No, it isn't
modern to think of yourself as the projection of the people
who've gone before you."

"It's too painful," Weiss said, trying to divert him from
whatever mesmerizing he had in mind for us.

"Let me finish," Pierce said, causing Weiss to smirk like a
naughty child, and went on. "But we can't ignore it, none of
us can. We all behave like puppets, our limbs jerking to those
strings that are the hopes of a father or a mother—sometimes
fulfilling, more often disappointing, them." He looked from
one to another of us, relenting. "That is why I'm so fascinated
by this stuff of my old man's here and why you must forgive
me for going on so about it. You see, I'd hoped these relics
might make you wonder if I have given him any immortality
at all. We might make a game of it. Discover what survives a
man. Pin the tail on it." He picked up a small blue book with
the red and blue pennant of the Racquet and Tennis Club on

its cover and riffled its pages. "Clubs? Julie—belong to any clubs? The faculty? Ben, you're kind of a joiner, aren't you? I'm not. The old man, now, must have belonged to fifty. Men's clubs, country clubs, lunch clubs . . . Well, I know—but it told you something. That a man was a gent. That was important. It's what everything worked on."

"It was a different world," Weiss said.

"Oh, I *know*, Julie. It worked only because the world was a comic, simple little place, where some college boys who'd majored in team spirit could outguess the Navy Department and sell them their own flying corps and then go make out of that same stuff a business they all thrived on. No, couldn't do that today. World's too big and impersonal a place—and yet it still runs on integrity."

Pierce looked at Weiss meaningfully, and I grasped, with a mixture of disbelief and embarrassment, that he was prescribing—elixir for a sluggish conscience. It was naïve as only Jay at his most artless could be, but there it was—and it silenced us and made the room oppressive. Indeed, I craved the clash now, wanted Weiss to take him on, to parry, with wit or reason, Pierce's claptrap and get to the throat of their dispute.

But Weiss only nodded, as though to say he understood, and then smiled, not, I decided, at Pierce's accusation but at the notion of our being required to stand so long before the portrait while Pierce established jurisdiction and precedent. Yes, Pierce Jay, plaintiff, was going to bring some justice in the world.

But Weiss was not to be provoked. He moved along the table, inquiring politely about this group and that, and when was the initial flight of the flying boat to Brazil, to all of which Pierce scarcely replied. But he moved after him—closing, opening, bobbing like a boxer, at last planting himself in Weiss's path.

"Come on," Pierce erupted. "Lay it on the line, Julie. I need to know."

"What?" Weiss picked up the journal and turned its pages slowly, reading snatches.

"We've been partners for seven years and I've taken your word for the real tender between us—not the legal crap between Ben and Jack Snyder. Now, what am I to believe? That you are confused and inattentive? Did you imagine that running Microdom is only a hobby with me—or are you really trying to screw me out of control?" He watched Weiss turn another page, not reading but pondering a reply, and Pierce must have got the impression he had an advantage, for he pressed on quickly. "Come on. What are you, Julie? A man of spirit or"—he tapped a nostril, sniffed—"do I detect a whiff of that odor you detest? What was it again? The man who smells of money? Oh, I know that money smell, Julie, the foulness of cheap perfume on clothes that have been slept in. But it isn't the money, Julie. Money is odorless. It's the lust for it. That's what you meant, didn't you? Because greed has a real stink."

Weiss turned another page, then spoke evenly, without a hint of ill will. "Well, for one thing, you tend to load all these very ordinary business dealings with a big freight of emotionalism. It's best not to let the heart run what is essentially a machine. It is surely injurious to both. Business doesn't interest me for this very reason. Business is not a matter of the heart or loyalty. It is simple expediency. If one were to act in a business situation as one does in a love affair, out of affection or sentiment, one would instantly become entangled in the machinery. That is why one employs a man like Snyder, who is a professional at it and has, presumably, a calculator for a heart, and leaves it up to him." Weiss snapped the album shut and raised both hands defensively. "I am not prepared to talk business tonight. I didn't come for that. I thought it was to be a party. Is it not?"

"I'm not talking about business," Pierce insisted. "I'm talking about us and I'm talking about what makes an association of men strong—the trust between them. Loyalty—you know what that means?"

"Don't pause to explain. I'll look it up later."

Pierce nodded at Weiss, stared at him, occasionally licking

his lip. "I used to think you were the smartest man I'd ever met, Julie. I told Ben that, didn't I, Ben? You were that perceptive about our institutions—saw right through to the core of them—to dazzle a dunce like me, but now I find something has made you miss the main point."

"Oh? I always hate to miss that."

"When the man you're with reveals a weakness, you cover for him. You don't take the opportunity to knife him."

"Oh, the code of honor. But I know very well. Fair play— to hit here is fine, but there a foul. But I didn't realize it is the main point. I thought it more the caste mark of affluent men and nations—to talk about rather than abide by, for they know too well that if they are to endure, they must act out of self-interest. Well, I'm not prepared to talk about that either." He turned to Lily and said, whimsically, "You didn't tell me it was to be a debate."

Pierce, his legs spread wide, was fueling up with rancor as though from a hose. It sloshed and brimmed, so that he menaced us with the swelling weight of it.

"Oh come on," Lily said, rising from the window. "Let's go climb the tree and have another drink. Dinner will be ready in a few minutes."

Pierce led us downstairs, two steps at a time, and I noticed an old trait, one I had nearly forgotten, an impatience in step and gesture, as though his limbs were indeed ruled by a twitching string.

And there was a new, headlong abruptness to his speech. Halting us on the porch, he peered up toward the platform, where candles still flickered and where I'm sure we all longed to go and be cloaked from one another in its merciful shadows. "Too dark," he announced. "Couldn't see out there. We'll stay here and drink."

On the brightly lighted porch, there was no eluding him, and his voice was raw with irony as he made us fresh drinks. The dark one he poured himself honed his tongue sharper. He mimicked my appeasing smile, made a mirror image of the lopsided expression which shields a crooked tooth. Even as I kept my patience and humor, trying to coax him back to decorum, he nipped away at the sensitive spots, my priggishness, fearfulness and caution.

Then, as we sat down to dinner, he turned to Lily. "Marvelous, marvelous, what you do with a few flowers and soft lights. All the magic of the theatre here on the table, and that only the background for the hundred splendors of the meal itself. Oh, you can laugh all you want, but believe me, it isn't easy to spend all day polishing the silver and cooking these delicious—what is this lovely sauce, Lily?"

Lily, who had been watching with a cautious smile, said, "It's mousseline—but save your compliments for Mrs. Saylor. She made the dinner."

"There you are. So modest. Never wants any credit for all the chores she does so skillfully. Really remarkable, my wife. Sometimes I have to stop and congratulate myself. Mother: bathes, feeds, comforts and teaches my demanding children; nurses them when they're sick and puts them in and out of snowsuits, rubbers, whatever, a dozen times a day. Professional woman: instructs at a great university. Veteran of a big dig in the Middle East. A master's in anthropology from Harvard, and well along toward a doctorate. Think of it, at thirty-two . . ."

"I'm thirty-four," she said, and we laughed gratefully.

But Pierce was still at his fingers. "Federalist," he said, ticking off another zone of accomplishment. "Tireless secretary of the Cambridge chapter. The denser the war clouds, the harder she labors toward a peaceful world. Oh, you are indispensable to the movement, Lily dear. That consoles me. Who wouldn't be consoled by that?"

Lily looked up from her plate with some mischief left and a determination to make this play. "Well, yes, I *have* been worried about that. I think a woman who tries to be everything—governess, hostess, reformer, competitor and bedfellow, all those nice things—tends to spread herself thin, don't you? I don't care for thin women. I wonder which I should give up. It's a problem."

"Oh yes, I can see. A really tough decision," Pierce said, helping himself to more of the sauce. "Would you know, Lotte? When is a woman happiest—when she's telling her husband what to think, or when she's barefoot and pregnant?"

"I'm sure I don't know," Lotte Weiss said and lowered her eyes.

"Of course you do. You know everything."

"Well"—she made a helpless gesture—"on a beach in the summer, I like being barefoot. It makes me feel a little girl again. Very carefree. But surely not in the city. I don't like dirty feet. And I've never been pregnant."

"No?" Pierce paused in his persistent eating, put down knife and fork. The joy of discovery gleamed in the pupils of his eyes. He folded his hands under his chin to gaze at Lotte. "Why is that?"

She did not hesitate. "We would like very much to have children, but thus far we have not been so fortunate."

There was a numbingly quiet moment during which I decided that was surely the end of it and struggled to find a new course for our thoughts, when, to my horror, Pierce said, "How is that? It's not so hard." It was the Pierce of the Fence Club bar, the Pierce of Bailey's Beach, breaking out of his smooth shell, bloody of eye, ravenous, claws already slashing, like a predatory hawk. "How come, Lotte?" He had a hold on the Weisses now and he wouldn't let go. "It isn't a matter of fortune, you know. It's . . . scientific."

"It's also very personal," Weiss said. "If you're really interested—come around tomorrow and I'll explain."

"But why not now?" He smiled at Weiss, nodding with mock amiableness. "We're all good friends here—aren't we?"

"Because you're not inquiring, Pierce. You're quarreling. I don't want to quarrel." Hypnotized, Weiss was watching Jay's upper lip as it bowed with amusement and contempt, and the tongue which lubricated it in slow passes. "In fact, I want to go. May we go, Lily? I'm sorry, but it's really getting quite late."

"Class tomorrow?" Pierce asked. He struggled to his feet, pushing his chair back. "No, can't go yet, Julie. I've been saving this wine for a very special occasion—and that's what we've got." He was crouching by a painted cupboard, withdrawing bottles of burgundy. "Yes sir, Julie. Very important occasion." He squinted at the label. "Hospice de Beaune. 1942. Very suitable. Very old Beaune for very old friends . . ." He uncorked a bottle and went through the ceremony with a steadying concentration—a splash in his own glass, a smile of approval, and then he started around with it, filling Nancy's glass, then Lily's, which he overturned clumsily with the neck of the bottle. He ignored the dark red stain creeping across the linen and passed on to Lotte Weiss, who, at his approach, turned her glass down.

"European custom?" he asked, bottle poised.

"Perhaps. I don't want any more wine. If it's so lovely, it would be a shame to waste it."

"It's my wine to waste. I don't like to see empty glasses around a table. Particularly one that's upside down. I *abhor* the sight of a turned-down glass. It's one of the ugliest sights I know."

She righted it and he filled it to the brim, but her eyes were resolutely downcast and the indication clear she would leave it untouched.

"Lost the taste for wine?" Pierce, still hovering over her head, bent like a penitent's, asked, "And what are we supposed to make of this chaste collar?" His hand rested on it, clasping the back of her arching neck, and she seemed to freeze at his touch. Across the table, Lily was folding the napkin in her lap with concentration. "You used to be such a lover of life, Lotte. *Game*—we used to say of girls like you. But you don't seem very game tonight. You're different, somehow. What is it, Julie—a sea change?"

"No," Weiss replied. "Lotte does not change. She is very constant."

"But she seems different." Pierce moved along to fill my glass. "Wouldn't you say so, Ben? How would you account for that?" He drew back to enjoy my discomfort. "Say something, Ben. Speak up, boy. Don't you remember, or can't you think of the right word?"

Rising, putting his chair neatly back to the table, Weiss said, "Well, if you wanted the last one—if that was the point of all this—I think you have it. There is no more to say, surely, about anything." Lotte was rising too, mumbling her goodnights to all.

Pierce, the bottle still in hand, stared at Weiss. "No, no— wait, Julie. Not the last word at all. I have much more to say. Wait . . ." But they were moving toward the door. "If you don't stay to hear it now, I'll tell you in court."

In the doorway, Weiss turned. "What are you talking about?"

"I'm going to sue for control."

Weiss glanced at me for verification and I felt Pierce's eyes on me too, goading me to some bravado—but my tongue would not move.

"I don't think you'll prove anything," Weiss said and urged Lotte ahead of him toward the door.

"I'll prove," Pierce shouted after him, "to anybody who cares, just what kind of a scientist you are."

Nancy, Lily and I sat in the rubble of the dinner, listening to the diminishing clamor, the sunderings and crashings of final demolition. His reckless footsteps pursuing the departing Weisses, their car starting in the driveway, and then Pierce's voice howling after them, echoing along the silent paths and gardens on Linnaean Street, "You can't take it from me, you fucking Jew!"

PART FOUR

1959

 16

Bluejay's tall white mast and spoon bow had a welcoming look, that of an old acquaintance who seems untouched by the years. She was riding in a nest of cruising boats alongside the float in Camden. We had driven down late in the afternoon of the first Friday in July, and as we approached with our duffel, I could see Pierce standing in the hatchway, elbows resting on the coaming, drink in hand, gazing with salty contempt at the tourists around the picnic tables of the lobster pound.

"Where have you *been,* for God's sake?" he wanted to know as we came over the side. "I thought you were going to be here by three. There's been a fair southwesterly the whole frigging afternoon. We could have been through the Reach by now." He scowled up at the telltale, still swimming across a glossy, infinitely clear sky.

In the cabin below, Lily was stowing the icebox from a grocer's carton, and she looked up to say, "I've been having a lovely time shopping but Pierce has been in agony, thinking you'd deserted us." She wore shorts and a Greek sailor's jumper and her hair was tied up in a workman's blue kerchief. When she smiled her teeth were very white against a

skin already flushed with sun. She had a corsair look about
her, without artifice, every sleek inch for use, not admiration.

"Well, I've been toiling for you in the office all day,
Cap'n," I said, "and I expected to be piped aboard and
handed one of those things before I get chewed out for a lousy
two-hour delay in reporting . . ."

Pierce's real impatience to get under way faltered. He had
been looking at the lines and fenders, thinking what to let
go first, but he looked up, alerted, trying to guess if I had
brought him any good news. He stepped aside to let Nancy go
below. Turning, he called after her, "You and Ben can have
the forward cabin if you like—it's more private."

"There's no such thing," Nancy said, squeezing by Lily
with an armful of clothes, dropping them and kneeling beside
her to help.

Pierce was waiting, expectantly. "You want a drink?" He
looked below where splinters of excess ice lay heaped in the
galley sink. "It's all there. Help yourself. Every man's his own
bartender on this cruise."

"Oh, I can wait," I said. "Everything can wait. Let's get
under way. Can we get someplace tonight?"

He nodded. "North Haven, anyway. I wouldn't want to
spend the night in here. Got to get away." He crouched to the
panel in the cockpit and turned a switch. A fan whined softly
below deck. "You want to change?"

"Later. I'll give you some help with the lines."

"There's time."

I went along the deck, dropping my duffel bag into the forward compartment and following it to change from the business suit, for I had come directly from the office, into cotton
trousers, sweater and sneakers. When I came up, *Bluejay*'s
stern was slipping into the current. Seeing that I stood by the
bowline, Pierce tried to start the engine. It coughed and snor-
keled, obstinately fell silent twice before it caught, setting up
a purring in the planking, and I cast off.

Onshore, a kid leaning on his bicycle and an old man in
dungarees and a couple, arms entwined, watched *Bluejay*'s

nose swing slowly around Camden Harbor and then point to
sea.

We went by the plum-red yacht club, so close I could see
through the kitchen door to where a woman was slicing toma-
toes. On the porch a man in khaki was hanging Japanese lanterns, and I could hear the New York voices of some blond
teen-agers walking up the dock with their sail bags.

Lily came forward to help me with the mainsail, and when
we had it set, it bellied out to catch the still-fresh following
wind. The marvelous first moment of being away overwhelmed me. With the engine shut down, there was no noise
but wind and water, and yet *Bluejay* was soaring as though
she too had been eager to be free of the land. Astern, the
Camden hills, topped by a stone tower, began to turn a majestic, smoky blue.

The first sea swells caught us, and with them, it seemed, the
shore-borne cares, the persistent anxiousnesses loosened their
grip on me and there was some promise that in the week
ahead I might elude them altogether.

Pierce had given the helm to Nancy and he frowned at the
folded chart, giving her a compass course southward to the
whistler where we would round Islesboro into East Penobscot
Bay. There was a quarrelsome set to his mouth, suggesting
that the bloody-eyed bird still rode his shoulder, but the news
I carried, which seemed to me more cheerful than he had any
right to expect, was going to be an antidote and there was no
reason to withhold it any longer.

I made Nancy and me a drink, and then, with all four of us
assembled in the cockpit, I said, "I don't know what to make
of Jack Snyder. I thought him incapable of any sort of conciliatory noise, a turtle of a man. And yet it was Snyder, all right,
amiable as you please."

"He called you?"

"Yesterday afternoon. Then he came around to see me this
morning. I wish you could have heard him. It was important,
he told me, for all concerned that Mr. Jay not get the idea he
was to be slighted in the expansion. His name and presence

were as essential as ever, more so, if that were possible. That much had to be clear, and if he had given any other impression, he was at fault." I laughed. "What have you *done* to those guys?"

"Nothing."

"You've talked to Weiss."

"On the phone. Once. Maybe a couple of times."

"Well, I don't understand, but they're apprehensive. They want to please you. They're persuaded you're indispensable."

"Does that surprise you, really? I am. What did he want to talk about? Was it all just bullshit?"

"Well, he wanted to know if a title was important to you. Yes, often is, he told me. Often makes a great deal of difference. Executive Director? How did that sound?"

"What else?"

"He had in mind that the new issue could be of a different class in order to prevent any dilution of the present stock."

"Okay. There's something, all right. That's a concession. He didn't happen to touch on whether they still intend to steal my company?"

"Oh come on, Pierce, for Christ's sake. This is a total reversal. I cannot understand it. I mean, I heard you say unforgivable things to Weiss. If ever a man had grounds for vindictiveness . . . Just out of curiosity, did you apologize?"

"For what?"

"I don't understand. He seems to be totally without spite."

"Or pride—one or the other."

"Pierce, you're talking like a man on top. You're not—not now. They're making it easy and agreeable for us. Don't you understand?"

"Do we keep the voting trust?"

"Well, no. Of course not that. Snyder said he could not alter his distaste for that."

"Then I hope you told him to go fuck himself." We sat around Pierce silently, listening to the sea streaming along our sides. Southward, I had a glimpse of the beginnings of a fog hurrying along the shore and blurring its profile. "Well, what did you tell him?"

"That I thought I could persuade you. I said I'd call him sometime when we got to a phone."

"Now you know what to tell him."

"We'll talk about it again," I said. "Later, when you're in a more reasonable frame of mind."

"Oh, you're wrong, Ben. I'm in a very reasonable frame of mind." He rose, and reaching around the cabin bulkhead, snatched a bottle and added whiskey to his glass. "But I don't think you know how it feels to conceive of a structure and then go build it, pole by pole, and hold it up when it threatens to fall down and then, in the moment it proves firm and useful, to have it hijacked. I don't like it, and what I want from you now is not a lot of crap about how agreeable they are and how nice it's going to be for me, going back to work for my own company as the executive janitor. What I want from you is not common sense, if that's what you've been talking with Snyder, but your loyalty and some courageous plan to get my company back. I've been screwed—and I want you to do something about it."

Nancy, alert, was only pretending an absorption with the compass needle. Our wake was askew, unrolling shoreward. Lily went below, to reappear promptly in a peacoat. She sat down beside Pierce and patted him on the knee. "But listen to what Ben's saying. He knows all that, and he also knows what's practicable."

"Oh, good, Lily. I didn't know you had any view of this at all. Now what do you mean? Are you for me or against me?"

"You know very well I'm for you, Pierce, but you make it so difficult for me when you behave like this—either in the destructive way you're starting out now, as though you'd bring down everything in a great crash if you can't have it all your own way, or in what you say to people, to me, or Ben or—oh God, I still can't bring myself to think of it—Julie Weiss."

Pierce looked at his wife steadily and said, "People are either for you or against you."

"Pierce," I said, "what do you expect me to do?"

He stretched his legs, regarded the toes of his sneakers. "Whatever would work. There must be ways of getting control back, obvious ways."

"You mean split them? Of course. Sure, if the Class A is going to be the voting stock, all we'd need is one of them to keep control. Do you think there's the remotest chance of that?"

"Each has his price."

"I'm told everyone does. In this case it might be high."

"I don't agree." Jay's upper lip puffed out angrily as he leaned across the cockpit, spittle flying. "I would think that was clear, that Blum would do anything for money. Automatic for him. He'd spread his legs like some old whore for a lousy two bucks."

"Well, if it's a grudge fight, and money is no object, you could always go buy up everything they make available."

Pierce leaned back, watching me, his head rocking. "You're kidding, but it could be done, couldn't it? Buy everything in sight. Straw man. You'd only have to get them once to get them good—right?" He, too, now noticed the fog pursuing us, packs of wispy hounds coming up over the horizon, and he watched it moodily before he added, "But it's impossible, for Christ's sake."

In the eighteen years I had known Pierce he had never denied himself anything because of its cost. "Good," I said. "That's good sense."

Lily was watching him, too, as his eyes trailed astern again, gray now like the fog, expression fading from them. He turned thoughtfully back to me. "There's got to be another way. Your way. Can't you think of something?"

"Perhaps." I nodded. "There's generally something you can do. But let's leave it at that, can we? If we talk Microdom for the next couple of days, it's not going to be a vacation for any of us. There'll be time enough when we get back."

Astern, the fog licked the rim of the lowering lavender sun and its long curling tongues were catching up, touching us with chill and spreading a smoky field around *Bluejay*. As we rushed on into the first blues of evening, I was hoping that Pierce's seamanship was a match for his eagerness.

The whistler on which Nancy had been steering blurred even as we came abeam of it. "New course here?" I asked.

He looked as though I had asked him an irrelevant question, but he rose and, clutching the deckhouse, peered ahead. "Yes, we come northeast now."

Nancy hesitated, and I put the wheel over for her, watched the needle turn and steady on 045 before relinquishing it.

"Where are we going, Pierce?" I asked.

"The Reach. With this breeze, we can get through before dark."

"I'm cold," Nancy said. "Will somebody take this while I get a sweater?"

"Fog doesn't bother you?" I picked up the chart and followed his pencil line ascending into Eggemoggin Reach and guessed it was another three-hour sail. "You wouldn't settle for some place short of that?"

"Oh yes," Lily said. "We don't want to anchor in the dark."

"Got to get on," Pierce said. "Been waiting all day for a run and now you want to go in."

Nancy, pulling on her sweater, shivered. "Oh, please. I'm getting cold and hungry. It's going to take us hours to fix dinner. Couldn't we?"

"We'd have to go back." He looked over his shoulder at the mainland, still visible, with dread, as though there were furies after us.

"Here's Pulpit," I said, putting a finger on the chart. "We could make Pulpit in less than an hour."

But Pierce did not hear. He held *Bluejay* to her northeasterly course and brusquely asked Lily to make him a drink. When she had and he had taken it from her without thanks, none of us spoke for a while. We sat in a sullen circle, watching the sun sink farther, feeling the urgency drop out of the wind, as though it had joined our mutiny. Ahead, the fog rose its steep silvery banks.

"Oh, all right," Pierce said abruptly, "Pulpit then." He held out his hand for the chart, and after the briefest glance, headed *Bluejay* southeast.

North Haven, like a long green slipper on the water, lay ahead now, spreading its welcoming arms, yet the closer we approached its shore, the more the pearly fog inched up its slopes like incoming tide, sometimes engulfing it entirely, then receding to give us a provocative glimpse of a field or a clump of spruce.

When we were no more than a quarter of a mile offshore, it came out to meet us and wrap us, to within a few feet of *Bluejay's* whispering hull in its tall curtains. Her bowsprit disappeared. Though the sky was bright above us, we sailed on within a gauzy well.

"Christ," Pierce said. He looked anxiously ahead, then at me, as though to say, "This was all *your* idea."

"It's still patchy. You'll probably run out in a minute."

"Take a look." He kicked the fallen chart toward me. "It's unmarked, your Pulpit Harbor. We have to look for the frigging rock. Are we down far enough?"

I found Pulpit, halfway down the coast, and nodded. "You want to take in sail and poke in there a bit?"

He looked over the side, where the gray water slipped by forcefully, and bent to start the engine, but after repeated attempts, each less encouraging, it failed to turn over. "Shit," he said.

I went forward, and straddling the bowsprit, peered ahead, watching the water and listening, hearing only the cry of a gull, like an angry child, overhead, and the dark water licking at the hull. I felt her behind me and turned to find Lily sitting on the deckhouse. "You think we'll hear the surf?"

"Hope . . ." And in that instant I saw a white lace of water coming toward us and cried out, "Come left, Pierce!" *Bluejay* swung eastward obediently and the fog broke, giving us an alarming view of a head of land close aboard, but we looped safely under it and moved off along the coast—in close when we could, searching for some break in the ridge and veering off gingerly when the fog closed.

As he cried out from the wheel for assurance, there was a rising fretfulness in Pierce's voice that matched the crying gull's. Unsure and angry at the engine and at all of us for the conspiracy that had brought him here to feel his way through the perils, like a blind man in the city, he looked as miserable as Nancy, shivering from time to time with a mixture of cold and anxiety.

Just at dusk, as I stood at my lookout station, accepting the likelihood we might not find it at all and that Pierce, to say nothing of the rest of us, had no notion of an alternative, Lily sighted Pulpit Rock. It rose, like a phallus, from the ledge that reaches across the mouth of the harbor, and as *Bluejay*'s nose swung toward it, through parting curtains of fog, we cheered.

I walked aft to the cockpit and in the fast-fading light tried to read the chart. With a flashlight I studied it just long enough to see that Pierce was leaving Pulpit to port.

"No, you can't," I told him. "That's the bar. You can't cross it. You have to go around."

He squinted ahead, nervously, sweeping the water, and it *was* hard to believe. He shook his head in doubt. The Pulpit appeared snug against the eastern shore, impossible to circle it.

"All right, look at the chart."

He held his course, looking at me, then at the chart with suspicion. The sails snapped with a fresh gust, sweeping us forward and distracting him, but again he tried to follow my finger under the light. He headed off momentarily, and *Bluejay* faltered, her sails flapped fretfully as though they felt the urgency of the fast-fading light.

"You want to take it?" There was uncertainty and an edge of anger in Pierce's voice. It was a challenge. "You take it in? Come ahead, you've been reading the chart."

"All right." I put a hand tentatively on the wheel and handed Lily the chart and flashlight. "Hold it so I can see it," I said and headed off, leaving the Pulpit to starboard.

My hand on her helm, *Bluejay* rounded the Pulpit obediently, crept up under the lee of the headland, where at my command Pierce let the anchor drop into the quiet of the estuary called Cabot's Cove. With the splash and the dropping of her sails came that buoyant relief of land people who have matched their superficial skills against the capricious, Olympian sea. Our apprehension drained away, to be replaced by some small confidence in our wits.

The dark was sudden and total. We could make out a lobster boat riding at a mooring a hundred feet away, silhouetted in the only lights, those of three houses on the distant northeast shore. Otherwise we were encircled by soft, velvet blackness. Overhead, *Bluejay*'s mast swung through a field of small stars, and on my cheek I could feel an aromatic southerly breeze.

Below, there was a pleasing domestic scene. Lily, freshly combed, was pumping up the galley stove, and beside her, Nancy filled a saucepan. Yellow paths, spilling from our portholes, wandered off across the gently stirring surface of the cove. It was an altogether gratifying time, with its sense of safety gained—the comforts of food and companionship on the way and those of drink already in hand.

Yet, beside me, Pierce was sullen. He complained about the harbor entrance which had confused him and the Coast Guard for failing to buoy it, and I realized that what was really vexing him was that he had relinquished the helm. Though I tried to make a joke of it, I could not reach him. He was working up one of his thunderheads, feeding it with ever-darker drinks.

Then, as though it underlay every thought, he reverted to Microdom and wanted to know what I planned to do. If I had it in mind to call Jack Snyder from here, it would be a good bit of exercise getting to a phone—five miles, anyway, of water and fields, between me and my friend Snyder.

"We have a week ahead of us, Pierce," I suggested. "There'll be time enough to talk about it, but while you're angry it's useless." Though I was too wary of Pierce's mood to propose it now, he had put the idea into my mind of a minority stockholder's suit as a means to better terms and I intended to return to it.

But he accepted my argument, and as we went below for dinner he turned to grumbling about our short run and how, by doubling back, we had lost a whole day of sailing, cutting his expectations of reaching far up the coast.

I decided the seating arrangements by touching Lily's hand. This brought her next to me on the port bunk, her own, leaving Nancy and Pierce to face us. In that first instant beside me, Lily dropped her lovely head to my shoulder in a childlike, trusting way, to murmur how sleepy sailing made her. It was an unconscious act of submission, and across the table, Pierce looked away, trying to ignore it.

But Nancy parodied it, nestling against him, and made him laugh. With so favorable a start in fetching Pierce from his glooms, she flirted in her broad, teasing way. She told him he was particularly appealing in sailing clothes, how she doted on the little jungle behind his ears, wished she could keep me from the barber, preferred long hair on men and always longed to touch it.

Pierce was diverted by her playfulness until Nancy made the facetious proposal we switch partners for the cruise. "They do it all the time on yachts, don't they?" she asked. "I thought that was the whole point." She thrust her fingers into his curls, and at her touch, Pierce recoiled as though it repelled him.

"No?" She pouted, acting elaborate injury. "But then what can we do about Ben and Lily? Ben's been in love with Lily for years, you know. What can we do about that?"

"Yes, I know," he replied. "Do you think it ought to bother me, Nancy? Does it bother you?"

She shrugged, maintaining her frivolousness. "I was just wondering."

"I tell you, Nancy, now you ask . . ." He pushed back plate and spoon, as though for some negligent waiter, and poured himself more wine. "What bothers me is flouting it. I don't like to watch people going to the bathroom or making love in public."

"You used to." I could not resist it. "Or is it just French people you like to watch?"

"You know what I mean," Pierce warned.

"If it's the audience . . ." Nancy looked out through the hatchway.

"No, it isn't just the audience." Pierce slurred the word. It emerged as "audiench" and Nancy laughed. "No, goddam it. It's the playing at it that I hate. I don't like people putting hands on my wife . . . squeezing her flesh."

We had been leaning against the bunk cushions, Lily and I, and my hand had fallen across her shoulders, my fingers brushing her upper arm. Entirely unconsciously I had sought to touch her, and the smooth, tanned skin seemed to welcome my fingertips, offering itself up as to a warm sun. I withdrew my arm as Pierce said, "There's a kind of suburban, middle-class party where it's considered very Saturday-night for a wife to sit in somebody else's husband's lap. It lets everybody know they're having a good time. Supposed to be very gay and wicked and daring. Well, it has the opposite effect on me. It makes me sad. They want to be unfaithful but they haven't the guts. It's a reversion to childhood—they *play* infidelity."

No one said a word, and Pierce pressed his attack on Nancy. "You like watching Ben feel other women, Nancy? Does that stimulate you, for Christ's sake?"

"It doesn't bother me." Nancy was tense now, but still smiling determinedly at him.

"I do believe you like it. You get some kind of cheap thrill out of it, is that right? You bored with him?"

Nancy, losing patience, said, "Oh, don't be disgusting, Pierce."

"Or is it me? Washington—is that it? I offended you, didn't

I? You wanted to run the show and you didn't get to—right? That pissed you off, didn't it, Nan? Come on, say it. Spit it out. Get all that nasty stuff out of your system. You want to see me punished."

"No, dear." Nancy gave him an indulgent pat. "Punishment isn't in my line at all."

Pierce withdrew his hand and stared at her curiously, as though he'd never examined her thoroughly before. "Jesus, it isn't, is it? So long as you have a good seat for the show, you'll watch anything." Resentment of her spilled from Pierce like a jinni out of a bottle.

Lily had moved away from me now, and from her corner regarded Pierce with a curious melancholy.

For a moment no one spoke, and then Nancy said, "Flirting's a perfectly harmless game. You can read what you like into it but any evil is most likely in the eye of the beholder. Anyway, it's the whole point for a woman—being alluring. It makes her know she's alive. It's her pleasure and, sometimes, her only protection. Yes, often at a party my mother would warn my father by being affectionate with another man. Of course, she was never serious, while he generally was. Mother's a professional flirt, isn't she, Ben? But it never did any harm to her marriage. It often held it together. When my sister Natalie was having a miserable time and thinking, after only a year of marriage, about divorce, Mother told us what her life had been like . . . that Daddy had had affairs with other women, often when problems in his business and paying the bills at home were at their worst. But she accepted all this, that with his charm went weakness, that he might wander off, but she also knew he would come back, that no matter how much it pained her, it was her responsibility to keep the marriage whole—that we girls, a household, just the unbroken circle of the family was more important than any temporary injury to her pride."

"But you don't believe that, Nan," Lily said. "Nobody believes *that* any more."

"Natalie's still married—and reasonably happy."

Pierce's head swung back and forth, like some zoo animal's behind bars, as he stared at Lily. Her arm, as she sat up, lay tangent to mine. "Bring me a tall glass," he told her brusquely, pushing the wine away, "and the bourbon."

Lily brushed my legs on her way to the galley. "But that's old, old stuff out of the attic, Nan. Surely you don't believe in that—the double standard?"

"I believe nothing ever really changes." My wife smiled as she quoted me. "It only seems to. Morals *can't* change much. They vary a little, up and down, like skirts, but you can't do away with them. Women will always be scorned for promiscuousness and men will always be forgiven for it."

Lily laughed in rich and mischievous contradiction, and that golden sound in her throat teased and excited me.

Setting Pierce's glass and bottle before him, she knelt beside me on the bunk, groped in the locker and produced a Scrabble set. Then she spread the letters on the table for us to draw. Though we began to play, the argument over morals continued and no one of us was persuaded, nor, in the end, even listened to the others. It seemed that beneath what each of us was saying lay newly inflamed emotions and they were becoming more difficult to discipline.

The cabin had become stuffy, heavy with the smell of oil and faintly steamy with the liquor we had drunk. Through the haze of Pierce's cigar smoke, swirling in the light from the swinging yellow lamp, I felt that our accustomed inhibitions had loosened their grip. Nancy, even in our most intimate talks, had never spoken of her family so freely. And she seemed to have openly condoned my attraction to Lily. Even as I wondered at it, my hand had found Lily once more, my fingers seeking the plumpness just below her elbow.

We not only touched, but smelled each other. Lily's moist mustiness beside me and a saltiness on warm skin. There was some spicy oil from Jay and the liverish odor of tobacco leaf on his breath. I was very much aware of confinement now, of lack of choice, not even an illusion of the infinite decisions which persuade a man he is free. Here—riding in our warm, lighted ball, tethered by a slender line to a precarious hold on the earth, fathoms below—we swung, the four of us, in eternity, with only the bottle, the flickering lamp and our own four bodies to assure us that we lived and another day would come.

It seemed to me that somewhere, on the sea perhaps or later, here at *Bluejay*'s cabin table, I had lost my will, that it had been pooled with the others and surrendered to some force outside us all which had already begun to guide my hand, even as I moved the squares with their letters back and forth on my rack to make a word. Pierce's too as he reached for his glass again, making us each recall its relinquishing of the helm. It was festering in his thoughts now.

It was as though roles had been assigned and none of us could play another. My own, as I tried it on, pleased me, just as Pierce's clearly did not. I could feel him fuming at it across the table.

Lily and I, who had drunk the least, began to win the Scrabble game. We built elaborate words and quickened with our success. Nancy grew fuzzy and sleepy, losing interest, as Pierce, brooding, began to play a variation of his own. He was spelling out words which had a particular appeal to the bloodiness of his thoughts—first, obscenities, at which we laughed; then, grimly, for half a game, he sought the letters to spell *ghetto* and *pogrom*—then shoved the board away, drowning Lily's reading of the score by saying with special truculence, "Oh sure, I know it isn't fashionable or enlightened. Around the Brandeis anthropology department you could get your Ph.D. lifted for it. And to be honest, I can't help hating myself for it some—but goddam it, I've been there and I *know*. A Jew can dress up in a Brooks suit and a crew cut and stand in the middle of Harvard Square, yet underneath the disguise there's that ancient, hook-nosed Fagin with greed in his veins ready to screw everybody that isn't a blood relation for the smallest advantage. They're like some fucking fungus—a parasite. They'll always destroy the tree."

"You're safe here," Lily said, putting the pieces back in their box, "because we know what you mean by that—or at least I do."

Lily's rational tone reflected my own thought of Pierce's railing, that it was a groaning need, one rooted in his balls, to find villainy and thus explain to himself and to us the blunt fact of failure. Pierce, too, thought she was calling him out and sat up. "What?" he asked her. "What do you mean?"

"That you want to provoke me." She smiled sweetly, deftly. "But it's too late and we're all too tired . . . and too drunk." She reached for his glass, but he drew it to his chest. She gathered the others and rose to do the dishes.

Nancy went to help her, and Pierce and I sat confronting each other. He seemed to be struggling against Lily's cool, patronizing reason and an awareness he had drunk more than the rest of us and now had to prod sluggish wits and an unresponsive tongue. But even as his eyes threatened to close and Nancy, yawning, went off to bed, he struggled on, trying to make something of it.

"Goddam it, it's easy enough to take the intellectual view. I can talk that talk as well as anybody. I could even believe it, until I worked with them."

"I've worked with them," Lily said.

"Sooner or later . . . shit, I've known it all along . . . every Jew believes the world is a hostile place. Their distrust of their fellow man is going to destroy the world in the end. The evil is in the hypocrisy, that shopkeeper's hypocrisy, old as Shylock, that deceives you into believing they are otherwise. You know what my old man used to say about them— never get into a pissing contest with a skunk." His eyes blinked heavily, painfully. "When I was in communications school in the Navy, we'd take the tests in series, and there'd be five minutes between when you could talk to the guys who'd just taken a part you were going in for and the Jews would deliberately give you the wrong answers. No, I know as well as you do what the liberal line is—only I have to trust my instincts. Sometimes my mind deceives me, but not my instinct—and by instinct I recoil from Jews, from Jewish looks, from the sound of Jewish voices—affected, quarrelsome women, never content. They have no *pride*, for Christ's sake, no serenity, always agitated, because their values are all . . ." He made the money sign with his fingertips.

"I'm afraid that's a universal way of keeping score," I said. "Do you ever stop to think that good manners—grace, not making waves, making it look easy—was another useless subject they taught in college? They might better have taught us some straining and pushing."

Pierce shook his head. "No, the rules don't change, Ben. Straining and shoving means you lose. Those are still the rules. Better to fail than lose your dignity—a man without dignity disgusts me."

"You have to win. Style has no meaning unless you do."

Leaning across the table, he glared at me. "You agree with me, goddam it. Why are you arguing against me? You warned me that day in Watertown. Come on, admit it. You wouldn't trust a Jew, would you—even if he was a friend of Lily's?"

In the galley, she turned to us slowly, a melancholy in her lovely face.

"But I don't agree," I said, "that there's some special black villainy born into every Jew. If they're less trustworthy, it's only because of circumstances. Yes, I did warn you, but only that you can't expect them to play by Ivy League rules. No, not even in Cambridge, not even David Blum would be bound by them."

"There, you see," he shouted in boozy triumph. "You do agree."

"No I don't. They'll learn, and meantime, you must play by their rules if you're going to play with them, and we must, in every business now."

Pierce sunk back, overcome. "Oh, fuck you, Ben. You're

saying that just to agree with her." He looked back and forth at us, resentfully, and then pulled himself up to grope in the locker where Lily had put away the liquor.

*   *   *

Nancy was a dark shape in the starboard bunk, and when I spoke to her she murmured and turned to the bulkhead. The cabin light was alarmingly weak and I turned it off. A paraffin lamp flickered in the head directly aft, shedding enough light for me to find pajamas and sleeping bag.

But when I closed the cabin door and stretched out in the darkness, I found my bone-weariness and the gentle rocking of *Bluejay*'s hull were no match for the drink. It swirled uncomfortably in my gut and throbbed up in the roots of my brain. Waiting for sleep, my mind was clear and I was thinking once more of the effect of these isolated but confining quarters on all of us, how buttock to buttock our feelings intensified.

It occurred to me that all of us had the presentiment, Pierce most acutely, the knowledge that Lily and I were committed to acting out his collapse, bound to gang up on him—in Scrabble games as in the piloting of *Bluejay*—in each new evolution of the cruise. The sole force which might have sustained Pierce, Nancy had withheld. Nancy had licensed our bullying flirtation, believing it was innocuous, to herself at least. Listening to her regular breathing in the adjacent bunk, I wondered if, as Pierce had suggested, it was Washington at the root of her delinquency, or the permissiveness she argued, or some emotion she could not even comprehend.

Was it trust she offered me? I doubted it. Nancy tended to cynicism where men were concerned. Writhing miserably, listening to her breathing, regular now but thin and adenoidal, I had pity for her, for her abdication of pride and spirit, but rather than gratitude, I felt indifference.

Lily was still with me, the smell of her in my nostrils, and again I tasted the prescience. Custom and rectitude and the fear of consequence that chastens behavior were giving way to exhilarating possibility.

Even as I allowed myself these thoughts, I suspected them for the fantasies of drink and the wakeful dreaming of a mind that readily reverts to adolescent pattern. I knew well enough where reality lay and yet I could not get illusion out of my throbbing head. Seeking reason and perspective, I thought of the meeting of the Beacon Hill Association we were missing tonight, of the postman who at eight would be shoving the day's notices and bills through the slot in our door, and of the thirty-odd people at the office who soon would be busy with their dictation and telephoning, but it seemed illusion itself. The reality was *here,* afloat—expectant in the dark.

The compartment began to close, stifling me, and I opened the overhead hatch to find the night had turned calm. Hoisting myself onto the deck, I looked aloft into clear heavens, sewn with such a richness of stars that the shoreline stood out in profile all around us and we floated in the center of a silver lake. It was breathless, and *Bluejay* lay so still she might have been alongside a wharf.

Reaching down through the hatch, I grabbed up the sleeping bag and carried it aft with me along the cool, dew-moist deck to the cockpit, where deep cushions, running fore and aft on either side of the helm, were long as bunks. Spreading my bag on the starboard one, I heard Pierce's voice, weary but contentious.

"All right, foxier then, foxier than I am. But foxiness is no fucking good to anybody. You can't build anything out of foxiness. Foxiness devours itself. It chews on its tail and then it can't stop until it chews up its own eyes and its own crafty brain."

Light filtered through the hatchway door, and when I knocked, Pierce's voice paused. Lily was in her bunk, but she raised up on an elbow, grateful, I thought, for the interruption. Pierce, still dressed, was as I had left him an hour earlier, sprawled on the edge of his bunk, one arm behind his head, foot propped on the chart table, drink in hand. He frowned, nettled at my reappearance.

"I was suffocating up forward," I said. "I'm going to sleep on deck."

His heavy lids closed twice over painfully red eyes. "Bugs. Mosquitoes'll get you. Won't let you sleep."

"No. No bugs. It's lovely up here. Lots of room. Come on up."

"No thanks."

"Lily?"

She considered it, with a glance for the glare of the lamp, then for Pierce, questioning him. Then, agilely, she slipped out of her bunk and climbed the ladder to look out, her head beside mine. "Oh, it is lovely," she said, hopping down the ladder. As she rolled up her sleeping bag, she turned to say to Pierce, "It's stuffy in here. I'm going to try it outside. Sure you don't want to?"

"I said I didn't want to go out. It gets light around five, for God's sake."

Lily wore boy's white pajamas, and from my bunk I watched her, a child ghost in the starlight, making up hers and sliding quietly into it. For a moment it was breathlessly still, and looking aloft there was a stunning sight—our mast and spreaders, a soaring, protective cross against that brilliant awesome heaven.

By raising my head I could see Pierce below in the cabin. Draining his glass, he made his way to the icebox, where he cursed and chipped away at the dwindling block, and with a glass replenished, sat down on his bunk as though he meant to sit up the night with his furies. Presently he went forward to the head, and on his return to the cabin, he came to the hatchway and looked into the cockpit—but none of us spoke. For another ten minutes I could hear him shuffling about in the cabin and then, when I had given up all hope of it, the light went out and *Bluejay* was still.

"Asleep?" I asked softly.

"No."

I could see her face—luminous, marble-pale against the cushions. I stretched a hand, bridging the cockpit, and after a moment I saw hers creep from the covers to meet mine. Our fingers touched and then our palms closed in a miracle of promise. I listened, straining to hear some continuing noise, but there was only a gentle licking of the sea and a lazy murmur of halyards overhead.

Releasing her hand, I slid from my bag, knelt beside Lily and kissed her. She was not surprised, and her mouth received me, warm and open, as though we were habitual lovers, safe in our bower. There was a tiny moan from behind her lips, telling me that hers was the same blessed relief as mine.

I felt for the zipper of her bag, and as I found it she stopped my hand and took her mouth from mine to whisper, "No."

The cabin door was black now, with the look of an empty cave. Bringing my mouth into the curls about her ear, I whispered, "You came out here to me—it's true. Stop thinking, Lily. Someone else is doing the thinking for us. Can't you feel it?"

"Yes. Who is it?"

"I don't know. But he's very able."

She laughed softly. "I'm not at all sure of that."

"But he'll have his way, however we like it."

"I'm not sure of that either."

The zipper opened for me sibilantly and my hand leaped to Lily's bosom, but she was rising forcibly against me. To my dismay, her knees rose and swung past me, out of her bag.

"What are you *doing?*" I whispered, trying to restrain her.

"Going below."

"Oh Christ." I held her wrist and we hesitated in the chilly night, bright now as daylight, Lily half out of her bag, one hand clutching the front of her pajamas together, looking at the black, open door of the cabin. And I went angrily back to my side of the cockpit.

*   *   *

As Pierce had promised, first light and its gulls woke me early.

By my watch it was quarter to five. I had been asleep less than four hours, but in that time the infinite clarity had been replaced by cold, enveloping fog. Lily slept, only her head, turned into the cushions, showed above the green caterpillar shape of her bag.

Still groggy, I was startled fully awake to see Pierce's haggard, red-eyed face peering from the cabin door. It vanished so quickly I began to doubt I had seen it at all. And to be sure, a few minutes later when I got up to look, he was in his bunk, head buried in a pillow.

The fog was thickening, dripping like rain from the rigging, and I went back to my bunk in the forward cabin, there to doze. Each time I woke, it was to find the fog a great cushion around us and the prospects more cheerless and I returned to my bunk, where the queasiness in my stomach was more endurable, to await some brightening in the sky.

At about eleven I was awakened by Pierce's voice coming from the deckhouse overhead. "What did you do?" he was asking, a loony, antic edge to his voice. "What did you do out there in the dark? Did you let him have a little feel? Come on—tell me."

"Oh, stop it, Pierce."

"No, really." He was on the point of laughter. His voice bubbled, nearly choked with it. "No, no. I want to know. Did you let him play with your tits, Lily? He was longing to the whole evening. That was plain enough. He couldn't resist touching—even after I told him not to."

"Oh, *please,* don't be disgusting."

"Does it disgust you, Lily? I don't believe that. You like it. Come on now. Well, it doesn't disgust me. As a matter of fact, I find it very stimulating. You're very desirable to me right now. How about it . . . or are you saving it for him?"

"Shut up. Shut *up.* We didn't *do* anything."

"I saw him with you, Lily."

"Well, that's all you saw. That's all there was."

"Sure. I believe you. I know you didn't sleep with him, because I watched you all night."

"Oh, Pierce. You idiot. Why didn't you come out?"

"Because you didn't want me to. Oh yes, that's true. You wanted to be with Ben. You wanted to lie down beside him. Oh yes you did. It stunned me, that you could lie down beside him for the night. You didn't feel strange about it?"

"You were awful," she began, speaking so softly I couldn't hear the end of it.

He laughed in reply, a giddy sound that split the thick silence, and said, ". . . unless you want to make love to him. Do you? What happened when he was there with you?"

"We kissed. That's all."

"Long one?" The laughter erupted again, choking off as he answered himself. "I don't suppose you could see your stopwatch."

Lily spoke carefully, weighing the words. "It wasn't conscious, going out there to be with Ben. Still, you're right. I am attracted to him. I have been, all along."

"Have you ever . . ."

"Slept with Ben? No."

"But other things?"

She murmured, and I could not make out what sort of confession it was but I knew it would be the truth.

"Oh God, I wouldn't want you to make love with him. Not even in your dreams. Perhaps most of all, in your dreams." Pierce spoke slowly now. "I thought it was just talk."

"No. Not just talk. And yet it's always seemed innocent."

Pierce groaned. "Oh God . . . if you mean . . . No, Lily, I don't have a right to deny anyone pleasure . . . least of all you. I'm not blameless. Jesus, it's what makes me know I'm alive, looking at some girl, maybe a stranger in the street, and wanting to go to bed with her. It isn't much different with you, I don't suppose. No—I don't have that right, do I? To keep you from some pleasure. There's little enough. Only don't make me *look*." Pierce's voice had taken on an uncharacteristic nakedness, a fluttering, as though his words came on the beating of his heart. "I'm riddled with holes today, and they're letting in sadness, drying me out. The idea I might

lose you, even for a second, or that I already have, is unbearable, Lily. You're everything, you know? You're the core. You
make me go."

"Oh *no*," she cried. "But that isn't true."

"Don't let me see. I couldn't endure that. You going off,
knowing my sorrow was his joy—no."

"There won't be anything to hide," Lily said.

Nancy's insouciant voice carried from somewhere aft,
"There's coffee if anyone wants it."

*   *   *

Just before noon the sun made slight exploratory signals to
us. A glow and a warmth filtered through the gray ooze and a
hesitant breeze stirred the nearest veils. Pierce, his legs dangling from the cabin, watched the lobster boat emerge, its
new hull, clean and square, topped by a fire-charred super-
structure.

I was the first to speak, pointing out the clearing and the
possibility of getting under way, but Pierce ignored me.

"Shall we go home?" Lily asked.

No one replied. The four of us sat facing into the cockpit,
overcome with inertia—Pierce sullen, Lily avoiding my eyes,
Nancy reading, nibbling from a box of cookies, retreating
into a fictional world.

Now the shoreline cleared—Pulpit Rock, its nest and whirling hawks; then, on the far shore, a red barn with white trim,
and beyond, a cluster of weathered summer cottages, steps up
the pale green hill.

Pierce gave me a searching look, from which I guessed
there was to be no interview, no warnings or threats, no posting of his property. We were now too civilized and mature
for animal strife, for wrestling and bloodletting sure to end
in farce, and too proud of being men to talk or reason. And
it stood between us, ephemeral yet menacing, like the fog,
and inevitably waiting to be settled.

Gravely he went below, where I could see him unfold the
charts and spread them on the table, saw him run some

courses, then come topside to squint at the telltale, scarcely stirring at the masthead. He bent to start the blower.

"Well, we'll go on," he announced. "We'll go on to Mount Desert. We might still make it today, but we're going to need the engine."

A strong whiff of gasoline rose from underfoot and we waited several minutes before trying the starter. The engine caught on the first turn and I moved up to take in the anchor. *Bluejay* shuddered, and with Pierce at the helm, moved into the channel and, late and dispirited, back into Penobscot Bay.

Outside, the water was a dark brown mirror, flecked here and there with suds and whorls of kelp. Although we raised sail in anticipation, the canvas fell slack and we moved off under power toward the plump green hassocks of Great Spruce Head and Eagle islands. As we passed between Budd and Sheep into the East Penobscot, the wind came up, a cold, clear snap out of the northeast, clearing the sky, riffling the sea and turning it a deep blue.

Simultaneously, as though it felt no further obligation, the engine faltered, missing beats like a failing heart, and Pierce, relenting in his determined ignoring of me, told me brusquely to take the helm and went below. Returning, he reported there was gas in both tanks, though he had shifted to the port one, and asked if I had any suggestions. While I was below, noting again the strong fumes, wondering if it could be a clogged line and regarding its throbbing armor, the beast died altogether.

Thus, in order to keep our way we had to fall off to eastward, deciding Pierce to abandon the course for Eggemoggin Reach and to make for the Deer Isle thoroughfare, which, it seemed, we might fetch on a port tack.

Lily and Nan, sweatered now, brought up bowls of chowder and cold chicken, but Pierce refused it, saying he had no appetite, and leaving me with the helm, he went forward to slump at the foot of the mast and stare sullenly at the horizon. *Bluejay* heeled over and seemed to stretch into the growing sea and wind, but Pierce stayed on, hunched against the mast, clasping his long knees, unmindful of the bursts of spray that rose to sweep the bow.

Lily went up and sat beside him, but he did not speak to her. From time to time he put his head down in the nest of his own arms. But as we approached the nun marking the entrance to the narrow thoroughfare, he came aft and without a word took chart and wheel from me. Stonington's tall standpipe and hospitable harbor were coming into view now, just off to port. "We're going in, aren't we?" I asked.

He squinted at me. "What's the matter with you? We're barely under way. We'll never get beyond Schoodic if we don't sail more than a couple of hours a day." He looked at his watch. "It's only six and the breeze is holding."

"Somebody ought to look at that engine."

"Mount Desert," he said.

Both Nancy and Lily were looking longingly at Stonington's wharf. You could make out bright-colored storefronts and an Esso sign. "There's probably a movie," Nancy said. "Don't you think we could all use a movie?"

But Pierce's eyes, zealous for the next buoy, searched the sea ahead and he held his course. Nancy and Lily rolled themselves in blankets and watched miserably as Stonington disappeared in our wake and we headed northeast again into the building wind.

The swells came running in now to give us a real taste of deep water. Swift, steep banks challenged us, rising up under *Bluejay's* prow to split there and send us sharp-needled reminders of its fickleness. For an hour Pierce exulted in our discomfort. Jaw set, the collar of his peacoat turned up, his hair drenched with spray, some spirit was returning to him.

Nancy went after Marezene, tried to stay below but could not, and returned to huddle behind the deckhouse. Pierce was amused; but what had begun to concern him was our slow progress. The course, directly into the wind, caused him to pinch and lose way. And now we had commenced to pound, the hull colliding with such a weight of water we seemed to be barely holding our own against the weather.

From time to time he would look over his shoulder at the Deer Isle shore, to find that it had not diminished, just as Swans Island, ahead, grew no closer. A gaudy orange sun was sinking into the blue ridge along the western horizon. Otherwise it was a gray world, and I thought we had another hour or hour and a half of light.

"You're not going to make Mount Desert, Pierce," I said. "I doubt you can make Swans at this rate."

"Oh, please," Lily said. "Let's go back. This isn't any fun. Let's go back and start early tomorrow."

"God, yes," Nancy groaned. "This is a vacation."

For a moment or two I thought he wasn't planning to reply, that he intended to sail us on forever, and I knew him to be not nearly expert enough to enter any of these rock-studded harbors after dark. But he groped for the chart, and after a glance at it, said, "All right, I wouldn't want to spoil anybody's good time. We'll go to Isle au Haut."

He held out the chart to me, pointing out the narrow passage under Rich's Point, a back door to the anchorage on the leeward side of the island. It was no closer than Stonington, but he was going to have his way. We came about, and flying before the strong wind, watched Isle au Haut rise out of the sea.

Pierce asked Lily for a drink; she went below, then reappeared with one for each of us. Then, with a glass in hand and the prospects of making harbor before dark, I felt some degree of order and sanity had been restored and, surprisingly, I was looking forward to the evening. But as we approached Rich's Point, or what we believed to be Rich's Point, scanning the sea for the number five buoy that would lead us safely under Burnt Island and into the passage, we saw only the desolate coast, its scrub growing right to the surf line. There was no sign of human life along the shore as it stretched endlessly southward, and though I had gone forward with the binoculars, and clinging to the life line, scanned the inshore waters, I could find no buoys.

Then, instead of heading north, so that if we failed to locate the channel we could sail around the north end of Isle au Haut or even continue across the dangerous, but possible Merchant Row into Stonington, Pierce astonished me by heading southward, wasting what was surely the last precious hour of our light in the unlikely chance we had hit the coast too high. In the fading light I found a buoy, and as we approached I read the number—three—and called it out.

Pierce brought *Bluejay* about and we tacked slowly northward into the sea. I crawled aft along wet decks to look at the chart which Pierce had discarded and slid back and forth in the cockpit.

"I don't understand about the five buoy," I said. "We ought to be able to see it. Are you going around the top of the island or up to Stonington?"

He shook his head stubbornly and then, to my astonishment, swung *Bluejay* directly in toward the shore, passing into what looked, from the sloping shoreline, to be shallows.

"What the hell are you doing? Do you see the buoy?"

"I suppose it could sink, or wash away, but the passage couldn't. It's in there somewhere."

"You're crazy. It's up further." The alarm in my voice got Nancy and Lily to their feet, and we peered forward at the closing profile of Isle au Haut, like the bony back of some great monster asleep on the sea. It had turned from deep smoky blue to black, losing its rocks and stands of spruce, dissolving into one great, looming shadow in our path.

"It's shoal water in here," I said, looking at the chart again. "We'll go aground for sure, Pierce. Stay off. Do you want me to take it?"

"No. I don't mind a ducking. You mind a ducking, Mose?"

"Oh, for Christ's sake. Don't be an ass. Let me take it."

"I don't see any boats," Nancy said, looking around the horizon. "Nobody's going to know."

Lily was watching her husband with something like apprehension, but she said nothing.

"No," he said, his eyes shining, "I wouldn't do that. I wouldn't let you take it, Mose. If you want to be useful, go up and stand bow watch. That's all right. Sing out when you see the rocks. But I'll keep the helm tonight. Anybody doesn't like it"—he glanced at Nancy—"can take the dinghy." It lay upside down, lashed to the deckhouse.

I found the lead line and went forward again, shivering with cold and apprehension, wondering what I would do when we went aground in this gusting onshore wind or when, in a matter of minutes, it was fully dark.

We moved in swiftly, the wind and sea eager to hurry us into the fierce, dark, now enveloping shape of Isle au Haut, and I could hear the sound of surf and see it burst, little white fists in the shadows ahead. I kept looking aft, wondering how long he was going to hold this collision course with the beach. *Bluejay*'s nose swung to the north, swayed indecisively, but kept on toward the shore.

I swung the lead once, but we were going at such speed that the line streamed along the hull, tearing at my hands, and I reeled it in with difficulty. I saw a black shape in the water just off to port and cried out, but Pierce kept on heading for the dark thicket of trees on the shore, and while I tensed, expecting to feel the grating of our keel, I saw the thicket part, as though some projection of *Bluejay*'s bow was opening up the shoreline like a plow, and to my astonishment the Burnt Island passage, a winding silvery highway through the darkness, bringing some last light from the sunset on the other side, appeared miraculously, dead ahead. I was speechless— and from the cockpit came the sound of cheering.

With the splash of the anchor in the Isle au Haut thoroughfare, Pierce shook off the hostility that had clothed him all day. He made the drinks and watched with some pleasure as Nancy and Lily prepared dinner. Whiskey was effective in numbing the day's anxieties and revealing our appetites. We dined hugely, washing down the beef with three bottles of wine, and found our common disposition—so shattered in the day behind us—largely mended.

Pierce, now with Lily beside him, was jubilant over his discovery of the passage and entertained us with his theories about the missing number five buoy—that it had been towed off by souvenir hunters or by the Isle au Haut Mafia in some reprisal against the Coast Guard.

In this growing sense of comradeliness around the cabin table, with Pierce leaning back into the cushions, touching Lily from time to time as though to assure himself and me that she was there, it was hard to believe in the events of last night and the painful aftermath today. But the changing moods of the *Bluejay* were such that now, as we listened to the persistent wind and the chop against our sides, Nancy was able to say, "Sounds cold out—none of that sleeping on deck tonight"—and we all laughed, a bit nervously, but we laughed. And the missing sense of pleasure seemed to have come back aboard.

Only Lily was unable to shake her preoccupation. In a moment of repose, I found her eyes on me, wide and earnestly questioning. I noticed that Pierce's unaccustomed handling of her, as it grew more obvious, was making her uncomfortable. While we drank our coffee, he held her hand and stroked the inside of her forearm. She seemed indifferent to it, but found an excuse, some clearing and bringing on clean glasses, to break away. And all the while Pierce's desire for her grew, as though he had swallowed an aphrodisiac. I could feel the musky heat of it in the cabin. When Lily knelt on the bunk and reached into the locker for the Scrabble board, I anticipated his hand as it found her bottom and greedily palped it. Quick, unsmiling, she moved off, ignoring it.

We began to talk of marriage in the most general terms, Nancy resuming what she had been saying last night, about its being the woman's responsibility, and Lily broke her silence.

"I don't agree at all," she said. "It's no more the woman's responsibility than her husband's." And with an arresting urgency, she went on. "My mother was once, just once in her life, unfaithful to my father. She's told me that it happened with no real love for the man she went to bed with, nor any lack of it for Father. It was no more than if she'd admired a pretty dress she didn't need, and ordered it, or looked at those pictures they post outside a movie, and been curious and so, unexpectedly, gone in. She never intended it to be more than that, and it wouldn't have, except that in those days—it was 1936—the New York papers would list visitors. When there wasn't much going on, I suppose a society reporter would drift by a hotel and jot names off the register. And so a note appeared in the New York *Herald Tribune,* saying that Mr. and Mrs. Harvey Parsons of Boston were stopping at the Plaza Hotel. It was the weekend of Father's Harvard reunion, and Mother was missed, as was a classmate of Father's named Henry Symonds. He'd been her doubles partner. You see, she was incapable of the cleverness of some sordid hotel on Eighth Avenue. In Boston, people have snickered about it for twenty-eight years—really. I still hear it. They forget the names long enough to tell the story in front of me, and then are horrified as they recall it's *my* mother they're talking about. There was to be a divorce, but it was never completed. They meet now and again and they're very well mannered, like distant cousins—and Mother is still bewildered over how something so trifling has altered so much."

"Trifling?" Pierce asked.

"Well, no, of course it wasn't trifling to Father. His tolerance, his unorthodox views applied to everyone but us. I remember"—Lily laughed—"I remember when I was only eleven, and had the first swellings here, how he was mortified to see me naked in the upstairs hall, and how he detested anything the least bit off-color said in front of any of us. It was such a surprise from a man who condoned every kind of odd and curious behavior beyond his own threshold, a man who was himself such an experimenter with life."

"Then what do you mean?" Pierce asked.

"That it's wrong of him never to have forgiven her her

single night of being with another man. It wasn't that she loved Henry Symonds, but somehow he was important to her struggle to be herself, to prove her own vitality and attractiveness. That was hard, you know, against Father's strength and his rigid hand-me-downs about morality. Just like your mother, Nan, she could have forgiven him anything. Oh, why should it always be the man who's free? What a dirty trick. Why must we put up with that? It's not my idea of the marriage contract. You both observe the terms or it's meaningless." Nancy was smiling at Lily as though to say she wished she were right, and it induced in Lily a final affirmation. "Oh yes. That's the real moral revolution of our day. Young girls, girls in college would agree. They have very different ideas than we did."

"How *can* there be any fundamental change?" Pierce asked. "I suppose girls aren't afraid of pregnancy any more, but that isn't so important. There've always been ways around that. The real point is, nobody wants to share his woman. It's jealousy that keeps a woman from being promiscuous. That can't change."

Lily laughed, an angry, challenging sort of laugh. "Do you think we're less jealous?" When he didn't reply, she added, "Or less sexual?"

"Less opportunity," Pierce said.

Lily looked at him coolly. "I have *plenty*. Any woman who works has plenty of opportunity."

"Harder, slower to arouse," I proposed.

Lily laughed at me, her face flushed with derisive mirth, and Nancy joined in, taunting me in common female cause. "Maybe it's your arousing," she said as though she had been waiting for this glorious moment to find me vulnerable and with allies for the attack. "Men always like to think that if there's anything wrong with their love-making, it's the woman's fault. And yet they get to think of them as some appliance for their satisfaction that should turn on with a button. That's what women dread about sex, that men make a routine of it. A woman arouses quickly enough if she's surprised, stroked . . . made aware of her body."

Whereupon Nancy went off to the galley, and Lily, rising to help her with the dishes, said, "All right, Ben—what do *you* think? You haven't said whether you think morals are freer now—and if they are, whether you like it that way."

"I agree with Pierce. The form, the rules can't change. It's for the protection of women. It's a rare one who's still alluring after forty—while a man's still attractive."

"That isn't true," Lily said.

"The courts believe it. And divorce law, property settlements and all are designed to protect flabby ladies and punish their defecting husbands. In California—"

"Oh, I don't want to hear about California. What a disappointment you are, Ben. I thought you were on my side."

"I am. I'm getting around to it in my own way. Society rarely lives by every line of the code. Morals are too personal a matter. We all must make our own rules. You're better at that than most, Lily." I found Pierce watching me, and I asked him, "Do you have any regrets, by the way, for anything you've done?"

He gave me a little grin, one that acknowledged my accusation yet conceded nothing. "Oh, I've done lots of stupid things," he said with a warning thrust of his chin. "I'm as aware of that as you, Mose. But no, I don't regret a single damned one. My old man used to say that you never regret the things you've done, only the things you haven't. That's true, you know . . ." He shaded his eyes against the light near Lily's face, squinting at her. "I do hope I'll do fewer stupid things in the future. I don't want to be an *old* clown."

She watched him thoughtfully and then turned abruptly back to the drying of the dishes.

The wind was continuing to blow, sweeping a fine spray down through the thoroughfare, and I went forward to see if we were dragging, watching a pair of lights on shore until I was sure we were secure, and then climbed down into the forward cabin, closing the hatch after me. Nancy did not speak, though I could tell from her breathing she was not yet asleep. As I undressed in the dark I seemed to feel her hostility and I could hear Pierce's voice, whispering but audible and quarrelsome. I could not make it out precisely but I was as certain as if I had heard every word that Lily was putting him off, telling him it was late and there was not enough privacy.

I strained, leaning out of my bunk, for some giveaway sounds, the groan or sigh or cry from her lips that would be evidence of his success, for I knew Pierce would want me to hear. But there was only the regular snapping of a halyard against the mast.

Throughout the night the wind moaned in the rigging and *Bluejay* swung and shivered at her chain, so that I had a sense of peril and slept little, but toward dawn the wind slacked and the day began with a dense chorus of sea gulls, staccato cries and soft, plaintive chatter, and then laughter, ripples of it, and I peered out through the hatch to see that they were rejoicing at the glow of red in the east, already dissolving the last night shadows. A light breeze gave the pale water a delicate, feathery texture, full of promise.

We were all up early, and as we gathered around the table for a hasty breakfast I noted that Pierce and Lily were remote, waspish with each other, and I was certain now that Lily had thwarted him, perhaps in punishment or perhaps because of me.

Below us in the thoroughfare I could see half a dozen boats moored and a building at the shore which could be a boatyard, but Pierce would not hear of any delay. He knew island mechanics. They took their sweet time over their dinner before they showed up and then they talked your ear off and lost their wrenches in the bilge before they found the trouble. He was itching to get under way, and tinkered impatiently with the engine—trying to start it—until the battery wearied. But at eight we had sail up, feeling along on a light southwesterly, back through the rocky Burnt Island passage, and as we marveled over how we had come through it in near-darkness,

Bluejay touched bottom, thumped twice and came hard aground on the second right-angled turn.

Even as it became clear that the tide was ebbing and the wind blowing us onto the reef, Pierce balked at taking down sail, and the more I argued for it, the more obstinately he persisted in trying to sail *Bluejay* off. He relented finally, and as Lily and I struggled to get the mainsail down, he shouted at Nancy to help him launch the dinghy.

Lily rowed around *Bluejay*, sounding the water which shoaled steeply ahead to two feet. There was no sign of help in any direction. A quarter of a mile eastward a boy watched us stoically from the edge of a dock, and Pierce began to row toward him. With no optimism I turned on the blower, and after it had run half a minute I pressed the starter, heard it groan, and as I pressed again, it sounded weaker, and then with its last ounce of strength it jolted the engine to life.

In reverse, the propeller churned the clear water under our stern, and I watched kelp, tipped with yellow beads, moving lethargically along the side, swirling like dark blond hair. Then, as I advanced the throttle so that the hull vibrated angrily, *Bluejay* scraped free with a grinding thump of her keel and we inched back into the channel. Ahead, Pierce turned and rowed toward us, calling out to keep way on, and I took the chart from Lily's hand, praying that the engine, faltering and throbbing with infirmity, would persist until we cleared the passage.

Lily caught Pierce's painter and he crawled over the stern, but he did not reclaim the helm. Indeed, as we passed safely under Burnt Island and moved out to sea, he went forward to raise sail and then sat on the deckhouse and watched as the sun came through a wide ruffled wake of turbulent clouds fanned across the downcast sky.

I shut the engine off, and ahead, all three of them sat silently, feeling the swell begin to take us and a firm, gentle wind heel us far over, and then, as we headed east, make up dead astern. The main bellied out, well fed, and the genny slipped and slid against itself and the spreader and sometimes snapped taut with an uncertain flap or a drumlike crack. The sea was becoming choppy and deep green, with occasional frothy crests, and the bow wake made deep, breathy, satisfied sighs.

We left the Merchants and Fog and Heron islands astern, but before us was an infinity of other islands. They lay in our path like scattered caps and slippers strewn by some careless child. Each one virgin, no mark of human life, present or past, upon them, and as we passed close, they seemed to lure us in. There were square ones with rectangular cliffs, forbidding as saw blades in violent oranges and blacks. Others were soft and worn, roundly feminine in ocher and umber and, in certain lights, fleshy pink. As I sailed in close, Lily came aft to sit in the cockpit and share the glasses with me, peering at the dark stands of spruce, and below, the knee-high bay and blueberry and juniper that crept right to the rocks at the shore. And there was one island, treeless and uninhabited, except by a herd of plump black-tailed sheep who, baaing, hurried up their slope as we approached.

It was then that Lily and I decided we must stop to explore an island, and she went forward to propose we anchor for lunch at Long Island, but Pierce, huddled again at the forecastle, vetoed it with a shake of his head, and Lily returned to say he wanted to be in Southwest Harbor by dark and couldn't take a chance on the wind.

Wistfully we watched Long Island slip by, catching a tantalizing breath of its perfume, yearning for a walk on the long, curving arm of double beach that reached out to us, beckoning, and at the velvet, lime-green clearings that climbed its breast until they were swallowed in the dense black shadows of its balsam pelt.

At noon, as we turned north, the wind slacked and a fan of mackerel clouds climbed into the eastern sky, veiling the sun, letting through shafts of light that put me in mind of that old maxim about "drawing-water." Lily, who had been sunning herself on the deckhouse in a dark blue bikini, put on her sweater and went below to make lunch.

Off Great Gott Island, the wind died altogether, leaving us to wallow to the maddening snap and slack of the mainsheet and the fretful swinging of the sails. The engine would respond to no coaxing, but issued a cloud of noxious fumes which hung over the cockpit like a tent.

Later in the afternoon a light, fickle wind came down out of the northeast and Mount Desert rose out of the sea ahead to tower over us, and well before dusk we passed under the shelter of Cranberry Island and into Southwest Harbor.

Alongside a crumbling, oily dock, clustered with work boats and strewn with paint cans, we watched an inarticulate mechanic, a man with short white hair and a pink, ageless face, disassemble the carburetor and scoop out fingers of green sludge. While he reassembled it we went off on separate errands in the village.

Walking along the main street with fresh bread and a blueberry pie, I saw Lily in the laundromat and went in to wait with her while our clothes whirled in a vat. I looked up in the midst of describing the bakery, a housewife's kitchen, to see Pierce in the window, staring at us, stricken, over his sack of bottles from the package store. It was as though he had discovered us at some new treachery. Though I waved, he moved on quickly, and we returned on board *Bluejay* to find him nursing a fresh hostility.

He was so abrupt with the mechanic that I suspected the man would fix our engine so it would never run again, and indeed he set about further tinkering and presently announced it would require another call in the morning. I followed his red and black mackinaw up the dock, hoping to undo Pierce's damage, but when I asked about those vivid streaks in the west—they were filtering through a palisade of black, rolling clouds, turning the horizon luminous—he told me with evident pleasure that we were in for some bad weather and I had a feeling he was going off to arrange it.

This was confirmed in the morning. I awoke to leaden skies and a drizzle. After breakfast I turned on the radio and groped along the broadcast band listening to half a dozen forecasts of rain and strong northeast winds. At ten-thirty I walked up to the village, hoping, vainly, for some promise of clearing. Just before noon our mechanic arrived to complete the engine repair, but he would give us no encouragement about the weather. "Slow clearing" was his prediction. By that he seemed to mean it would rain again tomorrow. As to the following day, he would say no more than "mebbee."

With the rain pattering on the deck overhead, we had the first of our arguments about whether to abandon the cruise. It was Nancy who first proposed it, saying that personally she was miserable and wanted to go home. Why couldn't we leave *Bluejay* here at the dock? Surely the captain could be persuaded to pick it up here. As I joined in, pointing out that the weather did look unfavorable, Pierce, who had been lethargic all morning, overruled Lily's tentative agreement. "Fair-weather sailors," he cried, rousing himself, digging out foul-weather gear from the lockers for all. "You'd never be able to live with yourselves, don't you see? The little suspicion of cowardice would plague you the rest of your days. We're going to get past Schoodic Point. I promise you." He was unrolling the charts, clearly intending to resume our voyage, calling off the names: "Petit Manan, Rogue Island, Great Wass, Moosepeak Light—don't they get to you, the names—make you want to see them?" And here Nancy protested firmly, threatening to go off onto the dock now if he put to sea in this weather.

When Lily and I voted with Nancy, he agreed grudgingly not to proceed east today, but impatient to leave the dock, he cast off and under power we moved slowly out of Southwest Harbor and up the fjordlike Soames Sound. Between steep banks, thick with spruce, the sound probes into the heart of Mount Desert like a narrow alpine lake, and we stood in the cockpit, gawking at the squat houses with their wide porches and gambrel roofs and their tall white flagpoles growing amidst the trees. As the rain came on stronger and heavier, dripping off our slickers into our shoes, we envied every house its fire and dry clothes.

We found a mooring in the clear water off the service wharf in Northeast Harbor, and Nancy spoke of going ashore to find a movie, but waiting for a break in the downpour, we began to drink and it grew dark and late and we stayed aboard. After dinner we played gin rummy. It was odd how any game around that table in *Bluejay*'s cabin made Lily and me behave like children, sometimes squabbling between ourselves, sometimes ganging up on Nancy or Pierce. After a few hands he dropped out and lay back in his bunk, head propped so that he could get to his glass, and already so drunk that he frowned with the effort of focusing his eyes.

*   *   *

A hangover added to my afflictions in the morning. While Pierce slept intermittently in his bunk, Lily made breakfast, and when it was eaten and cleaned up, there was nothing to do but wait to be hungry again. I peered out from under the hatch at even darker skies and a thick film over the shore. At its nearest point, a flagpole emerged and receded endlessly in the opalescence. There was a furry stillness over the world, and at hand only the persistent sound of dropping water and the fat flies buzzing in the cabin.

Warm, cheery studio voices spoke of more rain and northeast winds of fifteen to twenty knots. What an endless day lay ahead. There was a pervasive, funky smell from the bilge and curtains of rain swept by the hatchway, filling the porthole covers, trickling down the mast in glistening worms, gradually soaking clothes, sneakers, towels, and chilling my heart with the certainty it would never end.

Pierce was in a torpor, but from time to time he would look at me or Nancy as if he expected to detect some change in our attitude toward him, something sticking out he could grab at. Around the table, we grew silent and increasingly aware of the other's eccentricities in feeding. Some peculiarity with tongue or lips, the slightest greediness or solicitousness for another, a carelessness in the galley or head, all ballooned into an incubus. I remembered Nancy's casual disposal of an orange peel into water so clear, each rock on the bottom was visible, magnified.

Pierce passed the time by taunting Nancy. From time to time he would heave himself from his bunk to stare at the little shingled house on the service dock fifty yards away and say, "Go on, Nancy, take the pram in and find out about the bus schedule. There's a phone booth there. I can see it from here. You and Ben can go—all of you. Lily and I can sail *Bluejay*. We'll get beyond Schoodic alone."

He turned to see how we all reacted, testing us. Lily was first to assure him of our loyalty, then Nancy, and of course now there was no possibility of either persuading or deserting him. And I recognized, as he did, what had changed. Mixed with my irritation at his displays of arrogance was a new awareness of his vulnerability. There was unspeakable, yet tangible, pity in the close air of the cabin—something from which to avert our eyes.

During the long afternoon he spread charts on the table and plotted courses eastward while he drank. Nancy and Lily were huddled in their bunks, reading, and in the quiet I offered the calumet. "Look—we'll do something surely, Pierce. I have some ideas on how to make trouble for them."

"You do?" He did not look up from the chart. "It's about time." Although I offered to explain, he had no curiosity. As the darkness fell again and the rain pelted down, determined to flood the earth, he was possessed with thoughts of his mutinous crew.

"And you'd go too," he accused Lily. "I know that. Just along for the joy ride and you're miserable now and sorry for yourself. Don't give a damn about seeing what's farther east, places you've never seen, places really wild." His finger sought them on the chart. "Moosabec Reach, Mistake, Quoddy Head. No, you don't care. You'd go with 'em, wouldn't you—if you could? If you weren't being such a brave scout—or nurse." The thought touched his sullenness off into anger. "I don't need you. Maybe Ben needs a nurse. Not me."

"I know you don't," she said.

"Go with them in the morning. I'll get beyond Schoodic alone. I don't need you."

"You can't, Pierce," I said. "You can't handle this boat alone, sails and navigating—surely not down there. You can't be serious. You'll reconsider in the morning."

Pierce clawed at a two-day growth of beard. "Oh, screw you. I'll reconsider nothing. You can all go tonight. Get yourself a nice warm bed up at the Kimball House and be on your bus in the morning. Go on," he shouted. "Go on—I want you to. I want you all off *Bluejay* tonight. I'll row you ashore right now."

But the drink which had fueled this outburst turned to opiate, and we sat around silently, watching his mouth, still working over orders to pack up our gear and get out, grow still, as he fell peacefully, boyishly asleep. With my help, Lily put him to bed.

I woke repeatedly in the night to suffer that anguish of head and stomach from having drunk too much again. The remorseless thrumming of the rain increased my feeling of captivity, and like a prisoner, I was losing track of time. Was it three days we had lain here, or but two? I had never been elsewhere and never would be freed.

Then, at six, I had a quickening awareness of merciful change. We lay motionless in the water and it was quiet. The halyards had ceased their strumming, and the dripping, to which I had grown accustomed as to the tick of a clock, had stilled.

I thrust my head through the hatch to find the sea a black mirror, the sky a field of gray winter slush, but bearing in the east a border of brightness like hope itself. The silence was broken by a lone, plaintive gull cry, then an insistent honking —outrage at some discrimination—and I saw them standing on a stone jetty in a row, facing seaward on their long sticks, hunched. They took off on command, legs retracted, in synchronized pumping of their tentlike wings.

With the clearing, the three days past vanished from our

recollections like a nightmare. We were under way before eight, motoring into a flat calm of a morning. The bell off Bear Island swung in its black tripod, tolling farewell, and Pierce acknowledged it with determined cheer. He refused breakfast in favor of black coffee, but welcomed me to the wheel, and in apology for last night, asked the advice of both Nancy and Lily for our course on Frenchman Bay.

Bluejay furrowed across the brown glass into which Mount Desert dipped her opulent flanks. The massive humps were worn softly round, and glowed, as though from within, with shades of umber, russet and pink. Fringed at the tide line with black kelp, the huge rocks were monster eggs, spilling into the sea, or there, disappearing, whales.

The sun came through suddenly, turning the sea a pellucid green near us, shading to blue as it reached to shore and horizon and glinting with tiny jewels. As the clouds dissolved, we raised sail—and to fill them came the kindly, following southwesterly, pushing us along Frenchman Bay toward Schoodic and making the pram swish serenely astern.

Overhead, the benign sun diffused, warming the air, whitening the sails as they spread against a sky now a vast, pale powder-blue dome, nearly white overhead, deepening in the quadrants and then turning white again at the horizon. One gull glided across it, very high, the trailing edge of his wings translucent as glass.

What an efficacious balm the sun was, dissolving all viciousness, all sense of disaster, restoring us to our holiday. Under it, Nancy and Lily had shed sweaters and pants and spread them to dry on the deckhouse. Towels tied to the handrails flapped and fluttered. In their briefest bathing suits, they stretched on the deck for the basking, and the frivolous, aphrodisiac smell of the oil was rising once more from their skin.

I had been steering east across the wide mouth of the bay for Schoodic Point and Pierce's wilds beyond. But in the middle of this benign morning, all of us so newly eager to please, Lily pointed out the islands that lay to the north, clustered off Winter Harbor and the low-lying eastern shore. She passed me the binoculars to see the one nearest, a handsomely plump cushion with an inviting inlet. I found it, Turtle Island, on the chart and altered course slightly to head for it.

Pierce, who had been forward with his camera, clinging to the bowsprit to capture the turbulence of our bow wake, noticed and came aft to inquire. "You want to stop there for lunch?" He looked at the chart, then at Lily. "All right. I'll eat anywhere . . . if you can find an anchorage."

While our wives prepared a basket lunch, he made a thermos of drinks and seemed agreeable, if not enthusiastic, about the shore excursion. Then, as we approached Turtle Island, I realized his doubts were not stubbornness. On the windward side there was a possible anchorage in the rocky cove, but the wind was too strong to consider it, and circling the island, it was clear that instead of shelving, the steep shore of the lee side plunged into twenty fathoms of water to make a peril of anchoring and landing the dinghy.

I had given Pierce the helm and was unwrapping a sandwich, feeling Lily's disappointment. Nancy, too, looked as though she had been denied a promised pleasure, while Pierce, indifferent, was relieved to be on our way. Watching the bow swing east again, Lily said, "There's always something between us and an island. You wouldn't think, seeing them out there, so many of them, they're so unattainable."

"They're not," Pierce said. He was standing above us, amiably, holding the top of the thermos in one hand, steering with a foot, and he pushed the wheel over, heading us north again. "We'll try some more. What's the next one, Mose?"

There was another, larger than Turtle, several miles beyond. "Ironbound," I said, finding it on the chart. "Some coves on the east shore, but they're deep."

Approaching, Ironbound seemed uninhabited. Through the glasses, its two long beaches were narrow and rocky, with thicket growing on them. Beyond, however, up its slopes, lay inviting clearings, hillside fields linked with groves of hemlock, as though it had been farmed or grazed.

Pierce moved along the island's coast, heading up for me to drop the lead, but I could find no bottom, and presently he said, "Okay. You go ashore. I'll have a sail by myself. I don't care about going in, anyway. Take all the time you like."

And so it was quickly arranged. While Pierce headed *Bluejay* into the wind a hundred yards offshore, I hauled in the dinghy and boarded it, unshipping the oars as Lily took the stern seat. Nancy, her sneakered foot dangling over *Bluejay*'s side, steadying us, held the painter.

"Come on," I said, "if you're coming."

She was looking down at us thoughtfully, with the faintest smile, first at me, then at Lily, who, in blue jeans and sweater, hair tied in a blue bandanna, peered eagerly ashore. "Well, I don't think I will," she said. Abruptly she let go the painter and shoved us off.

Rocking in *Bluejay*'s lee, I asked, "What's the matter?"

"Nothing. I think I'll stay behind—with Pierce."

"Don't you want to go?" he asked her.

"Not really." She shrugged. "The beach is all rocks and those clearings are going to be gardens of bullthorns and poison ivy. Why? Don't you want some company?"

I didn't think from his expression that he did, but Nancy had decided and I began to pull for shore, getting the feel of the oars and enjoying the elation of being set free.

Lily had turned to gaze at *Bluejay* reaching lazily toward the mainland, treating herself to the sublime sight of the sloop. Her delight made me think it akin to a gratifying reflection of her own figure.

"Do you really think you can help?" she asked remotely. "Or were you just being cheerful?"

My own thoughts had gone ahead, searching out a landing place along the rocky beach that would not batter the dinghy's bottom, and for a minute I could not think what she meant. "Oh no," I said. "Not just being cheerful at all. There are a number of things we could try. I was thinking of injunction. There's an action, not at all uncommon, called a derivative stockholders' suit, or a minority stockholders' suit. With it you can enjoin a management from an act not in the company's best interests. I think we can try that. There's no certainty—in fact, it's a remote chance—we could win, but that's not the point. What we want to do is make a nuisance. The more we make, the better. It's the kind of thing Pierce would have a taste for." I turned to see we were heading for a place where the shore was made of rocks like bowling balls. To the south it looked more hospitable, and I pulled toward it through the swells.

"Only what?" she asked.

"Is he all right? I wondered last night—I wondered any number of recent nights—whether this is just a particularly unpleasant phase he's going through. There's every reason to believe that, isn't there? I had no idea about the money. I'd always assumed that was inexhaustible."

"Well, of course it isn't a phase. Good Lord, Ben, you knew him before I did. When he's threatened and unsure of himself, he's a bandit. He shoots anything that moves. But he's not crazy. If you'd asked me a week ago, I'd have said some new taste of success, some reassurance his luck hasn't run out, would fix what's eating him."

"No longer?"

"I don't know, Ben. Sometimes it's *me* that makes him misbehave. What *is* that? The jealousy of my work, people I like. It's intensified the whole wretched business that he thinks of Julie as *my* friend."

"Oh, Lily, no. You can't take the responsibility for any of it yourself—as though he were a child."

"Still—I wonder. If only I could have been some good to him with Microdom—if you'd *made* me go to Washington . . ."

"Is that the trouble, Lily? His little whatchamacallit with Lotte Weiss?"

She looked beyond me to the pebble beach, where stones the size of golf balls rattled with the waves, and pointed to a flat shingle beyond. I pulled straight for that until we thumped, and I leaped over the side, with Lily following, and we half carried, half dragged the dinghy high and weighted the painter with heavy rocks.

Finding the thicket of spruce impenetrable, we started along the shore toward the sweeping bluff at the far end.

"When was it?" she asked. "In Washington?"

"Oh hell, I'm sorry. Nancy said you knew."

"Yes." She moved ahead of me to climb the rocks leading up toward the first of the terraced fields. "I think perhaps I did."

There was a thick droning of summer insects, evoking sadness and fleeting childhood memory as we proceeded. Lily turned once to face me. "What a curious pair you are, you two. I used to think the relationships between women were complicated, but they're nothing to what goes on between a couple of old Blues, are they?"

"Tell me."

"Well, of course you worship and envy him, out of some old yearning habit. Oh, yes you *do*." She laughed. "It's what attracts you both to one another. It's a really tidal pull."

"I envy him you. That's all. My God, *no*."

"Yes, even now. I can see it in your face, even when he's behaving at his worst, even as he angers you and makes you want to hit him, you're still in awe, even as you pity him, as you did last night. Yes, I think that's true." She turned to look at the sun-soaked field in which we had arrived. It was thick with low gorse and clumps of wild raspberry bushes, heavy with fruit. She plucked a handful and shared them with me as we stood looking across the broad reach of the bay to where little Italian-cherub clouds hung in a delicate blue sky. A white lobster boat had paused to pull a trap and we could see the lobster man hauling, tossing back the culls, then the splash, and the puff of blue smoke from his stack as he moved on.

"I wonder what it would be like," Lily said, "all that isolation. The way he knows it. I don't mean today. It's glorious today. But I wonder how he likes it in the winter and in the storms, being out on the sea. It seems so lonely when we come to those buoys, perpetually rising and falling in the big seas. I get a terrible feeling of pity for them." She laughed. "Particularly the nuns."

"It's just a day's work. Once in a while, when he hears the cannery whistle blow, he's glad it's not for him."

"Yes. I suppose all this, the stunning, glorious, big quiet, doesn't move him at all. That's for people who've been where we've been." Meditatively she loosed the knot at the nape of her neck and shook her hair free in the sunshine. Then, kneeling, she spread the kerchief and began to fill it with the fruit.

At the edge of the clearing I found a fallen birch, and peeling a foot of bark from the dark, fibrous flesh, twirled it into a horn and fastened it with my belt. We picked silently, side by side, for a few minutes until we had a generous dessert for four.

Then, carrying the berries, we crossed the field to where a silent trail led farther up the ridge. We followed it through knee-high grass, peering off to the sides where thick groves of fir trees shaded deep, spongy carpets of needles. And ahead we saw the trees opening into a broad clearing. We went on eagerly, hoping it would be the top and command a view of the whole of Frenchman Bay.

Emerging, we found a weathered shack, stove in at the roof, and we paused, alert for human sounds. There was only a hushed whisper from the treetops, and we moved forward past the doorway and its glimpse of rusting stovepipe, some nests and scattered nutshells, toward a timber tripod astride a pair of huge, ancient cogwheels. From its peak hung a brown cable, frayed at one end but at the other still arching forth to some grand purpose and disappearing into the earth ahead.

In a moment we stood at the brink of a huge crater in the body of Ironbound Island. Granite steps, sized for a giant's foot, led down steeply on two sides, to make an amphitheatre and suggest that half a pyramid had been excavated whole for

delivery to some pre-Columbian majesty. It had the awesomeness of ruins, some place where priests have sent blood spurt-
ing across flat stones to propitiate an angry sun.

The floor was a dark green pool reaching to the escarp-
ments, a pair of steep shadowed rock faces opposite, like the
prows of tall steel ocean vessels moored together, and between
them a passage led to more wonders beyond. At the far side,
where it was in deep shadow, the water appeared to be bottomless, but on the east, where shafts of sunlight reached to
meet a shelf of sloping rock, it was inviting.

"Wouldn't that be heaven?" Lily said. "Do you suppose it's
icy?" Putting down the kerchief of berries, she ran ahead,
leaping from step to step, spiraling to the shelf at the pool's
edge. She knelt and dipped her fingers, then frowned into the
depths, before she looked up to call, "It's all right. In fact, it's
quite lovely."

I followed her down, and trying the water myself, found it
cool but far warmer than the sea water. Beside me, Lily had
taken off her sneakers to dangle her toes in the water. "Do
you suppose we could?" she asked, and her eyes moved along
the edge of the quarry as though she expected peepers.
"Could we skinny dip?"

I peered doubtfully into the opaque brown depths.

"Yes," she said. "I was wondering that too—if there's something down there with a long arm and suckers on it that will
reach up for my fine white leg and have it for his supper."

"Want me to go first?"

"Will you?"

"Go for a little walk. Just up there."

She left me at once, and bravely, silently I set down my
birch-bark cornucopia and undressed, then slipped cautiously
into the water. I paddled to the center of the pool, finding it
warm and clear, and from there I could see that the passage
between the two steep faces opened into another quarry,
smaller than this, its rim gleaming white, as though snow-
capped, with gull droppings. I lay on my back, floating and
paddling, watching Lily saunter around the upper tier, bend-

ing to look at a clump of wildflowers, then standing tiptoe for a look seaward.

"See the *Bluejay?*" I called.

She nodded and pointed southward. Pierce was sailing around the island. Coming out of the water, I climbed to the second tier and stretched out on the sun-warmed stone to dry, at first making a pretense of not watching Lily as she undressed deftly below me and dove, one swift leap, her hair and long legs flashing in the sun.

But then as she splashed about, calling to me that it was glorious, I rose onto one elbow to watch her. She was swimming back and forth across the pool, with graceful, professional strokes, her white buttocks glistening as they rolled in the froth. And when at last she hoisted herself back onto the rock, she twisted so quickly that I had only an instant's view of her breasts, then her back was to me.

She shook her hair to dry it, combed it with her fingers and tucked the damp strands behind her ears. As she sat with her legs dangling in the water, her arms were raised, so that I got knee-weakening glimpses of the long, slow curve of breast and thigh, and my own body languished, became inert as the earth, and my penis budded forth from its lair to grow by a few tentative millimeters. And then, in a miracle of extrasensory communication and blessed, joyous relief, I watched Lily, still kicking the pool water, stirring a turbulence about her knees, turn her head to me with that joyful, shameless, vital laugh, and as though she knew all, kneel, then rise, gloriously, to stand facing me, beads of water still glistening in the thick brown clump below her belly and on the breasts—white and rigid and textured from the cold water.

Then I was stumbling toward her, bearing it clumsily, ponderously and ludicrously across four yards of uneven rocks, a great tower of aching, agonizing yearning and violence that had been ripening in me for as long as I could recall.

Still with that pleased, calm smile on her exalted face, she simply held her arms slightly away from her wet, warming body so that I could embrace her, and then, groaning with my sublime agony, I dragged her down upon the flat cheek of stone where we stood. And she was belying her benign face, ready for me—so warm and moist that there were but four exquisite, glorious thrusts and I burst inside her in an explosion that split the earth beneath her and swallowed us both and we went plunging down into the dark at its center. When I floated back up to the light, Lily was whispering into my ear, "There, you see—I keep my promises."

"Never, ever," I said, "was there anything so grand."

"Yes." Soothingly, she stroked the back of my head.

"Was it good for you?"

"Yes." It was the answer, but it lacked an enthusiasm I sought. I rolled over onto my back so that my head rested in the soft part of her arm, enjoying the last shameless moments, the two of us, spread-eagled like children on the smooth, warm shelf, Lily's legs still wide, receiving the sun between them, her eyes closed as though she slept.

"Better?" I asked. And when she did not answer, "Not so good?"

Her arm folded slowly, shading my face, and the fingertips closed over my lips. "Oh, Ben, no. Don't do that." Her eyes remained closed, but the faintest smile played on her mouth. "I'm an unfaithful wife today—but not disloyal."

*　　　*　　　*

Rowing back to the *Bluejay* through gentle swells, I was exalted and sang out a farewell to Ironbound and a promise to return. It seemed I had reached a pinnacle in the topography of my life, one from which I could look over the gullies and woods where I had been trudging—to find this majestic view and confirm my oft-doubted belief that for those who find the way, it can be so always. Everything was possible now. I was Hercules, the oars matchsticks in my hands, and I was going to live forever. This enviable, unattainable woman, now blotting her hair with a blue kerchief, her knees holding the birch-bark horn and rubbing against mine with a sumptuous easiness that was continuing surrender, had given herself to me.

It was only as I looked over my shoulder to see *Bluejay* running in, looming larger with each surge of her bow, that my thoughts turned to Pierce. I had a glimpse of him, standing on the lazarette, one arm stretched to the backstay, steadying himself as he turned the helm. It was an anxious pursuer's stance.

I felt one long, enervating shaft of remorse for the perfidy. But even as I hesitated, holding the oars aloft, watching the widening pattern of the drips from my blades running shoreward, I was remembering Pierce's own advice. It came in his own voice, so fresh it could not have been locked so very deep in my recollection—"I always assume that if a girl is willing, she has all that stuff in hand."

For an instant the past was the present and Dilys Given was restoring her lipstick and smiling at me in a Savoy Plaza mirror. And Angela? Where was Angela Rice? Had she ever existed? The spinning time-wheel was dizzying. Angela was awaiting my call in a dark apartment on Sutton Place. And Pierce? There were times when I failed to see, on him or me, the smallest mark of the passing of time. Were we not the same men as always? I could believe we were going back to the *News* tomorrow, that this vacation would end in our return to a room in Timothy Dwight, where my clothes—I recalled the beloved rusty tweed jacket with elbow patches— still hung in a closet.

"What's the matter?" Lily asked. She was trailing a hand in the water languidly, but looking up with first anxiousness at the approaching *Bluejay*.

"Nothing," I said and dug my oars into the sea.

There was quick-darting curiosity about us. Pierce's black eyes were frisking us before the dinghy touched the side. Behind him, Nancy prattled—her caustic whimsy, wondering what had taken us so long. Did we realize we had been ashore over two hours? That she and Pierce had been on the point of calling the Coast Guard? What had we been *doing*?

"Oh, for Christ's sake," Pierce said. "Can't you shut up?"

I made the painter fast on the stern cleat and turned to find

Lily watching me, anesthetized. For an instant I thought she was unequal to the deception and was turning to me for help.

"It's a magnificent island," I said. "You should go have a look."

"Yes. Oh yes, it was lovely," Lily agreed. "Covered with wild raspberries. And see—there'll be enough for dessert."

"You went swimming?" Nan asked.

"Yes. There was a quarry." Lily touched the damp curls at her neck and then held the horn out to Nan, who helped herself, then to Pierce.

Under the leathery surface of his skin, the flesh was turning gray. He was searching her face, trying to find some other reason for the dazedness, the lingering catatonia, while the sail flapped overhead. His eyes went to the horn of plenty. He took it from her hands and spilled it into the sea. He flung the pieces of birch bark away and stared at my belt before returning it.

We stood in the cockpit, rocking slightly, waiting for Pierce. His eyes had gone round. They were those of a warrior just stung, experiencing the strange numbness, like nothing he'd ever felt before, and hesitating to touch it for fear of what his fingers will find.

"What else did you do?" Confronting Lily, Pierce's face was ugly with impotent rage and his voice trembled. "What besides berrypicking? What besides swimming?" He gathered a hank of Lily's damp hair in his fist and wrung it. "Anything else? Come on, tell me. I want to know. Did you kiss? Sure. You did more than that, didn't you? I can feel what you did. Come on, tell me. I can see it and I can smell it."

Then he reached for her as though he meant her harm, and I grasped his arm. "Stop it, Pierce. For Christ's sake, don't be an ass."

He wheeled on me. "Oh, *you* . . ." His huge hands clapped against my chest to send me spinning onto the cockpit seat, and he closed, hovering, clawing the air above me, eager for my throat. "You laid her. Come on. *You* say it. I want to hear you say it."

"Stop it, Pierce," Nancy cried sharply.

"I'll say nothing"—looking into his tear-brimmed eyes, my own voice was high-pitched and unfamiliar—"because there's nothing to say. Believe whatever you like. Let your whiskey-soaked fancy run—but don't ask me to verify it."

We stood there, all four—*Bluejay* moving slightly underfoot—the world at a stop.

Pierce still trembled, measuring us all, and I was drawn and repelled by the sight, moved strongly by an overwhelming pity for him. It was not guilt, for it seemed that what had happened on Ironbound, our coupling, Lily's and mine, was no more my doing, nor Lily's, than his own. It was a rite—feral and inevitable—acknowledging Pierce's collapse as man and abdication as master. It had to be performed as surely as blood ran in our veins and yet it left me queasy with disgust for all of us.

Lily was watching Pierce gravely. Her head was thrust forward—not in penitence, but inertly, as though she had been stunned dumb and required some touch, some signal from him to reactivate her. She looked older by years, and stripped, not only of my own illusion, but her real, enduring beauty. She had lost even womanliness, and desire for her, the slightest solace from it, was gone.

I felt equally immobilized. I stood in awe of my own foolhardiness. It was as though on a challenge I had been walking the parapet of a vast building, and now gazing into the chasm, I could only reel at my jeopardy. Sanctuary was nowhere in reach. It lay as far ahead as it was behind.

My initial punishment, if that was its name, was to be confinement with these shipmates, my sentence an endless confrontation with them, the three glasses of a triptych mirror providing infinite, unwelcome, unexpected images of myself.

"We'll go back." Pierce broke the spell with these, just audible, words and put the wheel over.

A light breeze caught the sails, the bow swung and *Bluejay* began her inbound voyage. But Pierce, as though he could no longer bear the sight of us or sea or shore, went below, leaving me the wheel. I could see him lying in his bunk—his back turned to the passageway.

For two hours I steered southward, close-hauled, out of Frenchman Bay. Lily sat alone in the bow, hugging her knees, staring ahead at the afternoon sky as it lost its warmth and turned a delicate greenish-blue, then gathered streaks of thin cloud in a fibrous pattern like the skeleton of a fish. The water took on the deep-sea look, bottomless and heaving, its surface veined and wind-streaked. A path to the lowering sun glinted with wintry brilliance.

Nancy sat in the cockpit, back to the cabin, legs wrapped in a blanket, her intense gaze roving, lighting, now on her book, now aloft in the rigging, now the horizon, yet never on me, and I could feel the new deafness between us. I didn't know if it was to be abiding, but it was a perceptible thickening of hearing and a blight on all the senses.

"Nancy," I said finally, "will you slack the jib?" She regarded the cleated halyard for a moment before she complied, allowing it to snake around the winch until I said, "There— that's it."

Still not looking at me, she asked, "Where are we going?"

"Bass Harbor. I think we can find something there, a bus or a taxi, to start us home."

After a moment she said, "Imagine. Well—I won't count on it." Her voice had a hollowness, but the resilience was there and I felt some hope.

Toward evening Pierce came topside and went forward along the deck. He stood beside Lily, steadying himself against the shroud, and kneeling, took her arm, not roughly, but urgently, while he spoke. I thought she nodded. She turned her head to reply and then he released his hold of her and came aft, stumbling once and catching the life line. He paused at the edge of the cabin, looming over us both, then passed by, ignoring us, on his way below. I could see him sitting on the edge of his bunk, smoking.

At seven, with a gray dusk falling and the sun slipping down behind Deer Isle, we passed Bass Harbor Head and I swung northward on an easier course for the harbor entrance. Pierce emerged and took a look at the approaching shore. "What in hell are you doing?"

"Bass," I said. "We'll make it comfortably before dark."

He pushed the wheel against my hand, heading us back into the wind. "Not going in any place. We're sailing to Camden."

"Tonight?" I held the chart out for him, indicating the Casco Passage ahead, squeezed through the rocks and islands north of Swans and marked with a single light at the westward end of York Narrows. "We can't make that at night."

Pierce stared fiercely into my eyes, but knowing mine was reason's side, I tugged against him, struggling to keep *Bluejay*'s nose shoreward. Whereupon he seized me by the arm, fingers digging into my flesh, and yanked me from the helmsman's seat with such force I was flung to the deck. Only the life line kept me from rolling overboard.

"I've got the wheel now," he said. "And I'll decide where we go and when we do it. Now stay away from me. Both of you."

I picked myself up, and goaded by a stinging where the stanchion had caught me, climbed back into the cockpit. "You're insane," I said. "There's no sense in putting our lives in danger."

Nancy, smiling from the hatchway as though she had not seen or heard the struggle, said, "Anyone want a drink?" She beckoned me. "Come chip the ice for me, Ben. You want a drink, Pierce?"

Pierce did not reply, but sensing Nancy had intervened purposefully, I went down the ladder into the cabin and opened the top of the icebox.

"It would be wise, I think," she said, taking the splinters of ice and dropping them in the glasses, "to follow the captain's orders."

"He's deliberately putting us on the rocks. He's going to split the hull tonight. I'm certain of it."

She shrugged. "You can swim. The captain is reasserting

his command. Let him." She climbed the ladder and called forward, "Lily? Want a drink?"

She didn't, it seemed. When I put my head through the hatchway she was looking ahead and I watched the entrance to Bass Harbor disappear over our starboard quarter.

Feet braced against our pitch and roll, Nancy began to slice some onions into the bottom of a kettle, and without even asking my help, pumped up the stubborn shipmate and lit its flame. She produced meat and vegetables from the icebox and sliced them, adding them to the now-hissing kettle with zealous concentration. I saw her, knife in hand, touch a lock back out of her eyes. It was such a familiar gesture of absorption in necessary tasks, and through it I recognized that it was Nancy alone who could hold us in some semblance of accord until we reached shore.

When the food was ready she called up through the hatch to Pierce. "Captain? Is Captain Bligh ready for his supper?"

Pierce didn't look at her. "I don't want anything."

She sniffed the bowl. "It smells delicious. You'd better have some if you're going to sail all night." She set the bowl and a fork at his foot and then, indifferent to his hostility, stood beside him, hands in the pockets of her peacoat, gazing out to sea as though at last enjoying the sail.

Nancy took food to Lily in the bow, and presently I heard their voices murmuring, soft and melancholy, like mourners. I wondered what further confrontations there must be, or if, somehow, Nancy's insistence on returning to a former pattern of relationship could lead us off intact.

When Nancy came below, it was with two empty bowls. Then, standing beside her in the galley, watching her ladle out our portions, I was moved by fresh admiration and gratitude to touch her tentatively on the arm. She shied from my fingers in a warning that this avenue—that of hand to heart—had been closed.

Nevertheless, as we sat across from each other at the cabin table, she looked up and said with her glossy grin, "I was just wondering if the children have been having a good time too.

Well—we won't tell them what they've missed. We'll tell them it was awful." She laughed. "Do you suppose we can do this every year?"

*   *   *

At nine o'clock, just as the night closed solemnly ahead of us, drawing its cover over the rugged fists of granite jutting from the sea, our silence was broken by Pierce's calling to Lily, "It's the number three can we want. Somewhere off to port. Can you keep lookout?"

"Yes." Her voice floated aft, plaintive, yet even.

"You'll want a light," he called to her. "Nancy will bring it up." Putting his head down the hatch, he pointed it out to her and told her to douse the cabin light, that we must all get adapted to the dark. "Except for you, Ben. You're reading the chart."

This manifestation of his being master of the *Bluejay* once more, the manning of stations, did not quiet my anxieties. I continued to feel the menace in him and determined to keep vigilant. Before I went below I tested the release on the horseshoe life belt which hung from the port shrouds.

Beyond the anxiety about Pierce himself, there was a flourishing resentment among all of us. As we passed each other our grievances surely would have burst had it not been for the compelling need to work together that the moonless, starless night and the search for a safe passage through it now thrust upon us.

Pierce did not lower sail, and in entering the York narrows, he shut off the engine and felt his way on the fickle wind. Lily, hanging to the forestay, probing the infinite thicket of the night with her feeble beam, only rarely found one of the red nuns we sought to keep on our port. She would call off its number, and I, in turn, would locate it and call a new course to Pierce for the elusive flasher where we would turn northwest.

To my relief, Pierce's thirst was for coffee, and Nancy made it strong and black to his order and brought us all fresh cups of it to keep off the penetrating chill and the wearing weariness that plagued us as we lost our way. We went northward under power, but more often under sail alone, straining at the rail to hear the bell that would take us into the Reach. Hearing nothing, seeing nothing—until, after midnight, we heard surf breaking and in the next instant were shaken as the keel struck and staggered along a ledge, heeling us far over before we broke free.

In Lily's light I made out a small island, low in the water, and guessed at Smutty Nose on the chart. Bruised, but intact, we beat westward and then faintly heard a bell. Tacking this way and that, losing it, then hearing it again, nearer, we ran it down to find it the number eight off Devils Head. We passed it close aboard and into Eggemoggin Reach, dropping the sail now, for some stars had emerged, enough to reveal the steep banks of the passage, the lights ashore and, far ahead, the impudent towers of the Deer Isle Bridge, winking, high as Orion.

It was during this three-hour passage, in the darkest hours of the night but with these man-made reassurances close, that we eased our vigilance and were reminded it was the very net that sustained us, this necessary comradeship of wheel, chart, lookout and coffeepot, and kept us from the miserable undoing that awaited us.

We made the turn just under the Thrumbcap flasher and were feeling southwest along the narrow corridor of cans to the bell which clears the Reach when, at four-thirty, a first flourish of red streaked the heavens astern and another day began. As the sun crept up and gave shape to Isleboro, it lost its warmth and made a white path across the water to us and there were long brush strokes of gray cloud against a colorless sky. There was no wind, and as we started across Penobscot Bay on the last leg into Camden, the sea was black and slick and strewn with oily ovals.

*　　　　　*　　　　　*

Pierce, carrying Nancy's duffel bag, walked with me toward

the coalyard where I had left the car. We had not spoken on the way up the dock or along the quay—but his stiff-legged walk and the grim headlong stare told that the time of our confrontation was at hand.

I was light-headed and the earth heaved under my feet. I had an exceptional feeling of being in the limbo between wakefulness and dream, of entering that fantasy of life ashore I had not considered since Pulpit Harbor, and leaving the real one on board the *Bluejay*, behind. Indeed, I turned for a wistful view of her, rocking at the edge of the pier below us.

Pierce's red-rimmed eyes were intense. The sleepless night had left him fired with raw urgency. He heaved the bag through the tailgate window, then stared at me, forcing himself with all his will to an ugly task.

His eyes questioned me and remembered, looked away again. "Did you think you could, Ben? Did you really imagine you were man enough for her? Or did you only want to spoil it." He shook his head. "I can't believe it. I tell myself it's a fact. It really happened. And yet . . ." He sagged against the back of my car. "I came up here with the idea of harming you. I've rehearsed it many times. Killed you. That brought me some pleasure last night—but now I find I can't. Can't touch you. I'm paralyzed. It's hard to talk to you, even to look at you. I can't clear my instinct of the idea you're my friend. The habit's too strong. Twenty years—Jesus. If you're not, I don't believe I have one." He laughed without mirth. "Well, for one thing, I'm going to get myself a different lawyer."

"I suggested that once before."

"I'll look around. I'll call you when I've decided." He pushed himself from the car and started away, but after a few uncertain steps he turned and came back. His long, craggy face wore a painful look of regret. "But we'll have lunch sometime." He put out a hand and I took it.

He walked along the quay toward the dock, hands in his pockets, head down, weary but still big, loping along, and I envied the man—everything.

On the dock, Nancy was saying good-bye. I could see her sauntering toward the coalyard, pausing to admire *Jo-Mar,* a great hulk of chrome and glass from Florida, tied up at the fuel dock. Watching her, I had a new awareness of the finality of this particular parting with Lily and Pierce. It was the end of lovely young illusion, end of the time in life when I could believe that at any moment, tomorrow probably, next day at the latest, something marvelous was going to happen to me: that I might arrive at the office and find they'd make me a partner and were sending me to Paris for three months, or that I would turn some corner into the arms of a wholly un-expected love affair, one so sensuous and joyous it would be the equivalent of rebirth. My acquaintance with futility was now close. I had full knowledge of how the years that re-mained to me were circumscribed. Mystery and hope were gone.

On *Bluejay* I saw Lily pluck up a sweater that lay on the deck and carry it slowly below with her. Jay examined the bowline and stepped aboard. Preoccupied, he looked around the cockpit, moved a cushion, folded a chart, peered through the hatchway, then stepped over the coaming and down, into the cabin—pausing to close the hatch cover behind him.

Afterword

 **17**

But we did not meet again, Pierce and I—and the news of him gave me no occasion to try. He retained a well-known Boston firm for his suit against Microdom, yet it did not get to court. I sat beside a member of that firm at the Union Club Christmas dinner and learned from him it was because of Pierce's own growing indifference. With some difficulty they had arranged a meeting with Weiss and Snyder. Pierce had failed to show up.

Then, toward spring, some friends from Cambridge told us that Pierce had left Lily, that she had moved into a small apartment on Memorial Drive, and put the house on Linnaean Street up for sale. A week later I was in Cambridge and drove by it, half expecting to find him on the roof, enlarging the observatory dome, or adding a floor to the tree house. But the windows stared vacantly into the street and in the uncut grass a *For Sale* sign was planted, reminding me painfully of the cycle that had been completed.

Between ourselves, Nancy and I did not speak of the Jays. From the moment of leaving Camden the previous August, we never looked back. By a mute agreement, the cruise of the *Bluejay* lay isolated in our recollection, under the drifts of necessity and passing days. We were fruitfully employed with many interests. There was my work, of course, but the children, too, and the increasing enjoyment both Nancy's family and my own took in them. Other friends became as important to us as the Jays had been.

Then one morning—it was early February of 1960—Nancy passed the *New York Times* across our breakfast table. She had folded it to an item buried in the back pages. I read:

> Son of Airline Pioneer Slain in Harlem. Pierce Jay, Jr., son of the World War I hero and founder of the first commercial airline linking the Americas, was beaten to death in or near the 125th Street Station of the Lexington Avenue line yesterday evening. Police said he had been living with friends at 21 Bank Street since his arrival here last summer. He is survived by his mother, Mrs. Victor de Villepin of this city and Bellerive, Newport, R.I., and two daughters, Allison and Mia.

"I'll have to go," I said. "I suppose it'll be in New York."

"Do you want me to come?"

"Not unless you want to."

"Funny—I'm remembering him with great fondness now. I'm remembering all the boisterous, glorious ways Pierce had." Still reflecting, she gave one ear to sounds of a dispute about misplaced homework that drifted toward us from another room. "I think perhaps it would be best if I didn't come with you. That'll be all right, won't it? Lily would understand." She read Pierce's obituary again. "I wonder why she isn't mentioned."

"They seldom get things right. It's all so hard to believe. I wonder if it isn't . . . You know, some mischief of his."

"Yes," Nancy said, rising to get the children ready for school, "you'd better go alone."

*　　　　　*　　　　　*

Entering from the dazzling brightness of Fifth Avenue, the

chapel at St. Thomas' seemed a gallery deep in the earth and it was a moment before I could make out who was present.

Pierce was. His coffin, covered by a robe of white carnations, was already in place at the head of the aisle. Some candles glowed on the little altar, shedding a rich, soft light on the golden reredos. There was an undertow of organ chords, deep and earthy, challenged now by a passing subway train.

The mourners, some twenty of them, were emerging in the sooty amber light. Alone in the second row was a good-looking man in a tweed coat. He was about my own age, but a stranger to me. Next there was a phalanx of modish people, much fur and a sprinkle of derbies, whispering among themselves. I recognized Gordon Grimes and then Sandy and Dilys Given, faintly waxy but otherwise undiminished by the almost twenty years since I had seen them at Pierce's wartime farewell.

On the south side of the chapel were some Yale faces. Blodgett was up front with his wife. He was becoming the unofficial representative of our class at significant functions. Behind them was a pair of bareheaded young women, one plain, the other interesting. Glossy black curls framed a pretty heart-shaped face which was the more remarkable for its lack of color.

Behind them sat a young Negro couple, well dressed but with an air of contentiousness. They seemed to prickle at the environment, even as they sat staring straight ahead of them.

As I wondered who they were I felt a touch on my arm. "Wolfie, my God," I said, and we shook hands with an enthusiasm that shored up my waning spirit and drew us powerfully into the ceremony about to commence. We took the nearest empty pew, and folding our coats, piled them in one corner.

He knelt on the hassock beside mine and whispered, "When in Rome . . ." I could feel his presence, warm and reassuring next to me. Arms folded, he was peering through the arch into the cavernous nave of the church. A great mirror over the chantry looked into an empty choir stall, but on the near side a moving shadow gave away the organist's blind.

"It's hard to believe," I said. "He was only forty. That's no time to die. That's when life is meant to begin."

Wolfe's face was seamed and he was gray at the temples. I thought he had aged more than most of us—but agreeably, as though seasoning had brought him a full measure of wisdom and tolerance. "I don't know if it was beginning for him or not," he said. "Sometimes he thought it was and sometimes he was very glum. You know how Pierce was."

"You'd seen him lately?"

"A bit. Maybe once a week over the past few months. We were working on something. He turned up in my office one day last fall and said he was looking around. He was broke, you know, really stony. Think of it—Pierce. He wouldn't go to his mother and he didn't want to borrow from me either, but he was thin and seemed hungry. I'd take him out to Cherio's for lunch and he'd be ravenous, filling up. My place, you know, but the waiter would bring him the check. Even then, needing a haircut and wearing a dirty shirt, he looked to any waiter like the man who was going to pay the bill." Wolfe chuckled, enjoying it. "He had some ideas about manufacturing computer components, and they looked good to me."

"You know what happened at Microdom?"

"Sure. He told me. Oh hell, he was erratic enough. You don't need to remind me. But my *God,* Ben, you know what Microdom sells at now?"

"Pierce didn't keep his stock?"

"When he and Lily separated, he put it in trust for the girls."

"You were helping him then?"

There was denial in a slight motion of his head. "We'd found a place in Queens and were going to run it. *He* was going to run it and I was going to worry. I was staking him."

"Where was he living?"

Wolfe nodded toward the girl with the pale heart-shaped face, several stalls ahead. "With her." Looking closely, I saw she was a child, no more than twenty, yet with heavy-lidded, exotic eyes. "Jean Kaufman. He met her at some rally in the Garden. She works at the Civil Liberties Union, a clerk-typist, but a bright, earnest girl. They'd go off together, on the bus down to North Carolina for these sit-ins. He had a picture of Jean and him picketing the Woolworth's in Raleigh."

"Pierce?"

"I know." Wolfe shook his head. "Still, he was always one for burning everything down and starting over new."

"Was it some civil rights thing? Is that what he was doing in Harlem?"

"They had friends there, he and Jean, but no, it wasn't a meeting or a riot. It was in a lonely part of the subway, the stairs. And you know, he didn't look as if he belonged there. He looked like a rich white guy who forgot to get off at Eighty-sixth Street. With only a token in his pocket and his old, threadbare chesterfield, he looked like he must *own* the subway. Some guys mugged him and he put up a fight. They bashed him good and left him to die in the men's room. Stupid—isn't it?"

There was a change in tempo—some businesslike chords from the vast sheaf of organ pipes—and suddenly Lily appeared at the right of the altar. She wore a dark fur hat and gray coat and she was leading Mia, the younger of the two girls, by the hand. Allison followed, then Melissa de Villepin in a black hat with a short veil that shaded her eyes. She leaned on the brooding Victor.

The rector, bald and baby-pink, brought up the procession, nodding as he watched them file into the first pew. Victor seemed to doze at once against a stone pillar, while Melissa and her two granddaughters sat dauntlessly erect, eager to be first to their feet or knees, as it was required. On the aisle, Lily's head was slightly bowed as she looked at the pall of flowers, so close she could touch it.

" 'I am the resurrection and the life, saith the Lord . . .' "
The rector spoke over Pierce Jay's box. Could he be in there,

truly? I looked around to see if he wasn't pedaling up the aisle on a bicycle—but there was only the sallow undertaker's man, hands clasped, by the door.

" 'Lord, let me know mine end and the number of my days . . .' " Such a little box it was to contain him. How could they? Was he crouched in there? Embryonic? Well— why not? The perfect cycle.

" 'We bring our days to an end as it were a tale that is told . . .' " Or was it an illusion that he had been big— would need an extra-long, king-size coffin? Was he already diminishing, already down to five-foot-six, on his way to dust?

" 'For the trumpet shall sound and the dead shall be raised incorruptible . . .' " Oh *sure*. Why do they go on saying that? Because there's so little comfort in the truth, I suppose —and anyway, who's to know?

It was over. Beneath his white blanket, Pierce was gliding away from us on rubber tires, pushed by smooth men in striped trousers. The rector stepped aside to let the family return the way it had come, from the vestry. But Melissa de Villepin, a contrary plan in mind, moved down the chapel aisle, eyes sparkling, chin high, Victor hastening after, while Lily and her daughters disappeared with the rector into the dark labyrinth of the church.

As we moved slowly along the aisle, Wolfe asked, "Do you want to meet Jean?"

"If it's no trouble."

At the rear of the chapel, the congregation was queuing for a word with Melissa de Villepin, who stood at the foot of some stone stairs, Victor at her side, but the young women hesitated under the arch.

Jean Kaufman wore her coat like a cape, across her shoulders, and as we approached she was groping in her handbag. Even here in the half-light I could not avoid admiring her— the exquisite, smoky face, the delicate, tapering legs, the pronounced hips and breasts. And the sight of her brought Pierce alive for me. I could almost see them together, and I was drawn to her, felt I already knew her.

The other one, her sister, moved away as Jean looked at me through blurry eyes. "Yes, I know who you are." Her voice was rich and husky but it held no warmth for me. "He spoke of you."

"Pierce has been on my mind. A dozen times I've thought of trying to reach him. I wish I had." She did not reply, and I added, "It's some comfort to think you and he had some happiness together."

"Yes. I guess we did." And she turned away to see where her sister had gone.

I supplied my name to Melissa de Villepin as she spoke it, "Oh, Ben, I'm *glad* . . ." She took my hand warmly and held it, brightening, as though she placed great store by me still. "You know, I looked around once during the service and saw you there and I thought how it would have pleased him. Then I began to wish we'd all come around to him sooner. I was thinking of myself, really. One does at a time like this, don't you think? Yes, what grieves me is not that Pierce's life is over but that I might have done *some*thing . . . Do you remember how in Newport . . ." The others were moving on, through the great doors into Fifth Avenue, leaving us behind, and she watched them. "Yes, any of us—but I most of all."

"He was not an easy . . ."

"No, he wasn't, was he? No one is. And there are always the other pressing things that get in the way."

"They're waiting," Victor said.

*   *   *

On the street I saw her. She stood beside a giant livery Cadillac conferring with the man I had seen in the tweed coat.

"Lily," I said, coming up. "How are you?"

"Oh, Ben." It was matter-of-fact, as though we met daily. "I'm all right." She turned to the man in the tweed coat and introduced her husband. "Stay with the girls a minute, David." She walked a few steps away, leading me.

"So," I said, meaning her attractive husband, "it all works out for the best." But I watched her eyes slip down the street to where the box was being fed into the mouth of a hearse. "Yes—even him. I gather he'd found himself at last—that it was just his lousy luck . . ."

"Oh? Do you?" Lily asked. "Well, I think it was only another phase of the search. He was still trying to find the way. He knew there *was* one, to some heroic pattern for his life. He carried that belief like a shiny coin in his pocket, and when he rubbed it, I used to feel good too. *I* could believe it. He'd seen it in his father—and even while the illusions fell all around him, he never lost the idea there was some grandness just beyond his grasp. He dreaded ordinariness. It's what he was running from, the thought there was no such thing as a noble spirit, or if there was, he'd been gypped, that he was really a mutt at the dog show, passing himself off as a champion."

"He wasn't *that.*"

"I know—but he was never certain. Were you?"

"He was tragic, of course, but still—capable of anything."

"You believe that, Ben? You're not just saying that because of where we are?"

"You know how important he was to me. My God, Lily, I used to buy ties because they were like his. I tried to copy everything . . ."

"I know. You traded as you passed, you two."

"It seemed if I could only have the appearance, the spirit would come along. In a way I *am* him."

She looked at me with the briefest smile, and then away.

"I sometimes think Pierce was the most important person in my life," I said. "I used to feel I was no more than his satellite—just reflecting that light he burned."

"That blinding light?" Lily asked.

I saw the rector appear and move toward the first of the limousines. Lily's husband beckoned and she took a step in his direction.

"It wasn't us, was it?" I asked. "It wasn't the *reason?*"

"Ironbound?" She studied the cluster of undertakers, unmoved by their now obvious impatience to start. "Why?"

"I don't think I could bear that."

"No?" Lily asked. "Well, it's not easy, is it?—and anyway, there's no longer need."

She was a stranger. Life was long enough for that—for a woman to grow from acquaintance to friend, to become your lover, then become stranger again. Her hand was in a cloth glove with stiff, ridged seams and I could feel no warmth through it. As she left me she seemed the least bit heavier, but she walked lightly and proudly as ever and I could not fend off a familiar shaft of envy, even now, for Pierce's life and the women who loved him, even for this austere, dry-eyed rite.

I remember standing on the corner, watching the cortege move through the traffic in Fifty-third Street, past the Museum of Modern Art, to disappear into the Avenue of the Americas. Then I felt the loss in all its finality. He was gone. I hadn't believed until now that there wasn't to be a miracle.

I turned down Fifth Avenue, finding it took effort to walk, as though a force restrained me. As midday shoppers and businessmen passed, I felt I had ceased to exist in their urgent world.

I stopped to stare into a shop in Rockefeller Center and realized I had, at Lily's signal, assumed that burden, one I had come down to collect, and now, bearing it away, it was proving too much—not weight, but its gauzy, stifling envelopment.

What a pale world it was, now Pierce Jay had left it. Those of us who had gathered in that farewell, testifying to our closeness, that we loved him most, might have done better by him while he lived. Any of us might have reached out to alter the pattern of his days. Instead we had believed those grand heroics long after the evidence was in, believed he had no need, was proof against us and our aspirations. Again the instances of my own treacheries taunted me.

"But we couldn't help it—none of us . . ." I spoke into

the shop window. No, it was illusion, certainly, that any of us could have altered the headlong thrust of Pierce's life. He carried destruction in his breast, in those romantic, princeling notions of another time that kept him from adapting to his own. They denied him the thoroughfare of our times, where he wished, so desperately, to strive.

And then it burst upon me—that if it was true some of me had gone into the ground with Pierce, then some of him lived with me. I shouldered the burden and found I could breathe with it, that I had the strength for it now. I moved off with it down the avenue, rapidly for a man with no place to go, in imitation of his loping, long-distance stride.

About the Author

JOHN LEGGETT was born in New York City in 1917 and is a graduate of Andover and Yale University. During the Second World War he was a naval officer and served in the Pacific Fleet.

Mr. Leggett was an editor at Houghton Mifflin for six years before his first novel, *Wilder Stone,* was published in 1960. In the same year the author became a senior editor at Harper's firm which also published his second novel, *The Gloucester Branch,* in 1964. Since the fall of 1967 Mr. Leggett has devoted full time to writing. Short stories and articles have appeared in *Esquire, Ladies' Home Journal, Mademoiselle* and *Harper's.* He has been a Regents' Lecturer at the University of California, Irvine, and is a member of the Board of P.E.N. and the Council of the Authors' Guild. Mr. Leggett, his wife and three sons live in New York City and Manchester, Massachusetts.